The nomad w~~~~~~~~~~~pped off another shot, he~~~~~~~~~~e steppe pony the nomad rode wen~~~~wn as if it had run headlong into a fence. Päts shouted in triumph.

But the nomad had been in the saddle since boyhood, and knew how to take a fall. He lost his rifle, but hit rolling and came to his feet only a couple of meters from the boulder. At that point-blank range, Päts fired—and missed. Before he could work the bolt again, the nomad pulled out a knife and jumped on him.

He jerked up his knee. The Tatar twisted aside before it could slam into his crotch. In the tiny part of his rational mind that was still functioning, Päts realized that, while Bektashi's men might be bandits rather than soldiers, even bandits were apt to know more of hand-to-hand combat than farmers. Rather more to the point, he realized he was probably going to get killed.

A rifle roared, so close to Päts' ear that for an instant he thought it was the sound of his own death. But it was the nomad who jerked and convulsed, who splashed Päts with blood and brains and bits of bone.

Päts threw the corpse aside, scrambled up to his hands and knees—he remembered enough of where he was not to stand up. Sergei Izvekov was less cautious, or more foolish. Seeing as he'd just blown out the Tatar's brains, Päts could hardly complain. He did shout, "Get down!" A startled expression crossed Izvekov's face, as if he suddenly realized what he'd just done. He threw himself flat. "*Spasebo*," Päts added more quietly: "Thank you."

"*Nichevo*," Izvekov answered.

CODOMINIUM
REVOLT ON WAR WORLD

CREATED BY JERRY POURNELLE

with the editorial
assistance of John F. Carr

BAEN BOOKS

CODOMINIUM: REVOLT ON WAR WORLD

Copyright © 1992 by Jerry Pournelle

A Baen Books Original

Baen Publishing Enterprises
P.O. Box 1403
Riverdale, N.Y. 10471

ISBN: 0-671-72126-7

Cover art by Gary Ruddell

First printing, July 1992

Distributed by
SIMON & SCHUSTER
1230 Avenue of the Americas
New York, N.Y. 10020

Printed in the United States of America

CODOMINIUM

REVOLT
ON
WAR WORLD

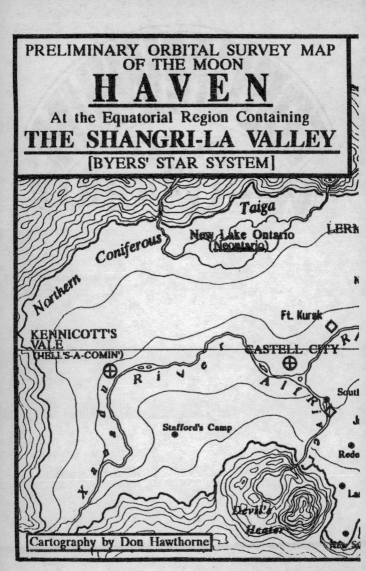

PRELIMINARY ORBITAL SURVEY MAP
OF THE MOON
H A V E N
At the Equatorial Region Containing
THE SHANGRI-LA VALLEY
[BYERS' STAR SYSTEM]

Taiga

New Lake Ontario
(Neontario)

LERN

Coniferous

Northern

Ft. Kursk

KENNICOTT'S
VALE
(HELL'S-A-COMIN')

CASTELL CITY

River

South

Stafford's Camp

Redd

Devil's
Heater

Cartography by Don Hawthorne

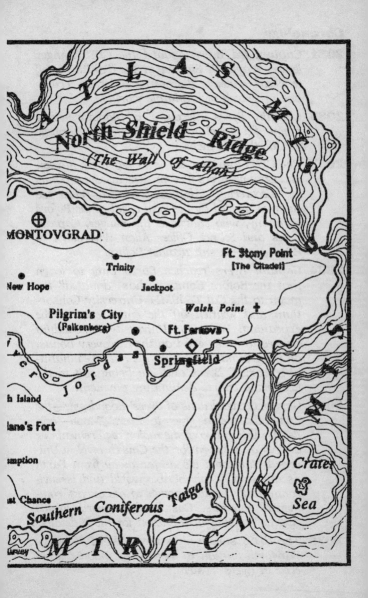

Chronology

2031 Captain Jed Byers aboard the CDSS Ranger leaves Wayforth Station in the Tanith Sector to chart a newly discovered Alderson Tramline in search of habitable worlds.

2032 Captain Byers discovers a planetary-sized moon of a gas giant, which is more a loophole for life than a niche.

2033 The CDSS Ranger returns to Wayforth Station and Captain Byers files for their discovery bonus for discovering a habitable world. When his claim is rejected by the local agent of the Bofors Company, who chartered the Ranger, Captain Byers and Science Officer Allan Wu return to Earth to file a suit against Bofors.

2034 Captain Byers reaches Earth only to learn that the Bofors Company has "donated" the moon to the Cal Tech/MIT University Consortium and written off the entire cost of the expedition. When the University Consortium refuses to make good on the discovery bonus, on the grounds that Haven is not an "inhabitable world," Byers and Wu bring suit in the California courts demanding payment.

2034 Garner Castell learns of Byers' Boondoggle—the name the media gives to Byers' Moon—and decides it has two of the major requirements he desires as a haven for the Church of New Universal Harmony: it's as far away from Earth as any known inhabitable world and is environmentally hostile enough to discourage commercial interests. Castell sends word to his "agents" at Wayforth Station for more details.

2035 The CDSS survey ship the Edward V leaves Wayforth Station to survey the moon discovered in Byers' System.

2035 *The University Consortium wins its case in the lower court. Byers and Wu appeal to the CoDominium Council.*

2036 *The CDSS Edward V returns to Wayforth Station after an incomplete and disasterous survey of Byers' Moon.*

2036 *Based on data supplied by the Edward V, the CoDominium Council declares that Byers' Moon is an inhabitable world, and that Byers and Wu are entitled to their discovery bonus. The University Consortium is given one year to raise the money.*

2037 *Garner "Bill" Castell purchases the license to colonize the world he names Haven. He dies of a heart attack later that year during a shouting match with church members who charged him with looting the church coffers to finance the colonization of Haven.*

2037 *Kennicott Mining learns about the rich hafnium ore discovered on Haven.*

2037 *Fueled by his father's death, Charles Castell finishes preparations for the expedition to Haven. Most of the Church's assets are liquidated to finance the expedition, leaving many of the remaining church members disgruntled and dispirited. There's even talk that the "lottery" to pick expedition members was biased in favor of Castell loyalists. The ship departs amid acrimony and accusations of favoritism.*

2038 *The first Church of New Universal Harmony ship arrives on Haven under the leadership of Charles Castell. Castell City is founded in the Shangri-La Valley and the Harmonies prepare for life on their new world.*

Table of Contents

THE LOST AND THE
FOUNDER

"Call me Bill," Garner Castell said as the cop lifted him off his duff and chucked him into the paddy wagon, which in this case was an ancient Ford Econoline 150 with no seats at all in the back and a wall of metal mesh separating prisoners from the driver and his shotgun-rider. Garner "Bill" Castell told everyone to call him Bill, and often added, "I'm a walking list of debts."

He clunked down on the corrugated steel floor and slid toward the front of the van. He slid toward the back when it accelerated. The charge was vagrancy, but Castell enjoyed the ride, his first in weeks. The van had been converted to electric, so it was a quiet ride, and he was able to think.

Tall, with bushy brown hair, bushy white eyebrows, piercing gray eyes, an ice-breaker of a nose, stern lips, and a strong, cleft chin, Garner "Bill" Castell, when he stood straight and inflated his chest and widened his eyes and boomed his big,

1

resonant voice, could intimidate. When the cop yanked him down from the van, Castell went into what he called his Posture Act, which was nothing less than a graduate-level crash course in body language and public speaking. "How dare you, officer?" he boomed.

The cop actually jumped back for an instant, startled by the transformation. A second ago this guy had been a quiet little vagrant. Now here was this strutting, command-voiced evangelist. Anger surged in the cop, as it so often does, and he grabbed Castell's nearest bicep with renewed strength.

Castell ignored the grip and scanned the crowd of passersby who had paused on the sidewalk outside Austin's downtown police station to watch some of the fun. To each and every one of the members of that crowd, who were mostly young people from the colleges around town, Castell said, "They create bad feelings the way a bad singer can ruin the hymns of a fine choir. They persecute those who, like myself, wish only to get along and be left alone. Having sought no trouble, I am beset by troublers."

Someone called out, and although Castell showed no signs of having heard, he said, "Yes, exactly, we must learn to harmonize, we must become notes of the grand song called life, existence."

The cop holding Castell's arm shoved him. At once cries of protest rose from the crowd. Some scuffling broke out, and the van's driver tried to help his partner hustle the rabble-rouser into the station house. Their way was blocked.

"I've never resisted authority, when it deserved its due," Castell said. "And yet they resist my very existence, even in this mild, pleasant climate, where a soul can live simply and at peace, in harmony with gentle surroundings."

At the word "gentle" a few college boys stepped

forward and tried to pry loose the cops' grips. This caused profanity and elbowing, and before anyone knew it Castell was loose, but headed up the station house stairs on his own power.

And power was the word, because he fairly bounded to the top. "I shall pay their penalty for simply being here, and then I shall go. In three days, if you care, please meet me here, please show them that we can gather and part peaceably, in harmony."

And then he turned and entered the station house, where he was incarcerated for three days on a self-confessed charge of vagrancy.

When Castell came out of the cell, his life had changed, and he knew it. He signed for his few belongings, thanked the sergeant on duty for his force's hospitality, and then walked out between the swinging doors to the cheers of a friendly, happy crowd of supporters.

"That simple," one of the police officers said, snapping his finger in front of his partner's face. His partner said, "Bull, nothing's that simple," and was soon proven right.

Garner "Bill" Castell walked with the celebrating kids, who grabbed at his release as an excuse for revelry just as they grabbed at virtually any other excuse. He walked downtown, let them buy him a simple meal of chile con carne and beer (an Austin college kid's staple, be it noted), then followed them back to the campus of the University of Texas. There he lived for a few days, but soon he moved into the hills surrounding Austin, and groups of young people trekked out to find and talk with him almost every day. Some never went back, and soon those kind multiplied in every way possible, including live births.

The sight of gentle, well-spoken Harmonies seeking alms became common around Austin and surrounding towns and cities. And they were not beggars, because they always did helpful things before accepting any money, such as wash windows, paint houses, clear streets of trash, and that sort of thing. Soon they were taking in huge amounts of money from a populace generally glad to see them, generally glad to take advantage of their bargain prices and cheerful work habits.

When youths were reported lost, they most often turned out to have joined the Harmonies in the Hills. This led to the kids being called, even by themselves for a while, The Lost.

Meanwhile Garner "Bill" Castell refined his ideas around the central concept of Seeking Harmony with All, and his rhetorical abilities grew with his wealth and influence. Strangely to some, he paid taxes on all income, which was recorded scrupulously, and sought no exceptions from any secular rule or law on religious or other grounds. He simply harmonized.

Eventually he bought land, then more land, and more. Soon he controlled several thousand acres of the scrub-pine hills outside Austin, and he began designing buildings. He always had them approved by reputable local architectural firms, to whom he paid generous fees.

Questions about his past Castell answered with shrugs and laughs, jokes and dares. "Find out if you can," he told one reporter who, seeking a human interest story if not an exposé of a new guru, had come all the way from New York City itself. The televised interview only served to enhance Castell's standing and increase his popularity.

He married a young woman of American Indian and Mexican heritage who'd been brought to him by some of The Lost. They'd found her beaten and abandoned in a clump of creosote bushes by a dirt road, and it was said that Castell never once asked her about her past, either. They had a son,

Charles, and were apparently a monogamous, contented couple. Castell abused neither his position nor his power to evoke enthusiasm.

He argued, swore, smoke occasional cigars, drank moonshine, played poker, and could plug the selected eyeball of a sidewinder at a hundred paces at dusk with a handgun. He displayed several accents in the course of even a single sentence, and spoke at least rudiments of English, Spanish, and German. He also kept his word, and earned respect daily.

Church of New Universal Harmony was incorporated, but continued voluntarily to pay taxes and fees and such from which religions were officially exempt. He rendered unto Caesar, and Caesar liked that just fine. The business deals, connections, and the virtuosity displayed by Castell's structuring of the Church's finances, holdings, and such led many to believe that their founder had once been a hugely successful businessman who had suffered a crisis of conscience. He had, they thought, wandered for a few years, until he understood about Harmony, and then he started organizing things again, this time along Harmonic principles.

Castell died from a stress-induced cardiac infarction during the negotiations for license and the actual purchase of colonizing rights to a new world, which he called Haven. Many rumors at the time linked him with CoDominium Intelligence, but such rumors never specified whether he was supposed to have been a member or simply talked to them as he'd talked to so many other groups of self-interested authorities. Certainly selective harmonizing, or Choosing the Right Song, as he called it, would be a likely route for him to have chosen in such a bitter battle to secure a new place for his Harmonies. Except for the one occasion of his jailhouse epiphany, he always tried to sing along with the loudest.

He left behind him a son, Charles, who proved a reluctant but eventually very able leader, and a Church that has withstood the test of time despite many transformations.

THE GARDEN SPOT

DON HAWTHORNE

Earth Date: 23.7.2034—WAYFORTH STATION; TANITH SECTOR—

A class action suit filed by the crew of a CoDominium exploration vessel was upheld today after six weeks' review of the case by CoDo arbitrators. The suit will now proceed to CoDominium Civil Court for eventual resolution.

Captain Jed Byers of the CDSS *Ranger* and his crew were prepared to bring suit against the M.I.T./CalTech University Consortium for breach-of-contract regarding the *Ranger*'s claim of a discovery bonus for the Byers' Star System. Though no habitable worlds exist in this system, the primary gas giant does possess a marginally habitable moon. The *Ranger*'s master and crew admit that this moon's qualifications for colonial use are barely within the parameters established by CoDominium law, but it was the University Consortium's position that the very fact of its being a moon rather than a planet rendered any discovery bonus clauses in their contract null and void. In addition, reaching the new system is by no means easy; it lies at the end of several awkwardly linked Alderson Jump points, and travel time from Earth is over a standard year. Even so, CoDo arbitrators, perhaps fearing to set a precedent that might discourage initiative

7

among exploratory vessels, passed the case upward in the Civil Judiciary, which is expected to hand down a ruling in favor of Captain Byers and his crew.

When asked his opinion on the future of the system which now bears his name, Captain Byers shrugged and said: "That's not my problem anymore. We found it. Now it's up to the Survey boys."

Willard Fahran, attorney for the University Consortium had little to say beyond this: "We don't see much point in pursuing this any further. The moon isn't much more than a rock, but the more time we waste on litigation, the less time the Survey groups have to find some shred of value in it."

Mr. Fahran would not comment on a statement by Allan Wu, Science Officer of the *Ranger*, that "ownership of an entire planetary body for personal exploitation allows very little chance of bankruptcy."

One Year Later . . .

"Geez, this place doesn't look too good." Frank Owens, the Navigator, grunted as he hunched over his screen in a posture that would bring misery to his back in years to come.

"What it looks like is borderline quality dog food," Brian Connolly, the First Officer, concurred. His voice had that fruity uppah-crust British drawl, and even in the gloom of the bridge, you could tell from its modulation that *his* posture was correct; his spine would never dare be otherwise.

"*Cold* dog food," Owens continued. He sat up and turned toward Captain Emmett Potter. "Christ, Captain; people are gonna try to *live* here?"

"Most likely." Potter was the end product of ten generations of Narragansett Bay fisherfolk. Though unusually loquacious for a Wet Yankee, he had to be in the mood, and right now, that mood was not on him. There was too much work to do. He finished tweaking a circuit board and plugged it back into the sensor module. The ship's master, Farrow, had very little money to spend, and in the months since leaving Wayforth Station Potter had become something of an expert in making do.

"Well, then, they're for sure gonna die here, I can tell you that right now." Owens grabbed his floating keypad and began making notes.

"Well, pickings have been pretty slim, lately," Potter continued. Which was something of an understatement. There'd been a lucky run of High Desirability planets discovered and placed on the A list in the last few years, and Survey Teams were assigned by seniority. The Explorers had been getting rich on discovery bonuses, the senior Survey Teams had been getting richer on all the "Priority:Rush/Habitation Study" orders, and the Companies had been getting richer still on their increased stock values for acquisition of high investment value worlds.

The only people who hadn't been getting rich were, as usual, the commander and crew of the *Fast Eddie*.

The *Edward V* was her name on the roster, but her first master had been a Canuck drunkard who insisted on calling her *Edouard Vee*; somebody heard the "vee" in a Montreal accent, thought it was "vite," which meant "quickly" in French, the joke made the rounds and the name had stuck like a leftover curse, far outlasting the short and undistinguished career of the ship's first, now dead, master.

Fast Eddie had a crew of eight: The master, Thomas Farrow, the flight crew, consisting of Captain Potter, First Officer Connolly and Navigator Owens, Chief Engineer William Liu and a black gang comprised of two engineers of indiscriminate but more or less Latin ancestry named Icaorius and Mi'huelo Costanza. Icaorius and Mi'huelo being something of a mouthful, they were instead known variously as "Ike and Mike," "the Cisco Kids," or more commonly, "those Christless Spaniards." They might actually have been Spaniards for all that the officers could decipher of their bizarre dialect, but in fact, they were Basques, and every reference to them as

Spaniards by the rest of the crew was followed by mysterious failures in cabin humidity, air conditioning, and most frequently, the mean temperature of shower water. Consequently or not, as time passed there were fewer and fewer such references.

Of the eighth man, the less Potter thought about him, the better he felt. Robert Miller was very low on his list of favorite people.

Captain Potter shook his head, thinking about how he had spent the last half of a year, and to what purpose? The ship was a patchwork embarrassment, the crew likewise, and as data began rolling in on the cheesy joke of a habitat beneath them, Potter couldn't help thinking that they were just the ship for the job. But he'd been with Farrow when the Wayforth Station administrator, Vilmer Hogan, had called them in for the assignment, and he knew the master hadn't had much choice.

"*Fast Eddie* is just the ship for the job," Hogan had told them. Potter had noticed that the administrator hadn't met their eyes when he'd said that.

"It's *Edward the Fifth*," Farrow had said tiredly. He didn't have much fight left in him, these days.

Potter had jumped in before the administrator could bully Farrow into submission. "And how can you say that, Hogan? She's been laid up for eight weeks waiting for parts that your service crews claim have to be saved for ships with higher seniority. And you want to send us to a rock that's over a year from Earth? We'll be spending the next six months burning fuel to get from one Alderson Point to the next and another half a year to get back."

"Your wages will accumulate, same as always. And you'll be reimbursed for your fuel expenditures."

Potter had given the administrator a sour smile. "Don't insult my intelligence, Hogan. You know as well as I that we can't come out ahead on this deal even if we hit the jackpot on a Survey Bonus." It had seemed like such a good idea for the crew to buy out *Fast Eddie*, once upon a time. . . .

Hogan had shifted in his chair, and for the first time Potter had noticed the sweat on the fat man's upper lip; he was very nervous about something. "Look, Farrow, Potter. Survey of this moon is very important to certain people. These people are eager to confirm the moon's habitability as soon as possible. I'm authorized to cancel all of the *Fast Eddie*'s outstanding debts, return her to full operational status at no expense to you, and absorb all your operating costs for the duration of the mission."

Potter remembered listening to the very quiet air conditioning unit in Hogan's office hum for some time.

"Why?" Farrow had spoken first, surprising them both.

Hogan turned to the *Fast Eddie*'s master, but Potter felt his attention on himself. "Wayforth Station is a hell-hole; we both know that. It, and places like it, exist only because they sit at intersections of Alderson Points. The CoDominium has written: Wherever two or more Alderson Jump Points are gathered together, there also am I."

Potter shifted uncomfortably; he was not a very religious man, but he was pretty sure Farrow was, and he resented Hogan's sarcastic blasphemy in the presence of *Fast Eddie*'s master. Hogan's attitude might also be taken as subversive by certain overzealous CoDo persons.

"Wayforth sits at the center of six such Jump Points," Hogan went on, leaning forward over his desk and steepling his fingers. "That makes it valuable, commercially and strategically. It connects to several of those Gold Rush worlds where all the other Survey Teams are even now making maps for the CoDo city planners and the corporate industrial developers. Earth-like worlds, easy to get to; prime stuff for the factions that can afford them, CoDo or otherwise. As for this moon, the Company wants to be sure it's not missing out on some lucrative mining potential; the Universities are still whining about a wildlife preserve; even the religious nuts are rallying under a common banner—Harmonies, they've started calling themselves—for a place to worship away from CoDo interference in their affairs. An out-of-the-way place like this moon appeals to all sorts of people by the very fact of its lack of easy access." Hogan leaned back, his bulk making the chair creak even in Wayforth's low gravity. "But there is another value to out-of-the-way places, too, gentlemen," he finished.

Potter had sighed. "I see," he had said, and he did.

Out-of-the-way places were for putting things out of the way, and the things that were most often put out of the way in the CoDominium were people. Earth was still crowded, and the better colony worlds were taken, or their lobbyists were still able to resist forced refugee assignment in the Grand Senate.

And you had to put them somewhere, he knew.

Enter the CoDominium's Bureau of Relocation, BuReloc for short, and arguably the hardest-working bureaucracy in history. Bureloc moved product like there was no tomorrow, and its product was colonists. Sometimes the colonists were willing, more often they were not. But willing or not, they moved.

"Poor bastards," Potter had said, as he and Farrow signed the contract for the Survey order.

"Don't worry about your crew," Hogan had said. "Better they have something to do for two years than sit around idle."

But Potter hadn't meant the crew of the *Fast Eddie*. He had read the discovery team's preliminaries on the moon of the Byers' Star gas giant, and he had been thinking about the people who would someday have to live there.

Now the *Fast Eddie* had arrived; the crew began the long preparations that would culminate, however reluctantly, with the first extended visit of men to her surface, and Potter's mood shifted into the low gear of indigestion.

"Pack your long underwear, boys," Owens pronounced, and transferred the last of the orbital survey data to the *Fast Eddie*'s shuttle computers. He turned at a chuckle from Connolly. "What?"

"Oh, just thinking about all the things people have said wouldn't happen 'til hell froze over." The First Officer pointed to a screen rippling with ground images and overlaid with environmental data. "They're all down there waiting for us right now."

"Cheery thought."

"All right, knock it off," Potter's admonition was quiet, almost weary; but not without a tinge of sincerity. Cat's Eye's moon was a NEW PLACE, words that filled the captain's mind in large block letters, black as death. Too many names were entered in Wayforth's Mariner's Hall as having never returned from NEW PLACES, and Potter had no intention of adding any more familiar names to that list, least of all his own. His temper was short, anyway; it was no longer possible to avoid going and speaking to Miller.

The eighth man of the *Fast Eddie*'s complement was not, strictly speaking, a crew member. Robert Miller was listed on the *Fast Eddie*'s first-ever passenger manifest as a "CoDominium Xeno-Geologist." While not welcomed by anyone since the day Hogan had forced him upon the *Fast Eddie*'s crew, Miller had made himself as unobtrusive as possible during the long flight from Wayforth, earning a grudging acceptance from the others that was best described as belligerent neutrality. Besides a gift for chess, he contributed nothing to the ship's activities and took what Potter considered to be more than his share of food and oxygen; Miller was an irredeemable athlete, given to spending eight hours or more in the *Fast Eddie*'s centrifuge ring and eating like a horse afterward.

Half a G seemed never to be enough for Miller, and Potter had three times found the rotation setting increased beyond its long-term design limits. He'd finally ordered Liu to program a lock-out on the ring's controls, and Miller had sullenly acquiesced.

Gripping the handholds above his seat, Potter pulled himself up and kicked off in the direction of the bridge door, continuing the zero-G acrobatics as he proceeded down the corridor to the living quarters module of the *Fast Eddie*. At the last door he floated to a stop and tapped the button.

"Yes." The voice from within was no less flat for being filtered through a wall speaker.

Don't say "come in" or anything civil, Potter thought. *Asshole*. "We're taking the shuttle down in about an hour. Bring your gear and come to the launch bay when you're rea—"

Potter was cut off by the rapidly opened hatch, revealing in all his glory Robert Miller, Company Man. Miller was already wearing E-Suit underwear and had a golfbag-sized canvas carry-all slung over his shoulder. "Excuse me," he said as he moved past Potter into the corridor.

Potter noticed the slippery grace with which the man moved as he insinuated himself into the gangway and moved off in the direction of the launch bay. *"Insinuated" himself*, Potter thought. *That's a good word for it; that's what he's done since the first day we laid eyes on him*.

"He's a part of your contract." Hogan was adamant.

"Then the contract's broken; no non-union, non-essential civilian personnel on Survey vessels, for their own safety and that of the crew." Potter felt his blood pressure rising; he was doing all of Farrow's fighting for him again, and it always gave him a migraine.

"You'll bear no responsibility for him."

"Damn right, 'cause he's not going to be aboard."

Hogan sighed deeply. "Potter, there are Company operatives aboard every ship in the Survey Fleet. You and I both know that, so let's cut the bull, shall we? At least this way you know who yours is. Miller goes with you."

"What the hell for, Hogan? We're a Survey vessel, we can't file any claims if something valuable is found anyway."

"You're forgetting the most important thing about the

Byers' Star moon. Its value as a dumping ground for undesirables. What happens if those undesirables turn over a rock one day and find a vein of gold?"

"You've got a lot of rich undesirables, so what?"

"Money is commerce, and commerce means representation in the CoDominium Senate."

Potter rubbed his eyes in weariness. "Rich undesirables who vote, right, I get it. Can't be having that, now, can we?"

Hogan shook his head and pressed a button on his desk. "I'm glad we understand each other. Eve, send in Mister Miller."

When Miller entered, Hogan had introduced him to Potter and Farrow, each man had nodded, and none of them had spoken another word to each other. With few exceptions, their first meeting with Miller that day had set the tone for all Potter's future conversations with the man. Which, he considered, watching Miller's back receding down the corridor, was just the way he liked it.

Potter returned to the bridge, allowing First Officer Connolly and Navigator Owens to head for the shuttle bay to make the pre-flight check.

He sat down with a surly grunt as they left, thinking how glad he would be when this was all over.

"Shuttle One to Bridge."

Potter acknowledged. From the shuttle bay, Connolly and Owens began calling off the pre-launch checklist in bored tones that belied their interest in the shuttle's operating status.

Alone among *Fast Eddie*'s accouterments, at least one of her two shuttles was always kept in perfect working order. They had to be: *Fast Eddie* might not be much, but it was the only way home, and getting back to the lumbering Survey ship waiting in orbit was only slightly less important than landing in one piece after leaving her.

Giving them the final green light, Potter threw the switches which detached the shuttle from its umbilicals.

The squat, ungainly form dropped away slowly from *Fast Eddie*'s forward ventral bay, dwindling in the dark distance, finally backlit by the bright flare of its engines as it moved into its descent pattern.

"God speed," Captain Potter said quietly. But for himself, the bridge was empty now, and lonely. Along with the First Officer and Navigator, the shuttle carried Ike, several hundred pounds of survey equipment, and Miller himself, stuffed unceremoniously and uncomplaining into an emergency deceleration hammock. Potter found himself envying the Company man even that. It would have been reckless to leave Farrow to oversee the operations of the vessel, and Chief Engineer Liu had enough to keep him and his remaining engineering lackey busy for months.

Potter sat back in the command seat, considering how much he hated being left behind, and how lonely the long trip home would be if anything went wrong down there.

The idea of things going wrong inevitably brought Potter's thoughts back to Miller.

The man was no more than a Company spy, Hogan had admitted as much; had admitted too that Miller's job was to be sure that Byers' Star's moon had nothing of sufficient value to prevent its designation as a relocation site for BuReloc.

Potter rubbed his chin. *All debts forgiven and a free ride for the* Fast Eddie; *if Hogan's on the level, then BuReloc is putting an awful lot of effort into getting a man out here just to verify that a place is worthless to the CoDominium government.*

"Right," Potter grunted. But in the last year, he'd had many opportunities to go over the available data on the moon, and there was nothing there to imply that it was anything more than an interesting exception in the Biosphere Rulebook.

Still . . .

He was nervously chewing the inside of one cheek when the shuttle crashed.

* * *

"*Fast Eddie,* this is Shuttle One down, mayday."

"Give it a rest for a moment, won't you?" Connolly's voice was weary as he massaged his temples, eyes closed.

Owens stared at his screens in tightly controlled terror. "*Fast Eddie's* probably in farside orbit from us right now; goddammit, I must've told Potter a hundred times to re-check those relay satellites."

"Well, he didn't, we don't have them, so if *Fast Eddie's* in farside orbit right now, we can't talk to them." Connolly opened a panel on his own console and distractedly pushed a few buttons.

"It's dead, for chrissakes," Owens surrendered in disgust. "Leave it alone." His own board confirmed his judgment that all the shuttle's port side controls were inoperative. They'd landed very hard and with a lot of noise, and every screen monitoring the port systems had gone dark the same moment that the shuttle had developed an ominous, sickly list to that side.

Ike arrived with the results of his inboard systems inspection; the shuttle was small, and it hadn't taken him long to ascertain that an outside inspection was necessary.

"Christ on a crutch." Owens' voice tightened by the minute as he struggled out of his seat against the unfamiliar gravity. "Well, that should make Miller happy."

"Miller?" Connolly frowned. "We've an emergency here, Owens; we can't have him toddling outside on a whim while we're trying to perform damage assessments."

"Oh? Why the hell not? He's going to be useless as tits on a bull, and it'll keep him out of the way while we work."

Owens was at the door when Connolly added: "Look, Owens, I can't say I've much use for the fellow myself; but we can't spare anyone to buddy with him; what happens if he wanders off and gets lost, or hurt?"

"Who cares?" Owens mumbled without turning around.

* * *

Thomas Farrow, Owner and Master Aboard of the *Fast Eddie*, stared at the screens with great, sad owl eyes. He'd posted himself to the bridge immediately upon hearing of the shuttle crash.

Pausing only long enough to drop three tabs of Hangover-Be-Gone, Potter uncharitably thought.

Potter had found his temper shortening with every discovery of a new dimension of his own impotence to affect the crisis. He had just learned that the second shuttle was inoperative; there could be no rescue from that quarter. Farrow had neglected to schedule its hundred-hour check, and Potter had found a dozen problems that were sufficient to ground it for full overhaul. He sighed again. But it wasn't Farrow's fault that they had no relay satellites; Potter had made the mistake of trusting Hogan's word on that one, and his ulcer was exacting payment for that folly, now.

Shuttle One was out of contact every ninety minutes for an equal amount of time as the *Fast Eddie's* painfully slow orbit carried her around the far side of the Byers' Star moon. Even when directly over the landing zone— Potter had forced the words "crash site" back from his mind so many times he'd lost count—the static generated by the gas giant, Cat's Eye, was enough to make an unholy mess out of communications.

"We're coming over the horizon again," Farrow said in a low voice.

Potter grunted acknowledgment. He had a feeling that Owens and Connolly were tiring of his demand for updates every hour and a half.

Too bad. He began calling for the shuttle.

"It's just great, that's all," Owens' voice was borne on a wave of interference, but the communications filters were doing their job well enough. "This place is a regular garden spot. Two hours outside in thin air with thin coats, and what's waiting inside but thin coffee. Anyway, it looks like we put down over a frost heave covered by snow; solid ground beneath one leg and lots of air three feet under the surface beneath the other. This whole area is a swamp marsh frozen solid for the winter. The landing leg collapsed and the whole weight of the shuttle came down on the port lift thrusters. They're half-buried, so I'd guess they're shot. Ike shakes his head a lot when I ask him how we can repair them, then he makes lifting gestures and shrugs."

"I've got Liu working on the other shuttle," Potter said. "Can't say for sure what we can accomplish, but we'll keep you posted."

"Yeah, right. Listen, Connolly wants to talk to you."

"Put him on."

"Emmett? It's about Miller."

Potter heard Owens bitching in the background at the mention of the BuReloc man's name. "What is it? What's he done now?"

"Well, the damn fool's gone off and started his bloody survey on his own. So far he's stayed in sight of the shuttle, but that's not the point."

Potter shook his head. Miller was utterly inconsequential, now, but he wanted to give Connolly and Owens something to take their minds off the strong likelihood that they would become the moon's first permanent human residents. "Is he any use to you there?" Potter asked. "In the repairs, I mean?"

He heard Owens shout *"No!"* in the background.

"No," Connolly admitted, "but it's damned dangerous. It's cold as a witch's tit out there, with snow to boot. If he falls and kills himself, we'll have to answer to the Bureau of Relocation for it."

"To hell with the Bureau right now, Brian," Potter said. "And to hell with Miller. Let him play with his drills and ore samples. We'll need all that data anyway, once we get you fellas orbit-capable again and ready to come home."

And if we don't get you orbit-capable, you won't be coming home, so it won't matter then, either.

There was a long silence. "Right," Connolly said

finally. "Got it, Emmett. See if you can't—" Connolly's voice faded out.

"Orbital path," Farrow said. "We're losing them again."

Potter boosted the signal. "Passing on, guys. Talk to you again in an hour and a half. *Edward V* out."

He leaned back against the chair's zero-G harness and tapped the console distractedly, looking out at the surreal patterns of the Cat's-Eye gas giant. "Tom, what's the latest on that storm front?"

Farrow turned to another screen. "Weather patterns on this rock are pretty strange, Emmett. Looks like they're tied in closely with the long full-night cycle, when one half of the moon is without light from either the system primary or the gas giant. The valley they're in is due for that night in about ten standard days."

Potter stared at the sepia-toned mass of gaseous soup outside, the horizon of the satellite a gray crescent along the top of the port. The moon's proximity to its parent world allowed enough radiant heat to compensate for its distance from the system primary, but the heavy gravity of the gas giant denied the *Fast Eddie* any chance of making geosynchronous orbit over her downed shuttle. They could only circle helplessly, and wait.

"Sit and spin," Potter said.

And pray.

A clipboard floated through the bridge hatch, followed by the clambering form of Chief Engineer Liu. "Emmett, we might have a solution to our problem."

"Well, amen, Chief."

"Huh?"

"Nothing, go ahead."

"Okay, here's a list of what's wrong with Shuttle Two, and here's what I can reasonably expect to fix in the next eight days."

Potter scrolled through the datapad screens, grunting occasionally as he passed items of interest. "That's great, Chief, but these are all quick fixes, and none of them bring the shuttle up to full spec."

"Well, no. But all together, they'll get Shuttle Two down in one piece, guaranteed."

"Well, hell, Chief, we've *got* one shuttle down there, practically in one piece; our problem is how to get that one back up."

"Relax, Emmett. The idea is we take the second shuttle down filled with as much repair equipment as it will carry, land it near Shuttle One, and then cannibalize the second shuttle for parts to fix the first. Ditch Shuttle One's ground car to save the weight of the extra crewmen and—" Liu wafted a hand toward the ceiling—"bring our boys home before the snow falls."

Potter looked at the Engineer for a moment, then went back to the datapad. "Nice work, Bill," he finally said in a small voice. He turned to Farrow. "Tom? You're Master Aboard, and we *are* talking about throwing away several hundred thousand New Dollars' worth of equipment."

Farrow shook his head in dismissal. "Don't be ridiculous. Those are our men down there." He gave a faint smile. "Besides, the CoDominium is picking up the bill, right? Let's think of this as an opportunity to stick them for all the taxes they've gouged us for over the years. Go ahead, Chief Engineer Liu. And don't spare the horses."

Robert Miller snatched at his flapping face mask, catching it before the wind could make off with it. He refastened it beneath his hood, and gave Ike a thumbs-up, after which both men returned to the task of lowering the shuttle's bay ramp into the thin snow covering the alien ground.

The shuttle had come down in the plains in the northeastern corner of a great equatorial valley. Surrounded for thousands of miles by soaring mountains, the resulting large, enclosed land mass was about the size of Earth's continental United States, and enjoyed the highest air pressure on the moon; close to that of Earth at fourteen thousand feet above sea level. Which made it just about tolerable if you were a mountain climber.

Which Miller was. He'd been on climbs on a dozen worlds, mostly on BuReloc business, but frequently for sport. That expertise had been the major reason for his assignment as the CoDominium's man on this survey mission. Thin air was not usually a problem for him, nor cold, but he most definitely did not wish to stay on this moon any longer than necessary; certainly not for the rest of his life. The shuttle crash had inspired his mind into a protective overdrive, and he'd thrown himself into his work with a fierce abandon.

Still, he'd learned all he could from his samples here on the plains. He needed to get to the foothills to look for exposed ore, and that meant he needed the ground car. Owens and Connolly had shown no interest whatsoever in anything he did, and that was fine with him. This Ike fellow was less obnoxious, and had readily agreed to help him with this much, at least.

Miller had noticed that Ike was largely unaffected by the thin air, and the cold as well. Obviously the fellow was of terrestrial mountain stock, but Miller had very little to do with anyone on the trip out here, and still less with Ike or Mike. He'd guessed Greece, or perhaps Turkey, but unlike the rest of the crew, Miller had made the connection between minor ship malfunctions and implications of Spanish ancestry for Ike and Mike. He might guess at their background, but he said nothing. He wondered if this Ike was the Company man aboard the *Fast Eddie*; his control officer had warned him there was certain to be one, despite BuReloc's efforts to get him out here on a "clean" ship.

Miller didn't anticipate a problem in any case; the Companies and their lobbyists in the CoDo Senate were powerful, to be sure, but they weren't foolish enough to confront BuReloc directly over one marginally useful world, whatever its economic potential. The Companies had the real power these days, but the CoDominium government still controlled the courts. The courts decided who was sentenced to "remedial colony support services," their euphemism for forced deportation, almost always for life, and the Companies had a lot of older executives with troublesome young children and grandchildren who frequently made the mistake of thinking themselves above the law. When he thought about it, Miller considered it a rather tawdry system of checks and balances, but it worked, and anyway, he didn't think about it much.

The ramp was locked in place, exposing the bulky ground car which had been idling within the bay for the last fifteen minutes. Ike helped Miller into the cab, and they drove it down the ramp. Miller was about to wave and drive off when Ike clambered into the seat beside him and shut the door with a grin.

Miller stared at the engineering crewman with a frown. "You don't need to come with me."

Ike shrugged. "No work to do; th' shuttle is *tota.*" He waved impatiently toward the mountains. "Let's take a ride."

Miller decided then that Ike was just obvious enough to be the *Fast Eddie*'s Company spy; still, he was glad for the companionship. He set the inertial navigation computer, put the ground car in gear and rolled off east toward the foothills.

Inside the shuttle, Owens cursed. "Well, great. That Christless Spaniard just took off for a joyride with the BuReloc spook."

"Oh, terrific. That's bloody swell." Finally losing his temper, Connolly threw a fused circuit board against the wall. After a moment, he calmed down. "Well. It's not like we'd a whole lot for them to do here, I suppose."

The communications panel chimed, and Potter's voice crackled into the cabin. "Shuttle One, acknowledge."

"Yeah, Emmett, we're here," Owens answered.

"I think we've got some good news for you."

Owens and Connolly shared a brief, hunted look. "Roger that, Emmett," Owens fought to control his voice. "What's the scoop?"

"Liu's been working on the Number Two Shuttle, says

he can have it ready in about eight days for a one-way trip to your site."

A strangled laugh slipped past Owens' lips. "Well— Jesus Christ, Emmett! What good is *that* going to do us?"

"Shut up, Owens," Connolly shouted, taking over the communications panel. "What have you got in mind, Emmett?"

Potter explained Liu's plan, and the four of them went over the details for the next eighty-five minutes. The *Fast Eddie*'s signal was beginning to fade as Potter added: "And please, Brian; be very thorough when you take soundings of that landing area. We don't want to hit another sinkhole like you did and have two busted up elevators in the basement."

Owens laughed an acknowledgement as he signed off.

Potter's signal had been gone for a full minute before Connolly put a hand to his forhead in panic. "Oh, my God . . . the sounding equipment; it's all in the ground car with Miller and Ike."

Owens began trying to raise the BuReloc man and their own engineering crewman, to no avail. "Jesus, they haven't been gone more than an hour and a half, how far could they get?"

Connolly sat back in his chair and closed his eyes.

"I suppose," he said finally, "that we can take some comfort in the idea that not very much more can go wrong on this trip."

Owens kept calling Miller and Ike, trying not to think about how wrong Connolly could be.

Miller and Ike were gone for five days, and the rest of the crew had given them up for dead. Owens and Connolly had begun clearing a landing area a few hundred yards north, taking soundings manually with a metal pole heated by a battery pack, for although there was snow on the ground, the ground frost beneath was quite thin. Despite the moon's miserable cold, it was extremely dry this close to the sheltering mountains that separated the valley from the sea winds. The clearing was done with no tools heavier than makeshift brooms and piled rocks to keep fresh drifts out.

Owens and Connolly had been sweeping clear the landing zone in a clockwise pattern, and had reached eight-thirty when the Navigator noticed his British First Officer staring off into the distance.

"Christ, Connolly, you're not snowblind, are you?"

Connolly dropped his broom and started running past Owens. "It's the ground car; it's Miller and Ike, come on!"

Powder clouds of dry snow puffed up around their feet as the two men ran toward the ground car, the thin, cold air of the wretched little moon raking their lungs in spite of their face masks. Owens thought that men might one day learn to run on this forsaken rock, but they would never enjoy it.

The ground car slowed and turned in their direction when they were within fifty yards, and both of them could see the carcass of some large, shaggy quadruped draped over its hood. Owens and Connolly staggered to a fast walk.

"What the hell is that?" the Navigator wheezed.

"Indigenous life form." Connolly too was panting as they closed the distance. "Herbivorous grazer, I suspect; likely inhabitant for this sort of terrain."

Owens shook his head. "First kill on the new world. Man has arrived."

Connolly threw him a sidelong glance; Owens was not the sort of fellow who made pronouncements on the morality of his species. And in any case, something about the animal carcass bothered him. Even as they approached, it looked wrong to him; too—lumpy. "Oh, bloody hell," Connolly said abruptly.

The ground car had chuffed to a halt as they reached it, and both Connolly and Owens could see all the details of the mooselike animal tied securely to its hood. And tied behind it, giving it the unnatural appearance Connolly had noted, was the body of a man wrapped in plastic. The feet protruded from one end, revealing the thick, CoDo issue explorer's boots of the engineering crewman Icaoruis, better known as Ike.

Miller popped the door and leaned out. "There was an accident," he said. "I'm sorry."

Neither Owens nor Connolly said anything, and Miller went on: "Get in, we'll drive him back to the shuttle."

Owens turned without answering and headed back for the clearing. After a moment, Connolly followed, leaving Miller standing in the open door of the ground car cab. Finally, the BuReloc man settled back into the cab and drove on to the shuttle. Owens took his hand from his pocket just long enough to casually raise his middle finger to Miller as he passed.

"What do you think happened?" Potter asked during the next communications cycle.

Connolly sighed. "I don't know, Emmett. Miller says they were up in the foothills, digging at some crystalline ore, when they saw this musk-ox-antelope thing. Ike apparently thought it would be good eating, so he shot it with one of the rifles from the ground car. Then, when he was climbing down to the carcass, some big predator jumped him out of nowhere, apparently trying to steal the kill. Ike lost his footing, and fell into a defile before Miller could do anything."

"How did Miller get the carcass away from the predator?"

"He says he drove it off with the other rifle. Possible, I suppose."

Potter's silence ate up a good deal of their precious communications time. "Do you believe him?"

"Hell, no," Owens said firmly in the background.

Connolly sighed. "I don't know, Emmett. The animal carcass looks pretty torn up, like a tiger was at it for a minute or two. Miller recovered Ike's rifle when he brought the corpse up. Both are pretty banged about."

"All right. Liu's a little ahead of schedule, he says the second shuttle will be ready in two more days. We've gotten a little sloppy in our radio contacts; that's not to happen anymore. I want you or Owens on this line every ninety minutes, clear?"

"Got it."

Owens leaned in and said: "And what if we have 'accidents,' too, Emmett?"

"Then the *Fast Eddie* writes off the Survey Team and heads home."

Connolly and Owens shared a look. "I see," Connolly said. "So we'd best hope neither of us slips into a coma."

"You or Frank on this line, every hour and a half," Potter repeated. "And make sure our guest knows it."

Potter signed off, and leaned back against the chair. He had to prop his feet against the console edge to do it.

In low gravity, as in politics, he considered, *leverage is everything.*

Behind him, Chief Engineer Liu stared intently at the silent communications console. "Bad," was all he said.

Potter nodded faintly. "Yup."

Connolly coined the term "muskylope" for the grazer Miller had brought back, and despite the mood of the camp being only a little less frigid than the outside air, all three enjoyed the taste; after their forced diet of survival rations, fresh meat was a welcome relief.

But once the steaks were gone, then Owens' and Connolly's distrust of Miller settled back in. They openly refused to sleep at the same time, an insulting statement which provided great moral satisfaction at first, but which only resulted in Miller being the one man in camp who was getting a decent amount of rest during the moon's seemingly endless day.

"Look at him," Owens said after waking Connolly for his relief. "Sonofabitch sleeps like a baby."

"Why not? He knows he's safe."

"But is he?" Owens asked Connolly in a low voice.

"Yes, I am," Miller answered, and Owens turned to

see the BuReloc man watching them calmly from his
sleeping bag.

Owens shook his head. "You spooks are pathetic;
America's in bed with the Russians in our glorious
CoDominium, so there's nobody left to spy on; nobody
except everybody. What did you find out there? Something too important to let poor Ike live after he'd seen
it? Or was it just for practice?"

Miller lowered his eyes. "It was an accident." The
BuReloc man leaned up on one elbow to look at Owens,
and Connolly wondered for the hundredth time if Miller
had a gun in that bag with him. "Whether you believe it
or not doesn't change the fact."

"Right, then. Frank, that's enough, yes?" Connolly said
from his own bag in the wall hammock. "Get some sleep;
the shuttle's due in eight hours. I'll come and wake you
then."

Owens stood up and pulled several blankets from a
locker.

"What are you doing?" Connolly asked.

"I'm sick of the company I've been keeping." The Navigator headed aft. "I'm going back to the ground car bay
to sleep."

"Frank, don't be an idiot, there's no heat back there!"

"Yeah, but there's a lock on the door." Owens stopped
before Connolly, pointedly ignoring Miller almost at his
feet. "Look, there's fresh batteries in the sleeping bags;
you come out to get me in six hours. Check me out
sooner if you get bored." He turned at the hatch, looking
down at Miller. "On second thought, considering your
company; don't get bored."

To Potter's surprise, the crew member who seemed
most affected by Ike's death was not his brother Mike,
but Farrow. The *Fast Eddie*'s master had taken to wandering about the ship with an apparent intensity of grief
that was a little frightening in a man who couldn't reasonably be kept away from air locks and orbital attitude
controls.

Farrow would often look out the viewports, staring down at the moon, and speaking softly under his breath. Rarely, Mike would come up behind the master and place a hand on his shoulder in a gesture of compassion. Seeing as it was from the man whose brother had died to his employer, and that the former appeared less affected than the latter, Potter found these occasional tableaux faintly distasteful, though he couldn't be exactly sure why.

As long as it keeps Farrow out of the way 'til we can get our living back aboard, Potter told himself. How Mike dealt with his brother's death was his own affair.

"Captain Potter, we're ready." Liu had finished the preliminary systems check on the second shuttle that morning, ship time, and had spent the rest of the day loading the gear they'd need to get Shuttle One flying again.

"Fine. Well, I guess it's pretty clear who's got to go."

Liu nodded. "I'll need Mike for the repair work; Owens and Connolly can keep busy, but this is drydock work, and command crew won't be much use."

Potter looked over his shoulder to be sure Farrow wasn't about. "Bill, this is going to be tricky; you need a pilot to get down there in one piece."

Liu nodded. "There's nothing for it. But we've got to take Farrow down with us; we can't leave him alone up here on the *Fast Eddie*. Hell, in his state he could walk out an airlock."

Potter ground a knuckle against his temple. "Yeah. Well, let's hope he doesn't wander off while we're down there. You recheck your repair estimates?"

Liu nodded. "Everybody working like coolies, worst case: three days. Most likely only two. We're up and off and back aboard *Fast Eddie*, headed home. The survey's scrubbed, of course; no bonus potential for a screw-up like this."

"Yeah, break my heart, why don't you." Potter looked over Liu's shoulder and out the port. "I've learned as much about this place as I care to already, Bill."

And I suspect, Potter finished to himself, *that our Mister Miller has, too.*

Shuttle Two drifted downward, and Potter found himself suddenly wishing there was an overhead hatch, so he could take one last look at the *Fast Eddie* above them. Involuntarily, he shuddered.

What a gruesome thought; unlucky, too. He began the minute adjustments that, magnified by their thirty-mile descent, would bring them into the general area of the first shuttle's landing zone. Liu was strapped in next to him, his eyes closed.

Can't say as I blame you, old friend. This is the sort of joyride that would have the Engineering and Machinists' Union howling for my blood if they knew about it. Behind them, Farrow had strapped himself in with a firm confidence that belied his earlier distress. Nevertheless, Mike continued a solicitous, if detached, attention toward his boss. *Good,* Potter thought. *Somebody else can hold his hand for a while.*

"Coming up on final, gentlemen," Potter tried to loosen his tightened throat with speech; it didn't work.

Air resistance increased around the shuttle, and the noise level from outside increased with it. In seconds the shuttle was a rock-filled washing machine of rattling pressure plates and popping seams. A giant of the air was slapping a pillow against the nose and belly, but the pillow weighed tons.

Potter saw Liu in his peripheral vision. The Chief Engineer had forced his eyes open to check his status panel. "How long, Emmett?" The vibrations made Liu's voice sound like a jackhammer was digging into his chest.

"Three minutes more."

"Have to be on the ground sooner; she's losing it."

"I meant three minutes to the landing zone. Another five to circle and land."

Liu rolled his eyes heavenward, and Potter hoped he wasn't looking for a good spot for harp playing.

When the shaking stopped, it was sudden enough to make Potter shout for a structural integrity check.

"Fine, it's fine," Liu was grinning as he checked his board. "She'll hold for that five minutes, but don't go longer than ten." Liu mumbled to himself in satisfaction, "*Heyah*, all gods bear witness, I can fix a rainy day!"

Potter passed over the western mountain range that sheltered the valley, their snowcapped peaks seeming barely below him despite his altitude. Shuttle Two's flat glide was taking it from one hundred thousand feet to a fifth of that in the course of their three-thousand mile flight path, and the view became spectacular.

The sun had broken through the thin cloud cover, lighting the valley from behind him, while Cat's Eye illuminated it before. And in that moment, as he looked across what would one day become known as the Shangri-La, he suddenly felt a great peace.

It's pure, he thought. *It's harsh in that purity, but it's a beautiful kind of harsh. People will come here, and they will live, and die, as Owens said they would. They'll settle it and cultivate it, fly over it and bury their dead in it, but they'll never change it, not really. In the end, like every pure place, it will change them. It will make them what it wants them to be, and they'll love it for that. The rest of this moon is cruel and ugly, but this valley is cruel and beautiful. Men will go to the other lands, and some will stay there, too. But those lands will never know the kind of devotion people will come to feel for this sheltered valley, this safe haven in a hard world.*

The moment passed; the landing zone was beneath them, a cleared circle of dead gray wintergrass in an unrelenting sea of shifting white, the crooked shadow of the crippled shuttle nearby. Potter was getting the feel of Liu's bastard child as he flew her, and the landing would be tricky.

Tricky it was, but perfect nonetheless.

One figure stood on the snow beyond the cleared circle; it ran toward the shuttle in a kind of loping shuffle;

long step, double-drag the other leg, long step. Potter cracked the hatch and pushed it open, freeing the debarkation ladder as he did so.

"Oh, my sweet *Christ!*" The blast of frigid air hit him in the face like a flamethrower; he actually recoiled a step, frantically gathering his parka closed as he fought to keep his balance. On the ground below, the figure that had come to meet them was struggling up the ladder. It stumbled into the shuttle and fell against the wall, sliding down to the floor plates.

Potter knelt in the howling wind, pulling back the hood of their one-man reception party. It was Connolly, and he looked half-dead.

"Mike, Bill, help me get him into a couch." Potter knew that after extended months with no more gravity than the *Fast Eddie*'s centrifuge, it would take all three of them to lift the First Officer, and maybe Farrow besides. "And somebody close that pneumonia hole before we all wind up like Connolly."

Potter's examination told them what they all knew already. "Exposure, of course. Frostbite on all his toes and all but two fingers. I'm no doctor, but I can see those'll have to come off." Potter lightly touched the blackened digits. "Hell, he's going to lose this whole foot." He stood and shook his head, helplessly. "I don't think we can save him," he said quietly, as if to himself.

"If he warms up enough to get circulation in his limbs, he's likely to get blood poisoning," Liu warned.

Potter nodded. "Keep the temperature down in here," he said. A boyhood survivor of Atlantic winters in lobster boats on Earth's Narragansett Bay, Potter had seen plenty of frostbite. "If he does start getting circulation into those fingers and feet, the pain alone will kill him."

Potter crouched beside his frozen shipmate, trying to get something out of him. "Connolly," he called quietly. "Brian, it's Emmett; where's Owens? Connolly, where's Miller?"

Connolly started babbling so suddenly Potter almost

jumped. "Frank went to sleep in the ground car bay, I told him not to, I said there wasn't heat, not there, he went anyway, I woke up and went to check on him, but he'd locked the door, he said he wanted to be there because the door had a lock, and I had to go outside and go around to the ground car bay door, and it had swung open somehow and Frank didn't answer and I crawled in and he was solid, oh God he was solid as a statue, he was like marble, like blue marble, God forgive me I let him die in there I should have stopped him, should have ordered him, I—" Connolly's voice shattered into a keening wail, sobs wracked his chest, their sound filling the shuttle as the dying man brought his ruined hands up to cover his face. In a moment, Connolly lapsed into unconsciousness.

Potter rose and went to the locker, removing a pair of comically thick insulated mittens with a single index-finger sewn in. He pulled a rifle out as well, a flat-sided accelerator model with rocket shell projectiles for vacuum or zero-G environments.

"Bill," Potter said, "take another rifle. Mike, Mister Farrow, stay with Connolly and do what you can for him."

Potter and Liu left the second shuttle and crossed the landing zone toward the first. Byers' Star had slipped behind the Cat's Eye gas giant, and this side of the Cat's Eye moon was turning away from its parent world. Night was coming to their hemisphere, truenight, and the temperature was dropping to welcome it.

"Emmett, this guy is BuReloc." Liu was trying to reason with Potter, but still matching his stride.

"I don't give a rip."

They closed with the shuttle, its port list exposing the belly to them. Beyond the body of the craft they could see a man's legs moving about, and some kind of pole pacing them.

Too angry at the man's cheek to give any thought of ambush, Potter walked around the nose of the shuttle, and everything seemed to happen at once.

Miller was there, with something in his hands and a pile of broken, frozen dirt on the ground nearby. There were two graves, each marked with crosses. It was all Potter saw before Miller turned toward them, the long black cylinder pivoting before him.

Potter heard Liu say: "He has a gun." The Chief Engineer didn't shout, but simply raised his own accelerator rifle to his shoulder and fired in one smooth, practiced motion. Miller spun about and went down, and it was only then that Potter realized he had struck Liu's weapon down with his hand.

Liu snapped the weapon away and back-stepped. "Are you trying to get us killed?" Liu was almost snarling, but he recovered his composure instantly. "I—I'm sorry, Emmett; but he was—"

But Potter was going to the felled BuReloc agent. The 9mm rocket shell had hit him in the groin; Potter didn't need a great deal of imagination to think that Liu had been aiming for Miller's head until his blow had dropped the weapon's aim point. *A little lower and to the left,* Potter mused, *and live or die, my friend, the Miller line would have ended with you.*

Miller's teeth were squared in a rictus of agony, but Potter wasn't feeling especially charitable toward the man just now, and anyway he was curious about something. He turned Miller over, eliciting a gasp of pain from the victim, and lifted the cylinder Miller had been holding when he turned toward them. There was a foot-square metal plate at one end, and Potter held it up for Liu's inspection.

It was a shovel.

Miller sipped cautiously at the tea. His beard stubble was blue-black, and together with the dark circles under his eyes and sallowness of his skin, made him look as bad in shock as Connolly looked in the last stages of hypothermia. Miller was aboard the Shuttle Two, the warmth of the semi-operational craft bringing some color to his features and a lot of pain to his own near-frozen extremities.

"He wouldn't come inside," the BuReloc man said. "He seemed to think that I'd gone out and deliberately opened the bay door to the wind, to kill Owens."

"And did you?"

Miller sighed and lowered his head. "Christ, Potter, look at where my sleeping bag is; I'd have to crawl right over Connolly to get to the damn door. It must have come open in the night; probably hydraulic failure. Owens wouldn't feel it through his sleeping bag until the batteries gave out; his own body heat would have bled away after that."

Potter said nothing for a time, looking out the shuttle's forward window. "You buried Owens and Ike?"

Miller nodded. "Connolly wouldn't have anything to do with it. He wasn't going to let me do it, but they couldn't stay in here with us, and leaving them out might have drawn one of those big predators down from the hills. It wasn't a sentimental gesture."

Potter turned at that. "Maybe not. But plain markers, or none at all, might make me believe that. Crosses don't."

"That was kind of you," Farrow said quietly from the back. Miller shrugged, wincing at the pain any movement caused him.

Potter sighed. "Right." He turned to Farrow. "Tom, would you look after Brian and Mister Miller? We're going to see about getting Shuttle One flight ready."

Farrow moved to comply as Potter, Liu and Mike left the Shuttle once more.

"I'm telling you, Emmett," Liu began when they'd left Shuttle Two. "This BuReloc bastard is going to be the death of us all."

Potter said nothing except: "Wait and see."

Placing lifting jacks beneath the hull and leveling it off, they found that Shuttle One looked far worse off than it really was. The collapse of the landing leg into the sinkhole had severed half a dozen cables, but

caused very little actual damage. Liu shook his head at
the irony.

"If they'd had jacks and an arc welder, they'd have
been back a week ago."

Shuttle One was operational and flight-ready in twenty
hours, which suited Potter just fine, as the truenight of
this hemisphere of the moon was now less than twelve
hours away. During his watch, he made a cup of tea and
sat beside the sleeping Miller, watching him.

"I think you're awake," Potter said quietly.

Miller opened his eyes. "What is it?"

Potter pursed his lips and studied the blank wall opposite. "Oh, many things. Like why was Ike up there in the
hills with you at all?"

"He invited himself. I assumed he was told to keep an
eye on me. Anyway, I didn't object to him coming along;
traveling alone in these circumstances is idiotic."

"Yup. It's illegal, too."

"Right." Miller sneered.

Potter sipped his tea. "What did this predator look
like?"

"Big. Shaggy mane. A lion with an attitude."

"Maybe like a bear?"

"Maybe. Probably. I don't know, I've never seen a
bear."

Potter nodded. "And you drove it off with the rifle."

"That's right, so?"

Potter didn't answer right away, but only went back to
his tea. "Do you hunt a lot, Mister Miller?"

"Not animals."

"I didn't think so. I used to hunt a lot when I was
young. Sometimes, on Survey trips like this one, I'll stalk
a local animal that looked game. In my years on Survey
duty, I've seen a lot of strange animals that do a lot of
strange things. But there's one thing I've never seen,
Miller. Can you guess what it is?"

"Why spoil your fun?"

Potter smiled. "I've never seen an animal on an alien
world that was afraid of man. They aren't capable of it,

you see. How could they be? They've never seen a man before. Our scent is different, but not threatening, assuming they even smell us at all. They don't see us as a threat, they can't possibly. Like the American grizzly bear. Do you have any idea how many settlers it killed, and how many *grizzlies* the *settlers* had to kill, before the bears learned that man was dangerous? That man's *rifles* were dangerous? And grizzlies at least come from the same genetic soup as we do."

Potter shook his head. "Nope. You have to kill such animals, Miller. They don't scare. And it isn't because they're too stupid to be afraid of Man; they just don't realize how dangerous human beings can be."

There was a long silence, during which Potter finished his tea before concluding: "But I do."

Miller watched him silently.

"That was a clumsy lie, Miller. That contrived gesture of crosses for the graves was another." Potter stood up and tossed his cup away. "And they'll cost you. I'd have been happy to blow your head off for killing Ike, or just getting him killed. But this is better. I don't even care how or why you did it, now. I'm just looking forward to turning you over to the CoDo Bureau of Investigation for murder. Who knows? You might get lucky; maybe they'll sentence you to Involuntary Colonization and you'll get sent right back here." He went to the door and turned, silhouetted for a moment in the hatch. "Won't that be nice?"

"Potter," Miller said, "you know that won't happen. You can kill me and leave me here, and BuReloc will have your ass on general principle. You can take me back and turn me in, and BuReloc will squeeze the CBI, and I'll walk, and maybe BuReloc will have your ass anyway, just to make an example of tramp spacers who get delusions of moral grandeur."

"I suppose there's a third choice."

"Of course. Keep your mouth shut. I don't profit from this escapade; it's my job. But you and your crew could stand to gain a great deal from what I learned out there. *If* you're smart. Just sit tight, shut up and wait for the Survey bonus checks to start rolling in. At the very least, I can promise you that your frostbitten Mister Connolly will even be able to afford some pretty advanced prosthetics and a lot of the very best physical therapy."

Potter looked at him, his face an impassive mask, then nodded again. "Good night, Miller."

It was six hours later, and darker than ever. The sky outside was black with snow-laden, lowering clouds that sealed the tops of the mountain ranges, a layer of ephemeral paraffin topping a jar of secret preserves. Neither the light of Byers' Star nor Cat's Eye's radiant energy penetrated to the land beneath. The valley was a great bowl, and the lid was on. The repaired Shuttle One was nearly ready for takeoff; aboard Shuttle Two, the survey crew's temporary home, most people still slept.

Miller awoke at the prick of a needle into his thigh. He spun about to grasp the handgun kept tucked beneath his left arm, but found only his armpit.

"Live a little longer." The voice was an anonymous whisper in the dark, followed by a flat *click* of a hammer being pulled back; Miller recognized the sound of his own pistol. "Convince me you're just trying to warm that hand."

"What is it?" Miller felt the pain in his hip going away, and with it any sense of urgency or resolve.

"What did you and Ike find up in the hills that was worth killing him for?"

Miller tried not to answer, but immediately realized there was no real point. He no longer had any control over what he said. "Ore—" The words grunted past his best efforts to stop them. "Crystalline—ore—in the rocks."

"Good. And what kind of crystalline ore was it?"

"Diamonds." Miller found himself unable to suppress a sly giggle.

"No, now really."

Miller's eyelids were heavy, but he wasn't sleepy. "Half-diamonds," he said, almost grinning now. Whatever they'd used on him, it was hideously strong stuff. "Half-life zircons." And this time he really did laugh out loud, but a mitten was abruptly stuffed into his mouth. Shortly thereafter, a finger burrowed hard into the bullet wound in his groin.

Miller returned from the euphoric place he'd been drifting toward with the subtlety of a train wreck. Tears brimmed over his eyes and coursed down his cheeks as he gasped for air, getting only more mitten. After long seconds, the gag was removed.

"Now," the voice said, and Miller's soaring pain rendered it still more anonymous: "One more time; what was the crystalline ore you found in the hills?"

Miller gagged, unwilling to believe that the pain was receding again, until the hollow ache in his bowels faded enough to prove it to him. "Zirconium."

A finger tapped his wound, light as a feather; it felt like an anvil dropped from orbit. "Nothing special about zirconium," the voice pointed out.

"Hafnium!" Miller gasped. "The ore is a new form of zirconium crytolite; it's loaded with hafnium, twenty times the amount found in the richest terrestrial samples. Almost eighty percent hafnium."

The voice was silent. "We *are* talking about the hafnium used in nuclear reactor rods, aren't we, Mister Miller?"

Miller nodded.

"And you took samples of this ore, to prove to the CoDominium that you weren't crazy?"

Miller asserted every iota of his will, finally sure he could resist answering. "Yes. Worth billions for energy, weapons technology . . . The moon's too valuable to use as a CoDo dumping ground, the deportees would wind up owning the Grand Senate in a few decades."

The voice said nothing, and Miller could feel the drug

pulling him farther and farther away. A tiny flare as another needle entered his arm.

"I don't think so, Mister Miller," the voice said. Then something like: "Not the deportees," but Miller couldn't be sure, for by that time he was dead.

Potter looked down into Miller's sightless, staring eyes.

He thought he should be able to compose some poetic statement on the irony of life and death and justice, but all he could think of was what a monumental fuck-up this mission had turned out to be.

Potter had awakened before anyone else to find Miller dead. Connolly too had passed away while they slept. Liu had taken Mike and Farrow with him to make the final preparations for leaving, and Potter had stayed behind to prepare the bodies for burial. He was the captain, after all, and it was his responsibility to bury his men.

Potter crouched next to Miller and tried to close the eyes; the lids kept parting, widening to finally expose the bright, blue, dead pupils.

I always thought they stayed closed, Potter mused. The Captain of the *Fast Eddie* turned to Connolly's corpse. *That figured, I guess. Underfed, no way for his body to keep itself warm. Your body never gets a chance to starve to death in this kind of cold. And we knew he'd lose that foot, maybe both, and most of his fingers. Poor Brian was probably better off. . . .* Potter stood up, looking back once at Miller.

But this is different.

On impulse, Potter opened Miller's sleeping bag down to the toes. Down flowed out, filled the cabin, floating to rest on Connolly and Miller and Potter alike. It looked as if Potter had won a particularly deadly pillow fight, or as if the snow had come in after all. The lining of Miller's bag had been slit open in a dozen places. Potter checked the heater packs at the feet and in the hood; both were still running high enough to rule out death from shock. The dressing on the BuReloc man's hip was bloody, but not enough to indicate he'd bled to death. Maybe, despite the heaters, the cold . . .

Potter felt something under the bandage; a hard chip about two inches long. He reached beneath the bloody dressing and pulled out a key.

Potter recognized it instantly as a storage box key from one of the ground cars. Scraping off the dried blood revealed the number "1"; no surprise there. Miller must have been carrying it when he was shot, then had the presence of mind to hide it under the dressing; not a place anyone would be eager to search.

Potter rose and pocketed the key. He would collect Farrow and Liu and Mike and get them to help bury Connolly and Miller, but first he wanted to check out the key. He left the shuttle and crossed the landing zone, giving a wide berth to Shuttle One, which craft's lifting jets were being test-fired for the next five minutes.

The ground car was resting outside; although they had no crew weight problem any longer, Chief Engineer Liu had decided it would be prudent to leave it behind anyway. Snow was beginning to drift around its fat tires already, a prelude to the moon's eventual claim on all that they would leave behind.

Potter brushed snow away from the door to get it open, looking forward to getting inside the cab and away from the roar of the shuttle's lift-jets.

The cold vinyl seats were blocks of ice, leaching the heat from his buttocks and the backs of his thighs. Behind the driver's seat, Potter found the right box, inserted the key and opened it.

Inside was a fist-sized lump of cloudy crystal bearing several marks in Indel-ink; numbers, angles, three-letter abbreviations. Survey marks. Well, it was ore, clearly, but as to what sort, he had no idea. He slid backwards out of the cab, still holding the rock up before him, and turned to look into the muzzle of a very large revolver.

Chief Engineer Liu's other hand was open and extended.

"I'll take that, please, Emmett."

Potter handed him the crystal without a word.

"What is it, Liu? What is that crystal?"

"Hafnium-rich zirconium ore."

Potter thought a moment, suddenly remembering what he knew of hafnium: Mixed with tantalum carbide, hafnium was one of the most refractory substances known, immune to temperatures below 7,000 degrees Fahrenheit. The alloy was used in nuclear reactor control rods throughout the CoDominium. More importantly, it comprised the ablative heat shields and armor for hundreds of CoDo exploration and military vessels.

"But," Potter voiced his thoughts, "why? It's common as dirt; literally. You can get this stuff from beach sand."

Liu nodded. "Yes. On Earth. But Earth is run by the CoDominium Senate, and you know how; no scientific research, nothing that might allow the Soviets or the Americans to gain any advantage over one another." Liu turned the rock in his hands. "And of course, there are all those political undesirables, and all those new colony worlds that are going to have to start showing a profit somehow." His eyes met Potter's. "That will mean forced relocation, or 'CoDo-sponsored colonization,' if you prefer. All those colonies will need power, and the CoDo isn't going to spend money on solar arrays or hydroelectric structures when it can just dump a pre-fab reactor station and move on. That means an awful lot of reactors, Emmett, and the ships which carry them have reactors of their own, and ablative shielding. And this," Liu held the stone up between them, "this is where it will come from."

Can I keep him talking? Potter thought. *Will the others see, realize what's going on?* "Did Miller know? Would he have killed Ike to keep it a secret?"

"Miller knew," Liu said. "Else why didn't he bring anything else back? As for killing Ike; well by the ounce, even by the pound in a one-planet economy, hafnium's not so valuable. But Miller's analysis markings say this stuff has *twenty times* the hafnium of terrestrial zirconium, and at an already higher purity."

"How is that possible?" Potter asked, trying to sound interested in anything but Liu's weapon.

Liu shrugged. "Higher vulcanism on this moon, probably, along with the godawful tidal pressures from the gas giant's gravity. Who knows? Xeno-Geology was Miller's field, not mine. Step back, please, Emmett. You can see it just fine from where you are."

Potter nodded, then looked up at the Chief Engineer. "So. Which Company are you working for?"

Liu smiled ruefully. "The one that's going to make me a Vice President."

"You're going to kill me, then?"

"Jesus, Emmett, I'm not a barbarian. Let's just go home and collect the Survey bonus." Liu smiled warmly. "If I get the kind of deal I think I will, you can even have my share."

Potter ignored him, concentrating instead on the fact that, despite his chatty, conversational tone, Liu had not lowered his weapon. "Did you kill Miller?"

After a moment, Liu nodded. "Mm-hmm."

"And Connolly?"

"No. No need." Liu caught himself. "I mean there wasn't any reason for me to."

"And if there had been?"

Liu sighed. "Don't be difficult, Emmett. I *can* fly the *Fast Eddie* home without you, if need be."

"Six months is a long time to be alone."

"I'll pass the time calculating my interest-income statements on the ship's computer." He caught himself again. "Besides, Mike and Farrow will be along too."

He's going to kill us all. Potter finally had to admit it to himself. Liu's aim had not strayed a particle from the center of Potter's chest. *Company board member or sole Survey bonus recipient; or both. Why share any of it?*

With nothing to lose, Potter sighed and reached for the pistol.

* * *

Mike came running at the sound of the gunshots. He could see nothing, but he knew the difference between the reports of an accelerator rifle and a firearm; there weren't supposed to be any of the latter in the *Fast Eddie*'s stores. Farrow raced down the ramp of the shuttle after him.

They passed under the craft to see Chief Engineer Liu and Captain Potter grappling in the snow, leaving a thin smear of reddened ice in their wake. Mike ran toward them, but his foot came down on something and his ankle twisted, throwing him off his feet. He hit the frozen ground hard and heard the gun go off again.

Mike looked to see that he had tripped on some white rock, and having no weapons he grabbed the stone and scrambled toward the men.

Chief Engineer Liu was pressing a gun against Captain Potter's stomach. Potter was already bleeding from two wounds, when Mike heard a third shot, this one muffled by the Captain's parka. Mike brought the rock down on Liu's skull, and the Engineer rolled off Potter's chest, stunned.

Liu hadn't dropped the gun, and seemed to be trying to regain his bearings, so Mike swung the rock with all his might against the Engineer's temple. The left side of Liu's forehead collapsed, his eyes rolled completely back, and he fell to the ground dead. Mike dropped the rock and went to Potter, lifting the Captain just as Farrow arrived.

"Emmett," Farrow whispered hoarsely. "Emmett, can you make it to the ship?"

Potter didn't answer; he was beginning to feel the cold through his parka, and tried to fumble for the coat's heat controls, but his hands wouldn't obey. "Rock," he said.

Mike and Farrow shared a look, and the Basque engineer gestured with a nod toward the stone he had used to kill Liu. The *Fast Eddie*'s master quickly brought the rock to Potter.

Potter tried to push it away. "Liu was Company man. Precious ore. Mountains filled with it." He wanted to tell

them to bury it, to throw it out the airlock from orbit;
never to let the Companies or the CoDominium know it
existed, but he was so tired; the fight with Liu had worn
him out, and he was so cold. He needed to sleep, just
for a little while.

Mike seemed to understand, though. Passing Potter's
bulk to Farrow, Mike stood and put the zirconium ore
on the ground, where the frozen marsh that comprised
the landing zone had been softened by the morning's
test-firing of the shuttle engines.

Mike put his boot over the bloody rock and pushed it
beneath the gluey, crunching surface. After a moment,
there was no sign it had ever been there.

Potter looked at the mountains in the distance, at the
dark, fierce storm clouds, the first snowflakes beginning
to fall.

No two alike, he thought. He closed his eyes.

"He was a good man," Mi'huelo said to Farrow.

Farrow nodded. "He was my friend, Eminence," Farrow said.

Mi'huelo looked back over his shoulder. "I wonder
what that stone was?" The Basque spoke idly, but his
tone was cultured, educated.

"I don't know, Eminence."

Mi'huelo shrugged. "No matter. If this—Company
man—was interested in it, than all the more reason to
deny his masters the chance to despoil another world."

He knelt to help Farrow pick up the body of Captain
Emmett Potter, who although not a Harmony, had yet
been an harmonious man. To the Harmonies, who sought
to harmonize with all things, such a man was highly
regarded; the Universe being ultimately in harmony,
those few with the capacity to harmonize naturally were
cherished as better parts of its Song. In that perfect song,
the Universe sent to the faithful just such voices the
faithful required to help them sing it.

And so, they believed, it had sent Emmett Potter, for
he was the means through which Mi'huelo Costanza,

Metropolitan of the First Church of the New Harmony, had been guided to this seemingly insignificant moon. For the Harmonites, too, had their secret scouts among the survey ships of the CoDominium.

Metropolitan Costanza now knew this seemingly insignificant moon could be made to resonate with that Harmony for which he and all the others of his order strove. Conditions on this harsh and unforgiving world would be a perfect place for the Harmonies to gather in solitude and security, for a little while, at least; for who else would want such a place? Metropolitan Costanza could see no reason for this place to stir greed among men, and here they might live in solitude, unmolested by the anthrocentric CoDominium, with its planet-raping Americans and their equally rapacious Soviet partners.

Metropolitan Costanza and Acolyte Farrow buried Captain Potter and First Officer Connolly next to Icaorius and Owens, who had been good, true friends; alongside Ike, who had also been a Harmony. The bodies of Liu and Miller they left for the ravens, or whatever their equivalents were on this world, to nurture any scavengers that might roam the skies of the new world, as those buried would nurture the scavengers that moved within the ground.

Then, preparing to leave, Mi'huelo turned for one last look at the land around them, now disappearing behind curtains of snow, falling faster by the moment.

"What did you say Owens called this place?" Mi'huelo asked Farrow.

Farrow thought a moment: "A garden spot, your Eminence."

Mi'heulo shook his head, smiling. "You see, Thomas? All things harmonize, if only we seek to accept them as part of the Song. Consider the four men buried there, and the two who lie exposed nearby. Theirs were lives claimed by this harsh world that might one day yet become a haven for we Harmonies."

"Creation willing," Farrow repeated, nodding. There was so much to understand, but he thought that perhaps today, he had just picked up one thread of one strain of the Music here.

"Remember," Mi'huelo went on, "as a part of the Song, this place may claim the lives of many more as it plays its part in that music." He put his arm across Farrow's shoulders. "The lives of men are only notes in that movement, and it is only the aggregate effect of those notes which may be fully apprehended. These six, Thomas, these six are the first strains in the movement that contributes the story of this place to that song.

"The deaths of these men are the first blossoms of Spring in this world, their bodies the bone-white seeds, and their blood the bright-red blossoms of the ultimate Harmony, the attainment of which we can only seek, and whose real nature can be known only to itself.

"Kneel beside me, Thomas, and let us seek some small measure of that Harmony."

The steel floor of the airlock was cold against their knees, its hardness a further challenge to their concentration. No matter; counterpoint was important, too.

Each sought his own path for a few moments; Farrow was devoted to Costanza, and though many Harmonies found some of the Metropolitan's interpretations—unsettling—still, he was regarded as a voice of vision.

For himself, Costanza fretted constantly over the Harmonies; they needed so much care and tending to protect them. They were babes in the woods, and they did not understand that those woods were full of peril. The Harmony of existence was a song of many movements, many parts, and though all, by definition, harmonized, not all were pleasant to hear. And despite the order's belief in harmonizing one's self to circumstances and events, Costanza knew that every great orchestration needed conductors.

His own song was thus sometimes a lonely one. But he was grateful that he and Farrow had been caretakers of this garden where such seeds of Harmony had been sown.

"Let the blood of those who lie here nourish the seeds of the Song thus begun, and let such fruits flourish and multiply in measures everlasting."

... *flourish, and multiply* ...

From *Crofton's Encyclopedia of Contemporary History and Social Issues* (2nd Edition):

Church of New Universal Harmony

The Church of New Universal Harmony espouses a kind of active pacifism that seeks always to "harmonize" with everything and everyone at all times. Such accommodations, conciliations, and compromises have rendered the Harmonies (also known, usually pejoratively, as Harmonites) vulnerable to many kinds of attacks over the years, but have also, somehow, managed to sustain at least the central core of beliefs embodied in their HARMONY WRITINGS, which include the Concordance of Referents and various attached holographic testaments, but very little, if any, actual ritual or dogma.

Although Harmonies are often called Peacemakers, it must be remembered that peace is not necessarily a harmonic of particular situations or circumstances. Although pacifist, the Harmony religion is not passive, and not without its inherent potential violence.

Garner "Bill" Castell, self-proclaimed wandering scholar, during his self-conducted trial for vagrancy in Austin, Texas, in the Old United States of North America, discovered that hoades of young people not only flocked to hear what he was saying, but offered him donations, services, and even devotion. His talks quickly took on the aura of revelation, and he apparently encouraged such feelings, at least tacitly. His Harmony ideas flourished, a meme gone wildfire, and soon his influence seeped into the secular arena as well. When he began structuring his talks into an avowed church, he found even wider acceptance. He quickly organized this outpouring of enthusiasm into an efficient fund-gathering organization, combining the best of both old style church tithing and contemporary business methods.

Castell was so good at this, that within a year of his trial for vagrancy, he purchased a plot of land on which he built the first building in what became the New Universal Harmony Complex, which covered four thousand acres of scrub-tree land in the hill country to the northwest of Austin. It is speculated that Castell, whose parents and origin are unknown, may have been a businessman who had earlier in his life walked away from a vastly successful corporation to "find himself," in period vernacular. Certainly his organizational skills matched his charisma in matters spiritual and philosophical.

Soon Castell's church exerted considerable social, and thus political, influence in the Southwest region of the old USNA. The church never abused its power, and was never seriously investigated or challenged by either regional or federal authorities. Unlike other cults, Castell's attempted to, as he put it, Harmonize with everyone and everything, and this attitude of compromise, conciliation, and comfort made his people quite welcome members of the majority of communities surrounding Austin at the time.

In other areas of the country, however, Harmonies met with considerable hostility and resistance, if not violence. Garner "Bill" Castell became a familiar figure in the halls of power, lobbying personally for toleration of his swelling flock and, as always, seeking a harmonious coexistence. It is noteworthy that this approach as often as not seemed to inflame the feelings of resentment, spite, and even outright hatred; Castell always quoted various philosophers when this happened, and the quotations usually dealt with the many flaws of human nature.

The Harmony First Prayer is as follows: "Be still as the silence/At the heart of the note/As it swells to fill the song." This is thought to mean that one should seek first to ascertain or understand, then respond to or harmonize with influences and forces in the world outside the mind.

Musical references abound in Harmony writing and thought. Zen influence is thought to be heavy, too, particularly in the lack of concrete dogma. Pythagorean concepts, such as the Golden Mean and The Music of The Spheres, are thought to affect Harmony thinking, along with such abstruse referents as the sciences of acoustics, quantum resonance, and fractal analysis of real-time object-events.

One might think of Harmony as a state of being, fragile or sturdy depending upon the individual weaknesses or strengths. One might also think of the Harmony religion as the human ad-libs required to maintain that state of being no matter what the world brings. This is perhaps the gist, although each Harmony sect tends to emphasize different elements in the seemingly myriad influences that contribute to the Harmony religion as a whole. The consistent element is the translation of the musical idea of har-

mony and harmonizing into real-world human events
and actions.

In short, Harmony thinking has, as it were, "harmonized" diverse systems of thought, from science
and philosophy as well as from many theologies. This
somehow stable mix owes itself, it is thought, to the
unschooled yet intense erudition of the church's
founder, whose intellectual curiosity was apparently
matched only by his spiritual longing for "everyone
and everything [to] get along in the same world,
damned or divine may it or we be."

And then, in 2032, a planet later to be called
Haven was discovered, and a few years later the acri-
monious dispute over the new world's habitability
exploded. When the lower court decisions favoring
the Cal Tech/MIT University Consortium were over-
turned by a CoDominium Council in a closed ses-
sion, it meant not only that CDSS *Ranger* Captain
Jed Byers and his Science Officer Allan Wu had to
be paid finders' fees for having found a habitable
world, it also meant that such fees had to be paid
within certain time limits.

Such fees are, literally, astronomical, so naturally
the media followed the proceedings avidly. Also, so
much fuss, and so many outrageous public claims
were made during the various levels of litigation, that
the whole thing played more like a holodrama than
an actual lawsuit.

The CoDominium Council's word, however, was
final, akin to the old-style Supreme Court decisions.
And Cal Tech/MIT University Consortium was suddenly faced with having to pay out more money in
one lump sum than they normally alloted for six
months or more of operating budget. Worse, University trust fund officers refused to allow capital to be
touched; the monies would have to be raised by outside means. And all this because the Consortium had
officially set aside Byers' marginal moon, Haven, as
"reserved for study," a vague classification many

members of the lower courts had fought against for years as being too vague, too academic, and entirely too static.

"Study how?" Allan Wu said during one of many public appearances and press conferences. "They've got no people willing, or qualified, to throw away two years in round-trip travel and an unknown number of years on the ground studying the moon, so how can they study it?" And Jed Byers stepped in to add: "And if they can be there all that time studying, then surely they've demonstrated our contention that we've discovered a habitable world, right?"

The Consortium tried to counter with arguments such as the following: "It is our considered opinion that several years at the minimum of programmed remote sensor scanning, mobile robot unit topographic mapping, spectroscopic atmospheric and geologic sampling and analysis, trial vegetable and animal survival experiments, biohazard controls, and other telemetrical exploration is necessary before the ultimate consensus opinion can be given as to whether this insignificant, far-flung chunk of rock is actually habitable in any way but by the most extreme, deep-space life-support system methods."

Into the fray stepped Garner "Bill" Castell. He made an offer to pay the finders' fees, as well as other, unspecified costs which were called, at the time, "good faith payments," a phrase now thought to have been a rather ironic pun masking other machinations having little to do with faith in any but the most venal sense.

Indeed, rumors surfaced that Consortium efforts to raise the required monies were being sabotaged by CoDominium Intelligence agents, although no specific allegations ever came to trial. Speculations also linked CoDominium Intelligence agents with Garner "Bill" Castell himself, whose past, after all, was not only a closed but a lost book.

And then members of Castell's own church began objecting to his actions.

Despite all this, in 2036 Haven was unilaterally declared habitable, and the very next year Garner "Bill" Castell bought the license to colonize the place he christened Haven. He died that same year, on the steps of his Fortress of Harmony in Austin, while having a shouting match with church members who charged him with having looted church coffers to finance a pie-in-the-sky promised land that only a chosen few might see.

In retrospect, it is now thought that perhaps Castell's church was given the license to colonize Haven precisely because he had not only the money to pay for the privilege, but the people ready and waiting for a new place to go.

When Garner "Bill" Castell died, his son, Charles, a scholarly man of thirty-six Earth Standard years, took over the leadership of the church, and actually led the group called The Chosen to colonize Haven, which his father had literally died to give them.

IN CONCERT

E R STEWART

I

They say Charles Castell knelt and kissed the ground when he arrived on Haven, but I know better because I'm the oaf who tripped him. My name's Kev Malcolm, and at sixteen standard years of age, I stood beside our leader in the open side hatch, half proud to be one of the reverend's acolytes, half scared to death I'd do something clumsy.

Sure enough, as the freighter's shuttle was winched against the dock, I somehow got my foot in the wrong place.

Castell smiled, I remember that. His gaze scanned the horizon of Haven, his world, his church's place of salvation. "Eden," he whispered. I looked up at his face so serious and serene, with its strong nose and jutting chin. Just looking at him got me giddy. Power was ours, I knew, because we were blessed. We knew the key-note of the Cosmos, and we Harmonized fully, our bodies and souls as one with the All.

Fishy freshwater breezes entered the hatch now, wafting away some of the stench of the transport.

The last leg of our journey had been accomplished in a freighter, with us as piggyback cargo. At nine hundred souls, we were too few to justify, or to afford, hiring an entire transport, which can carry, they say, up to fifteen thousand people. I'd hate to imagine such crowding, and turned my attention back to my immediate surroundings.

We heard sounds of water lapping, a lone bird or something calling out in harsh joy, and the murmur at our backs of the nine hundred Chosen, each eager for a first glimpse of the new, the promised, land. With darkness behind us, we stood in the hatch in orange light, squinting.

I studied Reverend Castell's eyes, seeking a clue. Did he see his destiny as he absorbed the first sights of his hard-won, costly last chance? Did he smell on the chilly air a cornucopia of plenty, or the stench of decay? Were any of his senses of this world, or all?

Someone said our First Prayer, "Be still as the silence/ At the heart of the note/As it swells to fill the song," as if intoning a hymn, and Reverend Castell broke his pose to step forward. The shuttle bumped the dock.

The next thing I knew a look of surprise crossed his face and he sprawled forward onto the dirt levee on which the dock was built.

So it was that my first step onto our new home was a leap of consternation and mortification. "Reverend," I said, along with three other acolytes, kneeling to help him rise. Knowing it had been my foot which had caused this undignified advent upon Haven, I blushed and tried to stammer an apology.

His electric gray eyes sparked a gaze toward me. That old familiar tingle of, what? Awe? Terror? It held me, that feeling, and my mouth fumbled into silence as he said, "We must all embrace our home, this Haven." And he gestured for us to lie down, too.

Word passed back in a chain of whispers as near to silence as the circumstance allowed, and the next few Chosen jumped down from the ship and fell prostrate for a few seconds. It was the inauguration of Reverend Castell's ritual of return, which he used at the termination of every journey thereafter.

Of course the ship's crew jeered and shouted catcalls. Our church had hired their transport ship and a crew, but we hadn't even made a bid for their support or loyalty. "Clumsy lot," one tough said. Another spat at us repeatedly. To them, we were rag-tag fanatics off on some wild goose hegira, a doomed group of dupes led by a megalomaniac with a simplistic Christ complex.

I'd heard all that and more, during our purgatorial months of motion between Earth and Haven, and not all of it muttered or whispered, either. We bore their assaults upon our dignity with stoic silence, some of us not even bothering to wipe the spittle from our faces or hair.

Some of us may have wondered of what use a tiny act of cleanliness might be to a group as filthy as we, after fourteen months in the transport vessel, washing only with gritty drysoap and handheld ionizers, perfumed only by the food-pastes smeared or spilled. Odors were among the least of our burdens, anyway. Old bruises from tests of our pacifism, administered by the ship's brutal crew bored between duties, kept some of us moving stiffly.

Also, at least one of our women was probably pregnant from a rape I'd unknowingly witnessed one sleep-period, when, in utter silence, the blanketed bunk-pallet beside mine had erupted into thrashing. Only when the crewman rose up from his victim had I realized what had occurred, and my shame and fury were such that I barely spoke for a week as I sought harmony with the event.

Now I shivered as I watched the others jump down from the hatch.

One of the men in a rowboat, still holding the rope by which the shuttle had been winched to shore after splashdown, called out lewd suggestions to our women and girls. I saw at least one of our men grow somber. His eyes grew hard and his mouth set sternly, for one of the prettiest women was his daughter, but none of us broke the peace as we sought to harmonize with the strains of Haven.

I stood with Reverend Castell to one side as he supervised both the advent of his flock upon Haven and the unloading of our supplies. "Each of us must do our part," he said once, bending to lift a parcel that a contemptuous crewmember had dropped. Smiling, Reverend Castell carried it to the stack of goods growing on the splintery bare-plank wharf. Although our supplies had all fit into the same shuttle that had brought us down from the orbiting transport vessel, they were sufficient to keep us going for as many as three years, even if Haven granted us nothing.

A shudder rippled through me as I avoided thinking past those three years. I bent to lift a sack of seeds, but a brother acolyte stopped me. "Let our beasts of burden do the heavy work," he said, gesturing at the laboring, infidel crewmembers.

Glancing at the joker, Reverend Castell said, "Take that man's place, and give him a rest." He pointed to a particularly loudmouthed space-faring lout, who had berated us worse with every load he carried.

Keeping my gaze on the hem of my robe, I balanced my conflicting humors and thought I understood the reverend's actions. "An aspect of respect is the ability to know another's lot in life," now made more sense to me. It was no longer just a tenet from the Writings.

A crane and several hoists helped complete our unloading, but it was past first, or Byers' dusk by the time we finished. By then we acolytes had done as much as anyone else, and the Kennicott crew was largely loafing or drinking in the one-room, rickety shebeen the wharf's ratty skeleton crew had slapped together a few yards from shore.

Faces showed fatigue, but a few showed more. Some openly grumbled, others gaped at the bleak landscape surrounding them as if trapped, and all of us shivered in our robes. My own hood I kept up, but many seemed to enjoy having their ears turn blue. Rubbing the tip of my nose helped, but only for a few seconds.

Aside from the cold was the air itself, which seemed somehow hard to breathe, unsatisfying to the lungs. A ringing in my ears and a dizziness assailed me, too, but I ignored such trifles in my earnest desire to be worthy of the reverend's respect and trust. Being acolyte to such a man is no small thing, and no small things can be allowed to interfere.

As the Shangri-La Valley was turned away from Byers' for a while, Cat's Eye peered down in quarter phase, its horizontal pupil balefully dark as the rest cast dim light over us. Jagged mountains tore at the bottom of the sky in menacing silhouette, while the lake itself glittered with phosphorescent blue-green flashes and orange Eyeshine. I think I saw Hecate, or Ayesha, or Brynhild, one of Haven's companion moons, but it may have been something else, or nothing outside my overloaded mind.

"Our balbriggens don't suffice," Reverend Castell said to me, having noticed my shivers. His use of Gaelic words meant he was in a good mood, I knew. "We must layer." He tapped the satchel I carried for him and I put it on the ground. He knelt and tugged out another robe, as plain and pocketless as the one he wore. "Pass the word," he said, a grimace of meaning on his face.

Sibilance behind us was the only hint that the Chosen had heard and obeyed. It struck me that some of us had been waiting only for an example, because no sooner was the Reverend Castell layered in the rough cotton cloth than many of the Chosen were pulling on their second or third garments. Surely they'd had them out ahead of time.

Such thoughts are best not voiced, however, so I donned my second robe and bowed my head, awaiting further commands. Patience is the lot of followers, who, if they know well their place and abilities, can be of far greater use than any number of discordant individuals howling on their own behalf, for in harmony is strength. So we teach.

"I must speak with the captain of our blessed transport vessel," Reverend Castell then said to me, as head acolyte. "Stay here and contemplate the start of our great salvation."

As he walked away I chanted the fugue called "Patience Is the Art of Elegant Timing," shivering only a little now, and worried more about my stomach, which rumbled and growled enough to pain me.

"Sixty-four and three quarters hours," one of the other acolytes said, in a tone of disgust. "That means when Eyeclipse comes, it'll be only light from the other moons for the next twenty hours or so." He sarcastically waved his hand in front of his face, as if blind in the dimmness of Cat's Eye. "No suntans here, eh? It's windtan or nothing, unless the frostbite gets you."

None laughed and the jester fell silent.

Haven's night interested me. Reportedly it would never get fully dark, but I thought I'd rather wait and see for myself, experience it. Those CoDo maps and lists and descriptions of habitable worlds tend to change after settlement, I knew. They changed especially drastically with the marginal worlds, like Haven.

Would the other two moons offer at least some light? I wished for a moment that I understood celestial mechanics better, then grinned and rolled my eyes. Fat chance of learning such things now. But, as for seeing one's hand always before one's face, surely that would be a boon, affording endless chances for good works. The right would always know what the left hand was doing.

With a shrug, I went back to concentrating upon my empty belly, and how best to ignore it, or at least nullify its demands. My eyes kept seeing, however, and my ears kept hearing, and curiosity flared in me like lashes of plasma from a furious star.

My senses tempted me into the new world, so I studied it a little. The orange-red tinge of Eyelight allowed sight, but with a diminished sharpness of image, as if details had been carefully erased to allow the world a greater freedom of generality. That idea shuddered through me, as I wondered what this place might show us if, or when, it decided to get specific with us.

My heart thumped and thudded. My limbs felt alternatively heavy and light, never normal. My eyes watered and I blinked away the tears. Cold seeped inward, confident of final victory on this bleak soulscape.

After the ennui, the torture, the oppression of the transport ship, however, that cold ground in the dim light beside our small hillock of stacked supplies was at the very least an edge of paradise to us, and few complained aloud. Mothers sang to children, while fathers hummed along. Children chattered and laughed, playing timeless games. Bodies shifted weight and the chill air cleaned us of one another's scents even as a few hardy souls visited the lake's edge for baths of an icier kind.

It was a moment of peace, and I was astute enough to savor it, even in my hunger, or perhaps because of it. Hunger imparts a meditative calm at times. At any rate, our peace was short-lived.

" . . . must be kidding," a harsh voice shouted from the shack where the ship's captain and his groundside crew drank and gamed. "It's your world, mister almighty Chucked-Out Charlie Castell, and my people aren't draft animals, and personally I couldn't give less a damn about how you'll move your supplies if they invented atomic damn-splitting."

It was the ship's captain, a cashiered CoDo NCO, whose voice roared forth. He bellowed at Reverend Castell, berating him, mocking his plan of colonization and mimicking his perception of our principles in a drunken tirade that would've spawned riot on any other world at any other time with any other audience.

The two leaders came out of the shack. The captain's fists came within inches of the reverend's face, but our leader neither blinked nor winced. Raising his hands to chest level, Reverend Castell said something in a firm but modulated voice, and that's when the other drunks roiled out of the shebeen, which actually rocked back and forth as shoulders pushed on the sides of the doorframe.

The captain yelled, "You can jolly well wait until your animals grow out of embryo, for all I care, but there's not enough money in the known systems to make me ask my men to do another lick of work for your bunch. Christ on a flapjack, you've got the arrogance of Lucifer himself, I swear."

Laughter and hoots of derision erupted in the mob outside the drinking shack. Our people, the Chosen, stood watching Reverend Castell as intently as audiences watch tightrope walkers, anxiety plain on our faces. I know many thought as I did, that to lose him now would fate us all to meaningless failure.

Several voices among our people said, "I told you he was crazy," or "Now do you see?" or even "Damn him, making them angry like that," but I held out faith in Castell, because he'd never failed us yet. Saying as much to my brother acolytes, I got them to circulate amidst the Chosen, spreading harmony and calm as best they could.

The captain and the reverend stood nose to nose as the opposite crowds studied them, some eager for blood, others seeking only peace. An electricity charged the scene, holding everyone static.

And then the violence in the air evaporated as Reverend Castell said something that made the infidels laugh and disperse. He came to us while they gurgled back down the drain, into their iniquitous sink of sins.

"They'll be gone in twelve hours," Reverend Castell told us. As usual, I was standing near enough to him to be able to study his features, and I swear I saw the traces of a satisfied smile there, as if he'd accomplished something difficult with less trouble than anticipated. He slapped me on the shoulder and smiled. "We're too excited to sleep anyway, don't you think, Kev?" he asked. Then, before I could respond in any way, he dashed toward our supplies and began climbing them.

His shipslippers let his toes grip the ropes and canvas on the crates, and soon he stood high above us. So high, in fact, that when he spoke we found that very few of us could see him at all.

His voice, a baritone coaxed and trained, modulated and resonant, fell upon us like manna. We fed upon the sound of that voice as much as on the messages it conveyed. It was a sermon like none before, rousing us to efforts none of us would have conceived.

We bent and lifted. We carried until our legs quivered. All the while, Reverend Castell stayed atop the diminishing pile of goods we'd brought.

Rocks twisted ankles, divots stole footing, and the light failed gradually but certainly as we moved our precious supplies away from the lake. There were trees, mostly sparse-set evergreens, but we stayed back from them, not knowing what might lurk in their shadows, under their deceptively familiar boughs.

A relatively flat area with harsh grasses that tore at exposed flesh with serrated stalks and sticky leaves that seemed to seal each wound proved the best place to create our first redoubt.

Directing the placing of crates and drums and barrels and sacks, we created a small fortlike square. Our supplies surrounded us, providing shelter as well as other necessities. Slit-trenches were dug by a few of our people who understood such matters, one of whom had been a CoDo marine until he lost his hand in a nameless battle, another of whom had been a mountain survivalist until swept into a city by defoilants and other government plagues. Deadfall was gathered and fires lit, and soon savory broths and other delicious if meatless sustenance sent out whisps of mouth-watering invitation.

Revererd Castell carried the very last crate by himself. He took it to the center of the cleared area and let it drop with a grunt. Such crates weigh more than forty kilos, I knew.

Hopping upon it, he said, "Chosen ones, hear me. This spot shall be our settlement, and from this spot shall we construct a place worthy of true and universal harmony. Here shall we found a place free of secular intrusions, free of the compromises so many of the churches have adopted of late on old, decaying Earth.

"As the silence at the heart of the note supports all aspects of the song, so shall this spot remain empty, a town square from whence shall radiate peace and chords of joy even as our settlement grows to fulfill all promises."

We hummed a chord and held it, and the single multiplex tone droned from and through us, raising our inner selves to new heights of strength and determination. No one shivered during that nine-minute chord, no stomachs growled, and no babies squawled. It was peace, it was truth, it was harmony.

The rest of that, I guess I must call it evening, Castell passed among us, squatting to chat here, pausing to give assistance there, spreading calm and confidence everywhere. His confidence radiated like a warmth more sustaining than the heat of fire.

After eating a tortilla rolled around celery with ten-bean sauce, I followed him on his rounds. My admiration for him may well have grown, if such was possible. He knew the right things to say to everyone, and knew all their names, all nine hundred of them. He even knew the names of the babes, not yet counted as Chosen, but certainly blessed by the harmonics of their parents.

When we returned to the center of the small square, Castell's crate was still there. I noticed that it was labeled with a Xeno-Biology warning symbol, a red triangle in a green square, with the legend HYBRID GRAINS.

Gesturing for me and the eight other acolytes to be seated, he treated us to a story about his father, Garner "Bill" Castell, adventurer, founder of our church, and our spiritual patriarch. As he wove aural spells of incident, plot, and character, I let my memory stray back to my only glimpse of Garner "Bill" Castell, lying in state in that old Victorian style mansion on the hill.

He had lain smiling faintly even in death as his son, left with the flock, left with the dream of a promised land, and left with just about enough church assets to assure new-found Haven's settlement rights, cried and ranted in a far corner at the unapproachable man's still unapproachable corpse.

Though he spoke now with affection, I knew Charles Castell still harbored complicated feelings for his father. "Be glad you knew yours," I whispered, sending out a prayer. And when the tale was told, all straining listeners smiled and nodded even as we acolytes laughed at the gentle humor of the ending.

Reverend Castell sat in a lotus position atop the crate and let his head loll slowly back until his face gazed upward. His eyes were closed to our sullied, sin-ridden world. His inner resonance held him rapt.

In three layers of unbleached cotton and rolled into a wool shawl, I soon fell asleep. We acolytes, in deference to the reverend's disdain of personal comfort, ignited no fire for ourselves. At sixteen, I fancied myself able to live up to whatever impossible standards Charles Castell thought fit to demonstrate for us.

I dreamed of milk, warm from the udder, and honey, hot from the hive.

II

We awoke to the ground trembling.

A throbbing moved the air in jitters, and I rolled to a sitting position, ready to brace myself. After so long in space, our reflects were those of travellers. My thoughts were of asteriods, or ruptured bulkheads.

Once I realized we were on ground, however, I instantly thought of quakes, and glanced over to see Reverend Castell still sitting on the crate, as if he'd not moved as we all slept around him. He was shepherd to the flock, and an example to those who would attain true harmony, and I tried to be like him, despite my alarm.

And then someone said, "They're just leaving us here," and I knew that the vibrations came from the shuttle departing. With that thought came louder sounds, and then a glimpse of the dirty white ship in silhouette as it roared quickly upward from the middle of the lake, dripping water, soaring into the dark and clouds.

My chest tightened. Dizziness swept through me. We were alone. We were the only people on the entire planet, nine hundred of us.

Despite my desire to avoid such daunting thoughts,

my mind's eye offered an imagined view from the departing ship: We'd look like less than a single spore of mold on the skin of an orange.

Tears welled. I stood and danced some tai chi to warm myself and calm my surging emotions. I missed Earth now more poignantly than I had just after departure, when the confinement of the transport had somehow crowded out any nostalgia.

Like many others, I stood gazing upward into Haven's dim sky long after the ship was invisible. Not even the clouds resolved into familiar shapes for us, and no birds flew over to bid us welcome.

Reverend Castell let his head loll forward, took a deep breath, and smiled as his eyes fluttered open. "So," he said. "At last." Rising from the crate, he jumped down and laughed, then rubbed his hands together. I thought the gesture more eagerness than a grab at friction's warmth. "We must awaken, and begin the tasks necessary to our survival," he said, his booming voice glittering with a hint of glee.

He strode from person to person in a widening circuit of our tiny meadow, his hands straying to touch children's heads and the many crates and supplies he passed. His manner was all encouragement and delight.

I ran to follow him, as was my place. My own hands now and then ruffled children's hair. I longed to emulate Reverend Castell in the deeper things, too. Giving blessings with total assurance must be a marvel, something rarer than humanity on Haven.

And then we came upon the rift in our wall of supplies.

It lay farthest from the lake, closest to the forest. The people there kept their gazes downward, and none spoke when Castell, his features frozen in an unreadable mask, asked, "How many?"

In a whisper I sent the other acolytes to count the Chosen. As they dashed off, I considered adding babes to the count, but the unworthiness of it blushed me and I was glad for once that my tongue had outpaced my thinking.

Reverend Castell stood motionless. He stared at the gap. Not even his eyes moved. His hands made fists and held them. Breezes shifted his robes, but inside those robes his body was still and solid as a statue.

Our count revealed that no more than twenty-three had decamped. The supplies, numbered and inventoried before departure from Earth and several times since, told their own tale. "They've taken only five crates' worth, Reverend," I reported, having checked the numbers myself. "Two of foodstuffs, one of embryos, one of farming implements, and another of medical supplies."

With each enumeration Castell's eyes widened a bit more, until, by the end of my list, his stare was maniacal. "Why?" he roared.

I jumped so hard I dropped the inventory scroll, which fluttered in a sudden gust of wind until I trod upon it, to keep it near. I dared not stoop to retrieve it.

"Why?" Reverend Castell demanded again in a quieter voice, his eyes narrowed to slits. Under his breath he began saying names, and I, being nearest, heard some of them. He was calling the roll of those who had absconded. My flesh rippled in awe at the man's perception, his memory.

Women and children started crying now, and the men pretended not to as some muttered fast prayers. Others began a soft harmonic humming, but Castell swept his right arm upward, cutting it off. He whirled, anger contorting his face, reddening it. "There is discord here," he said. His tones carried curses and damnation, thunder and fury, all wrapped in a desperate grip of will. His arms flew upward and he shrieked as if stricken, then he fell to his knees.

We acolytes rushed to help him, but a glare from him halted us as he said, "What must we do?" When his voice faltered in a sob, the Chosen held their breath, listening for his next command. We wanted guidance.

Water lapped on the shore and a chill wind sprang upon us again, from the water.

Standing again, Castell scanned each and every face visible to him, as if seeking a scapegoat. Many responded with whimpers.

When it was my turn, I held his gaze proudly, but my knees shook and sweat trickled down my spine. I was forced to look away, even though I was sure of my harmony with the reverend and his goals.

"Sacrifice," he yelled then, in a tone of revelation. His voice lashed out, struck us numb. "We have offered a few of our Chosen, that the remainders be the stronger." He pointed at the spot where the missing supplies had once been, as if accusing, then flattened his hand to swat away imagined pests. "We must not despise them, nor hold a grudge. Instead, we must wish them well and forget them. They are no longer of us but were once a part, like hair that's been cut, like fingernail clippings."

That last phrase came out of him in a lower register that imparted ripples to the flesh at the nape of my neck, but before I could dwell on the meaning of both words and tones of voice, he began smiling again. He clapped his hands thrice, signal for attention. Into the silence he sang a lament, then gestured for us to join in its repetition.

We created a layered hum and, at the end of nine minutes, as timed by a subcutaneous digital timekeeper under the skin of Castell's left wrist, the digits of which glowed a blue when scratched, we all felt better, as if losing the twenty-three had lessened our burden.

Reverend Castell then strode to a crate, bent, and tore off its top planks with his bare hands. A cheer arose, and we fell to opening our supplies and sorting them.

Children helped carry what they could, or fetched tools, while adults worked at whatever tasks best suited them. In use is ownership, and we sought to mesh our wills with the limitations of our tools. Some began setting up the incubators, to begin accelerated growth of embryos so that we might have beasts of burden to labor and breed, and freshwater fishes to feed us in later years.

Those people, specially trained and aware that their expensive equipment was the only of its kind to be had, did their jobs with the reverent concentration of monks. Others, of a more common ilk, joined in the chorus of work any way they could, remaining at the beck and call of more focused workers.

"Work well," Reverend Castell enjoined. "If no more should manage to follow us, then we shall have to suffice, and what we are shall be the future of this world, and of the greater Harmony."

His references to the outside possibility of other Harmonies scraping up the funds and begging or bribing the permission to emigrate from Earth to Haven fell like spattered acid, and in truth I'd heard him, during the months of travel, vent much bitterness about the many indecisive souls we believers had left behind. It galled him, for one thing, that they could remain behind, yet still call themselves Harmonies.

Some of us found likely places to begin plowing and harrowing fields to receive hybrid seeds. Exactly which Earth species would thrive, we did not know, so many small plots were rendered arable. Some set up an irrigation system, deploying the skeletal water wheels. Some of us dug holes in the ground, which was hard and rocky only centimeters beneath the tangled roots of grass.

My body warmed and my muscles, after fourteen months of nothing more strenuous than isometrics, cramped and throbbed deliciously. Also, I panted constantly, but savored the pains of hard work, knowing that each jolt of discomfort was a harmonic burden balancing the accomplishments of our faith. I viewed my visible puffs of exertion as misty prayers that would disperse on the many winds to eventually travel everywhere on Haven.

At one point that day I helped to demolish the shack by the wharf. We found a few bottles of spirits, and gave them to the doctors. We also found tri-pictures of naked people doing things with each other, which upset one of our coworkers.

Reverend Castell came over and looked through the tri-pix, then smiled and said, "These, too, may prove valuable, as we seek to populate this world." He gave them to the doctor, who somberly closed them into a medicine case. The upset man stood with face red and muscles bulging in his cheeks, but said nothing against Castell's decision.

We all got back to work, I drawing shovel duty.

From green wood that smelled of pine but proved harder and less knotty, from mud mixed with stickyleaf straw, and from oilcloths brought with us as wrappings around some of the supplies, we fashioned sunken cabins. Only about a quarter of each structure stood above ground, and the walls were lined with supply crate planks, stones, and unopened supplies.

We used the many flat stones to fashion an oven and even shelves and beds along the perimeters of each living space, and left a central hole in the roofing, to vent smoke. Some used big flat stones for roofing. Others used the pinelike boughs from the nearby trees to weave a kind of thatching.

Entrances were small, and often required crawling; they were easy to defend against any predators we might still encounter. Drainage was accomplished with lined, sunken furrows set under the stone or wood floors.

"These structures are based on those still to be found on the islands off Scotland's northern coast," Reverend Castell told us, "and they are in harmony with their surroundings and so can last as long as the stones themselves. Those in Scarabrae are over eight thousand years old and still quite comfortable."

His words inspired us, and gave us a sense of heritage, of being in tune with longer songs. He wandered from project to task to chore, advising and often pitching in to lend a hand.

His strength thrilled me, and I hoped to be as big and powerful as he, for I'd not yet begun filling out. Sixteen and scrawny doesn't last long in healthy lads, but at the time it seems forever.

"In times to come a city shall be raised on this site," he said, speaking less like a prophet than a professor. "This place is made for settlement, and we, in harmony, have come to fulfill its promise."

He happened to be near me as he said this and, without ceasing to shovel, I took a breath and dared to ask, "Reverend, do you see visions, hear angels? How is it you know about this place?"

He smiled down at me and said, "I studied Ekistics at university, it's the science of settlements." And then, in a quieter voice, he added, "I wish I'd paid stricter attention." And then he was walking away, to cheer and laugh and revel in the hard work of making a permanent encampment around which to begin our sojourn into future greatness, more intricate harmonies.

I bent and lifted more dirt, tossing it up onto the pile I'd made. The surface of the ground was at my chest now, and I knew I should go only a little deeper before beginning to shave the sides to enlarge the hole.

Ice, gritty like sand, which Castell called permafrost when I asked, and tendrils of some kind of fungus, too, made root shapes into what little loam there was, then spread flat where the rocky dirt layer began. It was like a vein of decay, maybe a motherlode, undermining the seasonal grasses above. It was as if the best of Haven floated upon the worst.

It occurred to me that my hole mirrored a grave at the moment, and that put me in mind of the Reverend Garner "Bill" Castell, our leader's father. Had the son studied Ekistics in preparation for his father's grand vision of a promised land where his church might exist in freedom and liberty? If so, then what had distracted him from the stricter attention he wished he had paid?

Shaking my head, I started widening my pit, trying
to slant the walls the way Reverend Castell had shown
us.

We worked for several hours, then broke off to rest
and eat.

It was after a meal of a small handful of dry rice
washed down with tea and broth, which made it swell to
fill bellies, that we had our first trouble with the patches
of stickyleaf grass.

Its serrated stalks sliced open exposed flesh, allowing
its sticky leaves to cling over wounds. We later found
out that some workers were using the stuff as makeshift
adhesive bandages. Unfortunately, the sticky stuff, clear
and odorless, worked like some snake venoms, breaking
down proteins in the skin and blood. Anyone with the
stuff on them developed ugly purple masses of pulped
tissue. Blood poisoning can result, and the affected areas
must be cut out, and quickly.

Allergic reactions are also not uncommon, including
anaphylaxis, which can result in quick, gasping death. I
knew about that one because I'm allergic to bees, which,
by the way, we'd imported, too. Without bees, few Earth
plants can cross-pollinate. Fortunately, the tough African/
Penn State hybrid was thought capable of colonizing any
planet, so there was little worry on that account.

As for stickyleaf grass, our medics figured it out and
explained it as a cousin to acid-secreting firegrass, but
only after several emergencies left more than a few of
us injured. One child, three and curious, had placed a
sticky leaf on one of her eyes, and another had been
eating them and died.

It was our first warning that Haven could, indeed, be
very specifically an alien world into which we were the
trespassers.

After that, we were all far more careful to take nothing
for granted. Not even the soil in which I dug seemed as
inert.

It seemed a trial of some kind, and I endured it by
working even harder. I made the acolyte house extra

secure by creating a zigzag entrance just big enough for one large man at a time to crawl through.

Nor was my dread of predators entirely unwarranted. A large part of our supplies, after all, consisted of the embryos of various foraging creatures, which we'd let loose. Once populations of these herbivores and omnivores thrived, we'd introduce the carnivores, a few of them, to act as predators and thus maintain a natural harmony.

An Earth-nocturnal cat from the Negev desert called a caracal, for example, was thought to be perfect for the dim lighting and relatively rainless conditions prevailing over most of Haven. It might raise havoc with our poultry, but could save grain from vermin, too. The high deserts and rugged mountains of our new homes would seem like paradise to such creatures, I thought. But encountering one might not be such a blessing.

Before any encounters might happen, though, there must be a thriving human settlement. On this world, man came first, bringing plants and animals with him, and although the harshness of the climate was a shock to many of us, even an insult, still, it was our place to be cautious.

In our hands lay Haven's fate, and we strove to be worthy of such responsibility.

In use lies ownership, and stewards of the land are keepers of the future, as our Writings tell us. On a more practical level, our church's resources had been spent to get us here, and the supplies we had were very likely all there would be. Haven's an out-of-the-way world, not on trade routes and in fact on the very rim of the CoDominium's interests and influences. And so we struggled onward. How fragile we considered our every possession, how gently we treated even stones.

Our laying out of the encampment proceeded at a measured and deliberate a pace. A few of us might have hurried to escape the bitter winds, or to gain privacy or other comforts, but haste would have created its inevitable waste, and that might well have meant doom. Colonizing a world requires patience.

Castell supervised us, and kept us patient, and we remaining Chosen labored hard. We quickly patterned our habits so that there was always work being done, even as others rested. With only variable nights, Haven invited such perseverance.

In several of my sleepings we had a place that seemed familiar upon waking, and some of the quicker animals were beginning to take on proper forms, among them the chickens. I found out by almost trampling a dozen yellow chicks that hopped by just as I climbed the four steps up out of the acolytes' house. To my look of surprise one of the genetics people said, "We let them breed a few cycles first, just to make sure."

"Then have you foodbirds?" I asked, my mouth watering.

He nodded. "Many have died, yes."

"Waste not, want not." Feeling lighter of step, I walked toward my day's duties. One of them was helping soothe the beasts to be slaughtered, by being among the chorus whose drones kept the birds calm even as the butcher graced each throat with his molecule-sharp, gently wielded blade.

Reverend Castell declared it Yule Season when he heard that meat was available. We celebrated with feasts and exchanged gifts of song, dance, and privacy. And our meals of roast chicken and eggs done many ways were, indeed, duly sanctified because we ate no meat that had not passed on its lifeforce first, and we ate no eggs that had not been candled and pronounced free of conception. Nature's cycles were kept in harmony.

Life began improving for us, as we harmonized with our new environment. Meetings were held again, as the work became predictable. Schools commenced classes. We sang, always we sang, and some began constructing instruments with which to enhance our music.

Once, as I sat with a group around a fire in the town square, the sound of a lone harmonica drifted to us from the woods. "The outcasts," someone said, and although a search was made, no one was found. Tales of the many odd items smuggled from Earth began to feature in our rest periods.

We contemplated the loss of regular dusks and dawns in one of Reverend Castell's sermons, and it moved us to think of the sacrifices sometimes necessary when better life beckons. On a more mundane level, shaving was largely forsaken, because facial and body hair added another layer of insulation, something to be cherished on chill Haven.

An influenza went through us at one point, giving most bouts of vomiting and fevers and worse, but no one died from it, and we pronounced it ship-borne, a legacy of lesser times, simpler tunes, when we'd lived in Earth's cacophony. Most negatives were blamed on Earth, while anything positive was a sign that Haven welcomed us, celebrated our arrival, and supported our efforts toward Universal Harmony.

Several women showed signs of pregnancy in the first months, and all would soon, we hoped. I often wondered when we acolytes would be permitted to choose wives from the girls, and I confess that I slept but fitfully all too often as I imagined this twelve-year-old, or that fourteen-year-old, naked and in my arms, her eagerness exactly matching mine, our knowledge equivalent as our bodies formed a chord.

Even Reverend Castell took a wife, Saral. His wedding was quiet and private, and she radiated both calm and good cheer when she stepped out of his house the morning after they'd plighted troth.

It was many sleeps before it dawned upon me that Saral was the woman who'd very likely been raped in the bunk beside me, during transport, and I could not help wondering if the Reverend had wed to save her from possible prejudice. Perhaps it was another of his lessons, too.

For a while we got along well, and bound ourselves in peace, but then the intruders came.

III

After a dozen Earth-months on Haven, I could go in shirtsleeves, and my body had filled out until I was bigger than Reverend Castell himself.

Walking between the rows of plastic-covered furrows, I crossed one of the fields north of town. The trick of covering the plants to create mini-greenhouse effects had increased our second crop yield by seventy percent, so I watched my feet, remembering clumsier days.

In my left hand I carried three small animals, all dead. They'd been discovered by three of our outlying farmers and I was taking them to the doctors for analysis. One looked like a salamander, green with red spots along its flanks, but it had a soft membrane across its forehead, and its eyes were multiplex, like a bee's.

Another of the animals I'd seen alive. It had a furlike covering that scraped off like moss, four legs, and twin tails with bristles at the end. Those bristles were more like tiny barbs, and caused swelling. I knew because I'd kicked one once, at the edge of a corn-crop.

Coming down the hill, I had a good view of the lake. Its beauty inspired me with pride at our world. Boats bobbed near the shore I approached, while our wharfs, now numbering three, showed much activity as nets were repaired and boats were sealed.

We used resin from the pinelike trees for a natural sealant, even inside our houses. It dried to resemble a plastic. Those trees, whose sap ran outside their trunk, added layer after layer in a seasonal cycle we had yet to parse. Resin could be harvested in liquid form, and kept pliant by heating, or it could be peeled in sheets.

I waved, but the small figures could not have seen such a gesture, if they saw me at all.

That's when thunder sounded, a rare sound on Haven. It was rarer still from a clear sky showing only sparse, high cirrus clouds, so I squinted upward, perhaps subconsciously recognizing the sound.

A glint became a glitter, and then the spot swelled and

I drew in a sharp breath. My pace increased, and soon I was running.

No one on the shore or in the boats seemed to notice, and I wondered if the sound had been baffled from their hearing by the very hills on which I now ran. My gestures and shouts did not carry far enough.

The spot had grown now. Blunt at the snout and wide in the beam, it was obviously a shuttle. Even as I glanced upward again the wings extended farther, to let it achieve subsonic speeds without tumbling.

I had to skirt a stand of oaklike trees, then cut through some more of the pines before I got another clear view of the lake. Some of the boats were making their way to shore. Others bobbed in apparent ignorance.

Increasing my pace, I grew light-headed. Thin air duelled with highland lungs, for I'd been raised in the Rockies, but my speed and rhythm suffered. The splashship was now big in the sky, and falling fast. It banked and I saw stains and signs of neglect. "Earthers," I shouted, my anger surging.

And then the last few boats began moving, their occupants rowing frantically, but it was too late.

I stopped running on the crest of the final rise. The animal specimens lay behind me, flung in frustration. All I could do was watch, squeezing my fists until my knuckles crackled.

The shadow covered three of the boats, but the splashship only struck one, driving it under almost gently. The old PanAmerican shuttle plowed a wake, and our other two boats swamped, but I saw swimmers. That first boat, however, showed no signs of surfacing again, and in fact, we never even found the body.

Looking left, I saw people running from town, and made out the tall, long-haired, bearded figure of Reverend Castell. He did not run. He did not even walk quickly. His pace was an angry, robotic stomp.

Looking right, I saw a few other boats coming down River East. River South showed no signs of activity, but my elevation and squint were insufficient for clear sight.

"It was slaughter," I said, wiping tears I hadn't noticed before. Drawing a deep but shaky breath, I started trotting down to the lake, vectoring to intersect Castell's stiff-jointed stalk.

When I came to walk beside and a little behind the reverend, I heard him muttering. His eyes seemed calm, but he was grinding his teeth. With each step he took and let out a breath, as if it were some meditation. We reached the old wharf and stood on the worn planks as the splashship lowered propellers and maneuvered toward us. A few people stood in an open cargo hatch on one side, and they waved. None of the Chosen returned the gesture.

Reverend Castell stood staring. His breath came in ragged gasps through his nose, while his lips writhed as if wrestling. When a light breeze rippled a fold of his robe, he swatted at the moving garment as if meaning to tear it.

The draft of a standard splashship is five meters absolute minimum, and a PanAmerican old-style shuttle requires more. The only wharf whose frontage had been dredged to accommodate such displacements was the old one, the one left by a CD geological Survey Team, the one we now stood upon. So it was that the newcomers came directly to us.

Behind Reverend Castell and me the other acolytes formed up. We were big now, and stood in a semicircle. None of us hummed or made any other harmonious sound. As for me, I avoided inner questions and simply looked to Reverend Castell for guidance.

The splashship's shadow covered us, conjuring chill, and then the ship itself slammed into the pilings and demolished a short dock we'd constructed. I steadied myself by taking a step, but Reverend Castell never moved. He gazed at the quintet of ship's officers standing in the hatch, his face utterly calm now, his hands hanging limp.

"Ahoy," one of the ship's ground officers called. "Would you be Charles Castell?" He jumped down onto the wood planks and tugged down the bottom of his tunic before extending his hand. I saw that his ranks echoed Marine ranks, not Naval ranks, which theoretically meant he was trained in all sorts of ground-side deviltry, perhaps even by CD Marines.

Reverend Castell, ignoring the hand, said "Peace is ours to offer." It was a formal greeting from the Writings, but his voice as he said it was strained and rough, as if he'd been crying.

Dropping his hand, the officer said, "I'm Major Lassitre, and—"

"Have you brought more of the Chosen, Major?" Castell asked. "More supplies, perhaps?" He enunciated every syllable with over-precise clarity, as if the sense of the words escaped him. It was more a phonetic mimicry of speech than true communication.

Major Lassitre smiled. His hair, combed back all around and graying at the temples, glistened as he nodded slightly. "Sir, my orders are to set up air traffic control for a field splashdown zone."

Reverend Castell swayed backward a little, but caught his balance before I could move. "You killed one of the Chosen."

The major met Castell's gaze. "I've killed none of your flock, Reverend; they committed suicide if they rowed under us, and I'm not authorized to stand around chatting in any case. We have shuttles coming down in four hours, and I've got work to do."

Turning on his heel, Major Lassitre waved to the other military people at the hatch, and they formed a chain and began handing down packs and field communication units.

Reverend Castell stepped toward the major and touched his arm. "Major Lassitre, may I direct your attention to that island?" He pointed to the big, wooded island situated somewhat west of the lake's center.

"What of it, Reverend? This wharf, if my briefing was correct, is CoDominium built and owned."

Castell swallowed and blinked once, slowly. "The island features prominences at all four quarters, and would serve as an excellent control spot for directing splashdowns."

"Sergeant," the major called to one of the men, who at once stood straight and said, "Sir." "Take a zodiac and reconnoiter that island; it may be a more functional control point."

"Aye, sir." The sergeant saluted, detailed three men to accompany him, and opened a panel on the shuttle's side. From it he took a heavy package which, when he pulled a cord, inflated into a keeled boat almost as large as our wooden ones. One of the sergeant's men attached an outboard motor, and they zipped away with much noise and too many fumes.

Throughout these proceedings Reverend Castell stood mute, but as the zodiac dwindled in the distance he said, "Major, what is going on?"

At once I dismissed the faintest hint of pleading in his voice as a trick of my hearing.

"At ease," the major told his remaining soldier, who at once actually took out and smoked a cigar. To Reverend Castell, Lassitre said, "Haven's about to get quite a population boost, sir. We've got three thousand, nine hundred and eighty-three more Harmonies for you, sir, and another eight thousand and five miners, merchants, and the like."

"What?" I blurted, unable to assimilate the numbers he'd mentioned, let alone grasp their situation.

Glancing up at me, the major grinned and looked me up and down more carefully. "Big one, huh? You've the makings of a fine marine, young man."

"I'm at peace," came the rote reply, but I noticed how he made himself sound as if he were a real CD Marine, and not just a transport company officer.

"Of course," he said, tone neutral. "If you call it that."

During this exchange, Reverend Castell simply continued to stare at the major, as if neither he nor I had said anything.

Redirecting his attention to Castell, Lassitre tossed a thumb toward the sky, to indicate a transport in orbit. It would be over us again in a little under four hours, I knew, remembering our own few orbits. "I forgot how isolated you are here, you had no warning, did you?"

"Haven belongs to the Church of New Universal Harmony. My father purchased settlement rights just before he died." His hand went to his chest for a moment, then dropped. "My people have sacrificed everything Earthly to come here." Reverend Castell spoke quietly, as if reciting from the Writings. "We've no further need of Earthly things. The Harmonies are welcome, but the others—"

"There are families aboard, sir. Men, women, and children. Your church didn't have the funds for a second expedition, so shares were sold. We can't expect you to like it, but it's completely legal. And besides, isn't charity part of your pacifist creed? Or at least basic hospitality?"

Castell took a step back from Major Lassitre. His eyes widened. He took a deep breath, and I winced, expecting a loud sermon to begin. How dare this infidel remind our leader of his own creed's duties? Instead, though, Reverend Castell let his breath out slowly and said, in a conversational tone, "Was the trip hard on them?"

At once Major Lassitre's body language relaxed, and he smiled. "Some died, I won't lie to you. You've been in the transport ships, even converted liners; you know how it can be."

"Squalid," Castell said. He, too, smiled, but with no relief there, no shared referents.

For myself, I could not understand our leader's attitude, his sudden relaxing. Had he conceded the CoDo's right to usurp his authority on Haven? Had he acceded to their right to rescind all those costly permissions?

Was he faltering?

"You understand, of course," Castell told the major, "that we have neither the resources nor the desire to take care of anyone other than our own."

The major laughed. "They may take care of you, sir. They've brought virtually no supplies and precious little know-how, if I'm any judge." When no one joined in his laughter, he coughed and said, "Yes, well. Fact is, Reverend, there's nothing we can do. Ours is but to do or die, eh? Although your chain of command's a bit shorter than mine, huh?"

And as he laughed again, the zodiac returned and the sergeant reported, with a note of surprise, that the reverend hadn't lied, the island was indeed a better place to set up a control point.

The shuttle sloshed back from the wharf and surged to the island, but it was long before the reverend moved or stopped staring.

Behind us the entire settlement had erupted in a cacophony of discussion and disbelief. Almost four thousand more Harmonies; what news would they bring of Earth? Old friends and new would arrive within a few hours. Excitement roiled among us, while we acolytes attempted no calming, feeling only upset ourselves.

"You had not the slightest appreciation of the difficulty in what you asked of me," Reverend Castell said at last, under his breath. He turned and glared at me a moment, as if angry that I'd eavesdropped.

With a blush I lowered my gaze, but my mind, always the independent part of me, wondered if the reverend had been subvocalizing a conversation with his dead father. It seemed to me futile to argue with ghosts that haunt only memory.

When Reverend Castell strode away I did not follow as closely as usual. His glare had sent sour notes through me, clashing with our normal attunement.

Later, the other acolytes began asking me what we must do as our numbers swelled fourfold. "Strive for harmony," I said.

For the first time in as long as I could remember, I was uncertain exactly what that phrase might mean.

IV

A communal symphony convened. We made music and let it take us into complicated realms of certainty and doubt, where Pythagoras fought with numbers and found the octave and the twelve chromatic semitones, our disciples, from whence came spherical harmony, as from chaos and cacophony a symphony universal evolved.

My fingers manipulated the rhythm sticks automatically and I hummed in tune, even as my mind kicked and screamed at the onslaught now facing us. We'd done fine for an Earth-year or so, and anyone joining us would be interlopers, even if they shared our faith.

Reverend Castell let the Chosen pulse with rhythms and song for only a few rondeaux verses before appearing in the town square himself, in fresh robes bleached white. In the orange of Haven's day he seemed covered in fiery blood. Raising his hands, he commanded silence. His gaze scanned us, and he shook his head, his face showing disgust.

"My efforts," he said. Then he glanced down for an instant and started again. "Our efforts to live in harmony with all forces of the universe have been blessed until today. Many have been injured, and most of us continue to marvel at the sheer harshness of Haven's environment, but we're still here. We have not thrived, but we have gotten by.

"Now the CoDominium has followed us, and its decay is spread even unto our crisp air and unsullied waters. This is cause for resentment, perhaps, but such negative feelings create disharmony, which shall, if indulged, prove our nemesis.

"We must welcome not only other Harmonies, but also the pitiable families transported here by the CoDominium. They purchased a share in our world and no doubt harbor dreams of better lives. They are more akin to the Chosen than most others from that rotting planet whose name is a synonym for dirt.

"Haven was the name of Tycho Brahe's island where he brought together the best astonomers of his time to form Uraniborg, the Heavenly Castle, an estate of science and truth, a refuge from idiocy and Earthly corruptions, and Haven is *our* planet's name, chosen and bestowed by my father, and a haven it shall ever be, to all those who must be clean of Earth."

The Chosen murmured amongst themselves and milled about, and Reverend Castell glanced at me and smiled, perhaps in atonement for the earlier scowl. "They're big enough," he told me in a soft voice. "They can accommodate even this latest of added burdens."

I nodded and returned his smile, squaring my shoulders. If such was Reverend Castell's new course for Haven, then such would I support, for I trusted him to sense the resonance, the harmonics.

The fact that we had no choice may have helped us be gracious in our first greetings when, a few hours later, the first clumps of miners arrived.

Those of us with boats helped ferry people ashore, while the rest of us either got on with urgent tasks or stood gaping up as shuttle after shuttle arrived. I figured there were five shuttles in all, working in a chain. They soon had the new arrivals on the ground.

Our women comforted the newcomers' wives and children, while our men harmonized with old friends and amazed colonists who'd expected a more settled world.

Some of the Chosen were eager for news from Earth, others contented themselves with the festive atmosphere that was developing as tours of our town and fields were given. It was as if we had visitors.

Visitors, however, soon depart, whereas this overwhelming number of people were here to stay.

To escape the confusion and conflicting feelings of giddiness and horror, I clapped hands outside Reverend Castell's house and was bid enter. Stepping down the four steps, I got on my hands and knees and crawled in through the curtain.

He sat in the dim light of a single wick-lamp, holding but not reading a copy of the Writings. "Kev," he said, "have you completed your circuit?"

I remembered my five-sleep walk, the people I'd visited, and the vermin I'd dropped on my run toward the lake, then forced myself toward peace, in order to better remember my tour. "Yes, Reverend, all the outlying farms are well. Some vermin and one possible raid from the outcasts are the only discords."

He nodded as if not really interested. "Can we increase our harvests by a factor of ten or more?"

Blood drained from my face. With all the confusion, I hadn't given thought to starving.

Reverend Castell blinked, and I saw tears flowing. "Maybe they've brought extra seed-grain, or implements, despite what the officer said."

I sat heavily, unbidden, on a pallet by the door as the truth sank home like an arrow in my heart: Even if the new arrivals took to farming in a trice, there was not nearly enough seed-grain to allow planting.

"They must spread through the Shangri-La Valley," Reverend Castell said. "How ironic that name's become. I wonder if the first surveyors foresaw this planet's strife?"

Not fully understanding his references, I remained silent.

"Muskylopes, perhaps," he said. "Or groundhogs, when we spot them. But we cannot slay them unthinkingly, as we did the American bison and so many other species."

I let him chatter to himself for a few moments, then said, "Reverend, you've always taught me that a note gains its power when it acts in concert with other notes according to the laws of harmony."

He glanced up at me, surprise on his face. A smile blossomed. "You are a good soul," he told me.

Unsure that he'd understood what I meant, I blushed but forced myself to say, "I mean, we can't abandon our Writings now," and gestured half-heartedly at the book he held. "I must tell you, there's already unrest spreading. Some of the newcomers describe themselves as service merchants. They have harlots, and gambling is on their every word, in their every thought. I have even scented alcohol on the breaths of some of our own, who perhaps shared a secular communion with less-strict brothers in Harmony."

It felt worse than a toothache to presume to tell Reverend Castell anything so crass, and I fidgeted and finally stood to excuse myself, preferring to let him think in solitude than risk being exposed to another of his rantings. Before I could move, however, someone poked his head through the curtain into the room and said, "Castell? That you?"

Aghast at such effrontery, I looked at the reverend, who appeared as amazed as I by such a breach of town etiquette. "I am he," the reverend said, standing. He placed the Writings on a stone shelf and folded his hands in front of his belt-line.

The man had curly brown hair and a dentist smile. He brushed off the dust from the short tunnel, then stretched up to touch the roofing. "Quaint," he said, more or less ignoring us as he surveyed the room's contents. He bent and brushed more dust from his trouser's knees.

Finally he said, "Oh, uh, I'm Julian Anders' secretary, Rollie Tate, and I was asked to bring you to see him right away, so can we get going?"

His words shot through me like high voltage.

Reverend Castell said, "Am I to understand that Anders is a Harmony?"

The little man nodded enthusiastically. "Sure what else? He's our leader, he brought us all to this dump.

Now can we get a move on? Reverend Anders doesn't like waiting."

My expression must have betrayed my inner turmoil, because Reverend Castell stepped forward and placed a hand on my shoulder. He leaned close and whispered, "A song always has more notes."

He meant that the notes left unsounded are as important as those we sing, a quotation intended to soothe me.

Did he also mean we should have seen this coming?

V

"A song always has more notes" is also what he told me a month ago when my baby died, and I wondered cynically if it were generic advice.

After three exhausting days my wife, Bren, had birthed a son, but the baby lived barely a moment. Looking up at me, one of the midwives shook her head, eyes wide.

My heart sank, and then my knees weakened. I sat on a stone covered by muskylope hide, gasping as if I'd run kilometers.

Concern for Bren shot through me then, as I caught a glimpse of the blood-smeared belly, still swollen as she struggled with the afterbirth. Standing, I rushed to her side. Her face was agony incarnate and incarnadine, her silken tresses lay matted, her eyes, when they opened, wandered dull and glazed.

"I'm here, Bren-love," I told her, grasping her hand, which squeezed mine hard enough to grind knuckles.

"Take," she said, "the baby," her neck's tendons taut, "to Reverend Castell," and she groaned, fought for control, and added, in a breathless whisper of pain, "blessing."

My throat was too choked by love and sorrow to answer, so I nodded. Leaning down, I kissed her salty cheek, then gathered the still bundle in my arms and trudged across the town square.

I passed the acolytes' quarters on my way, and heard

a droning from within. For an instant I regretted ever having left the warm community of bachelor acolytes, but I knew it was a strident disharmony. Besides, marriage was a rock-solid foundation for the soul, and in truth my love for Bren often threatened to overwhelm even my love for Harmony and all things Harmonious.

Spits of snow sent icy darts into my eyes, into my lungs. Haven's winter, although just beginning, featured blizzards to humble even our Russian taiga couple, Iban and Svetalma, who had taught us how to skin muskylopes and who often told tales of snow piled up to the sky.

At Reverend Castell's house I dropped to my knees. Hugging the still-warm bundle to me with my elbows, I clapped thrice and heard a faint, "Enter."

I crawled on threes, holding the bundle against my heart with my weak arm, the left. As my head thrust past the many curtains hung against the chill I said, "Reverend, our baby's dead." And with that the truth came home to me, and my tears flowed in a gush that blinded me like a bucketful of riverwater.

Reverend Castell came to me, stood me upright, and took the bundle. He sang it a short dirge, rocking it as if soothing a living infant to sleep, and then he placed it on a small corner altar, where candles already burned.

Coming back to me, Reverend Castell hugged me and said, "A song always has more notes, and your song is just begun. Our infant mortality rate is exceeding forty-nine percent, so such sacrifices carry little of the discord of surprise, Kev. We must bear the dead on life's shoulders." He squeezed tight, then let go and said, "Return to your wife, comfort her."

It was good advice, giving me something to think of other than my own misery, and the cold air outside revived me.

Only when I passed one of the midwives on her way to Castell's house did I falter. I knew she would take the tiny corpse and bury it in some unguessed farmer's fallow field, after doctors pronounced it pure. Looking down at

the ground, I hated its insatiable hunger for babies'
bones. A year had aged me ten.

When I got back, the strain was still evident on Bren's
face, too, and seeking to soothe her I tried to stroke her
forehead. She snarled at me, almost biting my quickly
withdrawn hand, then fell into heavy sleep.

"She must rest, but stay by her side, sing her gentle
songs," a midwife said, packing shiny things into a leather
bag.

It was bad for Bren, I knew. Just looking at her threatened to begin my tears anew, for the effort and loss on
her face, even as she slept, was awful in such a young
woman. Worse, strain remained on her face even days
later, after she was up and around.

We talked nothing of the lost child at first, then talked
of nothing but the lost child in the weeks following. Neither silence nor words did much good, but my love for
Bren deepened.

Still, I could not remove all of the guilt and bitterness
she felt. Of Earth-lowland stock, she could not risk
another pregnancy, so we took simpler pleasure in more
complicated ways and hoped no baby resulted from some
fluke. And of course all the while we each secretly prayed
for that fluke, because we none of us ever believe that
the worst is yet to come.

So quickly we grew older.

Such were my thoughts as Reverend Castell and I followed Rollie Tate down to the lake shore. On the way
we gathered the other acolytes with double-claps at
appropriate houses. As we walked, we heard howls of
furious celebration and shouts of dissension and anger.
It seemed our humanity was lessened in the acid-bath of
sheer numbers.

Following the scampering Tate, we passed a few merchants, some actually squatting in the street beneath
makeshift awnings, others hawking wares from collapsible
wheeled carts. Dice flung from hands better suited to
prayer than rough work clattered against stone walls,

rolled across once-clean sidewalks. We also saw a group of miners buying a pair of donkeys, looking like prospectors from histories of Alaska and California, outfitted with Kennicott equipment and preparing to trek into Haven's wilderness seeking who knew what forms of personal wealth.

Near the lake we neared a group of men, some ship officers, others dressed in relative finery, especially for Haven standards. A boat bobbed behind them, its operator a bored fat man, who yawned repeatedly and chewed some kind of cud between yawns.

There, standing on the pebbles beside Major Lassitre, was a tall, clean-shaven man with cropped gray hair and dew-lapped eyes glinting like coal pushed too far into a snowman's face. Tate approached the tall man and did a bow that incorporated a curtsey and other, subtler obeisance. "The bearded guy," Tate said.

Noticing us, Lassitre said, with some disgust, "He insisted on being the last to the ground." When Castell ignored him in favor of staring at the tall man, Lassitre stepped back a pace or so and fell silent. He watched with some amusement, his eyes glittering even as he shivered now and then.

Tate took a position behind the tall man, who stepped up to Castell and said, "Reverend, I'm Julian Anders, and I've led my people here to join yours."

Reverend Castell locked gazes with the man. I saw neither flinch and thought, *There's iron in them both.* Castell said, "You served under me, on Earth. One of my ministers, but I can't quite place where you served—"

"I'm a leader now, in my own right. When you took the first Chosen away, I rose to ascension by popular acclaim." He grinned. "I represent those strong enough to be left behind. We've come to Haven to bulk your enterprise and bulwark your fragile community against its own cowardice and weakness." He gazed across the landscape, eyes squinted, and added, "You'll be glad to have me here, from the looks of things."

"Haven neither needs nor wants a second-in-command,

Mister Anders," Castell said. He glanced at the military men, his gaze lingering on Lassitre, who affected not to notice.

"You're just lucky, I guess," Anders said, half his mouth curling upward. He looked around, sniffed the chill air, and added, "A trait I don't seem to share at the moment. I thought things would be, well, further along by the time we arrived. Have you forsaken all practicalities for constant prayer?"

The mockery and the veiled insult to our settlement caused several of us acolytes to bristle. Our bodies tensed. After all, we'd accomplished more than could reasonably have been expected, considering Haven's inhospitality and our own naiveté upon first arriving. And least of all did we expect to be insulted by one calling himself a Harmony, a so-called colonist who'd brought virtually nothing in the way of supplies or expertise. Here was arrant hubris indeed.

I looked at Reverend Castell, past the big black beard, past the bushy eyebrows, past the straight nose and wind-bronzed skin. I looked into his eyes, and I don't know what I saw, but a shiver descended my spine at the cold, hard glitter of it.

Unexpectedly, Julian Anders walked forward, brushing past Castell and parting the acolytes. "Let's find a warmer place to palaver."

Castell did not hurry after him, as a few of the younger acolytes did. Instead, he turned slowly and glared at the man's back. Charles Castell had a glare to melt glaciers, a glare to freeze volcanoes, a glare with all the charisma of creation itself concentrated in it. That glare could bless or curse, it could wound or cure. It only worked, however, if one saw it, and the reverend never looked back as he strode into our town.

"What must we do?" I asked the Reverend Castell.

He did not acknowledge me, but started walking back to town at that robotic pace, his eyes unblinking, that shuddersome glitter colder than even before, as if he'd ingested part of Haven's glacial heart.

*   *   *

"Yes, this site is nicely chosen, Castell," Anders said, leaning back against a pile of muskylope hides his aide, Tate, had gathered without permission from around the commons room in the acolyte quarters.

In the room's center a fire-pit full of coals radiated heat, while along its edges teapots heated water and small cauldrons simmered acorn-squash stew. A few blood-red heartfruits sizzled on hot, flat stones, and one culinary acolyte had a stuffed clownfruit baking, sans nose.

Lifting a silver flask, Anders took a pull, then smacked his lips and said, "Ambrosia, this brandy. Truly a balm for the soul. So, Castell, you can at least suggest a spot for our soul-troopers to bivouac."

Reverend Castell, standing by the door, frowned. "Our fields are vital to survival. We can spare no cultivated land. In fact, we need more."

"Oh, no doubt. But face it, old man, we need accommodations. Major?"

Lassitre glanced at Anders, brows raised but mouth tight.

Anders smiled at him as if reproving a child. "Major, you've given the situation thought. I saw you with your maps before we shuttled down."

"Along the river that runs east," he began.

Anders cut him off. "Major, I don't intend trudging through manured fields right now." He pursed his lips. "This town square we just saw, now that shows promise. We could expand the town—"

"Our buildings are all occupied," Reverend Castell said.

"Oh, these rabbit holes shall be demolished, of course. A dignified community requires real buildings. It cannot cower in neolithic bunkers. Major, your engineering programs can no doubt draw us up some suitable places."

"Places, yes. Not palaces, however. In fact, nothing as good as these." He gestured around us. I caught Major Lassitre's disgusted and helpless glance at Reverend

Castell. "You'll have to fit yourselves in here, Anders, or go off somewhere and fend for yourselves."

Laughing, Anders took another swig of his brandy. "Reverend Castell, does the major speak for you as well? Is this an example of Haven's charity?"

"There'll be precious little of that," Major Lassitre said. "If you'll excuse me, I've got to see to my groundcrew." As he walked to the door and got to his hands and knees to leave, Anders said, "My, he's certainly taking a more active interest in command these last few days."

The mocking tones stopped the major for an instant. "I was cashiered from the CoDo Marines because I happened to be caught in some political power moves. Bad timing's my only crime. And at least, Anders, I don't make grandiose claims based on ignorance and incompetence."

Pressing the attack, Reverend Castell told Anders, "Your presence I cannot dispute, but your behavior among my people I must condemn. Haven belongs to the Church of New Universal Harmony."

"Precisely," Anders said. "And the church neither begins nor ends with you, Castell. Leadership's not an inherited quality."

For an instant there was silence. Major Lassitre left the room. The acolytes tensed, offended by Anders. Others in the room, from Tate and the other newcomers to more of the Chosen, watched without comment as the two leaders stared at each other across the pit of glowing coals.

That's when Reverend Castell's eyes rolled back into his head. I saw it and got ready to catch him, thinking perhaps the heat or the strain afflicted him, but he neither swayed nor buckled.

Standing, he stepped over the rim and entered the fire-pit, his bare feet crunching down on glowing coals. I gasped along with the other acolytes, and no one else in the room made a move or a sound. All gazes fixed upon Reverend Castell; his mouth bore a hint of a smile.

He walked out onto the coals in the fire-pit and stood at its center.

Whisps of lazy smoke rose up from the hem of his robe, and I thought I saw small hairs on his legs withering, puffing into nothing. Then his garments burst into flame, and he raised his arms.

I cried out, terrified. Tears coursed down my cheeks. There were shouts of alarm and warning, and a few people stood and backed away from the pillar of fire. Raising my hand, I blocked the heat coming off Reverend Castell, and as I did so I glanced at Anders and saw the look of utter awe on his face.

Reverend Castell's beard and hair flashed, then crisped. His clothes and hair fell from him in ashes that wafted lazy on stray currents of rising air. With that final burst of flame, the light dimmed again, revealing the man at the heart of the fire. He stood naked, hairless, his body luminous in the faint glow of tallow lamps. It was as if he'd been reborn. He opened his eyes and glared again at Anders, and this time the interloper quailed.

"Peace is ours to offer," Reverend Castell said. His voice boomed. His eyes flashed. Every soul in that room felt stinging heat and electric thrills. "In concert is harmony's power found, and in harmony all shall thrive." Raising a hand, Reverend Castell pointed at Julian Anders. His fingers traced a staff in the air, then added eight symbolic notes in a scale.

Anders gaped. His flask lay dropped, leaking brandy onto his lap. He quivered. His eyes remained wide, but a new look came upon his features. And then he laughed.

In the silence it was a strident sound, and no one joined in. A sharp edge of hysteria cut the laugh short.

With an inhalation of breath that seemed to go on forever, Reverend Castell stood so straight and tall that he seemed to grow before our eyes, and in an even, singsong tone that broke each word into its component syllables, he said,

"Anger is the enemy,
"Act with thought,
"Strike no false note,
"Harmonize with all forces,
"Resonate with all events,
"Sing with all beings,
"Be still
"as the silence
"at the heart
"of the song."

With that he pitched forward, sprawling amidst hot coals.

Ashes swirled, confusing sight for a time. Sparks flew and some people swatted at their garments in terror.

Moving forward, I circled the pit and leaned inward. By stretching I reached the reverend's right hand and grasped it.

Leaning back, I pulled, dragging him through the embers.

Other acolytes helped by pulling on me, until another could snare the reverend's other hand. Intense heat had my eyes watering. I gasped for breath and inhaled ash and smoke.

When Reverend Castell's head came up above the fire-pit's clay lip, he shouted, "Help me, please."

A woman standing near grabbed a tea pot and hurled its water at Castell's face, raising blisters.

He shrieked and then bellowed, "Help me, damn you."

It was then that I noticed his eyes. They were staring upward, through the hole in the roof. His gaze followed the smoke and ash upwards, and I shuddered, because I knew then that he was demanding help not from us, but from his father.

A doctor rushed in and at once applied a salve to Reverend Castell's blistered face, which looked small now without the beard. After a quick examination, the doctor said, "He's not burned, not even his feet. The water boiled and blistered him, but the coals and flames did nothing."

Anders stood and left the room, taking Tate and several newcomers with him. I noticed a few of the Chosen following, too, as people crawled from the room on hands and knees in a childlike herd.

We would soon discover that Anders kept going when he left the meeting, taking eight hundred souls with him into Haven's wilderness, each carrying as much as possible in the way of provisions and equipment. The loss, echoing the first desertion when we Chosen first arrived, affected us little as the remaining three thousand or so integrated themselves to our ways in the warm glow left by Reverend Castell's flaming renewal of our faith in him, his cause. Whether planned or inspired, the gesture worked, for a while, to weave us back into organized, orchestrated harmony.

Flopping back, I rested until my breathing evened. I found myself gazing upward through the smoke-hole. I could see only Haven's wind-scoured sky.

VI

Reverend Castell thrust out his hand, in which was a crumpled ball of paper. His face, bare since the fire-pit a few months back, contorted in frustration and impotent rage. "We've been on Haven barely two Earth standard years, Kev. There is constant discord over living space, provisions, supplies, equipment, and even over the simplest elements of doctrine, since the four thousand arrived."

I looked at the paper in his hand. Paper was a fairly rare item. I owned none myself, other than my copy of the Writings. Only a few standard months earlier, one of our artisans had produced the first new paper on Haven, using rice and ancient Japanese methods his grandfather had taught him. To crumple such a precious commodity was almost blasphemous because it tempted waste to begin a melody all its own.

"These were to have been the expansions to our town," the reverend said. "Improvements, such as birthing pits dug deep to increase the air pressure, even as mine-shafts in South Africa did on Earth. I drew up the plans myself." He grimaced. "No doubt the miners can help with this."

"Shall we strike a chord of harmony?" I asked, seeking a solution as well as trying to console him.

He appraised me with mockery in his gaze. "You can't mean that we're lucky, even as Anders said." He shook his head. "No, Kev, Kennicott is not harmonious, they are cacophony." He stood and began pacing. The crumpled papers he tossed into the fire. "My careful plans, ruined in a mob-shout of BuReloc stupidity and Kenni-cott greed." He kicked the altar in the corner, tumbling a candle, which went out.

Hanging my head, I waited for his storm to pass. His rantings lasted longer these days, I noticed. They pro-duced less determination, cleared less mental air, too.

Reverend Castell had been raging ever since Major Lassitre, who had stayed on Haven, brought word from Splashdown Island that Kennicott Mining Company, in cooperation with the Bureau of Relocation, intended to set up a mining enterprise on Haven. Even as we spoke a shipload of immigrants got closer to shuttle-down.

My place as head acolyte had grown until I was Rever-end Castell's confidant. He confided doubts, dislikes, and discords to my ears more often than he talked to his wife, whom he saw only during sleeps. Now and then he thought aloud about creating for me a post of Deacon, but nothing had come of that yet.

Burdens stacked on me kept my brow furrowed most hours of my day, and I'd begun losing weight as worry affected appetites.

As the Chosen harmonized as best they could with the newcomers, my forays into outlying farmland became erratic, hasty jaunts, rather than regular journeys. In

town, now called Castell City by jest and general usage,
I circulated as best I could. At households where once I
found welcome, I'd lately begun finding suspicion. Some
called me Castell's spy to my face. Others hinted that I'd
been bought by Kennicott, or some other commercial
enterprise.

"We must organize church services again," Reverend
Castell said. "Secret meetings of the truly faithful." Bitterness warped that latter phrase into a self-condemnation,
so I said nothing. In my mind I railed against the
CoDominium. The thousands on their way would be
mostly from the United States, and many professed to
be Harmonies, as well. Lassitre's communications shack
even caught some cross-talk between BuReloc officials
and CoDo representatives aboard the immigrant ship,
and from it he brought us word that we would receive a
small food plant, to convert raw molecules into edibles,
reminiscent of Earthly shortages. It seemed they were
serious enough to try helping us slightly.

Reverend Castell said, "Have you nothing to tell me
of how our songs are being sung?"

I sipped some Hecate tea and savored its piney aro-
matics. "Our songs are quiet but strong," I said.

He chuckled. "You've been around me too long, perhaps, if you're learning the arts of such speech."

With a smile I denied that I could ever be too long
with him, then said, "My wish is only to hold my own
counsel until I know more details. I've heard many dis-
turbing things, and I'm sure my ears are among the last
to receive such grace notes."

A nod cast a shadow as sap flared in the fire. "If it's
about the mineral assays done by Byers' crew when
Haven was first discovered, I've dreaded the findings for
years."

"Only part of what I hear echoes Kennicott Mining
Company, but I'm sure they've a use for Haven or they'd
never have paid the freight for the North Americans who
wanted to come here."

He looked at me hard again, as if seeking confirmation

of a new trait, one not necessarily pleasing to him. "Politics is a shame in one so young."

"Forewarned is forearmed," I said, at once blushing. I was aghast at the militaristic quotation and doubly aghast that it should fly so readily from my lips.

Anger darkened his visage as he stood over me. "We seek harmony in all things, and in all ways. Peace is ours to offer only because we hold it so carefully, preserve it so carefully."

Bowing my head, I recited with him a short drone. A sharp pain stabbed me in the gut, from within, and I belched and tasted bile at the base of my tongue. Still, I made sure to fold my left hand over my right as I prayed, to cover the skinned knuckles and teeth marks I'd gotten by punching my way out of a debate.

The newcomers found more than enough work to do, making places to live, and trying to scrabble out more food. They went about the business of settling in, many contructing houses for themselves with our help, others moving in with Chosen families, still others fanning out across the Shangri-La Valley. A few who had been miners took their families to outlying farms, but scratching in the dirt differed too greatly from digging in the dirt to suit most of them, and I found on my long circuit walks that many of these became prospectors.

The few consumer products brought by merchants stirred up more greed than they pacified. Earthers used to buying things disliked making them, but there were too few manufactured goods to go around, and, until the Kennicott operation got properly started, virtually no chance of more being imported. And without factories and refineries, neither of which were planned so far as anyone knew, importing would be the only way to get such things during their probably shortened life span on Haven.

Handmade, utilitarian, and harmonious items just weren't as bright and shiny as manufactured consumer goods could be on Earth. Haven's quaintness wore off.

Tourism became torture when the newcomers and their families truly understood that they couldn't leave. Enthusiasms for collecting the charming handmade items evaporated when everyone used the things every day. And with more settlers on the way, even the hint of future scarcity was enough to push haggling into hassles and fights.

Theft and nuisance sabotage became, if not commonplace, then at least frequent enough to be considered ignorable. Each time I or other acolytes received such complaints, we promised to carry them to Castell, but I also advised, on my own initiative, increased security on the farms and in the shops. Prevention lessened temptation, I reminded them. We acolytes eventually learned some methods of keeping things safer, and taught those with whom we visited each stroll-period.

One evening Castell turned to me at a communal meal and said, "Our peaceful ways are chafing to those whose tastes run toward depravity."

Anger swelled in me, because I knew he referred to an incident I'd reported to him. While walking past the palisade's town square gate between my home and Castell's house, I had encountered a Chosen woman and a child. Both were crying.

"He touched her, she says," the woman told me, stroking the little girl's head as she hugged it. "Is there nothing to be done? Tell me how to find the harmony in such a vile act." And she ran from me before I could even ask her who had done such a thing.

When Castell heard, he was livid for an instant, then dropped into sudden, disconcerting calm. "The child must visit friends or relatives in the out-farms," he said. "And Chosen children must be in groups of three or more and accompanied by Chosen when inside the fort."

Outrage still roiled in me, but his words held such convincing harmony that I had bowed and crawled out to spread his words on the matter.

It was only the next night that a drunken man slapped an arm around my shoulder in the town square and asked me, with volatile breath and a leer, where he could find the brothel about which he'd heard such exciting things. Earthly corruptions flourished in Haven's miserly environment.

"Keeping our peace separate from their discord does nothing," I told Reverend Castell. "If anything, it weakens our song. Harmony cannot play counterpoint to cacophony and chaos."

Reverend Castell spun towards me and pointed at my face. "How dare you quote Writings to me, who helped my father compose them. How dare you interpret to me what my father and I wrestled into words."

"But you've got to realize that our settlement's fraying at the edges. Reverend, our children are beginning to mock the ethics of their parents, because they see such mockery every day around them."

"Yes, the secular always makes intrusions—"

"Incursions, more like," I said, so frustrated that I wasn't even aware that I'd interrupted him. "The Shangri-La Valley may soon be a bowl of blood."

"Your terms of war begin to try me," Castell said.

"Then I'll speak them no more." And I turned to go.

Having to drop to one's knees to leave a room makes melodramatic exits difficult at best. This was no exception, and before I got my head past his curtains he'd made me laugh by saying, "Oh, get up, for harmony's sake, I can't be expected to sing to your posterior."

Despite my anger, I laughed, and then I returned to my place beside him, and he said, "We must institute town meetings and community votes. Church membership shall be a requirement for voting privileges, but those lone voices who pledge to learn the ways of Harmony will be eligible to serve our cause, and can eventually qualify to join our chorus. Let each of the Chosen choose someone to indoctrinate, and distribute Writings to all who require them.

"And as for you and the acolytes, we must increase their numbers, as well. I charge you, Kev Malcolm, to be Deacon, along with the best two acolytes under your tutelage. For every acolyte choose two Beadles, from the newcomers, young people like yourself." Here his voice lowered and he leaned close to me. "Your new role is protector of the Harmonies. Deacons may decide upon strategies, ensuring their harmony with the Writings, and Beadles shall deploy tactics, to ensure compliance with Writings among the Chosen and the Pledged."

Swallowing hard, I nodded. My palms sweated and itched. My knuckles throbbed, too, and I wondered how much he knew of my many scuffles with disrespectful, resentful Earthers. I dared ask, "Does this mean we must set aside our pacifism?"

"Our church needs a buffer, and the Deacons and Beadles shall provide it," he answered. Then he scowled. "Our pacifism remains, but absolution for necessary lapses among those not yet full church members may be granted; we must always seek harmony, but we may adjust the strength of our voice to compete with the cacophony roaring around us." He put a hand on my shoulder. "I'm asking you to manage a group partly outside our beliefs and convictions, to ensure that we can thrive. In return, you'll be doing a service vital to the survival of the Church of New Universal Harmony."

Part of my mind thought it was a deal with the devil, but my bruises and sore hands argued otherwise, calling it a practical compromise in the face of uncompromising difficulties.

VII

No good deed goes unpunished, they say. In our Writings there is an entire chapter devoted to advice on how to avoid disgusting the infidels we must live among. Much of it is attributed to Benjamin Franklin.

One of the most important pieces of advice is to keep those around you out of debt, for nothing disgusts like owing something. Knowing this from our Writings, I would still have acted as I did when Reverend Castell, the acolytes, and I encountered the drunks.

In the lead, the reverend hummed as his long stride carried him across the town square and into one of the market streets, where goods and services were exchanged. We were on our way to the docks, where the shuttles had been bringing down immigrants, to officially receive the small food plant as a goodwill gift from CoDo reps and Kennicott executives.

It was midday, if peak activity among the populace meant anything. Crowds of newcomers mingled at the stalls, pilfering here and shouting there. Many were children, their faces wan, their eyes alert, almost feral.

"Hunger punishes us," Castell said, over his shoulder. "Have the botanists reported any progress, Kev?"

"No, Reverend." *They're not real botanists, only farmers elevated into research because of the population crisis,* I thought, pressing my lips tight to prevent the quibble from escaping. Along our quick walk we saw many failures of harmony, but Reverend Castell never paused. He never looked to either side, for that matter. The acolytes kept a wary eye, while we Deaks walked tall, for I'd chosen the biggest of us for the post of Deacon, and Beads patrolled more surreptitiously, melding with the crowds.

"What of the muskylope expedition?"

I rolled my eyes. "My sources extend to the island only occasionally, and I've heard nothing of late, but Major Lassitre sent only a squad. They'll bring back some meat, probably, but not enough to matter."

A few of the younger acolytes exchanged looks of surprise and alarm, and I regretted having to report to Castell in front of them. Three of our older acolytes had vanished, probably to join the outcasts, while one had been found dead, head crushed from a vicious beating. Any nudge in any direction was liable to cause overreactions these days.

That day, especially, we should have left the acolytes back in their quarters. Newly appointed acolytes should have been tending candles and helping set up for ceremonies, not being terrified by plainsong truth and unembellished bluntness of language, nor should they have had placed on their minds the oppressive facts demonstrated by the arrival of thousands of immigrants into a settlement that could barely support the souls already here. With each step we witnessed new variations of disharmony.

Violence, crime, and corruption rampaged through Castell City, now that the newcomer families found their last hopes waning. As population waxed, living space and cooperation waned. As the harsh realities of Haven set in, despair sparked fury and the urge to find scapegoats.

When Reverend Castell asked me if we were not close to the spot where one of our own had been found dead, I nodded. "There, in fact," I said, pointing into an alley. "He was found by that wall."

Veering from our agreed-upon route to the docks, Reverend Castell entered the alley. It stank of rotting vegetation tossed out back portals by slovenly householders. It also offered no Bead coverage, as they hadn't known he would visit this place.

Kneeling in the putrid muck and mud, Castell examined some of the loose stones fallen from the low wall. "These were used. They stoned him to death."

"It was worse than that, Reverend," I told him. "In his back were imprints of a hammer and curved cuts, as if from a scythe."

"Murder."

No one answered that word. "A constabulary is needed," I said.

Reverend Castell stood and turned to face me. He no longer towered over me, as I was taller, but his personal force caused me to step back a pace as he said, voice low and overly controlled, "I'll have no shattering of the peace by secular vermin open to the temptations of profit and pleasure."

The heat that came from him took away my breath. I nodded and bowed my head. Ever since he'd been in the fire-pit, Reverend Castell possessed an intensity beyond any human understanding. Although his actions and words that day remained unexplained and baffling, the fact that he'd withstood the coals pulsed around him like an aura of hellish divinity.

One of the young acolytes whimpered, and the sound caused Castell to break concentration. He returned to normal, although still he scowled.

He stepped over the low wall, into a tiny courtyard mostly filled by a dewpond, which was all but dry. "Perhaps he'd thirsted," Reverend Castell said, gesturing toward the small lens of water at the bottom of the dewpond.

"Reverend, this place is a brothel." I pointed up at the back of one of the buildings. "And I smelled distilled spirits on the body."

"You're accusing a brother acolyte of—"

"I'm reporting facts, Reverend, nothing more. Brigands might well have killed him here and poured whiskey on his body to scoff at our faith in Universal Harmony."

Reverend Castell's face relaxed. "Yes, that makes sense. Yes." He rubbed his hands together, neither for heat nor for eagerness but in a gesture of nervous indecision.

"Forgive my inept phrasing, Reverend."

He glanced up at me, then registered what I'd said and nodded, his hand coming up to touch my head. I felt his thumb making the sign of the octave staff upon me, but there was no thrill this time. Perhaps it was a sign of immediate doom.

As Reverend Castell led the way out of the alley, we found ourselves surrounded by a crowd of drunken newcomers. The reverend began a simple harmony, and we Deacons and acolytes joined.

When a group barred Castell's way, he changed direction. When he found all ways blocked by scowling miners, he stopped. I saw Reverend Castell's shoulders straighten, and he radiated warmth again, although not heat. He smiled benignly. "You have an interest in us, I see," he told the men, his tone light and friendly.

One stepped forward and shoved Reverend Castell on the chest.

Castell laughed. "You have touched us all," he said.

The acolytes cowered together in a knot behind me, probably because I'm the biggest, even among the Deaks. I stood just behind the Reverend Castell, trying to glare like him at the people hemming us in, hoping that I might intimidate them into leaving us to our peace.

Insults flew then. They called us Holy Joes and made jest of the harm part of harmony. They denounced our pacifism, mislabeling it apathy and inertia. "You've done nothing to help us, and you've given us nothing but a hard time when we try to enjoy ourselves," they said, in effect. "You Harmonies control things and get first pick of provisions, and then you put us down for taking the little we need to live on, calling it theft instead of simple survival."

"Peace is ours to offer," Castell answered. "Those activities you label enjoyments are but forms of disharmony. Can you not see the harm you do each other when you intoxicate yourselves and wrestle in lust without regard to increasing humanity? And as for—"

In the back of my mind I knew it was the wrong tack. This crowd needed no sermons on moderation. "Reverend, I see a group of CD Marines across the street, watching. Perhaps if we appealed—"

He interrupted me and commanded the acolytes to begin a song, and so we sang. The crowd, laughing and jostling us, tried to shout us down, but our combined voices cut through the hubbub with chromatic purity.

Even as I sang my gaze sought routes of escape. My heart thudded, and my palms were slick with sweat. And yet, as we sang, the mob began quieting, to listen. Reverend Castell's old magic almost appeared again. For a few seconds we serenaded our tormentors, and that's when Castell, giving us a sign to proceed, shouted, "Acknowledge, then, how the harmony of organized singing defeats the scattered cacophony of lone voices crying in this wilderness of pain."

I doubt if a third of the crowd understood more than

half his words, although they rode the crest of our harmonics to echo throughout that section of Castell City.

"You like peace?" someone yelled. "Then maybe you'll like being in pieces." Guffaws erupted at the pitiable jest, like stubborn donkeys braying in self-defeating frustration. It was like being back on the freighter, in transport to Haven, except far worse without the need to hide violence done upon us from the eyes of ship's officers.

A man almost as tall as I, belly flopping, dashed toward Reverend Castell and swung a fist.

The reverend collapsed, clutching his throat.

Stepping over and in, I raised my hands, but the man kicked the fallen man. The kick struck with such force that I felt the impact through the air.

Glancing down, I noticed that the attacker wore miner's boots, which are heavy and often steel-toed.

Reverend Castell moaned.

Around us, the crowd laughed and waited.

Kneeling, I helped Reverend Castell to his feet. He stood bent over, clutching his kicked ribs.

That's when the attacker leaned in to deliver a headbutt to Castell's face, which spurted blood and snapped nasal cartilage.

Red tinted my vision, but from within.

Reaching out, I grasped the man's throat and squeezed, trying to crush his larynx even as I twisted my left arm around to snag his right ear.

Part of the ear tore off.

As he croaked and coughed I let him bend over, then slammed the heel of my right hand up into his lower jaw.

Teeth shattered. White shards flecked with red spewed from him as he toppled.

Another man came at me, and I whirled away from him, timing it so my elbow would take him in the throat. I missed, but connected with his temple as he tried to duck under.

He fell as if poleaxed.

I panted now as hard as any human can, sucking in

air by the hectare as I sought to control my rage. I kept seeing glimpses of the Rockies, and fragments of my fights at the orphanage. Harmony eluded me. My vision remained tainted by my own unspilled blood.

The crowd of bullies backed away from us now. Some laughed nervously, while others kept up their verbal abuse even as they retreated to their bars and brothels. A few Beads, dressed in rags, kicked and thumped, but their efforts were drowned out by sheer numbers.

When a hand came down upon my left shoulder from behind, I turned to meet that attack as well. My fist flashed upwards.

It stopped millimeters from Reverend Castell's face.

He glared at me as I dropped my arm, but the glare held no terrors for me just then. "How dare you?" he said, voice cracked and whispery from the punch he'd taken. A bruise darkened his throat where his robe hung torn.

"They hurt you," I said.

His face contorted. "You'd so easily discard our precepts. For what? My corporeal safety? It means nothing if my spirit's in discord."

Hanging my head, I begged forgiveness.

Reverend Castell's voice dropped an octave, from baritone to basso profundo. "You are no longer attuned to Universal Harmony. Your warlike talk belies cacophonous thinking."

"I strayed," I said, crying. "I lost the melody and wandered, but I'm—"

"Silence. Our hands carry peace, which is ours to offer. Your hands dropped that fragile vessel. You shattered peace, and for what? So your hands could be raised to harm another? Your song has ended."

Nausea swept me to my knees, and after gagging I said, through tears, "Please Reverend." My forehead came down to rest atop his feet, which were bare and cold. Mud smeared my face.

His feet pulled back, and I glanced up. He cried, "This lone voice knows our song, and asks to rejoin our chorus of Harmony. His shouts, although disruptive of our melodies, flew from a good heart and noble intentions. His sour notes are absolved." And, after tossing back his head and laughing loudly, he clapped thrice, then reached down to help me to my feet.

Even as I stood and looked into his eyes I wondered if Reverend Castell had planned such theater all along, but the unworthy thought mattered little as I realized what we had accomplished.

From then on, goading violence from a pacifist would be like poking an overinflated balloon. And the crowd had seen me forgiven, absolved. That meant even lapses of pacifism might be condoned. We'd become unpredictable. Along with the buffer provided by the Beadles, such a reputation went far toward ensuring that we Harmonies would at least have a chance.

I followed Reverend Castell to Havenhold Lake, where we greeted uninvited guests who had come bearing gifts.

Maxwell Cole waited patiently while Marshall Wainright, Assistant to the Director of the CoDominium Bureau of Intelligence, studied his viewscreen. The holo-wall mural displayed a forest scene out of the Pacific Northwest instead of the stark lunar landscape outside. As Cole watched a squirrel run up a large conifer, he mused that he and the squirrel had a lot in common; they were both trying to set something aside for the coming winter.

Cole was a short timer, only three more years and he could put in for retirement. After twenty-seven years in the intelligence service, ten of them with the Navy, he was used up, tired of sticking his fingers in numerous holes in the CD's ever-leaking dyke. Let the younger operatives save the peace; his time was just about up.

Or was it? he wondered, as Assistant Secretary Wainright discreetly coughed.

"Agent Cole, we have a situation developing on

an outer world called Haven—a misnomer if there ever was one. It's a newly colonized world by some sect that calls itself the Universal Church of New Harmony. You've read the files."

Cole nodded. The anxiety that had begun to gnaw at his lower stomach, ever since he'd been sent that file, began to grow. Haven, an almost lifeless iceball of a moon, was all the way at the outer edge of the envelope of CD explored space—four Alderson Jumps away from the nearest habitable world. Haven was certainly, this close to retirement, no place he ever wanted to visit.

The Harmonies, one of the Neo-Millenniumite Sects, had bought the settlement license, so officially Haven was not part of the CoDominium. In reality, however, all human occupied worlds belonged to the CoDominium; the only question was whether they were or were not valuable enough for an "official" CD presence. Cole had a nagging suspicion that this iceball was about to change ownership.

"The Bureau of Colonial Government was not displeased to see the Harmonies settle Haven as long as it remained the worthless piece of real estate it first appeared. However, the situation has changed now that a large deposit of hafnium ore has been discovered."

Right, thought Cole, and now *somebody* doesn't want to pay the Harmonies a licensing fee for mineral rights they can get for a much smaller fee from the CD Bureau of Colonial Government.

The Assistant to the Director stroked the length of his long, thin nose. "It appears that we have one of those situations developing that requires a senior agent with great skill and discretion. Since, obviously, our part in the events that are about to occur on Haven must never become public knowledge."

Cole shook his head in agreement, wondering if somehow his superiors had agreed to blame the mess now developing on Comstock on him, the last agent assigned to that hellhole. If he'd learned nothing else in his lengthy career it was that in intelligence often what appeared to be a nod up was in actuality a shove down.

"Serendipitously, for all involved, it appears that the Bureau of Relocation also has a rather strong interest in the Haven question. It appears to be the ideal location for subversive elements within the confines of the terrestrial CD to be permanently isolated without invoking the offices of the Bureau of Correction or the Navy."

Good conondrum: When is a prison planet not a jail? Answer: When it's called Haven and is over a year's travel from Earth with little or no possibility of return.

"Your job, Agent Cole, will be to find legal justification for CoDominium intervention."

It sounded so easy rolling off the Assistant to the Director's tongue, Cole thought. What it really meant was he had to organize or foment a revolution; or what could pass for such on a forgotten planet like Haven. Thus providing, for the Grand Senate, an excuse to appoint a Consul General and send a contingent of CD Marines to restore the benefits of CoDominium order and civilization.

"You will be provided with a list of contacts and a review of certain 'unstable' elements there by someone who has just returned. I'm afraid that budgetary demands make it impossible to give you all the resources you might need; however, you will be given a rather 'free hand' in carrying out this operation. The Kennicott Mining Company has graciously offered their services in the way of funds and operatives when you arrive at Haven. I suggest you take them up on their offer."

Cole nodded. The Assistant to the Director of

CD Intelligence turned his attentions back to his viewscreen. Knowing full well that no objection by him would be tolerated, Cole cursed under his breath and left the office.

Janesfort War   115

...bewilderment, turning his attention back to the
... the captain, knowing full well that no electronic
... would be of any real value here. Water his
... Torth, Cat's Eye his chaser.

JANESFORT WAR

Leslie Fish & Frank Gasperik

The zodiac raft with the name *Black Bitch* painted on
her side growled away from the off-planet shuttle floating
in the lake, laden with crates marked Mining Equipment.
If one inspected the invoices attached, as the *Bitch*'s captain had bothered to do, one would find they were destined for one Max Cole, delivery at Castell City, or the
port thereof, to be placed in bond until called for. This
could have presented a problem, Castell City Port being
nothing but a rough pontoon dock, except that Max Cole
stood wrapped in off-planet cold weather gear, in the full
light of Cat's Eye, waiting for his cargo.

He wasn't alone.

The man accompanying him was as recognizable to the
locals as Cole was a stranger. His name was Jomo and
he was a thug. He inspired fear and the kind of respect
born of it. He was tall and broad and scarred and of
mixed parentage, the result of the usual problems one
found in the Transvaal. He watched the boat as it moved
towards shore and, like Cole, was dressed warmly. They
didn't speak but stood patiently as the cargo was
unloaded.

Cole identified himself and signed the receipt, and the
Black Bitch, reeking of the alcohol she used for fuel,
turned back to the shuttle for another load. A motion
from Jomo, and his crew—not dockworkers—began haul-

ing the crates onto handcarts and trundling them towards
the rough jumble of buildings known as Docktown.
Somehow it already had the undefinable aura of "slum"
that most port communities seemed to acquire.

Jomo and Cole slowly followed the handcarts toward
a largish, for Haven, building dug into a low bank with
a freshly painted sign proclaiming it to be the SIMBA BAR.
They trailed the crates inside after the unloading.
Another motion from Jomo, and the pair were left alone
in the main room of the establishment.

"I hope the shipment is as I require," said Jomo, with
carefully elaborate politeness.

"Better than you could imagine," Cole replied, just as
carefully. "You asked for arms to enhance your—ah . . .
'business' and I have done better than you asked. Look."
He produced an odd tool from under his coat and pried
open the nearest crate. "The latest CoDominium combat
weapon: the Sonic Stunner. Forty of them."

"A weapon that stuns? It does not kill?"

"You should find it most effective for your purposes,
Mister Jomo. No damage to the subjects, and they awake
in an hour or so with nothing but a headache."

Jomo lifted the bell-mouthed weapon.

"Yes, these will do well. . . . After all, a live captive can
always be made dead at a later date, but the reverse of
that cannot be accomplished."

Cole smiled, and shrugged. "This is the method of
loading and the manual for maintenance. Simple enough,
as you see."

Jomo smiled in turn, not prettily.

His purring whistle brought a man from the back
room, carrying a small box that had once contained boots.
At Jomo's gesture, the man put the box on the table and
stood attentively to the side.

In a single quick motion, Jomo lifted the weapon and
fired.

The sound of the stunner was only moderately loud.
The target crumpled in his tracks.

Jomo went to him, bent over and cruelly pinched the right earlobe. There was no reaction.

"Yes." Jomo grinned widely. "These will do well indeed."

"Ahhh, Mister Jomo, my remuneration?"

Jomo handed him the boot box. A brief inspection proved that it was full of CoDominium and Trade credits, a small fortune.

"Would you enlighten me as to how you acquire such tools?" Jomo nudged, studying the stunners.

"Such things are possible, if one knows just whom to blackmail or bribe. . . ." Cole shrugged again. "And as long as they're not found on Earth, or a planet under CoDominium control, they're quite safe to own."

Jomo nodded, put down the stunner and opened the manual.

"I must go now," Cole reminded him, "as I wish to ride the shuttle back to the ship. The sooner I'm out of this icebox, the better. I'll send down the rest of the ammunition with the next load. As it stands, you only have twenty rounds."

"I have no choice but to trust you in this matter," Jomo admitted. "But without the weapons the ammunition is useless. Also the converse. It is nice to do business with a professional."

They turned to the door and together walked back to the dock. Before boarding the zodiac, Cole stopped and turned to Jomo.

"You'll need this," he said, handing Jomo the very special tool. "You can't open the other crates without it. The security devices would ruin the control chips if you tried any other method."

Neither of them noticed that the zodiac captain, although turned away and occupied with unloading cargo, was close enough to hear.

They did not shake hands on parting.

Jomo mused on how much easier this would make the takeover of Docktown, the outlying farms, eventually

Castell City and the rest of the planet. Jomo considered himself a man of *great* plans.

Owen Van Damm was watching quietly while his immediate boss Maxwell Cole hung up his off-ship over-clothes and readied himself for the briefing. He felt that he was like that, layer on layer, persona under persona, and at the center? *I don't know anymore. I know that I am unhappy with Earth, and the government. The Fleet is a home, but I know too much to go back to being a Fleet Officer.*

"Here's the situation, Owen. . . . Jomo has the weapons and appears willing to use them. . . . He didn't press too much on where they came from and was willing to pay cash. . . . I imagine that we have the majority of hard cash on the planet. That means a serious retreat into barter, as Charles Castell doesn't seem to want money of any kind here. He might be a hell of a leader, but his knowledge of economics is primitive.

"With the breakdown of the economy it shouldn't be hard to nudge Jomo into a full takeover. . . . I'm afraid that the religious gambit is out. . . . They are still pacifists. Kennicott has an agent in place, and another from Reynolds Offworld is present. The Reynolds man is in Jomo's gang; the Kennicott rep runs a bar and whorehouse called the Golden Parrot. His name's DeCastro. Your job will be to provide some resistance to Jomo. . . . Make it bloody enough so it will hit the off-planet news."

Van Damm considered the options. "You mean put a bunch of farmers and religious nuts in a position to be slaughtered?"

"Exactly. You handle this one well, and I'll recommend you for a job on Luna in charge of the Haven desk. . . . It will be small, but will require a man with on-planet experience.

"Especially in light of the planned mining operations and BuReloc's policies.

"It will mean a promotion for you."

"So this whole thing is a setup for making a planetary prison mine for BuReloc and the mining companies?"

"Yes, and you have ninety days to pull it off. The captain of this ship can hold only that long, no longer. Kennicott can't afford to have a ship waiting and empty longer than that, so get to it."

Owen took that as a dismissal, and started to leave. Another thought made him pause in mid-step.

"Mister Cole? What if I don't pull it off?"

"If I don't get a report on the start of an uprising inside of ninety days, then you will stay here until you do it. Good luck."

"Thank you, Mister Cole."

Owen Van Damm considered that there was no choice here. In fact, field agent on Haven could be a better deal than assistant to some bureaucrat on Luna.

Kennicott, Reynolds and BuReloc . . . and probably a couple of big politicians behind it all.

There were greater dreams than Jomo's out among the stars.

Captain Makhno steered the *Black Bitch* back to the waiting shuttle, considered what he'd seen, and kept his own counsel. There was much to see here, and much to think about.

He eyed the last passenger he took ashore with the same sharp eye he'd turned on all the others. This one had the stamp of toughness about him, but not the sort Makhno was used to seeing: not the obvious bluster of the bully or the cold disinterest of the cop, but more the quiet confidence of someone who could use violence quite competently when needed. There had been another like that on the last ship, six months ago, but that one had been older, and talkative. He walked with a cane and was now in Castell City somewhere.

That one, unlike most of the voluntary settlers, was full of questions about the planet, the town, what kind of work there was to be found and where, the availability of lodgings, and the rest.

This one was silent. He was in his thirties perhaps, and he stood about 170 cm. tall, shaven of jaw and head with gray eyes and a scar on his left cheek. He was well muscled and seemed fit. He had a familiarity with small craft, and helped casting off from the shuttle and the docking.

The duffel bag he carried had an insignia freshly painted over, but looked to be that of the CoDo Marines.

Interesting, Makhno thought to himself. . . . Not in uniform. . . . Maybe a wounded retiree. . . . Perhaps senior enlisted. . . . Not the usual sort at all. Janey would be interested.

He had a lot of news this trip, and not all of it good. The sudden change of ownership at Harp's Place, for instance: how had Jomo managed that? What had become of Old Harp? Where was Harp's family, and how were they doing?

And just what was Jomo going to do with those loads of mining equipment? Jomo wasn't the sort to be interested in hard work of the legal variety, and running a mining operation took long hours and a lot of sweat. Maybe he got it cheap, and was going to sell it to the highest bidder; but that didn't fit either. Cole hadn't acted like a machinery dealer. The military type was another interesting factor.

Makhno's fees for hauling passengers and cargo in from the shuttle should be enough to fund a lot of pub-crawling, greasing a few palms, collecting all the news he could. Something had gone seriously wrong in Docktown while he'd been away.

Jane Wozejeskovich strolled through the upper field of South Central Island, examining her current crop and grinning in joy at the sight of the tall stalks, huge palmate leaves and already-forming flowers.

Of all the seeds she'd brought with her from Earth, this Illinois-bred hemp had adapted best. Something about the light/dark cycle and climate pattern had stimulated the plant growth to the point that she was getting a full, harvestable crop every other full cycle of Haven

around Cat's Eye. She knew—who would know better
than an organic gardener?—all the practical uses of marijuana, but the accelerated growth was a bonus she hadn't
expected.

Gods, yes: a very good crop, and a very good year.

Well, so much for the main crop: now on to the latest
project. Jane strode out of the field and up the guided
course of the island's sole reliable creek. Long before
she reached the new mill-pond and dam, she could hear
Benny Donato arguing high and loud with Big Latoya.
Jane grinned again. She'd bet a bushel of medicinal-
quality "euph-leaf" that Latoya was sweet on Benny, was
trying to get him housebroken to suit her before she
made any moves, that Benny had some idea what was
going on and wasn't exactly running away.

Benito Donato—volunteer settler, master machinist
complete with a Multimate machine shop—had been a
prize catch for her settlement, but he did need an occasional kick into line.

With his pal, Jeff Falstaff, he'd come to the island with
a head full of delusions about being the only man among
a co-op of eight women. The reality—that he was one of
three men, counting Makhno, and would have to work
his butt off like everyone else—had left him a bit miffed.
Well, he'd get over it.

Falstaff had caught on, and settled in, a lot quicker.
His little brewery was already producing a good enough
beer that the miners downriver were trading rough copper and zinc for it. He had been a general science
teacher Earthside, until caught teaching things not
required by the curriculum of the Greater Los Angeles
School System and the requirements of the CoDo—such
as original thought and Scientific Method. . . .

Her course took her through the main hall/dining room
and the kitchen beyond, where Maria-Dolores and her
mother tended the ever-burning fire and the still-kettle
set into the wall behind it. Granny calmly stirred the
stewpot on the fire while Maria-Dee fussed with her baby

in the crib and watched the temperature gauge on the brew-kettle.

Falstaff was in his laboratory down the passage. So were the kids: Latoya's big-eyed toddlers, Muda's gawky ten-year-old boy, the teenagers Nona and Heather—all of them staring in fascination at the current demonstration by Mister Wizard. Jane wondered if he'd ever had such devoted students back on Earth.

Falstaff—tall, bald, dark and reedy—looking nothing like his Shakespearean namesake, had designed and made a "caseless" ammunition to replace the dwindling supply Jane had brought with her from Earth. Right now he was busy showing the kids how to package the stuff. Even the toddlers were fascinated.

Hopefully, Donato would start teaching them gunsmithing next. He had modified her "coach gun" to use a piezo-electric igniter for the new shells, which were better than the ammo she had brought with her. The pair of them were a treasure beyond belief out here on Haven.

A quick stroll through the rest of the house showed little Muda and Lou fussing over the hemp-cloth loom, arguing over how much fiber they'd need to keep the settlement in clothes with the children growing so fast. The treasured cat that Heather had brought from Earth lay curled in her basket, buzzing contentedly as she nursed her new litter of kittens; the previous litter had sold for incredible prices in Castell City.

Jane paced up the stairs to her bedroom, her one indulgence, a semi-tower room whose glassless window looked out on the cultivated land, most of the island and part of the river beyond. She never tired of the view. There was the house and the home-acre, the outbuildings and kitchen-garden, the pens of rabbuck and pigs and cattle, the hemp-fields beyond, the trimmed and cultivated forest of nut, fruit, resin and timber trees beyond that, divided by ditches and greenthorn hedges, then wild forest down to the waterline. All her doing: her dream, her seeds, her labor. . . .

Hold on, there. Never forget the labor of the others: they'd been in it from the start. Those seven women she'd recruited at the landing had worked harder and longer hours than she had asked; even the children had worked too, as best they could. The men had provided needed skills the women didn't have.

And don't forget the help of the neighbors, all the squat-farmers on the river—little settlements hidden behind thick forest along the riverbank proper—living in dugouts, scratching bare existence out of the forest, hardly surviving before she came with her offers of seed and tools. They'd prospered too, repaying her in shares of their hemp or useful plants and animals discovered in the forest. Oh, yes, one needed to have good neighbors here.

Of course, what she offered them was worth the work: land of their own on her homestead, but who could have guessed they'd all do so well? Let the stupid CoDo bureaucracy sneer at "welfare bums," not that she would ever tell the CoDo about it; she knew better.

She wished the Earth-normal corn was doing as well, but her people wouldn't starve. The pigs she had traded from the Harmonies were thriving on local flora, as were the two heifers. One had taken to insemination, and she hoped the calf would be a bull.

Now if only Leo Makhno would come home soon, her contentment would be complete.

Tomas Messenger y DeCastro was no fool, as anyone in Docktown could tell you. He could see the writing on the wall—or on the new sign over what had been Harp's Place. He also knew how to move fast when he had to.

Therefore he had the advantage of surprise when he strolled into the Simba Bar and calmly asked to see Jomo. He drank a beer while various underlings slipped in and out of the back room. Eventually a flunky waved him toward the rear door. DeCastro coolly finished his drink and strolled to the inner sanctum.

Sure enough, Jomo was there—curious enough to ask what DeCastro wanted and listen to his answer.

"Very simple, señor," purred DeCastro, lighting a large off-world cigar. "Everyone in Docktown knows of your new, ah, equipment. Everyone in Docktown has also seen your, hmm, acquisition of this establishment. It is only logical to assume that your next target will be none other than my estimable self. Correct, Señor Jomo?"

Jomo answered with nothing but a smile. Only his lips moved.

"I see you have considered it," DeCastro continued, blowing an almost perfect smoke ring. "Certainly I have considered it, and come to the conclusion that I must join forces with you to survive."

Jomo raised an appreciative eyebrow, saying nothing.

"I ask not for equality with your most estimable self," DeCastro continued smoothly. "No. I ask to be your *segundo*, your *teniente*, your *caporegime* as it were. In exchange, I will ensure the loyalty of my men and carry out your every command with great efficiency."

He leaned back in his chair and puffed another smoke ring, letting his words take effect.

Jomo was silent for a long moment, then laughed harshly. "You expect me to believe this? You: a proud, independent Castillano, willing to bow the neck and swear service to another man? You expect—"

DeCastro was ready for this. "I am no *facisto* Castillano!" he broke in, calculatedly indignant. "I am Mestizo, ten generations' worth." His voice turned calm and ingratiating again. ". . . And I have the good intelligence to prefer being a small and wealthy frog in a large pond to being a big and very dead frog in a small one. You, señor, are clearly Going Places—and I wish to go there too."

Jomo nodded acknowledgement and considered the offer. He knew DeCastro to be smart and as good as his word when it came to holding a bargain; he had not progressed much because he was somewhat lazy, content to be comfortably wealthy and safely powerful, not terribly ambitious.

After inspecting the deal from all sides—and considering the value of one Paul Jefferson who currently held that position—Jomo pronounced: "I have a second in command already. It must be settled between you as to who will have the position."

DeCastro smiled, bent his head formally, and stubbed out his cigar.

Jomo got up from the desk and walked toward the door, motioning for DeCastro to come with him.

The only people now present in the bar were Jomo's men. Paul Jefferson was drinking at a table with one of the "safe" women. At a gesture from Jomo all noise and movement ceased.

"Paul," Jomo announced, "this man wants your job. Do you wish to give it to him?"

DeCastro raised an eyebrow as he recognized the Reynolds off-world man.

"Hell, no!" was the shouted answer, as Jefferson came up from the table, drawing his sheath knife.

Jefferson's next step was met with the roar of a large caliber pistol. He collapsed on the floor with a bullet hole through his right eye. The woman at the table carefully reached for her cup, and drained it.

"Discipline must be sure and quick," said DeCastro still holding his pistol in a combat marksman's stance. "Is there anyone else who wishes to dispute my authority?"

Nobody answered.

"No? This is good. I will now have a drink with each of you. We must get to know each other." DeCastro went to the bar, holstering his pistol.

DeCastro pointed at the first two men at the bar. "Dispose of that corpse, then come back and speak to me," he said.

Jomo smiled as he went back to the office; Jefferson had been with him for the last eighteen months but had been getting independent ideas of late. This had been the ideal solution.

Makhno threw the *Black Bitch*'s engines into fast reverse at the last possible moment and came to a foaming halt just at the edge of the north shore rocks. He killed the engine, threw out the anchor and reached for the dangling bell-pull in almost the same motion. The bell clanged overhead, louder than the laboring pump.

A grizzled head peeked over the ledge far above. Makhno waved frantically at it. The head withdrew. From above it came a creaking of gears. A rope with a padded loop at the end came snaking down toward the water. Makhno grabbed the loop, shoved his upper body through it and yelled: "Enough! Haul me up!"

At the ledge, hands pulled him in. He wriggled out of the loop before the crane's gears were properly locked, and panted: "Where's Jane?"

"At the fort, checking the stores," said Tall Lou, raising her gray eyebrows at him. "Why didn't you come around to the dock?"

"No time. What's the quickest way?"

"Up the new stairs, there. What about your cargo?"

"Haul the cargo up with the crane!" Makhno yelled back, already running. He clambered his way up the newly cut stairs, rebounded around twist after turn, ran panting to a thick steelwood plank door in the towering cap-rock and pounded madly on the knocker. "Jane!" he roared. "Goddammit, lemme in! News!"

Nona opened the door, batting her eyelashes furiously. In answer to his snapped question, she pointed fast directions to the storeroom. By the time she had the door closed and bolted, he was already yards off and running.

The dim-lit rock tunnel let out into a low-roofed rock chamber packed with rough-cloth sacks and homemade wooden boxes. Jane was there, just turning to see him. The ceiling-hung oil lamp threw startled shadows across her broad Polish face.

"Jane," he panted, bent over with the effort of sucking enough air. "It's bad news. Old Harp's dead. Killed. And Jomo's taken over Docktown. And he's got CoDo weapons."

"Whoa, hold on." Jane got up, tucked a stray lock of dark-blonde hair back into her tattered braids, and went to him. "Calm down, Leo. Take a deep breath and tell me everything, right from when I saw you last."

"Harp—" Makhno started, then choked again. He sat down on a box and rested his head on his knees for a long moment, caught in memories.

Harp had been the leader of the independent faction of Docktown, willing to do business with the Harmonies or anyone. When he had arrived, he had asked Castell himself if he could build a shelter, and a bank was pointed out to him near the lake by a warden of the church. Old Harp (had he ever been young?) had smiled, and had taken a shovel and started excavating into the hill.

By the end of the next two shifts, he had a room beyond it and a pile of rocks and soil blocking the wind from the entrance. Within a cycle he had rented his shovel for the use of an axe and had felled a couple of trees that he split for rough boards. Within four cycles more, he had added a brewing room and a bar and had a going business dealing in beer, food, and renting the main-room floor space for sleep during off-shift and full dark.

Harp's business had grown in leaps and bounds. He had become master trader and unofficial arbiter of deals between the independent farmers, growing Docktown and Castell City, respected by all sides as an honest man.

He had also been a voice of reason and a strength against the growing gangs in Docktown. He had refused to pay protection to Jomo or any of the others.

". . . They found his body washed up on the lake shore, just a couple shifts before I arrived. Jomo took over his place, changed the name to the 'Simba Bar,' moved his bullyboys in." Makhno ran a lean hand through his wiry dark hair. "Word is, he's taking over Docktown. He got CoDo stunners from off-world, and he's throwing his weight around hard and fast."

"Back up; you've just lost me." Jane sat down beside him and rested an arm across his shoulders. "Just who and what is Jomo?"

Makhno turned to stare at her, then remembered that she'd spent less than a turn at the landing-site before getting her land-grant, collecting her settler, and himself, and striking off into the wilderness. What she knew of Docktown she'd learned mostly through Makhno, and he hadn't told her everything.

"Okay, from the top." Makhno rubbed his eyes. "Remember the day you came in on the third ship, right after you got back from seeing Castell?"

"Oh, yes." Jane chuckled.

She remembered that well; as soon as she'd set foot on the lake shore, she'd gone after Charles Castell, finally caught up to him in a cow-barn, and asked him then and there for legal right to a full land-grant. Of course she could have just gone off and land-squatted, as so many did, but the fact that she bothered to ask the head of the Church of Harmony had impressed the old man. In return, he had bothered to ask her what manner of land she wanted and how she meant to work it.

In the end they'd struck a mutually profitable deal; Jane got a river island in exchange for a tithe of her crops for the next five years. A secondary deal for breeding-stock of turkeys, pigs and two cows for another half-tithe. She'd headed back to the landing-site, looking for a boat and whistling "Solidarity Forever," feeling quite charitably disposed toward Castell and his crowd.

"That's when I got hold of you and the *Black Bitch*, to take me down river."

"Right, right." Makhno had a vivid memory of the first time he'd seen her, a big stocky blonde woman in denim bib overalls, wrapped bundle of tools on her shoulder, huge pack on her back, plodding up to his ship. "You remember, after you stowed your pack and went out to collect volunteers . . ."

"You thought I was nuts." Jane grinned, remembering the skinny, grease-stained, hungover riverboat-captain who believed all the usual crap about "transportees," "Especially when I asked only women."

Makhno winced. Looking back now, it made sense; the

women had no illusions about their situation, good reason to fear what the bigger and badder elements might try on them. Damn right, they'd taken Jane's offer to get out of town and set up on their own.

"Well, that was part of the problem, you know," he reminded her. "There you were with a whole gang of women. A real prize for any pimp."

"I don't recall that we had much trouble with that," Jane frowned. "Just that one fool who came up and tried to bully us. . . ."

"And you hit him on the head with the shovel," Makhno finished. "That was Jomo. He won't remember you kindly."

That too was part of the problem. Jomo had always been a strong-arm man and a thug, but now he was a thug with weapons, and was moving to secure all Docktown.

His first obstacle would be the other, smaller gangs. Jomo commanded about thirty men. DeCastro had about twenty, but until now they had been better armed: three shotguns, one old-but-serviceable rifle and nine pistols of various calibers. However, getting ammunition for them was a problem. The rest of DeCastro's men carried clubs and knives and had shown great willingness to use them. Jomo, with his new weapons was a power to reckon with.

". . . He must have made that arms deal way in advance," Makhno concluded. "When he knew the guns were coming in, he took out Old Harp, grabbed Harp's place. It won't take him long to deal with DeCastro and the others, take over Docktown, maybe even Castell City. . . . Hell, I was the one who delivered those crates! 'Mining Equipment'—Goddam, if only I'd known, I'd have pitched the things overboard!" Makhno pounded his fist on the stone floor.

Jane caught his wrist. "There's no way you could have known."

"I could have saved Docktown. . . ."

"But not Old Harp. You said he was killed before the ship landed."

"Yeah." Makhno took a deep breath and straightened his back. "So how do we deal with this, Janey? What do we do when Jomo takes over Docktown, maybe all the settlements he can find. He'll try to make himself king of the whole valley before he's done. How do we survive?"

"We organize," said Jane. "Up and down the river, among all our friends, we organize. Then, we strike."

Jomo was talking with his accountant, and the news was not good.

"For the last two turns the take is down, and instead of cash, barter is being offered. Most of those clients insist that Old Harp always took trade goods, so why don't we?" The accountant, a small skinny man of unguessable age and race, paused to tap his pen against his teeth.

Jomo briefly rattled his fingers on the table before him. "Has any of the trade been in foodstuffs?"

"No, and no beer either. It has mostly been in timber, some furs and in a few cases, fish from the lake. What beer we do get is made right here and is of very poor quality. It's hard to tell if food is going to Castell City, for the Harmies appear to be living on lake-fish and the . . . paste from the synthetic-food plant, like the rest of us."

"So no real food is coming into Docktown?" Jomo frowned, remembering the taste of paste and baked lake-fish. "Not from inland or along the rivers?"

"No boats from anywhere up or downriver have come here for three turns." The accountant sighed. "In short, nothing coming in from out of town. The entire trade has dried up. I have not seen anything like this since I got here, and that was on the second ship."

". . . Then this is not the result of poor harvest." Jomo tapped his fingers on the table again. "I believe we are victims of a boycott."

"That is my impression also, Master Jomo."

"If the supplies do not come to us, then we must go to them." Jomo set both palms flat on the table. "Send me DeCastro on your way out."

After the man left, Jomo glanced down at the desk where his second-best treasure lay: a recent satellite-map of the entire Shangri-La Valley. With it he could find any structure or farm in the valley, and then no one could hide from him. With the stunners and this map he would take all of Haven.

Leo Makhno considered that of all the ways of wasting time on Haven, trying to make the Harmonies understand a problem was his least favorite. They simply didn't comprehend that some problems could not be sung away and that others must be dealt with immediately.

He had been trying for the last two hours to convince Charles Castell that Jomo was a threat to the Harmonies and their way of life, and had gotten nowhere.

"You are not in tune Captain Makhno. This Jomo person only affects Docktown, not us. We have complied with your request not to trade farm goods to Docktown because that is harmonious with our beliefs, but to use violence against him, or to even support violence is discordant with our way."

Makhno sighed. "Then you will not help us against him?"

"No, Captain, there is nothing we can do. Even if there was, we would not. Each must find their own way in the Grand Tapestry of the Universal Song."

Leo could hear the capitals and knew that further talk was useless.

"Good-bye then, Mr. Castell. I hope you survive what is coming."

"We will, Captain. Go in peace."

Leo figured it was time to see if he could find at least one of the Military types he had seen earlier.

If a deal to at least train the women at Janesfort could be struck, some progress would be made.

Owen Van Damm was hunting. It was his profession to hunt on occasions, and he took pride in his ability at it. Right now he was approaching the "lair" when he saw his quarry leaving. He followed unobtrusively down the street.

This quarry was difficult in that he didn't walk very fast, perhaps slowed by his lame leg, and was quite aware of his surroundings. Van Damm stayed about ten meters back and ambled slowly.

The quarry turned a corner at one of the newer buildings in Castell City (it had an entire floor aboveground and was made out of wood), and Van Damm followed. He made the turn—

—and stopped right there, nose to nose with his Target standing and confronting him.

"Are you following me?" came the question. The voice was polite but the body language said: I am armed and dangerous and you seem to be a threat.

Van Damm sighed, and answered. "Yes, I am."

"Why?" The man smiled, but his keen blue eyes never wavered.

Well, in such situations, the best defense was the truth.

"Someone has been asking questions about you and I, looking for us. I do not know who is asking, nor what connection he sees between us, and such puzzles are healthier if you solve them."

"Agreed." The man relaxed slightly, and leaned on his cane. "What do you think we have in common?"

"Your name is Nicholas Brodski. True?"

"Yes." No surprise, nothing else given away.

"You have the carriage of a military man, perhaps senior enlisted, likely of the Fleet Marines."

"Right again, laughing boy."

"I would also guess that you were retired for wounds?" Van Damm said, looking at the "penalty weight" the man was carrying, his gray hair and the cane loosely ready at his side.

"Right again. What's all this about? You ex-Fleet?" Brodski's blue eyes turned hard. ". . . or still working?"

"I am . . . retired from the Fleet, also. My name is Owen Van Damm." Truth enough.

"Okay, Owen. Let's get off the street and discuss this in more civilized surroundings."

"I agree." Van Damm allowed himself a quick smile. "If you know of some place where the food is not synthetic slop and the beer is better than the horse urine that seems to be all they serve now in Docktown, I will buy the first round."

"I've found a 'speak' that has some decent brew. Their sandwiches are pretty good too. Just let Ol' Nick Brodski show you where."

The speakeasy proved to be not far away, and connected by a backdoor to a recently used barn. Brodski knocked twice, waited, knocked twice more, waited, then knocked thrice. A voice came through the door: "Who's your friend, Ski?"

"Another old Marine, Charlie. Let us in; he's got cash to spend."

A Chinese of indeterminate age opened the door and let them in. Van Damm wondered, as he scraped goat manure off his boot soles, where the observation port was. He hadn't spotted it from the outside.

The room was lit by lamps that burned a sweet-smelling oil, one of the few places that still had lamp oil, and was warm, and—despite the crowding—quiet.

After the beer (a pitcher containing a liter and a half, for two tenths of a CoDo trade-credit) came the sandwiches: fresh meat and Earth condiments, all good.

"So," said Brodski, around a mouthful of meat, "tell me more."

Van Damm finished a swig of very good beer. "There is not much to tell. As far as I know, there is this man named Makhno, some sort of boat captain, who has been asking questions about us for the last six hours, at least. I thought that I would look you up and we could compare notes, so as to know more about what he wants."

Brodski turned a look toward Charlie who beckoned from behind the bar. Brodski said, "Excuse me," and went over to him.

Van Damm shrugged and went back to his sandwich

and beer, which were better than in any other place Owen had tried in the last couple of turns.

Brodski came back with a funny look on his face. "What you just told me was confirmed by Charlie over there. He says that Leo Makhno was looking for me earlier. He runs the zodiac that trades on the river."

"A coincidence, that. I came ashore on the zodiac, and since I don't think that there would be two of them on this planet . . ."

"Right you are. So let's add things up. Point one: We are both ex-Fleet. Point two: We are newly arrived on Haven. . . . I got here on the ship before this one."

"Point three," added Van Damm. "I understand that the flow of food and beer in Docktown has slowed to a trickle in the last few days. Who better than a cargo-boat captain to know why?"

"Good point," said Brodski. "You're not as dumb as you look. . . . Which brings us to point four. This shortage started shortly after one Jomo came up with a big batch of CoDo stun-rifles and began consolidating Docktown. Hmm, and have you noticed there's almost no off-world money around? Interesting."

"That means somebody—perhaps several somebodies—don't want to work for Mister Jomo, and they are not sending food into Docktown." Van Damm actually smiled as he let the idea expand.

"A . . . strike? Of the 'union' kind?"

". . . And maybe the strikers would like some professional help in case of strikebreakers," finished Brodski. "And a local shipping captain just might recognize a couple of old pros when he sees them. It fits. How do you feel about becoming a merc, Owen?"

"Not badly, after looking for work in this place for the past shifts . . . no, Turns."

"Turns is right, I've noticed the lack of honest work myself. I've been teaching Tai-Chi to some deacons for room and board."

"I had some idea of selling my skills when I came here—but I soon found that it was work for a gang or not work. The Harmonies don't hire much, and no honest Docktowners could pay anything—thanks to the curious shortage of currency. Since the only gang leader left is Jomo, I couldn't work there. He 'dislikes' people that are not of mixed blood."

"Umhmm. So what do you say to finding this Makhno fellow and applying for the job?"

Van Damm shrugged. "Since I have no job right now, and things are beginning to get rough here in Docktown, I think that I would perhaps like to see a bit more of the planet."

"Yeah. And I thought I'd quit being an armed tourist when I quit the Corps. . . . Well, Semper Fi, buddy," said Brodski, refilling both glasses.

" 'Til the Final Muster," toasted Van Damm. "Now, how shall we find our employer?"

"I have a funny feeling that if we just wait right here long enough, he'll show up. . . . Or do you have to go home and pack?"

"Ah, no." Van Damm pointed to his backpack. "I prefer to travel light—and ready."

"Wait here." Brodski got up and went back to Charlie, wrote something on a note and handed him a 5-credit bill, then came back to the table. "Just arranging for my duffel," he explained. "We may as well get acquainted until our new boss shows up."

They didn't have long to wait. Four leisurely beers, some gossip about mutual acquaintances in the Fleet, another sandwich and the arrival of Brodski's duffel bag later, the door opened (Van Damm still hadn't found where the peephole was) to admit Leo Makhno. He went to the bar, conversed briefly and quietly with Charlie— who pointed to Van Damm's and Brodski's table.

"Look alive," muttered Brodski, finishing his beer. "Here comes the recruiter."

The deal didn't take long to clinch, though the work was strange—training a small farmers' militia—and the pay was stranger.

"A . . . land-grant share?" Brodski repeated, swapping looks with Van Damm.

"And the profits thereof," Makhno finished. "Money's tight, but the trade's good and will get better. You want the deal or not?"

"Of course." Van Damm hurried to agree. "When do we start?"

"Soon as you're ready to go."

"Right now, then," said Brodski, pushing up from his seat.

Just then Charlie gave a low whistle and motioned to Makhno, who frowned and went back to the bar.

"Our new boss doesn't seem to want to spend time in Docktown," Van Damm observed. "Nor do I blame him."

Brodski didn't answer, watching Charlie lead the still-frowning Makhno through a backdoor. A moment later the pair reemerged, leading two nervous-looking young girls—both in their teens, both almost painfully pretty.

Makhno glumly marched back to the table. "Passengers," he explained. "Let's go."

He led the way out, the girls huddled close behind him, Van Damm and Brodski bringing up the rear. At the barn's outer door he paused to look up and down the street. "Come on," he almost whispered. "Quickly."

The direction he took was not toward the dock but northeast, up toward the river-mouth. He managed to look businesslike and nonchalant, but set a fast pace. The girls pulled scarves over their heads and did their best to look invisible in the dull light of Cat's Eye-set. Brodski and Van Damm automatically paced close behind, watching the shadows.

They'd made less than fifty meters when two skulking silhouettes came scurrying toward them. The whole party tensed and crouched, reaching under folds of clothing, but the two figures practically fell on their knees in front of Makhno and hailed him in quick whispers.

"Please, please, *Maitre—Capitan—*Makhno." Their voices, both female, jumbled together. "Take us with you— We don't want to work for Jomo—please—we will pay—some money—whatever you want—please—we've heard how women are left alone there—please—we can work—please . . ."

Makhno looked around, swore, motioned the two women into line behind him. "All right, all right," he whispered. "But keep quiet and keep together. We've got to move fast."

The women scurried to comply, and the party moved out again in the waning light of the planet above.

Brodski was in "drag" position of the little column when he heard the sound of a stunner being fired. Both of the volunteer women crumpled and lay still. Makhno and the two girls dropped flat.

Almost without thinking, Brodski drew his service automatic and nailed the origin of the sound with a 10mm slug, dropped his duffel bag, fell flat and rolled. He noted that his shot was rewarded by a ricochet sound and a yelp.

"Dammit, girl, get off my arm!" he heard Makhno snap.

The ZAP and flash of a CoDo stunner raked at the source of the last comment.

Brodski put two rounds at the spot the flash had come from, and rolled toward a low hummock in the dim light. This time a scream showed he'd made a clean hit.

There came a duck's "quack" from his left. *Van Damm*, he thought. *"Duck." Right. Well, it looks like I get a chance to see him in action.* He noticed a shadow moving from about where the quack had come from, and smiled. *I'll hold this flank and let him chase them out to me. I'm a potted palm in this one.*

There was movement almost dead ahead of him and slightly to the right. Their flank-man, possibly. *If I wait, he might give me a better target.*

Further to the left was another movement, and the quick gleam of sudden steel, but no sound. The spot he had been watching suddenly reared up and became man-sized; Brodski shot it. *Van Damm wouldn't silhouette himself like that.* The shadow fell.

At where he would have put the far end of the enemy position, something moved away—low and fast. Brodski considered it, but didn't shoot. The light was too uncertain and the range a bit much for the expenditure of a round.

For long seconds, nothing moved.

"Brodski!" came Van Damm's voice out of the gloom. "I think I've got it cleared here."

"Okay, Owen. Coming out." ... But where the hell were Makhno and the women? "What have we got?"

"It looks like there were four of them. Three dead. One got away," said Van Damm, frisking the body in front of him.

Brodski produced a pocket light, looked down and saw a corpse, expertly killed with a knife. It took a good man to get that close in what had been turning into a firefight. His estimation of Van Damm went up.

A powerful flashlight lit up the area, Makhno and the two girls just visible behind it.

"Did you get them?" he panted.

"Three out of four," came Van Damm's reply. "Not bad for this sort of thing."

Makhno's lightbeam hovered over the bodies. "Hmm, they look like Jomo's boys. . . . I'll wager they weren't trying to ambush us; more like, they were headed the same way we were—maybe chasing the women."

Brodski put his pocket light away and reloaded his pistol.

"Look what I've found!" chirped Van Damm. "A stun-rifle! I think you broke it though, Ski."

"Take it along, Mister Van Damm," said Makhno, climbing to his feet. "We don't waste anything."

"You take the woman on the right, Owen." Brodski sighed, thinking of the painful extra weight. "I'll take the other one."

Makhno sent the older girl (Mary) to search the bodies, and the younger (Rose) to bring Brodski's bag, while he helped the men pick up the stunned women. The little procession struggled its way through the darkened streets of Castell City, past the last of the outbuildings, up to the bent shore where the northern river emptied into the lake. There Makhno hunted through the underbrush until he found the disguised *Black Bitch*.

"So you hid her here and walked in," Brodski noted. "How come?"

"Didn't want to be noticed by Jomo's men. There's reason to think they'd grab the *Bitch* if they could." Makhno pulled the concealing tarp off the zodiac and began testing her engines.

"Not to mention what they'd make of these," said Brodski, holding out the sack Makhno had set down. "You must have half the portable CB radios on Haven in there."

Makhno grabbed the sack and stuffed it aboard the *Bitch*. "Yeah. Better we should have 'em than Jomo."

"Hmm, any idea why those bozos jumped us?" Brodski asked. "And were they really Jomo's boys, or possibly independents?"

"Jomo's goons," snapped Makhno, not looking up. "Maybe after the *Bitch*, maybe wanting the women. Saw us, jumped at the chance and started shooting."

"Why the women? Why your raft?" Van Damm pushed.

"The *Black Bitch* is the fastest boat on the planet, and the women . . ." Makhno paused. "Jomo's pulling all the whores in Docktown under his rule. These two used to be independents, who didn't like Jomo's working conditions. As for the girls . . . they're Old Harp's daughters. Do I need to tell you anything more?"

"Er, no. Not a thing."

The girls handed in three sheath-knives, a revolver and ammunition from the other man that Brodski had shot. "They didn't have any money on them, Captain Makhno," Mary duly reported. "Just these things."

"That's all right, Mary. Now, everybody, get those women aboard and help push off."

They slid into the river at dead slow, without the superchargers engaged. When they made the lake proper, Makhno opened the throttles, pointed the nose of the *Bitch* south and relaxed to the rising whine of the superchargers. They'd reach Janesfort at just about Eye rise.

Nobody followed them.

"You are quite sure," Jomo asked coldly, "that the women are nowhere to be found in the city?"

"I assure you, *mi Commandante,* my men searched the city most thoroughly." DeCastro started to reach for a cigar, then thought better of it. The supply was running low.

"We even managed to search some of the buildings in Castell City proper, under pretext of looking for two women who were contagiously ill."

Jomo raised one eyebrow slightly in appreciation of that trick. It was almost impossible to get any cooperation out of the Harmonies.

"Therefore I must regretfully conclude, that the delectable Ahnli and Zilla have fled the city." DeCastro's regret was genuine, and not just for the loss of income. He had sampled Ahnli's charms last shift, and wanted more of her.

"Then where could they have gone?" Jomo glowered. "There have been no boats in dock for the past three turns, no carts or wagons for the past cycle, and I do not see those two slits going far on foot."

DeCastro shrugged elaborately. "They must have fled with the assistance of those admirers who proved so effective against our search party. The survivor of that encounter was not able to recognize the men in the poor light. They could have come from anywhere, in a concealed boat or wagon, and taken the women back with them: to an outlying farm, or to some collection of the miners and prospectors to the west, or—who knows?—perhaps to the legendary Island of Women. In any case, they have gone out of our reach."

Jomo's frown deepened. "We must discourage further such defections . . . and it is time we extended our reach beyond Docktown. We must have land and river transport, DeCastro."

"Of course." DeCastro interlaced his fingers in thought. "When the *Last Resort* returns with her latest catch, we can . . . persuade the owners to put the ship at our disposal. As for wagons, I cannot predict when another will come rolling into our reach. We may have to march our troops into farming country to look for one."

"Better to use the ship to take us to farms along the river," said Jomo. "Indeed, we will have to visit those farms eventually. Best to start planning now."

"*Si, mi Commandante,*" DeCastro sighed, wondering how to persuade Jomo not to send him out on any such expeditions. DeCastro hated the wilderness, had spent all his life in cities, wished to be nowhere on the planet but nice, comfortable Docktown, getting rich off the spacer trade.

The trip upriver was long, wet, dark, and cold. Makhno took the opportunity to explain some of the facts of life at Janesfort, but the reception was mixed.

". . . Now we're into Central Forest proper. Behind the screen of woods, you'll find lots of farms—squatters, all of 'em, but what Castell doesn't know about doesn't hurt anybody else. The squatters along here are all friends of Jane. They're willing to help, but the real fortress is at the island. . . ."

The girls and women nodded acceptance, then huddled together in mute, miserable endurance.

The two men weren't nearly as patient. Brodski settled into griping and swearing; Van Damm joined him and looked sour.

That they'd be working for women, or that the trip was uncomfortable, was no damned excuse. Makhno grew steadily more irritated with both of them.

When they reached the north cliff-face of Jane's Island, Makhno took his own sweet time pulling up to the anchorage spot under the ledge-hidden hoist. Sure

enough, while Brodski reached, cursing, for the camou-
flaged bell-rope, Van Damm spotted the rising pipe to
the water pump.

"Weakness, that," he said, pointing. "Invaders could
climb it."

"Not likely," Makhno teased, hiding his grin. "Too wet,
too dangerous."

"Good troops could climb it," Van Damm insisted, taking the bait.

"Hell, I'd like to see you try," Makhno nudged.

"Fifty creds says I can."

"You're on."

Van Damm actually smiled, made a smooth leap out
of the raft and caught the pipe. Makhno had to admit
the guy was good, didn't even slip on the damp lower
stretch of pipe, shinnied up fast and smoothly.

"You just lost fifty creds fast," growled Brodski, jerking
on the bell-rope.

"Not yet I haven't," Makhno chuckled, his reply muffled by the bell. He watched as braid-wrapped heads
peered down from the ledge, grinned as they turned to
look at the stranger shinnying up the pipe.

Van Damm was better than ten meters up when he
came abruptly nose-to-nose with a shotgun in the hands
of Tall Lou. He yelled like a banshee, sprang away from
the pipe, and went straight back down into the water,
narrowly missing the raft.

Makhno managed not to laugh as he hauled the man
back aboard, but he couldn't help grinning from ear to
ear. Brodski, who'd been busy with the bell-rope and had
missed the whole encounter, asked what the hell had
happened.

"A woman with a shotgun," came Van Damm's reply.
"I couldn't even see her until she poked it up my
nose. . . . She was hidden by an overhang and a berm,
dammit!"

"Yeah. They keep watch on all the approaches." Makhno snickered. "You should've gone up the hoist, like a
proper guest."

About then the sling-hoist came creaking down to the raft. Van Damm shamelessly grabbed at it first, ducked into it and signaled to be hauled up. The windlass obligingly lifted him away.

"As I told you," said Makhno. "Jane's no fool."

"I'm beginning to get that impression," said Brodski.

The crew of the *Last Resort* never knew what hit them. One minute they were unloading a good catch of fish at Castell City dock, and then there came a crackling sound, and then they were waking up on the dock with ringing heads, bound hands, and a bunch of mean-looking Docktown goons grinning down at them.

Deckhand Joey Brown looked toward Captain Feinberg, and got a bleak look in return. He wondered what these goons wanted to rob them of; all they possessed at the moment were their clothes, dry suits, tools, and a load of fish.

The crowd parted and another man marched through. He was chunky, swaggering, puffing a thick cigar.

"DeCastro," Captain Feinberg muttered. "Damned if I'll visit his bar again."

"Señores," DeCastro announced through a cloud of odorous smoke. "Pray forgive this unorthodox greeting, but we have serious business to discuss. We need to hire the use of your boat and your estimable selves."

"What pay?" asked Feinberg, daring to stand up.

"The usual shares," DeCastro puffed calmly. "You will find that Señor Jomo is most generous to those who serve him well."

"Jomo's in charge of this?" Feinberg gaped.

"Shit," said deckhand Brown—and lay back down on the dock.

Makhno strolled down the line of exercising women assembled in the meadow below the fort, and considered once again that Jane had been very sharp in collecting her crew. After the initial gossiping and chattering, everybody agreed to work as a unit—and there was no dissension thereafter.

For once, almost all of them were assembled in one place. Granny, Falstaff and Donato were off minding the little kids, the radio and the cook-pot, but everyone else was here: Tall Lou with her short gray hair tossing at every stroke, big grumbling Latoya with her original fat diminished enough to show the respectable muscles beneath her coffee-dark skin, skinny Easter and batty-eyed Nona bending and dipping with teenage enthusi-asm, Muda methodical as ever, Harp's daughters grimly enthusiastic, the ex-whores Ahnli and Zilla struggling to prove they were as good as anybody else, even Maria-Dolores working soulfully while keeping one eye on the baby sleeping at one corner of the meadow. And there was Jane herself, blonde and big-breasted and stocky, the perfect stereotype of a Chicago Polack, unselfconsciously working harder than the rest of them, setting an example, all quiet competence.

Deadly practical, all of them. All willing to farm and grow the hemp, all of them busy making a good living this past Earth-year, now all of them willing to fight for what they'd made for themselves.

Willing to pay for a couple of good combat instructors, like these two.

Makhno strolled quietly behind the two men, watching. He'd hired them and brought them here, and now they were busy at their job, and he knew better than to get in their way, but he could take mental notes to discuss with Jane later. He'd learned much, just watching them.

Brodski might be gray-haired, fat and lame, but Mak-hno decided that he would never want to get in the way of that man's cane; it looked too . . . useful. In demon-stration of hand-to-hand fighting, he moved with a vicious economy that boded ill for any opponent. Van Damm was muscular, shaven-headed and blank-faced, could have been any age between 18 and 30, and spoke little. Makhno had seen him teaching the hand-to-hand and knife-fighting class, and had done some practice bouts with him along with the women; he had decided to stay well out of his reach.

Jane had been right: wherever these two had picked
up their experience, they were the best instructors to be
had for the price, most likely the best on the planet.

And "CD Marine" hung on them like halos. Exactly
what were they doing on Haven?

"Awright, enough!" bellowed Brodski, much to the
assembled women's relief. "Take a break, get washed up
for dinner, and then we'll talk about defense plans for the
island. See you back here in an hour. Diss . . . missed!"

The women bowed as the two men had taught them,
received a bow in return, gathered up their gear and
trotted off toward the wash-house. Brodski ambled to the
nearest woodpile, carefully sat down, rubbed his bad leg,
took out a battered pipe and filled it with genuine Earth
tobacco. Van Damm dropped to parade-rest and surveyed the scenery. Makhno sat down on the log and
offered Brodski his lighter.

"You two seem to be earning your pay," he began. "So
tell me, how're these farmers coming along and how
good are their chances?"

Brodski puffed blue smoke. "Well, understand that
we're not exactly starting with prime military beef, here.
They're mostly middle-aged, undersized women, with
kids in tow. Compared to the bulls in Jomo's employ,
they're nothing for size, weight or strength. They've also
grown up with a damned lot of conditioning that says:
'you're a natural victim and you can't fight.' It's hard to
overcome years' worth of that crap."

"That's the bad news. Is there any good news?"

"Hell, yes." Brodski poked inside his pipe-bowl with a
twig. "They're quick, tough, flexible, determined and
willing to learn. Van Damm's found a style of hand-to-
hand that they can use: get down low, come in fast, trip
and toss—and the ladies are getting remarkably good at
it. He's worked up a similar style with knives, and they're
very good with that—good enough that his padding's
taken a real beating, and we'll have to make him another
set pretty soon. As for shooting, well, those shotguns are
nice handwork, what with the caseless ammo and piezo-

crystal igniters in them: very good for the situation you've got. The ladies don't have any preconceived notions about how to use 'em, so they've learned quick."

Makhno chuckled. "I didn't think some of those scrawny little things could even lift a 12-gauge, but they manage. Did you see Granny picking branches off trees at fifty meters?"

"Yep. Damn good eyes on that little old woman." Brodski puffed thoughtfully. "Now mind, I don't know what they'd do in real combat. They don't have the arrogance of Jomo's bullies, but then again, they'll be fighting for their home and kids. Maybe they'll fold up in shock after they've shot their first man, and maybe they'll be so damn fierce you won't be able to keep 'em from killing everyone they see. Hard to tell."

"My money's on the women," Makhno decided. "They've been stomped on all their lives, and now they've got a chance to stomp back. I suspect there's a lot of revenge they want to get."

"Could be." Brodski shrugged. "The ladies are good at hiding and sniping. I confess, I can't figure out their table of organization, though it seems to work for them."

"What's to figure? Jane's top dog, little Easter and Nona are her aides, Latoya and Tall Lou are sergeants, Maria-Dolores runs radio, Granny takes care of supplies and the kids. The rest fall in wherever they're needed."

"And you? Where do you come into this?"

"Me?" Makhno glanced at him in surprise. "Hell, I'm just the captain Jane picked to bring her up here to her land in the first place. I kept on running up here because she paid me—first in timber, then in, uh, crops."

"There's a little more to it than that, I think," Brodski grinned through a cloud of blue smoke.

"All right! So I, uh, made a personal arrangement with Jane. So what?"

"Only Jane?" Brodski laughed, blowing more smoke. "Twelve women around here, and you the youngest and handsomest of the three men . . ."

"Dammit, you don't know what you're talking about!" Makhno almost yelled. "Did you ever try keeping up with more than one woman at once? No way am I getting it on with the rest. You're nuts!"

Brodski laughed until he choked, subsided into coughing and glared at his smoked-down pipe. "More to the point, what's your job when the Simbas invade? In fact, what makes you so sure Jomo's going to bother you at all?"

"Why should he even know about Jane and her people?" Van Damm bothered to turn around and ask. "We're a good long way from Castell City, and I assume you have not precisely advertised our position."

"Because of things I've heard in Docktown for years." Makhno chewed his lip momentarily. "This island's a natural fort, if you've noticed."

"I'd noticed," purred Brodski.

"And you've got some idea that the CoDo wants Haven, don't you?"

"Sure. Let some company get in on the ground floor and milk it to its shriveled little heart's content, and dump more BuReloc sweepings here for cheap labor."

"More than that: there's talk that CoDo's planning to move in its own governor, complete with troops to back him up."

"Uh, I've heard rumors to that effect," Brodski hedged. "Face it, Harmonies aren't exactly popular with the government right now, and if they have a planet of their own it's more than they deserve. Or so thinks CoDo."

Makhno gave him a cold smile. "Now, how do you think Jomo will react to that? By just giving up and meekly knuckling under?"

Brodski pursed his lips, and shook his head.

"Right. He'll plan some way to be profitable to the CoDo troops and governor. No way can he raise and train an army near town."

Brodski sat up straight, staring hard at the cleared fields around him and the meandering stone fortress.

Makhno caught the look, and grinned sourly. "That's right. They'd be happy to let somebody else do the clearing, planting and building for them—and then come in and take over."

". . . right," Brodski slowly agreed.

"And the fact that Ahnli and Zilla knew about this place means that word has spread around Docktown. Don't ask me how; I was careful to be discreet."

"Patient observers could add two and two," Van Damm considered. "You leave with several women, you come back with valuable crops. . . ."

"That's why we hired you two," Makhno finished. "The Simbas'll come, soon or late, and we have to be ready for 'em."

"I see." Brodski rattled his fingers on the log for a moment. "How do you think they will come? I doubt they'll walk."

"They'll probably use the *Last Resort*. According to Ahnli and Zilla, they were going to take her when she came in next, and we passed her on the way out."

"We had better figure out some kind of nasty surprise for them," said Van Damm. "We must talk to your machinist and chemist."

"All right, you can do that after dinner. But how do you fight a ship?" asked Makhno.

"By using its capabilities against it," replied Brodski. "More like preparing for the future. We put something together that will work under a lot of different circumstances and apply it when one of them turns up.

"So as I was saying, what's your position when the invasion comes?"

Makhno thought that over for a moment. "Well, hell, I've been a supply-runner and news source. If I'm here when it happens, I'll just go to Jane and ask her where she wants me."

"Good enough for now. I think Van Damm and I should start applying for jobs as gunnery and demolition officers. You'll need somebody who's blooded and seasoned to help you fight. I think I'll stay on here."

"Stay?" Makhno was jolted to realize that he didn't like the idea. The next instant he knew why, and kicked himself. Hadn't he been complaining about the pure hard work of being one of only three men among a dozen women? "Uh, we can't afford to pay you beyond what we agreed."

"No problem, son," said Brodski, reloading his pipe. "We plan to do just what the ladies have done: Take our land-share. Just when do you expect Jomo to make his try?"

"Well, the next ship is due in ten months. He'll want to have control solid before then."

"Mmhmm. We'd better join Jane's fief in a hurry."

" 'Fief'?" Makhno scratched his head. "More of a co-op, I think. Everybody's got their little patch, but we share the tools, knowledge, labor and resources."

"Come on, boy. Jane's really in charge here. She was the one who smuggled in the pot seeds, wasn't she?— Oh, don't jump like that; I'm not about to run and tell Jomo on you. Hell, I think it's the best thing to hit Haven since the Survey Teams! But it's her seed, her land and her rule, isn't it? And she lends—or more exactly, rents out—her tools and knowledge and seed and the other resources in exchange for shares of the crops, right? And it's her castle that everybody's going to hole up in when the attack comes, right? So just what would you call an arrangement like that?"

"That depends." Makhno grinned toothily. "The women may decide not to fight that way, you know. They may vote to spread out among the neighbors on the riverside, fight it out farm by farm, or go hide out 'til the Simbas leave, like they did when the miners were rafting down-river, or a dozen other things."

"Good Lord!" Brodski bellowed. "Ya mean they're gonna decide on defense by vote? Every last welfare-witch ranking the same as Jane, or you?"

"Why not?" Makhno's grin got wider. "You just said yourself that they made pretty good soldiers, so they're not that ignorant. They all wanted the land deal, so they're not that lazy. Besides, it's their land, their kids, and their asses on the line when the Simbas come—so who's got the right to dispose of all that for them?"

Brodski subsided into swearing and muttering. He was still at it when the dinner-bell rang.

Half the population of Docktown, and no few eyes from Castell City, watched Jomo's expedition depart. The *Last Resort*, loaded with three-fourths of Jomo's army— with food, supplies, and all of the CoDo stunners— chugged away from the dock and out into the lake. Some of the crowd actually cheered, and meant it.

DeCastro stood on the dock, watching them go, his smile only half forced. He calculated that Jomo's expedition would take at least three full cycles to sweep all three branches of the river, with brief returns to Docktown in between to unload cargo.

That meant that one Tomas Messenger y DeCastro had roughly one cycle to assure the loyalty of the twenty troops Jomo had left him. Such assuring would necessarily include thinning out the unreliable. With less than twenty *soldados*, DeCastro could not possibly hold all of Docktown. Certain adjustments would have to be made, troop-strength concentrated on the most important sites and the others patrolled often enough to keep them from becoming hotbeds of rebellion. Explanations could be made to Jomo at some well-chosen time.

The five men sat plotting and scheming and arguing at the cleared dinner table, Jane looking on from the head of the table.

"So what is it you want?" asked Falstaff. "Understand that we don't have a lot of resources."

"I was thinking through dinner," replied Van Damm. "What I think we need is a variable timed explosive charge that you could attach to their boat. . . ."

"You'll have to be careful of River-Jacks. They're nasty and hungry and they'll take care of any Simbas we miss," said Makhno.

"How will we get through them?" asked Brodski.

"Blue tree sap will do it. Just rub it on your body and it keeps them away."

"Yah . . . Painted blue like an ancient Briton," said Van Damm. "But what boat are they likely to have, Captain Makhno?"

"Since they couldn't grab the *Bitch* . . . the next best ship is the *Last Resort*. She mostly fishes on Lake Castell; easy prey for Jomo, I'd guess. Hmm, but she's just a diesel-powered trawler with a wooden hull."

"A wooden hull!" Brodski snorted. "How're you going to put a mine on something like that?"

Falstaff giggled, his white teeth showing sharply against his black skin. "I have a solution. One of the kids pissed in a pot of Eggtree sap I had been working with, and I tried to wash it out."

"So?" asked Van Damm.

"The stuff stuck my hands to the pot and to the wooden spoon. I had to use alcohol to get loose. I figure it'll do as an underwater glue. Hell, I was stuck tight in less than ten seconds."

"I . . . see . . ." purred Van Damm.

"Sounds good to me," chortled Brodski. "A real— heh!—'solution' for a real problem."

"Captain Makhno, do you know the interior of the *Last Resort*?" Van Damm plowed on. "Can you draw a plan showing where a small charge would fill the greatest open space, other than the engine room?"

"Maybe, but why not the engine room?"

"Because we might want to salvage her later."

Donato chewed his mustache and punched numbers into his rechargeable pocket computer. "I have some frying pans that are heavy cast iron; they'll probably do for the cases. Jeff, can you do something about the charge?"

"Well, I can boost the shotgun propellant some, maybe get a medium explosive. What I see as a problem is the timer. Any ideas?"

"There are a couple of clock chips in that stunner you brought back; they'll do, but . . . they'll have to be set before they go into the water."

"Keep at it, gentlemen." Jane, grinned, getting up. "I trust your sense of . . . timing."

She strolled off, leaving a table of assorted groans.

The lands along the eastern branch of the great river were low, flat, rolling, rich with tall grass and wandering herds of muskylope. Jomo and his troops only glowered at the passing scenery; it hadn't shown them lootable prey yet.

There was great joy when they spotted a rising column of smoke from a chimney, and the smokestack that was its source. Below it sat a turf-roofed dugout farmhouse surrounded by paddocks, storage-shacks, livestock-barns and a good-sized kitchen-garden. Five men, four women and several children were busy working therein. When they spotted the oncoming *Last Resort*, they stood up and waved.

Jomo smiled from ear to ear. "Fresh meat, Simbas," he said.

As the last dishes were cleared away, Brodski stood up and waved his cane for attention. "Awright ladies," he bellowed. "All those who . . . voted . . ." He managed to keep the sneer out of his voice. ". . . to go to the neighbors' farms and snipe from the shore, take these radios and pass 'em around. Set up schedules so there's always somebody on the radio reporting back to the island. That's vital, dammit, so remember it! I just hope everybody'll be awake and on the air when Jomo's boys come."

"Amen," said Jane.

Van Damm shook his head and reached for his beer.

Brodski sat down with a thump and reached for his mug, muttering under his breath about deciding strategy by town meeting.

Jane, still standing, turned to face them. "Now, concerning your land-grant . . ." she began.

Brodski and Van Damm sat up straighter, grinning.

". . . You'll have your share of the working land on the

island. However, for tactical purposes, we'll need you two on an advance listening-post downriver."

The two mercs looked at each other, shrugged, and muttered agreement.

"The best post I've been able to find is just north of MacDonald's, right on the bend of the river. There's a dugout house and some furnishings, a storage-barn, two paddocks and a kitchen-garden gone to seed. We can give you hand-tools and seed. Sorry, but we don't have enough livestock yet to spot you more than a few turkeys; you'll have to hunt for most of your meat, but there's plenty of game. Now, how much seed do you want, and what sort of crops?"

". . . Seed?" Van Damm gave her a blank look.

"Crops?!" Brodski followed him. "You expect us to be farming?!"

"Of course." Jane frowned, puzzled. "You're going to have to pose as standard river farmers. That means working in the field. Now, which crops do you want?"

Makhno couldn't help laughing as he saw the two mercs look at each other, saw the slowly growing realization on their faces, saw plainly what they'd expected out of life on Lady Jane's estate. They really had thought they'd always be fed, supplied, taken care of, paid even after their contracted work was done, coddled and fussed over like roosters in a henhouse as two of the only five men among more than a dozen women.

Falstaff caught it at the same time; he erupted into howling laughter. Donato only looked to heaven and waved both hands to some unnamed saint. Makhno laughed so hard he fell off his bench and rolled, whooping and yukking, on the stone-and-clay floor.

"Welfare bums!" He tired to hiccup explanation to the worried faces turned toward him. "Just sit on your fanny and whine! *Hic!* Oh, they've got a lot to learn about polygamy. . . ."

Nobody else seemed to understand what he meant, unless one counted the thoughtful look on Jane's face.

*   *   *

The last of Jomo's men came aboard, dragging the last laden sack, and waved his stunner to signal "all clear."

Jomo turned toward the first man in line. "Is this all they had?" he asked, very coldly.

"We searched thoroughly, Baas." The man automatically dropped into the Submissive Position of the Chacma Baboon.

Jomo frowned and turned away. "Poor pickings," he growled. "Let us hope that the next farm has more to offer. Pilot, haul away."

Former-captain Feinberg cast one glance back at the thick smoke-column rising over the remains of the once-successful lakeside farm, shivered, and turned back toward his engines. There was nothing he could do about this, no available escape short of getting his throat cut. He breathed a quick prayer to any gods who could hear him to give him an opportunity to run.

The *Last Resort* fired up her engine, and dutifully turned south.

Brodski and Van Damm were sitting in the hammocks outside their cabin, arguing over whose turn it was to weed the goddam vegetable garden.

"I've done it the last three times," Van Damm complained, nursing carefully on his next-to-last bottle of downriver beer. "I have blisters from the verdammt weeds. It's high time you did it."

"You should've worn gloves, like I told you," Brodski retorted, measuring out a half-bowlful of his dwindling tobacco. "Hell, you expect a lame man to go bendin' and choppin' all over that garden? My back would lock up before I finished one row. Besides, who's been doin' all the cookin' and laundry around here?"

"I washed the dishes, last time."

"Yeah? And who scoured the pans?"

"Scheiss! This is no proper work for a man!" Van Damm gulped the last of his stoneware-cup load, and glowered at the sky.

Brodski laughed until he ran out of wind. "Whooo!

Heh! What'd you think, that all those women would come over here and do the housework for us, for nothin' but a sight of your pretty face? Get real, Vanny: we got exactly what we contracted for, and now we're stuck with it."

"Shh!" Van Damm whispered, looking down river.

"Shh, what?" said Brodski, warily setting down his pipe.

"Boat." Van Damm jumped out of his hammock and sprinted for the cabin.

It took Brodski longer to get up; he was just struggling clear of the hammock when Van Damm ran back out carrying a pair of binoculars and the portable radio. He threw the radio to Brodski and peered out at the river.

"Which boat and which way?" Brodski asked, working the radio.

"The *Last Resort*, right enough," muttered Van Damm, peering low toward the river. "Heading upstream, and . . . loaded with armed men. Makhno guessed right."

"That tears it; the war's starting." Brodski thumbed down a switch and winced at the chatter coming through the earpiece. "Girls, clear the lines! We've gotta get word down to Janesfort. The *Last Resort*'s heading there right now, with Jomo's boys on it. Spread the word, warn everybody, get everyone into the fort, and be sure to tell Jane first."

There was an instant's pause for breath, then a wild jumble of chatter on the airwaves, most of it demands for more news. Brodski rolled his eyes heavenward, muttered something about civilians, then repeated his message slowly and carefully.

This time, only one voice answered. "This is the fort. We receive your message, Señor Brodski. Can you see Jomo's people yet?"

"Not yet. Give us ten minutes to get down to the water and we'll call you back. Ski out." Brodski thumbed off the switch, picked up his cane, slung the binoculars around his neck and started back into the cabin. "You get to carry the spare rations and water."

*   *   *

Jomo scanned the riverbank slipping slowly past, and considered where suitable farms might be hiding. Surely some of the squatters must have hidden in these thick woods; the cover, and the possible game, were too good to go to waste. He didn't like this alien forest himself, but he could tell a good hideout when he saw one.

Hey now, what was that? It looked like a thin streak of smoke against the sky, the marker of a farmhouse's chimney. How handy that everybody on this cold planet kept at least one heating-fire going all the time; it gave him a dead-sure way to find prey.

Jomo snapped his fingers at the pilot, then pointed a languid hand toward the riverbank.

Feinberg, having grown used to Jomo's little ways after all these turns, sighed wordlessly and turned toward the shore.

Van Damm poked his binoculars a little further through the screen of eggtree fronds, studying details of the Simbas' equipment. He smiled sourly at the bell-mouthed stunners. "Mark I's . . . lousy guns," he whispered. "No range, not designed for woods work, good for nothing but hosing down the near scenery. Doesn't anyone use good weapons anymore?"

"Yeah, Jane." Brodski tapped the shotgun and the silenced rifle on Van Damm's back. "Now let's fade back and keep watching."

They slipped back quietly through the woodlot. Where the wood gave way to the narrow plot of cleared land they hurried around the lone field, back into the woods again on the field's far side, and flattened behind an ancient half-rotted log. "Hey Vannie, you ever work for Intelligence?"

Van Damm froze for an instant, then rolled slowly to face Brodski. "What makes you say that?"

"I did some troop training at Camp Pendleton about six years ago," said Brodski, casually pointing his rifle in Van Damm's direction. "And we had a couple of spooks come through. I didn't have anything to do with them, but I remember one in particular. He was an Afrikaaner, and had a scar on his thumb—just like yours. I remember it because I watched his hands when he arm-wrestled with Bill Mason for the beers at the E.M. Club one night. He moved like you. That's a real hard thing to change, you know?"

"Ja, I forgot." Van Damm smiled thinly. "You know, that's how covers get blown."

"You working for the CoDo?" Brodski wasn't smiling.

"Yes, Fleet Intelligence." Again, Van Damm considered, the truth was the best defense. "But I'm thinking of settling down here. I'm getting to like the place. It grows on one."

"Van, I got on that ship one jump ahead of the cops and arranged my retirement on board. I'll only get twenty-five years instead of thirty, but what the hell, this place is a lot looser than Earth." His gun-muzzle lowered a little.

"I'll tell you one thing, Ski; I am not doing anything against Jane. In fact, I was sent here to do what I could to start trouble, give the CoDo its excuse. . . . Nobody knew about Jane back on Earth, but she has done a very good job on her own."

"How do y'mean? She hasn't hurt Castell or his claim."

"You don't understand." Van Damm shook his head in frustration. "CoDo wants Haven for—for, dammit, Kennicott's mining! They have found a rich strike of hafnium here, and BuReloc's dumping miners from Earth. . . . Does that suggest anything to you?"

"Where does Janey come in?"

"Farming!" Van Damm almost wrung his hands. "Aside from the Harmonies, who farms? Squatters, trying to live off the land, barely surviving—how could they feed the numbers BuReloc wants to dump here, even with the synthetic food factories? People would starve. BuReloc or the CoDo wouldn't care. . . . Scheiss!"

"Why, Vanny, can a spook actually have a conscience?"

"Their training did not take that from me." Van Damm

looked away, automatically checking the empty field. "Jane ... She makes farming successful, even for squatters. Surplus of food, not to mention the cloth, oil, paper ... She can make poor squatters rich, Brodski."

"More precisely, she's creating an independent middle class."

"If she succeeds ... then many people will not starve, will even do well, who would starve otherwise. I have seen a famine, Brodski. I ... do not wish to see it again."

"Okay, Owen, that's good enough for me." Brodski took position and shifted his gun-muzzle toward the field. "Let's get ready; here they come."

"Warn the others," said Van Damm, all business again.

"They're coming," Brodski whispered into the radio, seeing the first of the Simbas emerge, branch-slapped and dusty, from the trees near the river. "Any last-minute changes?"

"No," Jane's voice whispered back. "Lie low or thin them out. Up to you."

"Right. At our own discretion." Brodski switched the radio off and watched, feeling Van Damm shift restlessly beside him, while the Simbas leveled their stunners and ran, howling like banshees, toward the empty cabin. "How goddam brave of them," he muttered. "Van, you sure you got everything out?"

"Everything but the furniture." Van Damm squirmed as the Simbas kicked open the cabin door. "Idiots! We left it unlocked. They'll break the hinges. . . ."

They waited, watched, listened as Jomo's men piled into the cabin, leaving only two men outside. Van Damm winced at the sound of shelves and benches being slammed around.

"I count a dozen," Brodski whispered. "They must've left the rest to guard the boat. How many do you figure we can pick off?"

"These two now, the others later." Van Damm shrugged. "If we wait 'til they come out, we can get their head honcho."

"Then how many, total?"

"Given what we've seen of their training ..." Van Damm scratched his chin. "Three, maybe four. Then they'll wait awhile, come out in a big rush and shoot up the trees wherever they think we are."

Brodski grinned, calculating. "Give 'em a little longer to find nothing, then let's drop them when they come out."

"Deal," said Van Damm, casually drawing a bead on one of the outside men.

They waited until the cries and curses changed to the sound of furniture being smashed. Then the door opened again and the Simbas began filing out of the cabin. One of them snapped at the two outside men, pointed back toward the river and bellowed orders at the rest.

Bingo! thought Brodski. He shifted his rifle's aim, pulled the trigger, and dropped the boss Simba.

For an age-long second, the others stood in a rough circle and stared, drop-jawed, while their squad-leader jerked, folded and fell.

Then Van Damm took out two men together, one behind the other, with a single throat-shot.

"Not bad," Brodski whispered, aiming again.

At that point, the Simbas had the sense to either run back into the cabin or drop and pull up their stunners. Van Damm and Brodski got two more in the yard, though they couldn't be sure if the shots were clean kills, while the Simbas looked wildly around them for the source of the gunfire.

The survivors in the yard started crawling toward the cabin door, firing in all directions without concern for ammo expenditure. A few shots hit close to Brodski's and Van Damm's hidey-hole, and they ducked. The last survivor in the yard scrambled into the cabin, and the door slammed shut.

"Think they spotted us yet?"

"Maybe." Van Damm shrugged. "We got four kills, maybe three wounded."

"Good," said Brodski, slinging up his rifle. "Let's fade."

They backed a little deeper into the wood, then slipped

laterally down the length of the cleared field, almost to its end, and took positions behind thick standing trees.

"More distance here," Van Damm grumbled. "Less visibility."

"Harder for them to pick us out, too." Brodski opened his pack and hauled out some homemade jerky. "We may as well relax until they get up nerve."

"Or they radio for help and the reinforcements come," Van Damm gloomed, accepting one of the meat-strips.

"I somehow doubt they'll send the whole reserve," Brodski considered, munching. "Gotta have enough left at the boat to make sure it doesn't go anywhere."

"We should wait, then." Van Damm gnawed thoughtfully. "Let them come out, shoot at trees, get no response, mill around for awhile, then start breaking up into smaller packs."

"Then we harass them." Brodski rolled onto his back and pulled his hat down over his eyes. "Wake me when they come out," he said, and promptly went to sleep.

". . . but they hadn't gone," Under-chief Pucey panted on with his report. "Shot at us when we moved into the field. Same thing again: disappeared when we returned fire, waited 'til we started to move, then shot us up again—always from a different quarter. We pulled back to the river, and they waylaid us in the woods. If you hadn't sent that second squad out—"

"Of course," said Jomo. "I head the racket on the radio."

"Good thing, Baas; we could've been pinned down there for God knows how long. Must've been a dozen of 'em. They'd got ahead of us, somehow, in the woods. . . ." No point mentioning that he and Osgood had argued over whether to keep on toward the river in the face of that relentless sniping, or fall back to the farmhouse and wait for reinforcements. The sound and sight of approaching Simbas had settled the question. "We lost seven men, and there's ten wounded."

"We must take precautions. They will not catch us napping again."

Pucey threw a glance of silent appeal to Osgood, who cleared his throat and stepped forward. "Uh, Jomo, since we don't know how many settlers are involved, shouldn't we, uh, get reinforcements before proceeding?"

"Reinforcements?" Jomo's glower made the man take a step back. "Against how many dirt-farmers?" He picked up the marked satellite-map and shoved it under Osgood's nose. "Look! How much cleared land does that show? Scarcely enough for a dozen farms, if they support no more than four adults on any of them. Squatters, with nothing but whatever weapons they could sneak aboard the ships. Now just how much resistance do you think they're likely to put up?"

"Sir, they got seven of us." Osgood couldn't help sounding desperate.

"They caught you flat-footed because you weren't prepared. You will be from now on." Jomo sneered as he rolled up the map.

Osgood and Pucey traded bleak looks.

"No, we are not going to go back to Docktown, aborting this mission, just because a dozen farmers shot at you with a few leftover weapons. Now, I don't suppose you managed to collect much in the way of goods?"

Pucey shrugged, and solemnly held out one knapsack full of half-ripe cabbage tops. "That's all we got before they started shooting," he said.

"Janesfort, Janesfort," Brodski whispered into his radio. "They're coming on up the river, still keeping close to the west bank. Looks like they'll hit the next farm in another hour, maybe hour and a half."

"That's ours!" wailed a male voice, somewhere in the net.

"Everybody who can, take positions at Sam MacDonald's farm," said Jane, calm as ever through the static. "Thin the bastards some more. But be careful; they'll be wide-eyed and paranoid this time."

"Going now, Brodski out." He leaned around a tree to tap Van Damm's shoulder. "Time to hike again, down to Sam's for the next round."

". . . Simba bastards," Van Damm muttered, slinging up his rifle. "We could have eaten those cabbages in another week. After all the time I spent weeding them. . . ."

"Uhuh. They could've torched our cabin, too," Brodski considered. "Y'know, Vanny, I'm beginning to appreciate Jane's point of view about citizen-soldiers."

"One does tend to appreciate land one has worked on. . . ."

"Right. You go stiffen the resistance, Van, while I look up the captain."

Osgood had the dubious honor of leading the three-squad assault on the second farm, and he was determined not to make any incautious mistakes this time. He kept his radio on simultaneous transmit-and-send mode, never mind how that drained the batteries, and his stunner ready. His orders were simple: advance spread out in a line, nobody more than three meters apart or less than two, keep your eyes open, and shoot anything that moves.

Consequently, ten minutes after entering the deep, dark wood, his troops had shot two tree-hoppers and a red mole, and all hope of surprise was good and gone. Osgood, having nobody else to blame for this state of affairs, sighed and ordered the troops to pick up speed.

Van Damm had laid another neat surprise at the farm; once again the Simbas found nothing, no crops, livestock or people, but when they began their return they were ambushed. In the thick woods, the Simbas could find no targets. They hurried back to the boat, leaving four dead, carrying six wounded.

Jomo considered that, and ordered the expedition to proceed to the island. Foraging in the unlimited forest was just too dangerous. On the limited land of that river-island ahead, the pickings should be much safer.

At the *Last Resort*'s best speed, he could be there in another turn at most.

Jane, Makhno, Van Damm and Brodski were discussing strategy after supper and before turning in for the shift.

"We better make some contingency plans in case we win," said Makhno.

"Make that when we win, Leo," said Jane gently.

"Okay, when we win. What are we going to do then? Docktown will still be in, uh, enemy hands."

"Continue the boycott." Jane shrugged. "We can set up our own trade-spots along the river, tell our friends. . . ."

"That'll be rough on the people in Docktown."

"Rougher on the gangsters."

"We must kill them all, you know." Van Damm spoke up.

Makhno turned to give him a long look. "I'd be interested in hearing your reasons, Owen."

"This planet has no prison," Van Damm explained carefully. "No police, not even any courts. That is why you have this problem in the first place. You have no protection from thugs and crooks, and that is why you must kill them."

"How does that follow?" Jane asked, studying him.

"It follows that you cannot punish the thugs with prison, nor force them to pay just compensation, nor even exile them," Van Damm went on. "If you drive them out into the wilds, they will band together, and raid farms for subsistence. If you leave them alive in town they will try to invade again, sooner or later. You have to kill them, the ones that take part in the raid, who know the way here and see what valuables you have."

"We know we can't let them get away to tell that the 'land of women' really exists," Jane said levelly. "That will just make us targets again. But why should we go after the thugs left in Docktown?"

"Likewise, to keep them from trying for you again. Also, you cannot boycott Docktown forever. Sooner or later you will need the off-world goods available only there. You cannot leave Docktown in the hands of the enemy."

"True," Brodski noted. "But remember, there just aren't that many Bad Guys. The whole population of Docktown isn't more than a thousand people. There's only a limited amount of the 'crook' mentality to recruit there, and Jomo brought a big chunk of them on this trip. I say we should send some kind of message to whoever Jomo left behind, see if we can't scare them into behaving themselves."

"Are you sure that there is someone left behind?" asked Jane. "Wouldn't he bring his whole force to attack us here?"

"Jomo's greedy, not stupid. He must have left some sort of garrison to hold what gains he made. I read him for wanting the whole planet. Since he can't take the Harmonies yet with the kind of strength he has, he turned to finding a fort to build up his forces—or, thanks to your boycott, to hunt for food. He plans to come out and take on Castell eventually, but he needs a base first."

"We know that too. So how do we keep the garrison troops from coming after us again?"

"We send whoever the second-in-command is a message he can't ignore." Brodski grinned. "At the same time we arm the Docktowners with all the weapons we capture. I've noticed that, aside from the stunners, the firearms they have are mostly pistols of different calibers, probably stuff they brought with them. Ammo for them will be something of a problem, but in the hands of the Docktowners they can let folks defend themselves and deal with the Baddies themselves."

"We could even sell ammo. . . ." Jane considered.

"And if the CoDo comes in, cleaning up Docktown will give their security force something to do," added Van Damm.

"So we're obliged to carry the war to Docktown," said Makhno. "Ah, what the hell, you've got my vote." He turned his attention to the tan light showing through the window. "Right now it's technical midnight," he murmured, "Cat's Eye's waxing and setting. That means . . ." He doodled briefly in the margin of the map on the table before him. ". . . they've got to get here within twenty hours, start the assault soon after, win within forty, forty-three hours after that. So, we've got maybe sixty hours to settle this war, Jane."

"Why the time limit?" she asked, wiping a spot of grease off her chin.

"Because after that we'll be into second orbit, sunset, and turned away from Cat's Eye. Full night for forty-plus hours, remember? No light but the moons. Even Jomo has better sense than to attack unknown territory, in the dark."

Jane nodded slowly. "Right. So, sixty hours against . . . what, forty men? That means we have to kill roughly one every hour and a half."

"Uh, right," said Makhno. Van Damm and Brodski traded startled looks.

"Well, if we're agreed in this, I'm for bed," said Jane. "Coming, Leo?"

Makhno laughed, and shoved his chair back. Brodski and Van Damm looked at each other again.

"Y'know, Owen," Brodski considered, "we're gonna have to start seriously courting some of the ladies around here."

"I think," said Van Damm, shoving his plate aside, "that as soon as Captain Makhno is out of bed, we should have him take us back to our posts on the shore."

Jomo glowered at the passing island shore, scarcely noticing the grumblings of the troops on the deck behind him. Greenthorn hedges everywhere he looked: from the waterline on up for five meters at least, nothing but greenthorns. How had the pesky settler ever gotten through them?

Well, with luck maybe the settler was long gone and they could take the island cheaply. If greenthorns were the only problem, he wouldn't complain. There were no signs of any human habitation so far.

Whoa, there was something: just as they came around the southern tip of the island, where a natural jetty of rock jabbed out into the river, dividing the stream. There was a piece of pontoon-dock pulled up on shore, almost hidden under the hedge of greenthorns.

Strange. Why had the settler done that? Expecting company, maybe?

Jomo shrugged and gave up on the minor mystery. They were coming around to the shadowy western shore of the island now, and he'd have to keep his eyes peeled if he wanted to spot anything in all these shadows.

The western shore of the island was likewise edged with greenthorns from the waterline to about five meters up.

"Where can we anchor?" Jomo grumbled to the pilot. "Can't see a motherless thing in this light."

"Best pull into the lee of the north shore," the pilot noted. "Looks pretty steep; probably nothing'll attack us in the dark. We can wait there 'til sunrise."

"Fine. Do it." Jomo walked back to his personal cabin to get some sleep. He'd look at the map after a good rest.

"I don't believe it," Makhno whispered, peering down from the ledge. "The fool's just sitting there, waiting for daylight. I swear, those sentries never look up. We could lob one of the mines down on the boat from here, blow it to kingdom come. . . ."

"We might not get them all. Then all they'd have to do is reach Docktown, come back in greater numbers."

"Okay, okay, so we wait. Damn." Makhno eased back on the ledge until his spine touched the rock wall of the capstone-fortress. "I just don't like the idea of letting 'em walk in here tomorrow."

"Just remember," said Jane, stroking his arm, "the important thing is that they never walk out again."

"Is everybody in place?"

Brodski glanced meaningfully at his radio. "That's what

they said. So now we wait." He stretched out behind the log and pulled his hat down over his eyes.

In the dim light of the moons, Captain Feinberg crept softly across the deck of the *Last Resort*. It was dark, it was late, the sentries were nodding off at their stations, and he'd never have a better chance to escape than this. Just a few more steps to the gunwales, then over the side, then—

Then the zap of a stunner ripped out of the silence. Feinberg jumped, jerked, and flopped to the deck.

Jomo, smothering a yawn, strolled out of the shadows. The sentries straightened up and did their best to look as if they'd been giving Feinberg only enough lead to condemn himself. Jomo favored them with barely a sneer. He snapped his fingers and pointed at Feinberg's body.

"Pick up that garbage," he said. "And throw it over the side."

The sentries paused for only a moment, then hastened to comply.

Feinberg's body hit the water with a loud splash, floated a moment, then turned over and sank. A brief flurry of bubbles marked his fall.

Jomo slung the stunner back on his shoulder and strolled back to his air-mattress on the ship's stern, never once looking back. The sentries watched him go, none of them daring to mention that they'd just lost the boat's single experienced pilot.

"Goddammit, gimme a hand here!" Brodski panted, limping behind the others. "Got a damn bad leg."

"Can't wait for you," Van Damm retorted from somewhere up ahead among the trees.

"We be there when they come," agreed Muda, pattering along after Van Damm quick and sure as a goat among the thick foliage, for all that she was bent nearly double under the weight of her own gun and ammo and the swimming gear too.

"Here, lemme help." Joan MacDonald shifted the ballast-weights on her back, took Brodski by one arm

across her shoulders, and half-carried him through the
screen of trees.

Brodski bit his lip, used his cane as much as he could,
and didn't complain.

Benny Donato worked his wrench under a blanket-
shrouded light, tightening the seal-bolt to the last turn.

"It's ready," he puffed. "That makes two of them. I
have them set for fifteen minutes before dawn." He
turned off the flashlight and crawled out from under the
blanket, grumbling about the dangers and inconveniences
of bomb-making, and why this couldn't have been finished in his nice comfortable shop in the fort.

"You get the packing tight enough, Benny?" Falstaff
cut in on him. "I'd hate to have them leak."

"Any tighter and I'd break the case."

"Then let's get them down to the customers."

"Easy for you to say. These damned things are heavy."

Falstaff wasn't the quietest person moving in the dark,
and Donato was little better, but they didn't have to
travel far. Mary Harp met them with a whistle, and
guided them to where the rope stretched down to the
river. They bent and unloaded their packages and tied
them onto the rope. Another whistle toward the water,
and the men turned to hurry back through the trees,
their mission accomplished.

"Let us know if you don't get the mines to them in
an hour," Donato tossed to Mary, looking at his watch.
"I hope I don't have to take those fool things apart again.
That'd be a real bitch."

"Don't worry so much," Falstaff panted, tugging at his
arm. "We have other work to do. I've got confidence in
those two and the women with them."

"Well, maybe . . ." Donato grumped. "But cross your
fingers about those mines."

From under the greenthorns on the east bank of the
river, Brodski and Van Damm peered out with their
optics, studying the sleeping ship.

"Hmm, looks all right, Ski. Your plan better work."

"It will. Besides, what else do you have to do on a cold morning like this?" he said, rubbing Blue Tree sap on his exposed body.

"Look up an Island woman and promise to protect her for the rest of her life."

"I never believed you were that much of a politician. You ready to swim?"

"Ja." Van Damm glanced at the dark water, and shivered. "It ain't gonna get no warmer. Let's go."

Brodski gave two tugs on the line, and both men walked gingerly into the water. The bags of rocks that hung from their belts held their feet on the bottom, and the river's current was negligible at this point. As the water crept over their heads, they held up the plastic tubes that would allow them to breathe. Aside from the cold, the work was easy so far.

Following the shore line until they felt the distance knots in the rope, they pulled their heads clear of the water and looked downstream. Against the dark bulk of the *Last Resort*, they could see the binnacle-light in the chart-house. Nobody was moving on deck.

Brodski patted his way along the rope toward his preassigned position. "Hell of a mess," he muttered. "Me, a mud marine, playing frogman!"

"Ribbit, ribbit," Van Damm grumbled back. "I like this no better than you. Cold water, no proper gear and painted blue to boot. . . ."

"Let's get on with it," Brodski whispered through his chattering teeth.

They waded silently downstream until the bow of the *Last Resort* loomed above them. They patted over the rough wood surface, hunting for the proper spot.

Brodski moved down the hull until he felt the warm water of the engine's cooling exhaust. Now, just five armlengths more, he considered. He could be a little long in his measurement, but too short would be disastrous. He gave the hull an extra forearm-length for luck, and pressed the flat of the mine against the side of the fishing boat. He counted to ten, waiting for the glue to set, and again added a little more for luck.

Done. Brodski walked slowly toward the stern, waited for a forty-second eternity until a touch on his right arm—and another on his right bun—announced that Van Damm had reached him. With another signal-tap, they half-swam/half-walked toward the agreed-upon point around the downstream hook of the island. The deepening mud told them when they'd reached it, whereupon they headed towards shore. Neither of them spoke another word until they were up against the greenthorn hedge on Jane's Island.

"Did yours stick?" Van Damm asked, scraping water off his skin.

"On time, and like advertised. How about yours?"

"I thought I was going to have to piss on it to make it work!" Van Damm snapped, with almost enough emphasis to make it noticeable five meters away.

"Well, just so long as it stuck. Let's move."

Unmindful of the scratches, they lifted the mass of the natural barbed wire and crawled under it.

"The towels should be on our right."

"Ribbet!" challenged a voice ahead of them. "How high's the water?"

"Knee deep!" replied Brodski, in his best frog voice.

"Knee deep," Van Damm echoed, right behind him.

"How do you manage to keep that Afrikaaner accent on a frog croak?" Brodski asked.

"N-natural talent," Van Damm replied through clacking teeth.

A feminine giggle answered them. Soft footsteps pattered down to the hedge.

Van Damm and Brodski traded invisible grins in the dark.

They were greeted with warm towels—and warmer female arms, and a kiss each (who can prove anything in the dark?), and were led uphill.

"Heroes' welcome," Van Damm muttered.

"Patience, Owen. It gets better."

When they reached what seemed to rival the inside of a cow for darkness, Jane's voice asked, "Did you do it?"

"If we didn't, it's the devil to pay with the cook out to lunch!" Brodski replied. "One thing's going for us though; if one falls off, it's liable to do more damage than one on the hull. They're in damned shallow water."

"Good. . . . I mentioned the tradition of the divers' return, didn't I?"

"Right here," came Makhno's voice, followed by the sound of liquid pouring into cups. "Divers' return, or death to us all," he said, lifting his glass.

As whiskey, it was poor; as simple blood-warmer, it was right on target. Brodski and Van Damm gulped it gratefully.

After dressing, they shook hands. "I'll see you when it's over, Owen," said Brodski.

"Ja, you'll owe me drinks if this doesn't work."

"And I'll pay up, if either of us is still alive."

They parted company in the dark, and went their separate ways.

It was just before dawn when the charges went off.

They blew a large hole in the forward hold of the *Last Resort*, and one in the aft net stowage. With one hole to port and one to starboard, she sank quickly—and on an even keel—leaving only the wheel-house above water.

Of the troops aboard, half a dozen were knocked into the water by the initial blast. The rest, including the two deckhands, stayed long enough to realize that the *Last Resort* was sinking fast—then grabbed gear they could reach, and slid off into the chilly water.

Jomo, after a final furious look at the sinking boat, was last to leave. He found the water shallow enough that he could wade, holding his stunner over his head. He shouted at the others to do likewise, keep those precious Enforcers dry, but wasn't sure they heard.

The water ended at a bare rock cliff-face, too steep to climb, especially in the dark.

There was no help for it; the survivors had to wade

along the cliff until they came to easier land. Jomo bellowed and chivied them to the left, recalling that the land had sloped sooner toward the east side of the island.

The Simbas groggily complied, struggling through the cold, swift-running water. One of the *Last Resort*'s deckhands tried to sneak off to the right, and Jomo shot him. The rest of the survivors picked up their pace, trying to see rather than feel their way along the steep shore in the dim light. At length the water grew shallower, and the outline of vegetation appeared above the greenthorn.

The survivors clambered up the narrow beach of stones and started pushing into the greenthorn hedge just as Byers' Star peeped over the horizon, silhouetting them against the background of the gleaming river.

Directly ahead of them, half a dozen women stood up behind the greenthorn hedge and fired at them, from less than five meters away, with shotguns.

At least six of the Simbas went down in the first volley, and the second came an instant later. The survivors turned and ran, a few back out into the water, the rest to the left along the narrow pebble-beach. Gunfire followed them.

The Simbas running into deep water started screaming.... The River-Jacks had found them.... There was a flurry in the water where the "fish" fed.... The worrying of the bodies pulled them into deeper water.

Two men raised empty arms and shouted promises to surrender. Jomo, cursing, shot both of them. A shotgun blast tore the ground beside him, narrowly missing his foot. He dropped and rolled under the nearest cover—which was the greenthorn hedge. From where he lay among the thorns, he couldn't see if anyone else followed his example.

On the other side of the hedge he heard a woman's voice snap: "They're running down the east bank! Come on over and help us pick 'em off!" Another female voice replied, distant and staticky from a radio: "Soon as we can, Lou. Keep after 'em 'til then."

Two ideas occurred to Jomo just then: that this island

just might be the rumored Land of Women, and that he'd best keep quiet until those shotgun-toting slits ran past him on the other side of the hedge. He muffled his breathing and lay very still.

Jomo, hearing the battle run past him, peered under the hedge. He couldn't see anyone through the thick and thorny foliage ... but he did note that the hedge was mostly horizontal branches.

He poked experimentally with his stunner barrel, and saw that the branches lifted easily. Damn, this was his way out! He lifted the branch, crawled under it, and came out on the other side of the hedge. Beside the hedge lay a path.

Jomo followed it, going uphill, away from the armed women and the running battle, keeping low. As he ran, he could hear the sounds of his Simbas being slaughtered. Never mind them; all he could think about was finding cover, some safe place to rest. He was cold, wet, and more frightened than he'd been in years. If this was the legendary Land of Women, he no longer wanted any part of it. Dammit, they didn't fight fair!

The last of the Simbas were quickly picked off by the mercs or the women with them. . . . One or two tried the river but the "Jacks" made a quick and messy finish to them.

Jomo studied the greenthorn hedge crossing his path—and the path leading right into it. He poked at the hedge with his boot and a whole section of it lifted. He smiled bitterly, and crawled under the hedge.

A quick look showed the path went further uphill. He chose to follow it, move further away from the shore and all those hunting bitches. There was better cover in this forest, anyway.

The path let him out in a planted field whose crops grew taller than his head. It promised good cover; he started to sneak through it.

He was less than five yards into the field when he

noticed the odor and shape of the leaves. He stopped, stared, then burst out laughing.

"It's Ganja! Growing here on Haven. . . ."

Then he realized that "euph-leaf" wasn't a local herb at all. It was nothing but good old marijuana, grass, hemp—growing right here on an island full of women, and from what the sat-map had showed him, there were plenty of cultivated fields around here, maybe most of them growing hemp. What a prize!

If he could only get back to Docktown with the news, he knew he could raise a large enough army to come back and take the island.

Brodski and Van Damm met near the path in the converging hedges above the water.

They'd been giving "last mercy" to the wounded gangsters on the field. They started up, looking at each other—then recognized the lack of expression on each other's faces. Both shared distaste for the business.

"Have you seen Jomo?" Brodski snapped, sounding angry.

"No," Van Damm answered. "How about you?"

"No luck. Let's check the boat; he might still be in the wheel-house."

"Good idea. Big Lou will take care of the rest here."

"Alert her that there might be stragglers from the beach," Van Damm warned.

"Amen." Brodski shivered and turned away. "Their land, their fertilizer. . . . Shit."

As the two mercs plodded to the side of the river, their radios crackled to life.

"Where are you, Señor Owen?" came the question. "Are you and Señor Brodski all right?"

"All's secure here, Granny. Tell Jane we're going to check the boat for sign of Jomo. We haven't found him yet. Could you send the *Bitch* to take us to the wreck?"

"I'll relay Captain Makhno to you. We shall keep watch for Jomo from up here. Senora Jane says, do not be too late for breakfast. Granny, out."

"Just like a woman." Van Damm laughed. "The world

can be falling apart around them, but their major concern
is that you get to the table on time."

"So what's more important than survival? And what's
more valuable to survival than food? Let's get a move
on, Vanny."

Crouching and creeping along the path beside the second ring-hedge, Jomo worked his way northward. If he
could get safely far from the battle, he could maybe swim
the river, reach the far bank, hike his way back to Docktown. One of those squatters along the river had to have
a rowboat, or raft, or some damn thing that would float—
not to mention supplies for the journey. Or maybe, if
there was time, he could chop enough wood from the
wreck of the *Last Resort* to make a raft, find enough
food to hold him while the raft floated across river.

In any case, the hunters were least likely to be back
at the point.

Little Easter had insisted on following the two mercs,
and Makhno had no complaint. The *Black Bitch*, engines
roaring wide open, hauled them up to the point in a few
minutes' time. Makhno circled the tiny harbor. Nothing
was moving.

"Well, that leaves ship and shore," said Brodski, cen-
tering his optic on the smoking hulk. "The only man in
the wheelhouse is the corpse of the pilot. There's no sign
of life aboard."

"Then we should go back to the landing," Van Damm
insisted. "We may still have some unfinished business."

"I'll pull in at the east corner," said Makhno, heading
the *Bitch* around, "right where the hedge starts. They
couldn't have got ashore any sooner than that."

They grounded just under the start of the hedge, got
out, hiked the branches aside and began searching uphill.

Little Easter was following Van Damm, carrying her
shotgun at high port, when she saw a leg move under
the Orange-Berry bush.

The roar of her shotgun brought the men around with weapons pointed.

"It's okay," Easter chirped, smiling. "I got 'im in the head."

Van Damm checked the body and pulled it out to the open. "We owe you one, little sister," he said. "Hmm, if this one got through the hedge, we can assume others did, too."

Easter took a look at the man she had killed, bit her lip, then hurried into the bush. The sounds of her stomach emptying came back to them.

Brodski resolutely turned away. "How many do you think could have made it through?" he asked.

"We have to assume that Jomo did, since we have not found his body."

"That's what I like about you, Owen; you're such an optimist."

Jomo had stopped for a moment as nature called him, when he heard the shotgun blast below. He dived for cover beneath the hedge, not waiting to zip his pants, and peered back toward the shore.

Below him he saw a hunting-party searching the forest-belt, beating their way slowly southward. Below them, beyond the hedge, the zodiac was nosed into shore.

Jomo smiled hugely. The answer to all his troubles gleamed black on the beach: the famous *Black Bitch*! It couldn't be difficult to run, and it was the fastest boat on Haven. He checked his .44 pistol and started back down the slope.

Brodski and Van Damm had spread out keeping Easter in the line between them, and were working their way through the forest, each hoping to catch Jomo alone. They had plans for him.

Makhno, seeing them go, decided to leave the search in their hands and head uphill. It was time to check in with Jane and get the latest report.

"We didn't get off free," Jane grimly informed him.

"They shot back, not just with the stunners. Muda's dead, and who's going to tell her son? Ahnli got a little too enthusiastic, showed herself, and caught a bad one high in the chest. She probably won't make it. Tall Lou got clipped in the leg; she says it isn't bad, but knowing her, it'll probably leave her lame."

Makhno ground his teeth; he'd liked Muda. ". . . Hell, we didn't expect to win scot-free. Cheap at the price, I guess . . . if that's all there's going to be. . . ."

"What do you mean, 'if'?"

"We still haven't found Jomo. If he gets back to Docktown he'll raise another army, and he won't make the same mistakes. I don't know if we could stop him a second time."

"Don't worry, Leo. Even if the worst happens he'll need a boat to get home. We could still hunt him down with the *Bitch*."

"The *Bitch* . . ." Makhno jerked upright in sudden alarm. "Nobody's guarding her! I left her on the beach—" With that, he turned and ran back downhill.

"I'm coming, Leo!" Jane shouted after him through the radio. "Just let me tell the others first." She picked up her shotgun.

Makhno didn't hear; he was too busy racing for the anchorage.

When Van Damm heard the call he had been working his way along the hedge, looking for tracks. He hadn't found any, but he'd had hopes.

Brodski had made good progress upstream, and was looking over toward the stretch of beach when he got the call.

"Time to go back, girl, for all of us." Brodski stopped a moment and considered. "Let's get under the hedge and down the beach."

"Why, Mister Brodski?"

"I'll have a clear shot at him when he comes down to

the landing-point. I might put a hole in the *Bitch* but we'll stop Jomo."

Makhno dived under the lower thorn-hedge and came rolling out on the narrow beach. He got up and ran northward along the shore, heading for the *Bitch*.

"Goddammit, Makhno," Brodski's voice crackled from the radio. "Get out of my line-of-sight!"

Having no idea where Brodski was, Makhno ran on. There was nobody near the *Black Bitch* when he came pounding up to it. Panting with relief, he started to shove off. The best way to keep the *Bitch* out of any surviving Simba's hands was to take her out into deep water and keep her moving.

Then the ZAP of a stunner crackled out of the forest. Makhno fell sprawling in the bottom of the raft.

Jomo grinned down at the raft on the beach, regretting only that the stunner wouldn't kill, that he wasn't accurate at that range with the .44, and that interfering fool hadn't fallen into the water to be eaten. Well, he'd correct that. Meanwhile, best wait and see if anybody came. He could afford to wait, for a prize like this.

He grinned again, pulled a handful of crumpled leaves out of his pocket. With these for proof, he could recruit an army a half thousand strong out of Docktown.

Van Damm heard the ZAP ahead and below him, and dropped to a crouch. He waited a moment, then slipped forward, quiet in the thick forest, not nearly fast enough to suit him. So there was a Simba left in the wood-belt, maybe Jomo. Now was he moving or holed up somewhere? There was no further sound. . . .

Damn, but this was going to take time.

Brodski crouched behind a boulder on the beach, held his aim on the top of the *Black Bitch*. Where the hell was that damned Simba? When would he break cover?

Mary Harp squatted beside him, trying to match her

shotgun's aim to his rifle, making no sound. Good girl, that. "Don't fire unless I miss," he whispered. Mary nodded, waiting.

So much for her, and Makhno—and Van Damm was somewhere uphill, coming down through the woods. Dammit, where was Easter?

He heard the sound of light but clumsy footsteps sneaking away through the woods beyond the hedge, heading toward the point.

Brodski swore under his breath. The girl's tactical sense was good, but she was making too damned much noise! Whoever it was had to hear her coming, and what then?

Jomo heard the approaching footsteps below, and smiled. So, Makhno did have a backup, one of the women, no doubt. This part would be enjoyable.

He waited until he could hear the steps directly downhill from him, then fired. A thump and a sound of crackling brush answered him. Got her.

Jomo slipped out of hiding and made his way downhill. A moment's searching found the girl sprawled in a tangle of eggtree fronds.

Why, surprise: she was white, a blonde in fact, quite young and good-looking. She'd make an excellent incentive for recruiting fresh troops, worth dragging along on the trip downriver. Jomo scooped up the limp body, settled the girl on his shoulder and continued on down the slope.

Van Damm heard the footsteps in the forest below him, and crept forward with care. There: the target came into sight ahead. It looked like Jomo, all right—and, dammit, he was carrying one of the girls on his shoulder. No clear shot, not at this range, not that he could guarantee to take Jomo without hitting the girl; nothing to do but follow, hoping to get closer.

And who was that now, flitting down the slope behind

him? Whoever it was knew how to move both fast and quietly in this forest. . . .

Flaming hells, it was Jane!

Jomo reached the riverside greenthorn hedge and paused a moment to wonder how he was going to do this. The hedge was thick, and he'd have to lift the branches. Best to put the girl down, drag her through behind him. He dumped her on the ground and bent over to shove his stunner under the hedge.

Then he heard running footsteps behind him. Before he could yank his stunner out of the hedge and whip it around, a booted foot caught him square in the rump and kicked him head-first into the greenthorn hedge.

Jomo flailed wildly in the thorns, trying to ignore the deep scratches. The stunner was snagged in the branches below; he abandoned it to scrabble for his pistol.

"Jane, get out of the line of fire!" yelled a voice from upslope.

Jane?! Jomo wondered, then thought to roll over.

For an instant he saw the big, stocky, blond-braided woman standing over him. In an instant's flash of memory, Jomo recognized her.

—A year ago, Docktown, just off the ship, walking away with all those slits in tow. The one who—

And then her shotgun blast stopped his mind forever.

DeCastro was sitting in the front room of The Simba, considering fate. His plan of consolidation had worked as well as anything else had on this planet, but now he was down to all of fourteen men, which was not enough to hold Docktown thoroughly in control. He had entrenched at his Golden Parrot Cantina and here at the ill-named Simba, but neither establishment had enough supplies to entertain customers. Business was not merely poor; it was dead. Jomo would not be pleased when he returned, and the object of his wrath was most likely to be one Tomas DeCastro. At least the elimination of the Reynolds agent was a plus.

Try as he might, he could see no way out of this. There was nowhere he could hide in Docktown. The next ship wasn't due in for seven or eight months. There was always the run to the wilderness, but survival required serious supplies, and there were no supplies to be had. DeCastro remembered the good days in his then-profitable little cantina, and hoped that Jomo might be eaten by a Tamerlane.

There was a distant but growing sound of boat-engines out on the lake. The engines grew louder. . . .

In fact, much too high-pitched for the *Last Resort*. DeCastro held his breath. The engines cut to silence.

There came a shout from the dockside, then nothing. The three Simbas in the bar looked at each other, nervously fingering their rifles, but DeCastro kept perfectly still. He would wait patiently: it would not serve to appear excited.

He didn't have long to wait. The front door flew back on its hinges, and the man who'd been watching the dock came flying through it, on his back. He hit the floor, skidded, bounced, and lay still.

DeCastro and the three guards stared at the sight for a few seconds, but when they looked back toward the door it was too late; five unexpected guests had already entered. They were carrying shotguns, all of which were aimed at each of the guards, two at DeCastro.

DeCastro had better sense than to move, save to raise an eyebrow. He recognized the man in the lead with the sack on his shoulder—Makhno, owner of the *Black Bitch*—and the CoDo "Specialist" Van Damm, but who was the gray-haired one with the cane? And who were those arrayed beside them, the black woman and the stocky blonde? He might have seen those men in Docktown, but never those women.

"Ah, *Capitan* Makhno," DeCastro ventured, "to what do I owe the honor of this visit?"

Makhno grinned. "To an encounter with Jomo," he said. "I have a message from him: move out of this place, right now."

DeCastro set his empty hands on the table. He asked, "And how shall I know, señors, that this message is from my employer?"

"He can tell you himself," said Makhno, stepping forward. He put the sack down on the table, then stepped back.

Suppressing a mad hope, DeCastro opened the sack. Jomo's head grinned up at him from its depths. It took effort for DeCastro not to grin back.

"A wise guest knows when it is best to depart," he said, smiling. "I shall retire to my beloved cantina and former status."

He got up from the table, not too quickly, and started toward the door. An impulse of generosity seized him. He turned to the nearest Simba and offered: "Señores, if you are seeking employment ..."

The Simbas made haste to follow him, the latter two remembering to pick up their fellow from the floor and carry him with them.

"That," said Jane, "was almost too easy. Let's bring the girls in."

But the girls needed no summoning; they came in, shotguns ready, eyes wide with hope. "Did it work?" they yelped. "Are we safe now?"

"Safe, and in full ownership of Harp's Place again," Jane smiled. "You'd better repaint the sign soon ... and perhaps you'd best put *that* on a stake outside the door, at least for a few shifts." She pointed toward the sack on the table. "It'll be good news."

The office of Harp's Place wasn't in bad state; DeCastro had left a sizable amount of cash behind, and had not messed the files. The stock was down to nearly zero, of course, but Makhno's announcement of the end of the boycott and Brodski's trade share would solve that problem.

"The girls own the place, fair and square. You run it with them, and protect them, and in return you and Van Damm share half the profits."

"No complaints, Jane," Brodski smiled. "A nice little retirement business for me and Van. . . ."

"I can imagine," said Jane, through pursed lips.

". . . Uhmm, you know, sooner or later CoDo will come. . . ."

"I know. With any luck, they won't bother me and mine."

"True, but remember, with CoDo comes the Fleet, and they'll favor old Sarge Brodski with their business. 'Trust in the thirst of the Fleet, and you'll die rich,' as the old saying goes."

"Perhaps they'll like to sample the local euphleaf, too—" Jane smiled, getting up. "Take care of yourself, Mister Brodski."

"No fear of that," Brodski replied, watching her go. Yes, he could predict a profitable future for Jane and Docktown—and himself.

One way or another the Fleet took care of its own.

From the closed hearing by the *Interior Subcommittee* of the United States Senate, 1 September 2073.

Mr. Bendicks: Why, exactly, does the Administration want to cancel the treaties with the various Indian tribes and transfer the reservations to the public domain?

Sec. Pendleton: Seventeen years of free movement between national entities, ending in 2065, resulted in thirty-seven million foreigners, uh, extranationals, holding permanent residency permits within the United States. Fewer than six million of those persons have applied for citizenship, and according to figures of the INS, fewer than eleven million are competent in the use of the English language. There are twenty-eight different newsfax publishing one or more times a day in the United States, in eleven different languages. Throughout the several

states, there are innumerable enclaves in which the
principal languages spoken are other than English,
notably Spanish, Portuguese, Russian, Chinese,
and Arabic.

Mr. Bendicks: Mr. Secretary, one of us has obviously misunderstood the other. Let me repeat my
question. Why, exactly, does the Administration
want to cancel the treaties with the various Indian
tribes and transfer the reservations to the public
domain?

Sec. Pendleton: If the Senator will be patient, I'm
coming to that.

Mr. Bendicks: Please do.

Sec. Pendleton: Not only the United States of
America, but almost every other developed, indus-
trialized nation on Earth, has such enclaves of
unrepentent extranationals making their social and
economic demands but unwilling to naturalize.
This administration has gone to considerable effort
and expense to absorb these non-American populations that make up more than eight percent of
our total population.

Yet we have other un-Americanized enclaves of
much longer standing. I refer to a number of the
Indian tribes. In the first seventy years of the twen-
tieth century, major progress was made in Ameri-
canizing these people. Some tribes lost their
languages entirely. In most of the others, many of
the younger people had limited or no ability to
speak their tribal language. Then, in the last one
hundred years, and particularly in the last seventy
years, this healthy trend has been reversed. The
children are taught the tribal language from
infancy. Most tribes have modernized their languages for twenty-first century use by developing

new words from old roots, or "adapting" American words by adding native prefixes or suffixes.

If we are to exert legal pressures on these recent immigrants to adopt the American language and culture, we must first eradicate these cultural regressions by the Indian tribes, who, after all, have been recalcitrant for a much longer time.

Mr. Bendicks: It's reassuring to know, Mr. Secretary, that we have you in there fighting to Americanize the American Indian. Now, let me ask one more time: Why, exactly, does the Administration want to cancel the treaties with the Indian tribes and transfer the reservations to the public domain? I'd like you to state it explicitly, if possible, for the record.

Sec. Pendleton: Senator, the unfortunate cultural recalcitrance of these Indian tribes is rooted in the reservations. The administration has no argument with Indians as a whole. The number who live away from the reservations is five times the number who live on the reservations. Twelve times if we include those who identify themselves as Indian or part Indian and as having more than one-eighth Indian blood, so to speak. The majority of these are from mixed tribal stocks—Cherokee and Kiowa for example, or Jemez and Acoma. They speak only English, and essentially have been assimilated into the mainstream of American culture. To remove the Indian populations from the reservations would result in the completion of Indian assimilation.

Mr. Bendicks: Thank you, Mr. Secretary. I presume you're aware of the proposals by the Bureau of Reclamation for the large scale pumping of desalinized water to a number of the western reservations, and the establishment of urbanization projects on them. No doubt reservation land would become very valuable then. Who do you suppose would profit from this, if the land was first taken from the tribes and then made available for purchase from the public domain by developers? . . .

THE COMING OF THE DINNEH

John Dalmas

The army landed at Lukachukai on February 6, 2075.
Also at fifteen or twenty other places on the Navajo Reservation. It was a Wednesday. Not that February or
Wednesday mean anything now; the calendar is more
complicated here. But I remember those things because
I am an old man. I forget yesterday, but I remember
well what happened long ago.

My wife and I lived at Mescalero, New Mexico, then,
but sometimes we did consulting, mostly on Apache reservations. Strictly speaking, the Navajo are Apaches.
Were Apaches. The Spaniards got the name Apache from
the Zuñis, who used it for all the Athapaskan-speaking
tribes that raided them. The Spaniards called the biggest
of those tribes "Apache de Navajo," Apaches of the
Fields, because they cultivated corn and squash. The
Spaniards never did conquer them.

If you know much about Indians, you might guess from
my name, Carl Boulet, that I didn't start out as Dinneh,
as Apache or Navajo. I'm a Chippewa-Sioux mixed blood.
My great grandmother told me that the French last name
came from one of Louis Riel's métis refugees from the
Manitoba Insurrection in the 1860s.

But that's not what you want to hear about. You want
to know what it was like to come in exile to this world,
and what it was like here in the old days. I will tell you

the best I can. I did not talk English for many Earth-years till you came here. Once it was my best language; I had three university degrees, and talked it like you do, better than Chippewa. Better than Mescalero. Now it comes forth differently, even though my words are English. That's because I have come to think differently, living as we do here.

The September before the army came to Lukachukai, my wife and I—her name was Marilyn—established a program in applied domestic ecology in several Navajo schools, on a trial basis. It is strange to remember things like that. I was a different person in those days. At the end of January, we went back to see how it was going. On February 6, she was at Window Rock while I'd driven up to Lukachukai the day before.

It was noon. I'd eaten lunch, and was in the gym shooting baskets with a couple of teachers. I have not remembered shooting baskets for a very long time. Then the principal hurried in. The army, he said, had just landed at Window Rock, and federal marshals had arrested the tribal government. Troops had landed at Tuba City and Dinnehotso, too; they'd probably land at every town on the reservation that day.

Just then it was snowing hard at Lukachukai, which may have been why they hadn't landed there yet. The men I'd been shooting baskets with didn't even look at each other. They started for the door. Lemmi Yazzi paused long enough to call back to me, "Maybe you better come too."

I hesitated for maybe a second, then grabbed my parka where it hung in the teachers' lounge and followed them outdoors. They scattered; I stayed with Lemmi and we trotted to his pickup; we got in, he lifted it on its air cushion, and we left the parking lot in a hurry.

"Where are we going?" I asked him.

"A place we've set up in the Chuskas," he said. "One of the places."

Instead of going northeast into the Chuska Mountains on the maintained road, he drove west a little way, then turned north on a small dirt road, not made by engineers but cleared through junipers and pinyons by stockmen, for their trucks. You couldn't see very far through the snow, which was fine with us. The snowfall thinned and thickened but never stopped. As we got farther north, the land grew higher, and the pinyon and juniper began to be displaced by ponderosa pine. And there the snow wasn't just today's new fall. There was snow left from before.

I worried about Marilyn. It sounded as if, at Window Rock, there'd been no warning. I wondered if I was doing the right thing to go with Lemmi Yazzi. But if she was interned at Window Rock and I was interned fifty miles away at Lukachukai ... I turned the radio on in the pickup and got the tribal station out of Window Rock. It was playing "America the Beautiful." In English. That made it real to me; the government had taken over.

We'd been warned, kind of. The summer before, a rumor swept the reservations all over the United States, that the government was going to start taking over and selling Indian lands and relocating reservation Indians.

Ten years earlier, hardly anyone would have taken a rumor like that seriously. But in '72, the Soviets had begun rounding up some of the Turkic and Mongol peoples in Asia and relocating them by force to a world called Haven. It was scary to read about.

Countries had been sending volunteer immigrants to Haven for years, and once, out of curiosity, I'd read up on the planet. Not in the newsfax, but in technical journals. Haven sounded like a bad place.

Some tribes, the Mescaleros and Navajos among others, had set up unofficial committees of resistance. Not that we thought it would really happen, but just in case. Hideouts were built or dug in, in hidden places in canyons and forests, and supplies were hidden in them. It was to one of those that Lemmi was driving us.

We were the first ones to reach it. It was two hogans topped with a foot of dirt and twenty inches of snow, on one side of a shallow draw, shaded by pines and firs. The hogans would be hard to see from the air, with the naked eyes. Maybe an instrument search would show them.

Until that day there'd only been a rumor, and the Navajo Reservation hadn't seemed like the place where the government would start. The Navajos were the strongest and most populous tribe, and most of their land was poor. The White Mountain and Mescalero reservations had much better land. And the Nez Perce; even the Pine Ridge. I suppose the government decided that if they took the strongest first, and relocated its people, the other tribes would lose heart and do what they were told. I used to wonder if that's how it worked out.

Within forty minutes there were ten of us in the two hogans. Everyone but me had clothes stored there, and boots, and a rifle. I was lucky to have worn boots that morning instead of oxfords; the weather forecast had given me that. And two of the pickups had rifles racked in them, so there was one for me. I didn't know who I would worry with an old .30 caliber Winchester hunting rifle. Two infantry riflemen had more firepower than the ten of us.

Of course, the idea wasn't to get in fights anyway. It was to make little armed demonstrations, get on the television and in the newsfax, and get the American people on our side. That had been the strategy of the Indian rights movement for more than a century. But the government was paying less and less attention to the people.

It stopped snowing that night. Meanwhile the government had shut down all the tribal radio stations, and Navajo language programs on other stations, and banned any mention of what was happening. We tuned in Gallup, Flagstaff, Farmington, and Holbrook, and they never mentioned that anything was going on.

The guys I was with talked it over. They decided to sit tight and take it a day at a time. If we didn't hear anything tonight, maybe we'd send out pickups in the morning to visit the nearest groups. Maybe we could work something out.

No one asked my opinion; I wasn't Navajo. I wasn't

any kind of Apache—any of the Dinneh, or Tindeh . . . the *people* in the Apache languages. I was originally from the Red Lake Reservation in Minnesota, where the country was soggy muskeg instead of timbered mountains or rough, stony desert. I'd married a Mescalero, learned the language, and done my Ph.D. research on them. Also I spoke pretty good Navajo. But I wasn't really one of them. Not then. I even had enough European genes to give me blue-hazel eyes. But if they had asked my opinion, I'd have gone along with what they thought best. I had nothing myself to suggest. I was no chief then. I was an educator.

As it turned out, the army came to us, at about 3:30 in the morning. I suppose their instruments picked up the heat from our stovepipes, even though we kept very small fires. They'd have taken us entirely by surprise, except that I had waked up and had to urinate, so I pulled on my boots and went out of the hogan. And heard the soft, rumbling hum of landing craft settling into a meadow in the woods—what the Spanish and Anglos in the southwest call a *cienega*—a hundred or so meters downslope. I went into both hogans and woke everyone up.

We fooled them; we fought. It seemed unreal then that we'd do that. It seemed unreal to the army, too; that's why we did as well as we did. Some of us didn't even take time to lace our boots, just wrapped the laces around our ankles. The others strapped on snowshoes and went down the draw toward the *cienega*. I didn't have snowshoes; I just waded along the best I could in other people's tracks.

The troops were in no hurry. They were still in the *cienega*. They'd unloaded from the two light landers, I guess a platoon of them, and were forming up to move on us.

None of us had a night scope, of course, but the soldiers weren't wearing camouflage whites, and there was moonlight. With the snow cover, it was easy to see them. But it was too dark to use the sights on our rifles. We just aimed down the tops of our barrels and started to shoot from behind trees. We had time to shoot two or three rounds each before they started shooting back, but when they did, it was the most frightening thing in my life, before or since. It sounded like four hundred rifles instead of forty. I could hear bullets hitting tree trunks and rocks, and branches falling off the trees above and behind us. They fired for about half a minute, I guess.

Then they stopped, and started moving forward. Someone said later that they'd gotten orders through headphones in their helmets. They were to take us prisoner if they could, and they thought they'd intimidated us; thought we were ready to quit, and I was. One or two of our people started shooting again though, so the soldiers did too, and then the rest of us did. I shot two or three times more before Lemmi yelled to cease fire and surrender. After a few seconds, the soldiers stopped shooting again, too. They came up and arrested all of us. A few started to beat us with their rifle butts, but their sergeants swore at them and made them quit. We'd shot a few of them—I heard we killed three—and the rest were pretty mad. Five of us had been shot, and two were dead.

Another lander came down in the *cienega*, and they loaded us and took off. They didn't stop at Lukachukai. They flew us straight to Window Rock, where they'd set up a fenced compound with army field shelters, just for guerrillas, and mostly still empty. The other Window Rock internees were kept in the community college and high school auditoriums, and the livestock-judging pavilion.

The field shelters we were in didn't have any power cells in the heaters, so they seemed pretty cold, especially for sleeping. Especially when we lay on our cots in summer-weight sleeping bags, shivering and looking out through the transparent roofs, seeing stars through holes in the clouds.

Actually, most of us didn't know what it was to sleep cold. Not then.

The army let us know about our families—Marilyn was at the high school—but they kept us segregated. We were guerrillas. I never thought of myself that way, but we were. They kept bringing more people to the guerrilla compound, some of them women. This went on for several days. The Navajo Reservation is bigger than some states—about the size of West Virginia—with a thousand canyons, a thousand ridges and mesas, and a lot of its people live out among them on isolated ranches.

The army didn't know who or where the guerrillas were. So they waited for attacks, and killed or rounded up the attackers, and checked out little ranches for groups of men with weapons.

Quite a few White Mountain Apaches had driven up from the Fort Apache Reservation—seventy or eighty at least—and maybe forty or fifty from the San Carlos, connecting up with the Navajos they'd contacted earlier, through the committees. The police and the army didn't try to keep them from coming. Maybe they wanted them to come and get rounded up; they probably thought that those who came would be the hardcore resistance on the other reservations, and they'd get them now instead of later. There were also twenty or thirty Jicarilla Apache, and nine who came all the way from Mescalero in a van, expecting to get arrested and jailed on the way. There was even a work van load from the tiny Yavapai Reservation, mixed-blood Apaches and Yavapais who spoke only English.

Those numbers are not exact. I've estimated from hearsay, and from how many ended up in the guerrilla compound. The nine Mescaleros are the only ones whose starting number I learned exactly. Four of the nine were killed or hospitalized, or maybe escaped to hide out somewhere; the other five were interned with us.

The compound got more and more crowded until, after eight days, more troops arrived. Not the U.S. Army this time, but CoDominium Marines. Russian-speaking. Someone said the army wasn't happy about having to do that job, and that the whole thing had gotten out. Soldiers had told their families on the phone, also the news-fax and television, and the government couldn't pretend anymore that nothing was going on.

Then shuttles landed at the Window Rock airfield and they started loading us. I was lucky: I got a seat by one of the windows. After a few minutes we lifted, moving upward and outward till the rim of the Earth curved blue and white against black, and still outward till the curvature was strong. If I'd had a better view, I could have seen the Earth as a great beautiful ball. Finally, out beyond the outer Van Allen Belt, we docked with a converted freighter waiting to take us to Haven. I was feeling pretty bad; I thought I'd never see my wife again. But before they finished shuttling people up, they'd brought all the internees, Marilyn included, and we were together again.

The *Alexei Makarov* was not a Bureau of Relocation ship. It was a tramp ore carrier on contract to Kennicott. They'd put in temporary facilities in the cargo holds, to take immigrants on the return trip. We slept in stacks of narrow bunks, used long common latrines, and ate standing up.

At the start there were 2,436 men and boys, and 1,179 women and girls, thirteen years old or older. There had been more than three hundred younger children with the internees, but someone in the government got them taken away before we shuttled up. The woman in charge of taking them said they'd be settled with people on Earth; that conditions on Haven were too extreme for young children. That didn't help the children born aboard the *Makarov*. And it wouldn't help those who'd be born after we arrived on Haven. Or their mothers.

One of the first things Marilyn told me, when we got together, was that she'd started getting morning sickness while she was interned; we were going to be parents. She didn't know what that meant. I did—I'd read about childbirth on Haven—but I didn't tell her.

Meanwhile there were more than 3,600 of the Dinneh

living in badly crowded conditions on the *Makarov*. I got the numbers from George Frank, the Navajo Tribal Chairman, who was the prisoner in charge of prisoners. He was the man responsible to the marine commandant for our organization and behavior. Bad colds broke out as soon as the *Makarov* left orbit. Practically everyone got one, and quite a few went into pneumonia. The marine medics didn't have facilities to handle relocs, so only those whose condition was recognized as critical got taken to the clinic. Eleven died. We thought that was pretty bad. We'd learn later what bad really was.

George organized the Navajos according to clan, and the rest of us by tribe. Although I was only adopted Mescalero, the Mescaleros made me their spokesman because I could speak Navajo pretty well. From the start, most of the Apaches could pretty much carry on a conversation with each other, including the Navajos, each speaking his own dialect. But Mescalero is less like the others, and at first the Mescaleros had trouble understanding and being understood. And no one felt like speaking English; we felt betrayed by the English-language government.

More and more, the Navajos included us in. All of us were Dinneh, George said—we were all "the people."

It was the Russian language that complicated things. Like all Americans, we'd taken Russian in school, and the Russian marines and crew had all taken English, but not many on either side could understand what the other said very well. You had to talk very slowly and keep it simple. Marilyn was an exception. Her MA at the University of New Mexico had been in Native American Languages, but as an undergrad she'd had two years of Russian, on top of the three required years in grade school and a fourth year by choice in high school. So she was our spokesperson with the Russians, who liked her because she used their language so well.

Most of the Russians were all right. Whatever prejudices they had didn't include one against American Indians. But there wasn't anything they could do about too many people in too little space. It was always too hot in the hold. Water was rationed, and there weren't any showers. We could only wash once a day. After a while the holds smelled pretty bad. The food was poor and monotonous, but it nourished us all right, and on two meals a day, fat people lost weight.

To help pass the time, we'd sit in groups and tell stories. People would tell books they'd read, or movies they'd seen, or places they'd been, or they'd make up stories. At first only a few people would tell stories, but pretty soon more and more told them. Also we slept a lot. George set it up so everyone had a chance to do aerobic exercises once a day, in small groups. Most people did them—it was something to do—and it proved to be a good thing. But it did make it hotter in the holds.

Marilyn got to know the marines' liaison officer, a woman lieutenant named Toloconnicov, who gave her a little book about Haven. It frightened Marilyn to read it. It didn't sound as bad as the technical articles had, but I didn't say anything. We'd find out when we got there. It might not be as bad as I expected.

Something more surprising came from her friendship with Lieutenant Toloconnicov. One day the lieutenant gave Marilyn an envelope, and waited while she read what was inside: a formal invitation in English for both of us to have supper with the marine commander, Major Shcherbatov. Marilyn told the lieutenant that we'd like to go, but we hadn't had a shower or washed our clothes for nearly five months. The lieutenant wrote us a permission to use showers in the sickbay, and said there'd be clean clothes for us there.

It felt good to shower and put clean clothes on.

The major had been stationed in eastern Siberia for a couple of years, and gotten interested in the Chukchi people there. From that he'd gotten interested in American Indians, so he had lots of questions about the Navajo. When he learned that not all of us were Navajo, he had questions about the other Apache tribes, and the

Chippewa, and Sioux. We had supper with him twice, and talked for about three hours each time.

Marilyn asked him questions about Haven, but he claimed he didn't know much about it. I didn't believe him. He picked up his wine glass when he said it, which kept him from having to look at her. It didn't make me feel any better about what we'd find there.

It took the *Makarov* more than thirteen months to reach Haven. In that time we received four different series of shots, broad-spectrum vaccines to keep us safe from disease on Haven, as safe as possible. Also, Marilyn gave birth to a boy. We named him Marcel, after my grandfather.

The week before we entered the Byers' System, George said he didn't feel qualified to be chief on Haven, and proposed Tom Spotted Horse, a retired marine master sergeant in his forties. The council agreed, so Tom was our chief. He organized us into squads, platoons, companies, and battalions, and made sure we all knew what we belonged to. We picked our own officers and sergeants. That was tradition, and Tom didn't know most of the people.

A few days before we landed, Lieutenant Toloconnicov gave Marilyn a military topographic map of the district where we were supposed to land. Marilyn let me look at it before she took it to Tom. The latitude was subtropical; on a planet known for its cold climate, that was hopeful. The top half of the map showed the south part of a plateau that broke away into badlands. South of the badlands was a basin with the word *desert* on it. There were no towns or roads, but the plateau had a few thin broken lines with the words *livestock driveway*, and across it in large letters, the word *KAZAKHS*. The Kazakhs, I knew, were a people in Asia, and I remembered reading, years before, that a tribe of Kazakh traditionalists, herdsmen, had gotten the Soviet government to sponsor a Kazakh colony on Haven. This must be where it was.

An X had been marked on the plateau with a marker

pen. The only reason I could think of for that was, we were supposed to be put down there. I went with Marilyn and told Tom what I'd made of the map; he listened, and then made me his technical aide.

The next day, forming up to load into the shuttles, most of us were feeling glad to be getting there at last. Even I was. At least I'd know what we were in for. Instead of putting us down where the X was, they put us on a mesa isolated from the plateau by broken lands. Lieutenant Toloconnicov said the major was responsible for that. He believed that if he landed us at the X, the Kazakhs, who were armed, would attack us and make slaves out of the prisoners they took.

Then she marked on the map the mesa she thought we were on. I looked around. The ground cover looked a lot like bunch grass, shin high, with bearded purplish seed heads moving in a light breeze. Low shrubs were scattered around, mostly about knee high and stiff looking. It didn't look too bad.

We were told to unload some cases from the shuttles. Some were labeled *rations,* some *blankets,* and some *tents.* One small heavy case was unmarked. Lieutenant Toloconnicov said the ship's captain was going to keep the stuff, and not give it to us, but the major was in charge of us, and didn't let him. She told us this was all that the government had sent along for us here. She sounded apologetic when she said it.

When all the people and cases were on the ground, Toloconnicov gave Marilyn a package. She told her, "This is a personal gift to you and your husband from Major Shcherbatov. It is not to be opened till we have left." I think the lieutenant knew what it was, but we didn't ask.

On the ground, Tom assigned some people to start opening the cases and counting what was in them. The rations were marine field rations in individual packets, one meal per packet. The blankets were military, too. The tents weren't modern, individual field tents, but old, obsolete squad tents, too heavy to carry. To carry them, we'd have to cut them up, if we could find anything to cut them with.

When the shuttles lifted for the last time, we all stood and watched them get small and disappear. It felt very final. We felt abandoned, which was how we needed to feel. The CoDo Marines had given us every treatment they had to protect us from disease, but the Bureau of Relocation had left us to starve or freeze, or be enslaved.

Tom's supply crew kept opening cases. The unlabeled case solved the problem of how to cut up the tents; it held 500 trench knives in sheaths. Only 500 knives for more than 3,000 people, but we were lucky to have them. Then, privately, Marilyn opened the major's gift package. It held a big, 10 millimeter revolver in a holster, also a cleaning kit, and two boxes of ammunition, 100 rounds in all. That and a little kit for starting fire by compression. She gave the pistol to me.

There we were, 3,600 people, with blankets that still had to be counted, some old tent fabric for shelter, food for a few days, some knives, and one pistol. There was no store to go to.

It could have been much worse. It was summer. Also, the ship's captain hadn't been allowed to leave us with nothing at all. Before the shuttles had brought down the last of the people, Tom had sent out scouting parties to look for water and anything else useful. They didn't find any.

And it was almost hot, warm enough to sweat. The things I'd read had emphasized how cold Haven was. But there *was* summer, a long one. And when the sun is up for more than forty hours at a time, heat can build. I thought it might be early afternoon. The sun was high, but not as high as it should be at noon in the subtropics.

I told Tom what I thought. He squinted at the sky, then looked at me. "Forty hours between sunup and sundown? There was something about that in the little book your wife showed me, but a lot of it was confusing. Do we get forty hours of night, too?"

I'd known people like Tom: Intelligent, but only what they saw around them was real. Information about space or other planets was just noise. "It's not that simple," I told him. "This world is a moon. The planet it goes around, Cat's Eye, is big and hot, hot enough to glow in the dark. When Cat's Eye is up, we'll get both heat and light from it. When it's up but the sun's down; we'll have what's called 'dimday.' It will get cooler during dimday, but not as cool as during truenight." It also seemed to me that the sun would move around irregularly in the sky, because Haven circles Cat's Eye while they're both going around the sun. But I didn't tell him that.

He looked thoughtful, which was much better than if his eyes had glazed over. He was getting used to a new "here and now."

"It's complicated," I added. "We'll learn what we need to by experience." He nodded. Then the last of his scouting parties came back and told him they hadn't found any water. Nobody was surprised, up on a mesa like that.

"We'll go down into a canyon," he said to me. "If there's water to be found, that's where it will be. After we've found water, where do you think we should go? Down into the desert basin, or up on the plateau?"

"The plateau," I said. "We're going to need a lot of food, soon, and the Kazakhs up there are herdsmen. We need to steal some livestock from them. But they're armed, and they're supposed to be fighters. It will be dangerous."

His attention drew inward for a minute, then returned to me. "I'll send a raiding party to the plateau. Do these Kazakhs live in large bands or small?"

A raiding party. The Navajos had known about things like that, 250 years ago. Now— Now I wondered. "I don't know," I answered.

"We'll have to go and find out," he said.

He told his scouting parties to find a way down off the mesa into one of the canyons that flanked it. A way that the women could hike. The canyon needed to have good water and be one that men could climb out of, up onto the plateau. When the scouting parties had left, he went to see how the crews were doing cutting up tents to make shelter pieces. I went with him.

It seemed to me we were lucky to have Tom Spotted Horse as our chief. He sized up problems, made decisions, and gave orders like a marine sergeant.

The sun moved as slowly in the sky as you might expect on a world with forty hours between sunup and sundown. Tom's scouts had found two possible ways to leave the mesa. He selected one, then got the rations, blankets, shelter pieces, and pieces of tent rope distributed among the people. They made packs out of them. Then he formed them up in their units and we started down the trail, with scouts leading the way. The sun seemed almost as high as when the shuttles had left, a little more than three hours earlier by my watch. There were eight rations for each person—that was all we had—and no one was to eat until Tom ordered a meal break.

It didn't pay to think too much about things; you could go into despair. We had to make a decision and do it, and handle the complications as they came up. Or lie down and die. The Dinneh weren't known for lying down and dying.

We didn't have nice backpacks from Wilderness Suppliers. We rolled up our rations inside our two blankets each, wrapped them in a piece of tent cloth, tied it all together with a piece of tent rope, and slung it over a shoulder. Also there were a lot of people—almost all the women—who'd been interned wearing street shoes. Their feet were soon in trouble. Those who wore riding boots or engineer's boots were just as bad off. A few tried to go barefoot, but they put their shoes back on pretty quickly. Marilyn was wearing stout, low-cut walking shoes, but gravel and sand got in them. We took turns carrying Marcel. I offered to carry her pack for her, but she wouldn't let me. She said it would make her look bad to the Navajo women.

The canyon we worked our way down into was about seven hundred meters deep there, according to our map, and the way was steep, treacherous in places. It wasn't like hiking the Bright Angel or Kaibab Trails down into the Grand Canyon in Arizona. Those were surveyed, improved, and maintained—almost manicured; I suppose they still are. This was rough, untracked and uncertain. Much of it required scrambling instead of hiking. And we had people, especially women, who'd never hiked in their lives. Some weighed more than a hundred kilos, even after thirteen months on the *Makarov*. For them, the trail was hell; for some it was impossible. Twice we got cliffed out and had to wait while the scouts hunted for a way to continue. Then we all had to backtrack a ways before we could go on again. Once a scout fell to his death. We also lost eight people who fell when rock slid away beneath their feet and they couldn't stop sliding before they went over an edge.

All the scouts saw goatlike animals. One scout came face to face with something that looked much like a large mountain lion, with thick fur and a ruff—our first cliff lion. It backed away and disappeared when he yelled and threw a rock at it; it had never seen anything like him before.

The plants didn't look so unearthly either. I know now how strange some of them really are, but the strangeness wasn't conspicuous. It looked a lot like some canyon might in Arizona. There was a thing like grass with sharp leaves that cut when you touch them, and another with leaves that stung and burned like nettles, but quite a bit worse. Also there was something that gave people a rash; we needed to find out what it was, so we could avoid it.

The geology was different than I was used to. The rock strata seemed to be volcanic from the mesa top to the canyon bottom; there was nothing I recognized as sedimentary. Most of the strata were basalt; some were vesicular.

Even most of us who wore hiking boots had blisters by the time we reached the canyon bottom and buried our faces in the icy creek we found there. Lots of feet were raw, with bloody socks.

The hike down had taken us seven hours by my watch. I'm told some were still straggling in five hours later, and a few never made it, even with help.

Tom Spotted Horse was one of the first ones down. As others got to the bottom, he gave orders about sanitary practices, and had the people spread out along the creek. They could eat one ration each. During breaks along the trail, he'd had the platoon leaders find out who were the survival hobbyists—those who'd learned and practiced traditional survival skills. Now he sent them out to find material and make fire starters. Marilyn gave him the fire starter from Major Shcherbatov; it could serve to start fires till we had our own. She also gave him the little book about Haven.

Almost all of us took our shoes and boots off, and Tom had platoon leaders check on whose feet weren't too bad. All I had were a couple of blood blisters on the ends of toes, and blisters on the tops of my little toes, from walking downhill. They weren't very sore. Of the men with good feet, he assigned two hundred to be a raiding party. I'd shown him my pistol, so he made me one of them, assigned as an aide to Nelson Tsinajini, chief of the raiding party. Nelson and I already knew each other; we'd talked aboard the *Makarov*. He'd served in the infantry, making sergeant, and I'd done two years of ROTC at the University of Minnesota for the financial aid.

I didn't like to leave Marilyn and Marcel, but I knew if anything happened to me, they'd be taken care of. There were lots more men than women among us.

Nelson's orders were to go up the canyon, climb onto the plateau, find livestock, and drive them down to the people. Even Haven's day wouldn't last forever, so we were to leave right away. No one knew whether it would be too dark to travel in the canyon after sundown.

No one knew if it was possible to herd sheep or cattle down from the plateau, either, assuming we were able to steal some. We didn't even know for sure that a man could get up there from the canyon. But we didn't have any choice. If we failed, the people would starve.

We started. The top of the plateau wasn't much higher than the mesa top, but the hike was uphill. Judging from what I'd read, the partial pressure of oxygen on top was probably about the same as at 5,000 meters on Earth. That made breathing about as hard as on the Tibetan Plateau. We'd all been living at 1,800–2,500 meters on Earth—1,830 at Mescalero, I remember—but we'd just spent thirteen months on a ship with the oxygen pressure about like on Earth at sea level. So we spent a lot of time stopped, sucking air through our mouths and sweating. When we stopped for real breaks, Nelson would ask questions about Haven.

The afternoon sun didn't get down into the canyon bottom, which ran pretty much north and south, so it wasn't very hot, but the hard work made us sweat. I was glad we had a creek beside us most of the way, to drink from. I was also glad that the gravity on Haven is only 0.91 Earth normal.

Most of us were in our twenties or late teens—I was almost the oldest at thirty-four—but even so, some of them got pretty sick, probably what they call altitude sickness on Earth. On top of that, a Jicarilla named Juan Cruz, up in front a ways, was charged and badly bitten by something that looked like a short-jawed crocodile. It would have killed him right there, but two Navajos started hitting it with big rocks. A couple of the rocks they couldn't have lifted ordinarily. Cruz's right leg was almost torn off at the knee, and he lost a lot of blood before we got it stopped with a tourniquet. He looked more gray than brown. Nelson assigned three guys who'd been having altitude sickness to take him back to the people.

It seemed to me he'd never make it. I'd read about land gators—that's what the first settlers had named them. They're a kind of hibernating, warm-blooded version of the komodo dragon on Earth. Usually if one of them bites you, you get blood poisoning.

It was dusk in the canyon when Nelson and I climbed over the lip and onto the plateau. We were damp with sweat, but the air was already getting cold. The sun was setting when the last men reached the top—the last of the 182 that made it that day. There were others strung out behind for maybe a couple of miles, too sick to go on. It was pretty flat on top, and the vegetation was a little different than on the mesa; there was less grass, and quite a lot of a knee-high shrub. Here and there were small patches of a bigger shrub, chest high and with lots of thorns.

We had no way to make fires, and a raiding party in unknown territory shouldn't have fire at night anyway. So we paired up for sleeping, two guys huddled together, with two blankets and a tent cloth under us and the same on top. Nelson was my partner. Most of us had been picked up as guerrilla, and had gloves, winter caps, and jackets in our bedrolls. We wore those too. I could have used some water, but the nearest we knew of was a mile and a half back down the canyon.

Nelson assigned sentry duty, two men on a shift, using watches that were either luminous or would light up. It gets dark fast at that latitude, especially where the air is so thin. It was already deep twilight when we lay down, and in spite of the hard lumpy ground, I was asleep in a few minutes.

The first time I woke up, it was with a leg cramp. I scrambled out of the covers and walked it off, being careful not to step on anyone. It was dark, and through the thin, clear air, the sky was beautiful. It was also cold, and I was cold. When the cramp was gone, I walked out beyond where the men were sleeping, and urinated, then looked at my watch. I'd slept for two hours. That was the longest single, undisturbed piece of sleep I'd have that night. The rest of the night I drifted in and out of dreams and half-dreams. Even asleep I was aware how cold it was, and while I didn't get another cramp, my legs felt strange. They wanted to squirm. Also my thighs and buttocks were stiffening up from the hiking. It was impossible not to squirm and jerk, and Nelson was as bad as I was; maybe worse. Huddling together for warmth, we were closer than Siamese twins, which made the squirming and jerking even worse. Add to that being thirsty. . . . We weren't used to being so cold and thirsty. It got worse as the hours passed, and I was awake more and asleep less.

Even so, dimday took me by surprise. I'd dozed, and slept through the rising of Cat's Eye. It made a kind of dawn, and the gas giant loomed above the horizon, looking big! A lot bigger than the moon does on Earth. It was a thick crescent of reflected white, and in the cradle of the crescent, the rest of it glowed a dull, banded red, about as bright as the coals in a campfire. I could see a long way across the plateau top now, though not details; it was a lot lighter than full moonlight.

I nudged Nelson Tsinajini. "Nelson," I said, "it's morning."

He grunted, uncurled a little, and half sat up to look around. "Some morning," he said, and shivered. "When does the sun come up?"

I looked at my watch; it was about ten hours since we'd laid down to sleep. "In about thirty hours," I told him. He swore in English; Nelson preferred English for swearing.

I could tell from the thickness and direction of Cat's Eye's crescent about where the sun was on the other side of Haven. It agreed with what my watch told me. "Is this as light as it's going to get till then?" he asked.

"It should get lighter," I told him. "Cat's Eye should go through most of the phases before sunup. It ought to be pretty light out when it's full."

"Well shit!" Nelson groaned, folded back the covers, and got up stiffly. "We might as well get started," he muttered, and looked around. Then, changing to Navajo, he shouted, "Everybody up!"

It took a couple of minutes. When everyone was on their feet, Nelson made us all run in place to warm up.

It helped some. He took his knife and cut thorny stakes about a meter long from the biggest pieces of shrub wood he could find, and pushed them in the ground to mark where the trail was, out of the canyon. Then he had us roll our packs, keeping a ration out inside our shirts, and we started to hike again, away from the rim. He said we'd eat after we warmed up more. It seemed to me it must be near freezing, and I suspected it wouldn't warm up much, if at all, till sunup; it was more likely to get colder. After walking for about ten minutes—I remember that; I still had the white man's habit of looking at my watch—we came to a pool, and Nelson called a halt so we could drink and eat.

He was quiet while we ate. When we were done, he called three squad leaders over. "I'm going to hold most of us here," he told them, "and send your squads out to explore, to see if you can find where the livestock is.

"Frank, I'm sending Carl here with you." He put his hand on my shoulder. "Carl is Chippewa, adopted into the Mescalero, but he talks good Navajo. He's reservation raised, in Minnesota. And he knows things about this world; he read a lot about it, back on Earth. He knows when the sun will come up. And he has a gun, a pistol, in case you run into trouble."

Frank nodded. Frank Begay was the only man in the raiding party who was older than me. He'd been a medicine chief. Too bad I would never get to know him well.

"Take another ration each," Nelson said, "but leave your bedrolls here. I want you back when it's time to sleep again. At the latest."

One squad went along near the rim toward the west, another to the east. Frank's squad, eleven with myself, went straight inland. When Cat's Eye is only a crescent, Dimday isn't a good time for long-distance seeing, but if there were sheep around, we'd hear them farther than we could see them anyway. We'd hiked for nearly an hour and a half when we came to another pool. It looked shallow, but was about a hundred meters across, and

around it were lots of tracks that looked like sheep tracks.
As we walked around looking, we found pony tracks, too,
and tracks as big as cow tracks, but longer and narrower,
like young moose. I told Frank about muskylope, and
that some people on Haven had learned to ride them,
and use them as pack animals.

We looked at the trail where it left the pool. Frank
Begay had worked sheep all his life, and he said it looked
like a big band—about two thousand. They were going
east. We didn't see any dog tracks with them. Frank
decided to split the squad. He'd take five men with him
and follow the sheep. The rest of us would backtrack the
sheep and find where they came from. We were to keep
going till we either found the place, or for five hours,
whichever came first. If we found it, we would learn as
much as we could about it and then come back to the
big pool. If both halves weren't back in twelve hours,
the half that was back could go to Nelson Tsinajini and
report.

He put me in charge of the half squad I was with. He
said we were all Dinneh now, that the government had
made us all one. And that Tom and Nelson both had
confidence in me. One young Navajo didn't want to be
under me, so Frank changed him to his half and gave
me Cody George. Then we left.

I'd set my watch to zero on the stop watch mode, and
we backtracked the sheep trail for almost four hours
when we saw up ahead what looked like a long wall or
fence. By then it was lighter; Cat's Eye was still a crescent, but it was getting thicker. So we got down on our
hands and knees and crawled; the low shrubs would
make us hard to see.

What we'd seen was a fence made by uprooting and
piling the big thorn bushes. On the other side of it were
shaggy cattle, and I remembered reading that the Kazakh
colonists were going to take yaks with them. Yaks from
the Tibetan Plateau, that could stand severe cold and
thin oxygen. We followed the fence in more or less the
direction we'd been going before, west, and pretty soon

we could hear someone yelling up ahead, not an alarm, but as if he was yelling at the cattle. Closer up, I could see what looked and sounded like a young boy. He had a grub hoe, and seemed to be chopping some kind of plant out of the pasture. There was a gap in the fence, with only one big thorn shrub in it to block it, and when a cow would get close to the gap, the boy would yell and chase her away.

It wasn't just yelling; it was words. I was pretty sure it wasn't Kazakh. Kazakh is a Turkic language. This one sounded Indo-European to me. It reminded me of what Lieutenant Toloconnicov had said about the Kazakhs using slaves, and something I'd read about Balt and Armenian indentured laborers being shipped to Haven. If he was a Balt or Armenian, he'd probably learned Russian and English in school, so I could talk to him. He'd also probably not feel any loyalty to the Kazakhs.

I told my men to stay where they were and lie low, then moved to the gap in the fence and crawled through past the shrub that blocked it. Mostly the herdboy's back was toward it, so I crawled toward him on hands and knees, slowly, easily, making no quick movements. When I got closer, I could hear him talking to himself, as if he was angry. The hoe was a kind of grub hoe, and looked too heavy to be a good weapon, unless he was really strong. When I was about forty feet away and he still hadn't seen me, I rose up and started for him in a crouch, still quietly, only rushing the last few feet. I don't think he knew I was there till I was on him. Then I hit him from behind, throwing him down and landing on him. He didn't really struggle; I was surprised at how thin he was inside his sheepskin cape.

"Don't yell," I told him, in slow, distinct English. "If you're quiet, nothing will happen to you."

He didn't make a sound.

"Come to the fence with me," I said. "I want you to answer questions about your masters." Then I let go my hold on his head and got off him.

He half turned over so he could look at me. And
stared. "Are you—American?" he asked.

"I'm an American Indian," I told him, and watched
his eyes get round. He must have seen old American
movies back on Earth. "We don't have slaves," I added.
"Those we admire, we adopt into the tribe as warriors."
I'd seen some of those movies too. Sometimes they
weren't even all nonsense. He nodded, then picked up
his hoe, and together we trotted to the fence, he looking
back over his left shoulder as if for somebody coming. I
looked too, and saw something I hadn't noticed before.
I should have. By the light of dimday, I saw low buildings
humped in the distance. They looked like a large set of
ranch buildings.

Crouching by the fence, I asked him, "What were you
watching for?"

"Amud," he said. "It is his shift to keep watch on the
herd. He just went to the—ranch, for tea. He'll be back
soon, and if I'm not chopping puke bush, he'll beat me."

"We'll watch for him then," I said, and began to ask
about the ranch and the people there. His eyes were
gray, and looked too big for his thin face, but they flashed
with anger, and once I got him started, he talked without
urging. All I had to do was steer. His name was Janis,
he said. Most of the Kazakhs had left two truedays earlier—maybe 120 hours as I figured it. They had taken
the sheep to summer pastures. The lambs were now old
enough to be out during the cold of truenight.

Sometimes there was no truenight between truedays;
there was just day, then dimday, then day again. Sometimes there'd be a short truenight, with dimday before
or after. But now and then there'd be a long truenight,
and even in summer it would freeze hard then. The
waterholes would freeze over, and wet places would
freeze on top like concrete.

There were fifty or sixty Kazakhs with this ranch. Fifteen or sixteen of them were still here at their year-
round headquarters. There were also eight indentured
laborers—seven Latvians and a Russian—whose contracts

the Kazakhs had bought from the Bureau of Relocation. Indentured laborers were the same as slaves. Three of the Latvians were women or girls, and two of them were pregnant by Kazakhs. Their babies would die because the air was so thin, Janis said, and maybe the mothers. The Kazakhs didn't care enough about them to take them to Shangri-La for birthing. Besides, Kazakh women were supposed to arrive from Earth, later in the year, brides for the stockmen.

Of the Kazakhs still at the headquarters, three tended the cattle here in the pasture, one on a shift. Six tended the horse herd. The rest looked after the headquarters. Those not on duty would be sleeping or loafing.

And yes, they were always armed. They carried a short, curved sword and a pistol. Those out tending herds, like Amud, also carried a whip and a rifle.

That was as far as Janis had gotten when I saw someone riding out from the buildings. "He's coming," I said to Janis. "Stay here. Pretend you're napping. When he comes over to beat you, I'll kill him. I have warriors with me. We'll kill the rest of the Kazakhs, take their cattle and horses, and free your people. You can come with us if you want."

Then I crawled back past the gate bush and hid myself behind the hedge, to wait where I could see Janis through the gap. Two minutes earlier I'd felt confident. Now my guts felt tight and hot; it all seemed like a terrible mistake. Nelson had told us to scout; we were to learn, come back, and report. What I was planning to do was kill fifteen or sixteen armed Kazakhs and steal their cattle and horses. With five men, a boy, and only one gun—three guns if we got Amud's. Maybe I could still change my mind, sneak away and go back to the main force.

But Amud would whip Janis, and Janis would probably tell; he would feel betrayed. And— Did the Kazakhs have radios? Could they call in the crews from their outstations? Or police from somewhere, or marines?

The Kazakh rode up on his shaggy pony and uncoiled

his whip to wake Janis. I shot him in the chest, and he fell off his horse like a sack. The pony was well trained; he hardly moved.

I waved to bring my five men to me, and we crawled through the gap. The sight of his dead ex-master didn't bother Janis; he looked excited. The Kazakh was armed, as Janis had said. I gave the boy the sword, gave the Kazakh's military rifle to a Navajo named Arnold, and the pistol to Cody George. Then I told all of them what I wanted them to do, and nobody argued. They all looked as if they thought I knew what I was doing. After I'd put on the Kazakh's sheepskin cloak and cap, I got on the pony, helped Cody get on behind me, and told Janis to follow alongside. The others went back through the gap to do what I'd told them.

The ranch buildings were low and mostly oblong, and their roofs were rounded. They were made of construction flex, but riding up to them, you couldn't tell, because thick outer walls of sods had been built around them for insulation, and thick sods had been laid on the roofs. Their windows were small, and there weren't very many. Besides the finished buildings, there was almost a village of small round buildings nearby that weren't finished yet, for when the Kazakh brides arrived. The flex walls were up, and there were piles of turf waiting to be set.

Janis was skinny but tough, and used to the thin air. He'd jogged alongside me and had had breath enough to talk and answer questions. There was no radio at the headquarters, he'd said. That was hard to believe of volunteer colonists, and I still half expected to see an antenna on a roof, but all I saw was a windmill. The breeze had died, and the windmill wasn't moving. As we rode up, there was a smell I would come to know as the smell of dung fires. Somewhere a compressor was thudding; probably they had a power pump for water when there was no wind. I drove the pony with my left hand and kept my right inside my cloak, holding my revolver, in case anyone came out and saw that something was wrong.

As I rode in among the buildings, I could see a building with a lean-to on one side. A corner of the building was in the way, but I could hear a hammer clanging on iron; it had to be the smithy. The smith was Russian, Janis had told me, an indentured laborer whom the Kazakhs had given privileges. Janis didn't like him, perhaps because he had privileges, or maybe because he was Russian.

Janis pointed at one of the largest buildings, next to the windmill. "That's where the Kazakhs live," he said. Then he pointed at another: "And that is the horse stable." He started toward it, as I'd instructed him. His hand was inside his long cape, holding Amud's short curved sword; his job was to kill the stable boss, a Kazakh with an arthritic hip, and get his gun and sword.

A Kazakh came out of an outbuilding and crossed to another, not fifty meters away. He never paid any attention to Cody and me; I suppose he was used to everything being all right. Janis saw him too, and pretended he was going to another long building, maybe a lambing shed. Cody and I got off the pony just outside the door of the Kazakh bunkhouse, and I looped the reins around a hitching rail there. Then we walked in.

The door opened into a fairly wide, shallow room with pegs around the wall for cloaks and wet boots. It would keep cold air from rushing into the rest of the house when the door was open. Then we went through the inner door, my eyes sweeping around. It opened into the main part of the house, which was mostly one big room with sleeping robes around the sides, and at one end a kitchen not separated by a wall. There were men sleeping, and three men around a blanket in the middle of the floor, playing some game. We started shooting at once, first at the men gambling, then at others as they rolled to their feet from their beds. The two women working in the kitchen were screaming. There were six men there, and we shot them all, right away.

"Cody," I said, "go outside and see if anyone's coming." I hoped no one had heard the shooting through the thick walls. While I reloaded my pistol, I walked over to the women, talking Russian at them the best I could. They'd already quieted. Both of them were naked—the Kazakhs kept them that way—and one looked about six months pregnant; I don't think she was sixteen yet. I'd read the Koran; these Kazakh settlers weren't very good Muslims.

"Where do they keep their rifles?" I asked.

Both women began talking at once, then the young one quieted. The older woman was pointing toward a corner of the building. In that room, she told me, also in Russian. One of the men we'd shot would have the key on his belt. Carrying a butcher knife, she went with me to look for the key. After we looked at a Kazakh, she would slash his throat, even if he looked dead. She was a little bit crazy.

We checked out the three by the blanket without finding the key. I took the holstered pistol from one of them and put it on my belt as a spare. Then I heard two shots outside, not loud at all through the sod walls, and I ran over and opened the outer door, just enough to see out. Cody was crawling out from under a big man in shirt sleeves, and there was a hammer lying on the ground. The blacksmith, I decided. Cody was having trouble getting free; it looked like one of his arms might be broken. Then a Kazakh came running around the corner of a building, and I shot at him and missed. He ducked back out of sight. Cody didn't come to the bunkhouse like I thought he would. Instead he ran into the building across the way, which would let him find targets of his own. There was more shooting, I couldn't see where.

From where I was, I could only see in one direction, and it didn't seem like a good idea to go out. Besides, one of us needed to be here and hold the armory with its rifles. Back in the main room, I saw the older woman opening the armory door. The pregnant girl had put on a pair of pants from a dead Kazakh and was buckling on his pistol belt. I could see a ladder fastened to a wall, and a trapdoor above it in the roof. From the roof I'd be able to see around. But first I needed to see the armory and get a rifle. I couldn't hit much with a pistol except up close; with a rifle I could reach out.

In the armory were rifle racks, one of them almost full. I took one, an obsolete military model, and checked to see if the magazine was full. It was. I took two spare magazines from an open box, put them in a deep pocket in my Kazakh cloak, and went back out of the armory. The pregnant girl was standing by the inner door with a pistol in her hand, as if waiting for someone to come in from outside. I called to her to be careful, to kill only Kazakhs.

Then I went to the ladder and climbed it. The trapdoor opened below the roof ridge on the side away from most of the buildings. I could hear some shouting, but no shooting, and crawled to the ridge on my belly. From there I could see across the buildings and into the horse pasture on the far side. One of the herdsmen on shift was just sitting his horse about four hundred meters away, about as far as I could make him out by dimday. He seemed to be looking in my direction. There should have been another one, but I couldn't see him.

That's when I heard three shots below, in the bunkhouse, two of them almost at the same time. I stayed where I was, hoping that the women would take care of things down there. There was more shooting from a building near the horse stable. A Kazakh ran out, stopped around the corner of the door and waited, pistol in hand, as if he thought someone might follow him out. I raised my rifle and aimed as well as I could, given the distance and the light. Then I squeezed off a single round, and he fell. No one shot at me, and it occurred to me that if a Kazakh saw me, he might not be sure I wasn't another Kazakh.

Another one came trotting toward the bunkhouse, half bent over, also holding his pistol. There was another advantage for us: Except for herdsmen on shift, probably none of them had a rifle with him. I shot him down, too, and someone shot twice in my direction, someone I hadn't seen. One bullet hit a sod near my face and threw dirt on me, so I crawled back and rolled to my right a couple of meters, then moved back up just enough to peek over and see someone running from a shed and into cover behind another one.

It looked as if he was going to get around behind me. For just a second I thought about going back down through the trapdoor, but what good could I be there? I needed to be where I could find targets. So I stayed where I was. If someone did get around behind me, he wouldn't be able to see me from close up because of the eaves, and maybe he couldn't shoot well with a pistol.

One place I couldn't see at all was the ground close in front of the bunkhouse. Then I heard more shooting from inside. Right after that a window broke, as if someone wanted to get in that way. I knew the windows were double paned, because there was a sash at the outer end of the window hole and another one at the inner end. They'd be hard to crawl through. Then there was a shot from somewhere across the way, and I heard a yell of pain from in front, by the window. It had to be Cody that shot him—Cody with what I had thought might be a broken arm.

Right after that there were three quick shots from behind me, pretty far away—rifle shots, I thought. I didn't hear any bullets hit. From the corner of my eye I saw someone run from a building toward the Kazakh I'd shot near the stable. I didn't think it was a Kazakh; it was someone without a cap, someone baldheaded. He bent as he reached the Kazakh, just long enough to pull off his pistol belt and pick up his gun, then he shouted something and ran inside. I decided he must be one of the Latvians.

What happened next might have been from someone seeing my breath puff in the chilly air. There was a short burst of rifle fire, and one or more bullets hit just in front of me. One went through the sod, hit the flex below, and glanced back up through the sod again to knock off the Kazakh cap I was wearing. Then I heard feet trotting as if coming to the bunkhouse from in front, so I rolled over the top, and with someone shooting at me again, I slid down the other side feet first, to drop off the edge. It wasn't a long drop, less than two meters. My feet hadn't hit the ground yet when I saw the two Kazakhs, and when I landed, I emptied half a magazine in their direction. They both fell, and I ran to the outer door of the bunkhouse, hearing more shooting, and the dull thud of slugs hitting sod-covered flex.

I was in the cloakroom, panting as if I'd run a hundred meters, before I remembered the women. I called to them in English. "Its me! The American." But I still didn't try to go through the inner door. Instead I did some quick mental arithmetic. I'd killed a Kazakh in the cow pasture. Then Cody and I had shot six more inside. And I'd shot one near the stable, and two just out front. And Cody'd shot at least one other. That made eleven, eleven of, say, sixteen. And there'd been other shooting. How many were left? Had the women killed any?

So I called out, "How many from outside did you women kill?" The answer came in Russian: "One." So there shouldn't be more than four Kazakhs left, it seemed to me. Just then there was more shooting outside, and I stood beside the door, listening for whatever would tell me anything. After awhile I heard someone, Janis, call out in English. "Indian!"

I answered without showing myself: "Yes?"

"I killed two, and I don't know where there are any more. Some of my friends have guns now. What should we do next?"

"What about the herdsmen with the horses?"

"We just shot one of them. I don't know about the other."

That might have been the one who'd been shooting at me. "Get his rifle," I called.

"We already did."

Janis said he'd killed two, and then they'd shot a horse

herder, unless Janis had counted the herder as one of the two. There could hardly be more than two Kazakhs left to fight here—maybe none at all. I'd just told myself that when there was a shot from inside the bunkhouse, then screaming, and more shots. I went inside to see. It was the pregnant girl that was screaming, lying on the floor, while the other woman was swearing—it sounded like swearing—and emptying her pistol at a window in the other side of the bunkhouse.

I turned and ran out, around the corner of the bunkhouse, then around the back corner. Behind, crouched below a window but looking right at me, was a Kazakh. I don't think he knew what was happening, even then; he probably thought it was all a slave uprising. If he'd shot right away, he could have killed me. Instead I killed him with another short burst.

I stood there panting and shaking for a minute, till my mind started to work again. Then I replaced the magazine in my rifle. Was there another Kazakh? Or had we shot them all?

I went back to a front corner of the bunkhouse and called out in Navajo: "Cody! Are you all right?"

He called back to me from somewhere. "All right except for one arm. It may be broken. The blacksmith hit me with a hammer."

Another voice called in Navajo. It was Arnold, the man I gave the rifle to in the cow pasture. "Boulet! Where are the Kazakhs?"

"Most of them are dead," I called back. "Shot, anyway. Maybe all of them. Have you seen any?"

"Just one. He's dead now. He rode past me without seeing me. It was impossible to miss."

"Janis!" I called in English. "I think we've got them all. Let's be careful not to shoot each other now. But keep an eye open, in case one of them is still running around."

Actually there were four still alive, all of them wounded and out of action. We dragged them into the bunkhouse to leave them there.

We had thirty-six horses and about eighty cattle. Yaks. I was only a fair horseman, but four of the five Navajos, all but one who grew up in Flagstaff, were pretty good, and had herded livestock before. Four Latvians said they wanted to come with us. Another had been killed, and the pregnant girl had been shot in the chest. She'd gone into premature labor from the shock, and her breath came in and out of the bullet hole, making bloody bubbles that smelled bad. I was pretty sure she'd die soon, and so was she. The older woman said she'd stay with her. I think she probably killed the wounded Kazakhs with her butcher knife, after we left. She really hated them.

None of the other four Latvians—one a pregnant woman—had ever ridden a horse. The Kazakh ponies were well trained, but they thought that whoever was on their backs should know how to ride. Also, the Latvians didn't know how to control them, so the ponies took advantage of them, giving them trouble. Finally Cody made them double up, two to a horse. The added weight sobered the ponies up, and also made less for us to keep track of. It would be up to the Latvians to stay with us or follow us.

We all had guns now, a rifle and two pistols each. We also put a saddle or pack saddle on all the spare horses. Three of the Navajos knew how to load a pack saddle; they loaded the spare rifles and pistols, and all the ammunition boxes and swords, on pack horses. Also we filled the waterbags and canteens we found there. Then, with Navajos running the show, we headed east, driving the cattle ahead of us. The spare horses trailed behind, tied in a string.

We went slowly. We didn't know how these cattle would act if we hurried them, and with Cody injured, and two of us not as skilled on horseback as we needed to be, there were only three men qualified to handle the herd. We'd traveled as fast earlier, on foot.

There was time to think about the fight. How had we

won at so little cost? The Kazakh's had outnumbered us and had many more weapons. But they had suspected nothing. Even after we began attacking them, they didn't know what was happening; probably they thought they faced only their slaves. It wasn't warrior skills that won for us, or virtue, although their own evil treatment of their slaves had allowed us to attack them and win.

If we had fought them in other circumstances, it would have been different. The Kazakhs had a reputation as a tough people, and those who went with the herds almost lived on horseback. I remembered reading about the Kazakhs who wanted to be colonists: they were traditional herdsmen from the dry steppes around Lake Balqash. Probably they'd grown up in the saddle. I also remembered my reading on biogeography: wolf packs still ranged there; the herdsmen had probably grown up with guns, too.

Reading about them, I'd felt affinity with them. They had wanted to continue their way of life in freedom. Now I knew them and didn't like them anymore.

When we came to the big water hole where we'd separated from Frank Begay and his five men, Cat's Eye was swollen, gibbous, and dimday seemed about as light as a stormy day in Minnesota. I had not ridden for almost two Earth-years before, and my buttocks were sore from the saddle.

We'd had water to drink, from canteens, but we stopped to let the animals drink. One of my men rode eastward on the trail, the direction that Frank and the others had taken, to see if he could find sign that they'd returned before us. Then he came back, shouting that at the edge of vision, in that direction, he'd seen dust raised by animals. Either a herd was being hurried, or some Kazakhs were coming fast on horseback.

I took charge again at once, and told the men to get the herd moving toward the canyon. "Get them started," I said, "and drive them at a run! Get the pack horses there too! Nelson may need the guns!"

The three skilled Navajos began at once; the rest of us helped as well as we could. Even the Latvians tried. They'd been keeping their seats better than at the beginning, but now, as we began to hurry, and to harry the cattle into a gallop, one of the Latvians fell off his horse, and the others seemed likely to. One of them, the bald-headed man, shouted in their own language, and they stopped their horses. All but one, the pregnant woman, got off with their weapons. Looking back over my shoulder, I saw the other three lie down behind bushes. Their ponies stood by till one of the Latvians got up and charged at them, shouting. Then the ponies wheeled and started after the rest of us.

It seemed that the Latvians were going to sell their lives to kill some of their ex-masters. It wasn't easy to ride away from them, but we had to get the herds, the cattle and horses, to Nelson Tsinajini, so he could drive them down the canyon to the people. We'd sell our lives afterward, if we had to.

As the herd began to gallop, they raised a cloud of dust. The Kazakhs would notice, and come after us. Probably they'd seen Frank and his men scouting their camp, and killed or caught them. None of Frank's people had more than a knife. Maybe the Kazakhs had even made one of them tell.

I dropped back a little and to the east, out of our dust cloud to see. I could make out the dust cloud the Navajo had seen, maybe a kilometer away now, or a little more. The horses would run faster than cattle; the Kazakhs would gain on us if they wanted to. And as they saw our direction, they could cut the angle, and save distance.

I hurried and caught up with the others. Cody, riding with his one good arm, was leading the horse string past the cattle, with one of the other men harrying them from behind, to get the extra guns to Nelson. Behind me I heard gunfire, and for a minute I didn't know what it meant. They hadn't come to the Latvians yet. Then I realized: the Kazakhs had had prisoners with them, some of Frank's men, probably tied onto horses. And the prisoners were slowing them up, so they were dumping them off and shooting them.

How far had it been from the canyon break to the big pool? More than an hour and a half on foot through bunch grass and dwarf shrubs; seven or eight kilometers. Could we get there before we were caught? Surely the horses would, and the rifles, but would the cattle, and those who were driving them? I heard another flurry of shooting that quickly increased. The Latvians! How many Kazakhs would they kill, the three of them? Would the Kazakhs stay long enough to kill them all, or were they exchanging shots in passing, hardly slowing? Did they know how important a few minutes were for us?

The other Latvian, the one who had tried to stay with us, fell off her horse. I saw her trying to get up as I passed; it looked as if she was injured. For a minute I thought of circling back and picking her up, but my horse would slow too much, carrying two, and I was needed. I felt guilty anyway. I slowed a little and looked back. She had turned, lying on her belly looking back down the trail. Her rifle was unslung; she was ready for the Kazakhs. I speeded up again.

Soon the cattle began to slow. They were tiring. I told myself I should have tried to rescue the Latvian woman after all, but by then she was a kilometer back. So I rode out to the side again, away from our dust, to see how close our pursuers had gotten. It wasn't as bad as I'd feared; their horses had been running longer than ours. But even so, they were more than a dust cloud now; they were objects. Soon, even by dimday, they would appear as men on horseback. I decided to stay to the side. If it seemed they would catch the herd, I would drop back and begin shooting at them from the flank. Perhaps I could lead some of them away.

But not yet. We still might reach Nelson Tsinajini before we were caught, and some of his men would have guns by then, and be on horseback.

There were more shots, but they lasted only seconds. They'd come to the Latvian woman. Not long after that they began to shoot at us, just a short burst now and then. They could hardly be aimed, that far away in dimday, and there was little chance they'd hit one of us. It would be a waste of bullets to shoot back, and I'd have to stop. Or else shoot backwards, twisted in the saddle. I looked forward then, past the herd, and saw men coming on horseback. We were getting close; these had to be some of Nelson's men coming to help us. We closed fast, and in two minutes they were passing us, four of them, with more in sight ahead. Almost at once the four began to shoot at the Kazakhs, veering off to both sides. The Kazakhs would either have to stop, or split up, or run a gauntlet of rifle fire.

Then I felt my pony flinch, stumble a little, and begin to limp. I didn't know if he'd been hit, or stepped in a hole, or what. I reined him to a halt and jumped off. He stayed, obedient to his training, so I ran from him, throwing myself down behind some dwarf shrubs for cover.

The Kazakhs were coming up, maybe a dozen of them. Most would pass a hundred meters away, but one veered off toward my horse. He must have known I'd be somewhere near it. I shot at him almost face on, but his horse's head must have gotten in the way. It went down, and its rider unloaded from it even as it fell, landing on his feet but unable to keep them. He tumbled, rolling, and then I couldn't see him anymore. The others passed, paying no attention. I shot at the two hindmost, and one of them went down too, horse and rider crashing.

I started crawling, to get farther away from my horse.

Three more of the people were coming. Of the four who'd already come, I could see none, only three horses standing, moving in little circles. The Kazakhs swerved toward those who were coming. There was a lot of shooting, and when it was over, those three of the people were gone too, shot off their horses. There were nine or ten Kazakhs left. It seemed as if they shot more accurately from a running horse than we did.

I had crawled some more. Now the Kazakhs looked as if they weren't going to chase the people anymore. They gathered in a loose group two or three hundred meters away, as if talking to one another. Then they separated, and went to round up the horses they could see standing around. I started crawling on my belly again, till I came to a couple of big thorn shrubs. There I put a fresh magazine in my rifle. If one of the Kazakhs came close, I'd get up and shoot him, then shoot as many more as I could.

I got pretty cold, lying there on the ground. After a little while, when nothing had happened, I got to my knees. I saw the Kazakhs trotting off with some spare horses behind them. My horse was gone. When they were too far to see, I got up and went to look for the one whose horse I'd shot, who'd landed on his feet. I couldn't find him. I started walking toward where the people should be, and the cattle herd.

They had left the small water hole, and on horseback and foot were herding the cattle into the head of the small arroyo that grew to become the canyon. I was in time to help them. When all the cattle were in the arroyo, headed downward to where the rest of the people were, the armed men brought up the rear, in case some Kazakhs came. I was with them. Nelson saw me, and we talked. He'd heard what had happened, heard enough of it to know I was responsible. He said I was truly one of the Dinneh, a spirit from the old times taken flesh again.

When we got to the main encampment, we kept going, taking the herd down to the desert basin below. The Dinneh followed. Eighty head of cattle were not enough to keep the people; we needed many more. Tom Spotted Horse was still the chief, and he chose men to go back and get more livestock. Especially sheep—a big band of sheep that could be distributed to many people. I was one he chose. Half the horses and most of the rifles went with us. The other horses were used to scout the desert while we were gone, and the people were told to explore, to try eating every fruit, every seed, every root, every small animal. Quite a few people got sick and died. That was how we learned what was food and what was not. A few died the first time that truenight lasted forty hours, a night as cold as winter. Over the next few Haven days and nights, those who did not really want to live, died.

We brought almost fourteen hundred sheep down from the plateau. Pretty soon a force of Kazakhs came to punish us and take back their livestock. They used the same canyon we had used, but we had left men behind with rifles, to watch from side canyons. When the Kazakhs passed by, they followed them, and when truenight came, they crept into the Kazakh camp from up-canyon. The Kazakhs had sentries out below but not above, so our warriors went in among them and killed some of them in their sleep, with knives. Each time they killed one, they put his rifle in the stream. By the time an alarm was raised, about a dozen of the Kazakhs were dead. The rest left, went back up to the plateau. By then they would have seen that we were many people, and wouldn't know we had only the rifles we'd taken from them. Afterward we took their rifles out of the stream and cleaned them the best we could. The ammunition we had, we hoarded in case the Kazakhs came back.

After that we traveled for quite a while, slowly, driving our herds. Till the weather started to get colder. We wanted to be far from the Kazakhs, and perhaps find better land. Meanwhile we learned to make bows and arrows, and spear casters, and bolos, and learned to use them. We learned to drive muskylope into box canyons, where they were trapped.

Quite a few of the women who gave birth that first year died, and most of the newborn, but that was only part of it. We got so worried about the women that Tom Spotted Horse said only the men should eat unknown things. But that was too late for Marilyn. She died of a poison root. Then Marcel was killed by a tamerlaine, and for a time, I wished to die also. In the first long Haven winter, more than half of the Dinneh died from cold and hunger—mostly men. The women were given more food than the men were, and each woman was allowed to take more than one husband. Tom Spotted Horse said we would not butcher more than half our cattle, or more than half our sheep. For the rest of our needs, we had to use what the land had to offer. Some of the Dinneh wanted to have a different chief, but the council said that Tom was right. They said that any group that wanted to leave could leave, and take their share of the livestock with them, but if they left, they could never come back. So no one left.

That was a long time ago. Tom Spotted Horse was killed in a rockfall, and I was named "master sergeant," which is what the Dinneh had come to call their chief. Me! A Chippewa-Sioux mixed blood, chief of the Dinneh! I have lived through fourteen winters on Haven, and I am old. There aren't many left of those who came here on the *Makarov*. I think we get old faster here. I remember reading that there are minerals in the water on Haven that gradually poison you. For a time it seemed that the Dinneh might die out, so many died and so few infants lived. But some lived, and the yaks lived, and many of the sheep, which were also Tibetan. The horses had almost as much trouble birthing as the women, and we learned to ride the muskylope. Now we number 873, last count, which is up again, and our herds and flocks are large. We have found a lower valley where we take our women when their term is near, and mostly they live. Their mothers were ones who lived. The breed grows stronger.

The young people think this world is good. Except for the Kazakhs, years ago, you are the first outsider we've seen since the shuttles left us on the mesa. The CoDo Marines have never found us; I don't think they ever looked; I don't think they care. We may be here forever.

The lights in the viewing room dimmed, and the officers from the Bureau of Relocation shared final satisfied looks with the executives of the advertising agency.

This screening was being held for their very special guest; seated in the center of the auditorium was Edgar Paulsen, the representative from the CoDominium Information Council. Paulsen was a pensive, ferret-faced bureaucrat who frowned a lot without ever telling anyone what was bothering him. Most people who dealt with him considered Paulsen an easily distracted, even absent-minded man, which was a very grave mistake. In fact, he was certifiably brilliant, and if his moods and expressions changed rapidly, it was because he routinely summoned up complex problems he needed to deal with, brooded a moment, solved the problem in his head and moved on to the next one.

Paulsen was here today to review the latest effort

from the public relations department of BuReloc. Flanking him were Brian Callan, the junior BuReloc executive who had commissioned the ad spot, and Scott Saintz, senior partner of the Saintz-Raddison agency, which had produced it.

Neither man took the ad too seriously; BuReloc was not a public enterprise. As a CoDominium entity, its powers exceeded the constitutional authority of any nation where it operated, and it operated everywhere. Still, public resistance to BuReloc "excesses" was on the rise, and something needed to be done.

The result was the thirty-second holo-spot being premiered today in its final form. The project had been arduous, since Paulsen's office had insisted on location shooting and complete physical accuracy. Over the past year, Saintz-Raddison's people had worked closely with BuReloc execs, traveling throughout the CoDominium for locations, and the two offices had developed good working relations. Today's screening was as much a wrap party for them as it was a presentation for Paulsen, and they were all looking forward to the celebration that would follow.

Paulsen blinked slowly and nodded to Callan, a signal that he was ready for the film to begin.

Before them, the screen shifted spectra from neutral blue to a star-field dappled black, onto which came the bulk of a sleek CoDominium cruiser. The narration began just as the main thrusters of the CoDo ship came into view, and the camera angle swiveled around the gleaming ship.

"The new frontier."

Callan leaned over and whispered to Paulsen: "The narrating voice is performed by a computer-generated combination of three actors of the late nineteen-nineties; each voice was chosen for its qualities of recognition, sincerity and strength."

Paulsen nodded slightly and answered, as if

speaking to himself: "It's like listening to the cloned child of Mister Rogers, James Bond and Darth Vader." Without knowing it, he was two-thirds correct.

"This is the challenge that awaits humanity here, today, at the dawn of this new age," the inhuman voice assured its audience. The sincerity aspect was important for the public, but it was wasted on the BuReloc and Saintz-Raddison people; they knew what was being sold here.

"Centuries of strife have ended, to bring us to this golden era of peace on earth."

"Hasn't seen the tapes of the food riots in Tokyo this morning, has he?" another dark figure in the darker room asked. His companion chuckled.

On the screen, the camera's point of view had pierced the hull of the cruiser, and now moved down spacious corridors where people in coveralls moved purposely about undefined tasks, passing one another on opposite sides with crisp waves and cheerfully determined smiles.

A BuReloc woman in the audience snorted. "If this was shot on a CoDo ship, they used dwarfs for actors."

"It was." The Saintz-Raddison woman beside her finished lighting two ganjarettes and handed her one. "And they did." Their laughter sparkled, their smiles in the darkness reflecting tiny red pinpoints of light from the smoldering tips held carelessly before them.

"And these are the people who will shape this golden era, the people who will make this age-old dream a reality."

"If they can ever learn to wake up without screaming," a Saintz-Raddison man said, and the viewing room erupted into laughter.

Drowned out by the mirth, the narration continued: *"These are the men and women of the new frontier, whose bold spirit of adventure and dedi-*

cation to the future will literally win worlds for them and their children."

The camera's point of view had moved onto the cruiser's bridge now, and looked out a viewscreen that would make the one on which it was projected look like a postage stamp, had it ever existed. But it was pure fiction; the bridges of CoDominium cruisers were not built for the view. In the mythical viewscreen, a blue-green sphere loomed, graphic enhancements (and probably subliminal encoding) making it a hundred times more appealing than any tiresomely familiar snapshots of the blue-white old maid that was Earth.

"For this frontier is a place where all the old freedoms are alive and well." The voice paused, which was a mistake.

"Freedom to bleed, freedom to starve, freedom to die in childbirth, freedom to sell your daughters for scotch." The BuReloc woman was giggling as she counted off the points on perfectly manicured nails. Eventually she lost her composure, and her friend hugged her to stifle gales of laughter.

The camera pulled back to show a farmwork-hardened colonist straighten up over his hoe to stretch luxuriantly, and regard with pride the open fields, evidently his, that stretched on for miles.

"And where a man can have all the land he will ever need."

The entire audience, pushed to the brink by the past few minutes' comments, erupted into guffaws and howls of amusement.

"Yeah, a six-foot plot!" Callan couldn't help himself; the film was a huge success, and the party had apparently started early.

The camera panned up, into a starlit, indigo sky, and the Great Seal of the CoDominium faded into view, with the narrator's tag line:

"The CoDominium's Bureaus of Colonization.

Renewing the dreams of our forefathers, every day."

The lights came up as the laughter died down, the audience composing itself as its constituent members tapped out notes on datapads, chuckling to the person next to them.

"Oh, boy, that's great stuff." Callan pushed his glasses up on his nose as he entered figures for minimum police strengths required for the next days' round-up in London's Trafalgar Square. A rally to protest Britain's acceptance of Bureau of Relocation aid in various social programs would allow a vast number of English-speaking colonists to be gathered and send a clear signal to the rest of the United Kingdom. The police would be CoDo, of course; had to keep it non-partisan. And best to draw them from the Russian half. It would do everybody good to remind the world that the old bear still had teeth.

He looked across Paulsen to see Scott Saintz wearing a pained smile as he listened to Paulsen.

"But, Mr. Paulsen," Saintz was explaining, "you must understand; our people spent a long time on those CoDo ships and colonies. They're just blowing off steam."

Paulsen was shaking his head. "I still don't see what's so funny."

Saintz's gaze flickered to Callan in a clear plea for help.

"Is there a problem, Mr. Paulsen?" Callan asked neutrally; he liked Saintz, but surviving unexpected disapproval by superiors was the hallmark of the successful bureaucrat.

Paulsen shook his head again. "There's nothing wrong with the film; it's an excellent piece of work. I'm just puzzled by the reaction of Mr. Saintz's people. And yours too, for that matter, Mr. Callan."

Callan had to choke back a laugh of his own.

"Ah, yes. Well, Mr. Paulsen, in any public relations venture, a certain amount of embellishment is always necessary, to—"

Paulsen cut him off. "Embellishment?"

Callan's mouth was open; he shut it with an audible *pop*. What was Paulsen saying? That he *believed* conditions on all CoDo ships were like that? That all CoDo *colonies* were like that? Had Paulsen somehow missed the open secret—that those ships were, in fact, claustrophobic steel coffins bulk-freighting human refuse to backwater wastelands, pausing only long enough to jettison their miserable cargo, leaving them to scrabble for survival or die, and heading back to pick up another load of forced deportees?

Paulsen began closing up his own datapads and—an incredible anachronism—paper notebook. "It's a very good advertisement, gentlemen," Paulsen said. "Very good indeed. I see no reason to withhold Bureau of Information approval for its distribution."

Paulsen stood, looking down at them as he rebuttoned his jacket. "We've a lot of work ahead of us in the years to come. These riots and round-up measures are effective, from a bulk point of view. But the best colony worlds are getting the best citizens. BuReloc's getting the dregs of humanity, and that simply won't do if we're to build real worlds out there." Paulsen looked back at the blank screen, his smile almost wistful. "Something like this will encourage the brighter ones who can't afford citizenship on the better colonies to take a chance on the more marginal ones."

Callan was frowning, puzzled. "Excuse me, Mr. Paulsen; but what kind of person even remotely worthy of the the term 'bright' would willingly go to a place like Tanith, or Folsom's World, or Haven?"

Paulsen shrugged. "Oh, someone who saw your

ad and thought it a transparent lie. Someone who
thought they could go to those worlds and organize
a union, or form a political party." Paulsen smiled
down at him, and the dithering bureaucrat's tone
was so innocently matter-of-fact that Callan was
chilled to the bone.

"You know the sort, Mr. Callan," Paulsen concluded. "Troublemakers. *Smart* troublemakers have
always been the most difficult to deal with produc-
tively. But Professor Alderson's contribution to
society has changed all that. My sincere congratulations, gentlemen," Paulsen shook their hands as
he prepared to leave. "This film is going to be a
big help."

Callan watched Paulsen walk up the aisle.
Saintz was next to him, babbling in relief at his
ad having been approved. "Boy, that was a close
one," Saintz said. "I thought we'd lost the account
for sure. Times are tough in the ad business these
days; seems people change their agencies like they
change their socks."

Callan nodded distractedly. "Everyone is expend-
able, after all. That's what BuReloc's all about."

Saintz didn't respond to that one, just excused
himself to join the other celebrants. Callan sat
looking at the blank screen for a long time.

Politics of Melos

SUSAN SHWARTZ

It is desirable to be free if you can. It is natural
that the stronger power will subject the weaker.
These are not matters of right or wrong but of
logic, cost, and benefit. *The Limits of Empire*, Benjamin Isaac (Oxford University Press, 1990).

Maenads' shrieks from Lilith, dedicating a song to
"brothers, sisters, and citizens!" tore through Wyn
Baker's lecture yet again.

"You must think of the Fifth Book as more a dialogue
than a history," she said anyhow. "Think of two speakers,
a voice of Melos and a voice of Athens."

"Equality now. EQUALITY NOW!" brayed from a
bullhorn in the square below.

Eight thousand students disentangled themselves from
bottles, borloi, and each other to bellow agreement. Then
electronic guitars and keyboards clamored, and Lilith
shrieked once more.

A few notetakers, clustered near the front of the hall,
recorded her statement. No doubt they were intent on
grades, on winning scholarships they hoped would lift
them from Citizens' status to a post like hers: visiting
scholar and Personage. Wyn was too well controlled to
wrinkle her nose. She had, she knew, her tenured chair
because her family had endowed it generations ago, long

before people were divided into Taxpayers and Citizens. She had been born near the top of her world and had dutifully thanked God for that, for good health, and a powerful mind.

People like her might teach in a university in taxpayer country, fiscal and intellectual aristocrats. These days, the best a Citizen-turned-scholar might hope for was a position as major domo, a kind of nanny for adults who wanted culture on the hoof. And did she do well to encourage them?

"Awright, bros and sisters. We're gonna bring you a golden oldie from way-way-back-when. '*Be true to your school*—' For the People's University of Los Angeles!"

Another orgasmic scream from the students lying on the green four floors below. Hell of a way to have to teach. Her mind fleeted longingly to the dark wood and stained glass of Harvard's Memorial Hall.

Her colleagues would laugh at her if she gave up and went back in mid-semester. *"What did you think, Wyn? That you could pretend you were doing settlement house work? This is LA, not Phillips Brooks."*

No matter. It was her duty to teach them, and no Baker or Winthrop (her father had wanted two sons) shirked duty. "Think of it as tri-v, in which characters . . ." she had wanted to say "disclose and reveal themselves" but she revised fast . . . "tell you how they feel." Her voice sounded reedy even to herself, lacking all conviction against Lilith's passionate intensity.

"Two voices," Wyn had lectured. "The voice of Athens, harsh, authoritative . . . 'For we would have dominion over you without oppressing you, and preserve you to the profit of us both . . .' and the voice of Melos, a lesser state threatened with war unless it paid tribute . . . paid a bribe not to be attacked. 'But how can it be profitable for us to serve?' "

Outside, an amplifier malfunctioned. The bleeding electronic scream forced a groan from the protestors. The students nearest the window flinched.

That did it. Never ceasing her practiced flow of

speech, Wyn stepped down from her platform, stalked
to the window—her soft-soled shoes and long, jogger's
stride eating up the distance—and reached for the catch,
which hadn't been closed (or cleaned) in years. In the
grimy surface, she confronted herself: tall, with what
would have been a scholar's stoop if she permitted.
Cropped, pale hair and an old suit that firmly resisted
the Angeleno craving for the new and violently colored.

Wyn exerted the strength that forty summers of tennis
and sailing had built into her arms and forced it closed.
Amps, Lilith, and protestors faded to the sea-roar of a
conchshell held to the ear.

She thought of black ships, armored Athenian marines
landing at Melos and ringing it. Hopeless, hopeless, as
the Melians knew; hopeless to lecture at these students;
but she read out the passage anyhow. "Men of Athens,
our resolution is none other than what you have heard
before; nor will we, in a small portion of time, overthrow
that liberty in which our city hath remained for the space
of seven hundred years since it was first founded." And
more hopelessness in their counteroffer—"But this we
offer: to be your friends, enemies to neither side."

To her surprise, the students nodded. But then, they
knew from gang warfare: to be neutral was to be dead.

"Think of it as if it were today," Wyn said, her voice
falling out of the trained, platform speaker's cadence she
had learned almost as soon as she was allowed to join
her parents at the dinner table or their friends when they
sat at night and argued. "Of the people out there, who
is Athens, and who Melos?"

The Sovworld? The CoDominium with its marines and
its expatriates and its weight of distrust? Or her own life
in the rearguard of privileged Cambridge? *Answer that
yourself*, she ordered herself, and came up with no
answer. She wondered what answers her students might
have, if they dared to speak, or bothered.

Heads raised from the desks, and the notetakers laid
down their styluses and recorders. Attention flashed to
the windows, then back to Wyn.

"I made a mistake shutting the window," Wyn told them. "You don't study history by shutting out the world. Go and open it again. Look out there, listen—and *tell me!* Who is speaking with the voice of Melos now?"

She saw the way their eyes kindled with hope. *Am I doing this right? Does this all mean something that I can understand?*

The boy nearest the window sprang up to obey her. Wyn felt a shiver as she always did when her instincts told her she had caught a class's attention. The shiver deepened. The boy cried out in Spanish and leapt back as the window shattered and the building shook.

"Are you all right?" Wyn had run for years, but she had never moved as fast as she did then, brushing glass from her student (*hers! how dare anyone touch him?*) and blotting the blood on his hands with her scarf despite his protests that she'd ruin it. She comforted him in the Castilian she'd learned traveling with her parents.

Smoke and screams poured in the window. Beyond the square, a black column of smoke rose: the gate-control shack. Again, the building shook. Bomb or an earthquake?

The door opened, slamming against the wall with such force that two people cried out. Apologizing to the boy she held, Wyn strode toward the university rentacops. Real police muscle stood behind them.

"Taxpayer . . ." An imperious flare of her eyebrows drew a snicker from one student and made the rentacop correct himself. "Professor . . ."

"*Ms.* Baker," she identified herself crisply. In her world, everyone was a Taxpayer, and so many people were professors or had some such title that it was vulgar to use any of them.

"Begging your pardon, but we . . ."

"We've had a bombing. We're evacuating the building and moving our own forces in," said the policeman behind University Security, such as it was. He snapped up the dark visor of his helmet long enough that she knew it for a salute, then pushed it down over his eyes again. His riot shield and stick hung over arms and belt.

"My students?"

"All right, any Taxpayers here ... we'll see you out of the building."

"*All* my students, officer."

It was hard to stare down a black visor. She managed.

"Where you want'm to go, lady?" asked the cop.

"To their homes, of course."

A bark of laughter told her what the man thought of that.

"Then I will assume personal responsibility for them," she announced. She turned to face the students. "We are being evacuated," she told them. "I will see that you get home safely."

She walked between the policemen and her students out the door and to the stairs. Down and down and down the spiral stairs of the emergency exit they went. The Taxpayer students, fit from their exercise classes in garish health clubs, pressed at her heels. The Citizens, less fit and less well-fed, panted. In the half-light, their eyes started and bulged with fear.

But I said I would assume personal responsibility, Wyn thought.

Troops—she could not think of them as security or police—waited at the vaulted ground floor and the great arched double doors, forming a cordon of flesh and armor. Flanked by security, the Taxpayer students were led quickly off in one direction.

"*Señora,*" whispered the boy whose face she had wiped when glass had struck him, "you get the girls to safety. My friends and I ..."

This was no time for a lecture about the backwardness of "women and children first."

"We *all* will leave safely," she told him. She edged up to the helmeted man.

"Do you have an escort for us?" she demanded.

"Will someone tell me why this overgrown pain in the ass thinks she's a privileged character?" he muttered at the rentacop. "All I see is another prof. Taller than most; snottier than any. Give me one good reason why ..."

The man's eyes popped again. "Guest faculty. Professor Winthrop Baker from Harvard."

"Big . . . fuckin' . . . deal. Got an attitude out to there."

The rentacop hissed, drew him slightly to one side. As clearly as if she had a mike turned on them, Wyn overheard. "My God, do you know who her brother is?"

Her brother, Putnam, or as he liked to be called, "Put & Call" Baker, who managed her family's money and a good chunk of her university's.

The helmeted man shook his head. "Jeez. Just this once . . . just this once."

"Fire! Look!"

Adrenaline spiked, leaving Wyn calm and observant. She threw out her arms in a warding gesture, as if she could shield her students. Those who do not learn from history are destined to repeat it, Santayana had said. You can tell and tell a Harvard man, but you can't tell him much. Well, she was a Harvard *woman*, and these were her students, and no one was going to tell her she wasn't going to protect them.

Least of all a rentacop charged with getting them all out safely.

Amps and instruments twanged as musicians raced to shut down their equipment and escape. A blue tide of security, bearing the university president in its wake, flowed out from patrol cruisers onto the green. Bullhorns blared and interrupted each other. The president's eyes bulged. His cheeks puffed as he tried to make himself understood. Beads of sweat stood out on his bald head.

The building rocked from another blast. Across the green, flame shot from windows, licking the pink marble facade black. From the roof a man jumped. There was fire equipment nearby, but none in place to catch him. Wyn heard the crack as his bones broke. Behind her, a student dropped retching to his knees.

"Someone hold his head," she ordered in an undertone. She had to watch. Police cruisers landed, the whir of their airpads shrieking, then quieting as they touched down. More blue and armor marched onto the green, wielding nightsticks with a passionless precision that made her think of martial arts and weapons practice. Two techs stood by a cruiser, hoses at the ready.

A civilian in bright clothing—"Target!" screamed some damn fool and hurled a bottle that a policeman deflected with a blow from his shield—climbed to the roof of the cruiser and began to read.

"We got to get out of here," muttered one of Wyn's students.

"May they leave?" she asked the policeman quickly.

"What about you?" one student, astonishingly enough, asked her.

"I'll be fine. And we'll have class next week. I'll post a . . ."

"Outtahere!" the policeman jerked his chin. The girls in their midst, they fled.

The students on the green screamed down the negotiator, tried to rush the cops, and found themselves pushed back, back toward electrified barriers set up on two sides of the square.

Wyn saw her students caught up and engulfed. "No!" She cried, "No! Help them!" A nightstick came down on the head of the boy with whom she had spoken Spanish with. He toppled, blood pouring from his nose.

Wyn grabbed the policeman's arm. It was like grasping an industrial robot. "You promised they'd be safe! Go help them!"

"Go out in that, lady, and no one can help you. Sorry." He wasn't.

Four technicians drew hoses from a cruiser. As the police advanced, they shot foam, gray and slimy over their heads. It splattered on the feet of the advancing rioters. Where it fell, so did the protestors.

Again, clubs rose and fell. Wyn pressed forward.

"Get her *out* of here," ordered the cop.

"Come on, lady. Move it, Professor." Forming a wall between her and the battle on the square, they forced her out a side door. She was breathing in gasps, forcing herself not to weep, not to swear. She had seen blood on the faces of students. Her students.

And she was powerless to help.

Around back, she saw President Kerr-Truman, still sweaty, pale now as he realized that his East Coast trophy had damn near been a casualty in this stupid private war of his.

They bundled her into a van, carefully unmarked with the University's crest. It sped down side streets, careful to avoid the press.

She waved away the offer to go straight to University Health or straight to LAX and back to Boston-Logan Airport and the refuge of her Cambridge home.

All she wanted was a bath, a drink, and a chance to do some thinking.

Even at dawn, blood and smoke still tainted the air. Jogging in place, Wyn Baker glanced about, surprised at her own wariness.

The gray college Gothic buildings of Los Angeles University's central square looked as if some inept army had tried to fight a rearguard action and lost.

Splashes of paint stained the walls, the bars, and the shattered glass of the narrow windows. Lower down were splashes of slimy white foam and other things she preferred not to remember.

Hard to believe how silent the square was now, the quiet broken only by the high whine of bugs and birds on a May morning that would kindle into torrid noon. Charred earth and blackened grass marked where students and trespassers from the nearby Welfare Island had kindled yesterday's bonfire.

She had come out prepared to fight. Around her neck hung her panic button. All she had to do was press it, and a signal went out, alerting a private security force that charged a no-doubt-sizable fee for being at the beck and call of security-conscious Taxpayers like her brother, who had insisted she wear it. Her account statements revealed a hefty monthly charge for its use. Studying it, she saw other companies bought into her account: McDonnell-Nomura, Kennicott Copper, tax-free municipals from some government resettling organization or other (they all sounded alike). She supposed she had the prospectus for it somewhere. She was more interested, though, in the balance her statement showed: enough and more than enough in the month's income statement to sustain her for a year. She could well afford to post bail for her students.

Statement, ID, and debit card lay in her beltpouch along with a map, the location of the police station carefully circled. Best go in now, she thought, post bail quietly and get her students out. She had some notion of bringing them back to her on-campus house for breakfast.

Better not, she told herself. She might as well tell her colleagues and her dean, accept the escort of however many university lawyers they would probably unleash, and, dressed in her most formal suit, drive ceremoniously to the station. Where, no doubt, things would take forever if they happened at all. She had suspicions that the lawyers would express "grave reservations" and other such language designed to stop her from doing what she thought was right until her brother could be called.

A campus cruiser whirred slowly toward her. Jogging alongside was a cleaning crew in coveralls and sunvisors. Workfare recipients? she thought. They ran in step, without the sloppy individualism of the Welfare Island denizens. Almost, she thought, as if they were programmed. Their coveralls bore the University seal. One lifted his visor to wipe his brow. His face was very young, his eyes blank. Students had an ugly word for the maintenance squads: campus nulls. No one knew where LAU found so many of them. Student myth insisted they had defaulted on their loans.

She ran by them, noting from the corner of her eye the rentacop's surprised look. Damn! He'd probably call that in. She turned a corner, looking down as her running shoes sent broken glass cracking and scattering, and scuffed through stained, torn paper. Legs and feet assumed the rhythm of a thousand morning runs on the streets by the Observatory or on the beach by the big old family place at Manchester. The smells were painfully different—urine and fear instead of clamshells and the salt sea.

She began to perspire, and her thick old gray sweatsuit settled into its familiar folds. She passed a broken shard of glass and saw the same lean woman she had seen reflected yesterday in the helmet of a hoplite's riot gear: sandy-colored, rather than vivid, but wholly resolved. The street narrowed here. The station . . . that turn, or the next?

She stopped and drew out her map.

"Yo!"

Wyn crumpled her map with one hand. With the other, slowly, she reached for her panic button.

"Not gonna hurt you, lady." It was a boy's voice, reedy despite the tough street cadences. "What you doin' here? Ain' no place for you."

"I'm trying to help out some friends," she answered before she thought. *Don't let him know you have money, not him, and not whatever friends he's got with him.* "They were . . . got caught in the riot yesterday."

"You the teacher?"

"What?" She jumped at the voice and unfamiliar presence that questioned when she had expected threat. Something about its tones reminded her of her student she had come out to rescue, and she replied in Spanish.

"Speak Anglo, lady, *per favor*. I need to learn it good and blow this fuckin' Island like *hermanito mio*. An' I don' understand your kind of talk."

"Your brother?" Eyes and voice and face flickered as the boy rose from behind a scribbled-over, rusted dumpster.

"In your class. How you think I know you?"

"Want to go with me to the station?" Wyn asked. "He was arrested in the riot, defending some of the other students. I'm going down there now to bail him—"

"No WAY!" cried the boy. "You stay clear. He's gone now, you gotta think of him as gone. . . . I'm telling you the truth. Get outta here fast."

"It is the *law*," Wyn said firmly, "that a Citizen—not just a Taxpayer, mind you—but any Citizen may post bail and be released unless he's done something for which bail is denied. It is the *law*." Echoes—*we honor the laws, and we honor the laws that are above the laws*—rumbled like thunder in her mind. Or maybe that was the junker that clattered by on malfunctioning airtreads, forcing Wyn and the boy against a stained wall.

"Law don' work for us." The street-crawler's whine came back into the boy's voice.

"There is *always* law."

"For you, maybe. Rich lady. WASP lady. You go and talk, and maybe they give you coffee, maybe they call you 'ma'am.' But it won't do no good." The boy scrubbed a fist across his face. "They're gone. Gotta think of it that way. Even our mama, and she cry all the time. Don't go, lady. You don't want them to know who you are."

"He's your *brother*," Wyn said. Her voice went high and reedy. It nettled her: here she was, prepared to go bail out her students, and this child warned her away. His own *brother*, for pity's sake.

The boy looked down. "He's gone. And you're off your turf." He shifted from foot to foot, uneasy.

"People coming?" she asked, arching one eyebrow up.

"If we stand here too long."

"Walk me to the station," she suggested. The longer she stood here, the less she liked the walls with their smeared graffiti and windows covered by broken boards or the way they pressed in on her, or how old-style dumpsters provided the sites of a hundred ambushes. "Get me there, and then take off."

He thought about it, glanced around with a sentry's wariness, then nodded as if he were making an enormous concession. "Part way," he grudged. "Gotta get home. Don't want them to see me."

He turned his face away, but not before Wyn saw a dark flush of shame.

She was used to precinct houses that aped the Georgian brick of her university, to police who nodded to her and called her ma'am. She was not used to the boy's unease at approaching a police station or at the bunker that squatted between a garage and a locksmith's; and she did not approve, either of the fear or the reasons for it. Booths heavy with plexiglass and metal loomed up before it, well before it. The men and women in them stared down, not out. Wyn's guide hesitated. "They know we're here. Sense our body heat or something like that."

His feet shuffled, a strained, uncomfortable dance.

What would be the point of giving him a reward? They were being watched: if not by the police, then by his friends or his enemies. No point.

"I'll be fine from here," she said on a deep breath that made the lie believable.

"They're coming!" The boy's voice cracked. At Wyn's gesture, he vanished more quickly than she would have believed.

"He bothering you, lady?" The officers who edged up to her wore gear only slightly less formidable than the visored helmets and shields of their riot equipment. One held a bell-mouthed weapon Wyn identified with some amazement as a sonic stunner: *For me?*

"He was giving me directions. He was trying to help." She raised her voice, hoping the boy would hear her.

Their eyes raked her suspiciously. She wished for the protection that a car, a university escort, or the careful panoply of a dress suit might give her. She held her hands prudently away from the pouch at her belt.

"I'm from the University. Wyn . . . Professor Baker, on leave from Harvard." She managed not to wince as she brought out the seldom-used snobberies. "Classics Department. Some of my students got caught up in yesterday's disturbance. I came to bail them out." And, seeing their disbelieving eyes on her gray sweatsuit and tousled hair, "I have ID and credit on me."

They gestured her to proceed them into the stationhouse, a move that had everything to do with caution and nothing to do with courtesy. Her shoulderblades prickled every time she thought of the sonic stunner, of being clubbed down by a wave of inaudible noise, blinding, sickening dizziness.

She was sweating as if she'd run the Boston Marathon by the time she moved through the metal detectors and stated her business, first to a uniformed receptionist, whose flat eyes blinked, once, skeptically at her, then widened as she produced ID and platinum card. The sudden respect in her voice made Wyn tighten her lips, and tighten them further as the officers who had brought her in escorted her past the barrier. Her show of money and ID made them more respectful, but only slightly.

A flickering CRT and a bored officer faced her as she stated her business. She knew her voice had taken on its most glacial New England snap as she stated her business.

"All students who claimed Taxpayer status have been released to their parents. Unless, of course, they face additional charges." His stubby fingers hit the keyboard with bored efficiency.

"And the Citizens?" Wyn asked. "Several of my students had Citizen status only. I have their names and IDs . . ." She laid her list, culled from student records, on the man's desk. He gestured it away.

"Lady . . ." at her indignant eyebrow-lift, "Professor Baker," he corrected himself, "don't waste your time. All these . . . Citizens have been remanded to the proper authorities."

"What are these 'proper authorities'?" she asked, her voice frosting over.

"The Bureau of Relocation," he told her. "They'll be supplied with jobs, new homes, outside the urban infrastructure. It will give them new purpose and productivity." His jargon came out pat, by rote, designed to reassure and, if not to reassure, to intimidate. She might not know more of BuReloc but she recognized a pacify-the-tourists spiel when she heard it.

"They were *my students*," she insisted quietly. "They had perfectly appropriate jobs and purposes in life. I wish to restore what they had. How much?"

For a sick instant, she feared the duty officer might take that as an offer of a bribe.

"They're out of my jurisdiction, Professor. Why don't you go on home?" *Go back to your library*, Wyn heard. She flushed with anger.

"I understand. Very well, then, officer. How do I contact the Bureau of Relocation?" she asked.

"Lady, you don't. And you don't understand what you're letting yourself in for. Now, you look like a nice person who just doesn't understand the rules. So, I'm telling you: go home. Smith, Alvarez! Lady here can't go back to campus on foot; it was a crazy thing to come out here at all. Give her a ride back, will you?"

She could just imagine turning up on Faculty Row in a patrol car and having to apply CPR to half the cowards on campus.

"I'd rather have your escort to the Bureau of Relocation," she told them.

"Lady ..." One man laid a hand on her elbow. She jerked it away.

"Professor, you're upset; you've had a scare; you're not used to this. Why don't you let us take you to a doctor. . . ."

A nightmare vision of an outside physician, a diagnosis of nervous, overprivileged woman, a regimen of too many tranquilizers, blunting not just her anger but the keenness of her mind, tore through her thoughts. She was afraid, more afraid than she had been as she jogged through the wrecked streets.

She spun away, backing against the wall. They came at her as if they tried to tame a spooked horse. Their outraised, weaponless hands ... she remembered hands like that on clubs, hurling her students down, hauling them here, then tossing them to BuReloc ...

"Stay away from me," she demanded.

They kept advancing. Her back touched the wall. Her fingers touched the poli code and, as their hands fell upon her arms, she jerked one hand free and pressed the panic button.

She had just exchanged jailers, Wyn thought as she sat in the soft leather First Class of what she considered an unnecessarily luxurious LAX/Logan shuttle. Muscle from the private security firm her brother had engaged to protect her—or keep her from making a fool of herself—sat guarding her. A woman sat on one side; across the aisle was a male guard.

Even now, she didn't like to think of the scene that she had caused by pressing the poli code. A jurisdictional war between private security and the LAPD was only the least part of it. As the lawyers screamed, she had been hustled out of the station and back to campus. The dean's hysteria, her brother's outrage at what he called her recklessness, a veritable feeding frenzy of reporters . . . in the end, packers had been called in, and she had been whisked off-campus and onto the first available transport for Boston.

Her brother had wanted to charter a plane. For once, she had managed to overrule him on something. But a car would be waiting. She winced at the expense, at the needless, ostentatious care, as if she were some rocker or new rich who needed a vulgar display of paranoia to establish her importance. Her male and female companions seemed more captors than companions, and they muttered of her brother with the respect that a priest might use for a captious deity.

Glancing over at her escorts for what was, essentially, permission, she reached into the carryall they had allowed her to bring with her. A few books, some tapes . . . there was her financial statement. She pulled out the prospectus for the BuReloc bonds and began to read.

A very important and long-lasting anger smoldered within her. "Go back to your library." Most recently, her brother had reinforced that order, which was right out of her infancy. "Don't play with the children in the street. Stay in your own garden."

But there was blood on the roses. Even if she'd thought lifelong she wasn't good for much else, she had to wash the blood off those damn roses.

She looked down at the transaction record on her statement, found one of her guards watching, and turned the paper over.

Something about those bonds . . . a name on the prospectus . . . surely she had seen that name before. She turned to the description of a limited partnership, of which her brother had made her a silent, but voting partner. Sure enough . . . she recognized one name as a judge, another as a congressman. She remembered a dinner-table conversation about a few court cases; that is, she remembered hearing a few names—Bronson, Niles, Tucker—before she had turned her attention from what she had always thought sarcastically of as Important Business Affairs to faculty gossip.

Foolish, wasn't she? Her lips formed a silent whistle, and she recalled what one of her keepers had said. "It's a wonder they let her out without a leash."

A wonder indeed, if she wandered about with her eyes and ears sealed by ancient history. What was that sanctimonious stuff about law she had told the street kid?

The kid had known enough to run. But she wasn't a scared kid, she thought. That case . . . if she could find a conflict of interests or a bribe or some knowledge of inside information, which (she now recalled) had dealt one of the blows to the world's economy from which it had never recovered. . . . It would never occur to Putnam to think she would know that.

And for once, she would have a weapon in her own hands. She thumbed on her hand comp. It was a small unit, more used to writing than to database searches. She had always been a good researcher. By the time she landed at Logan and was hustled into a waiting car and the indignation of various family members, she had what she thought was a clue, a weapon, and an end to her naivete.

Over iced tea and poached salmon, her brother lectured her on discretion, security, and what she owed the family. Wyn disagreed.

May sunlight shone through the familiar, beloved ugliness of Memorial Hall's stained glass windows. It stained the old floor, hollowed by footsteps, with the color of blood; and blood was in the air.

In the year since her eviction from Los Angeles, Wyn had been in enough Welfare Islands to know when someone was being stalked. The pack was gathering; the hunt was up; and she was the prey.

She shrugged one shoulder, adjusted the strap of the old-fashioned green bookbag, and entered Sanders Theatre. Briefly, the smell of the ancient, polished wood overpowered the scent of blood. For more than a century, someone had taught the introduction to ancient literature here. She wondered how long it would take Harvard and the Department to name her successor—or if they would bother. Already, she had heard rumblings that the subject material was not just irrelevant to learning how to run a business or treat a cancer, but subversive. *Look what it did to Mad Wyn Baker.*

This sort of thing happened in the best of families. They used to shut the strange ones up in attic rooms, or let them rove about the big old country houses. Now, of course, there were drugs and rest homes.

She wondered what excuse would be found when whatever was planned actually happened. Because no threats had been made, no protection orders could be issued. "They don' mean squat!" one of the women in the Dorchester Project had assured her about such orders.

It had been a mistake to inquire about her students, now long vanished. She knew that her inquiry had been reported where it would do her the most harm, in those carefully lavish offices where her brother and his aides compiled a dossier on Professor and Doctor Winthrop

Baker and her troubled state of mind. *Did she seem . . .
composed when she pressed her police call button? Did
she perform her duties in a satisfactory manner upon her
return? Would you call Professor Baker's involvement in
the Literacy Programs on the Welfare Islands characteris-
tic behavior? Did you notice any . . . uh, behavioral
quirks when she was arrested on charges of civil
disobedience?*

Even her housekeeper had been questioned: Does
Professor Baker appear cheerful? Does she keep irregular hours? Has she ever said . . . ? The poor woman had
reported the questions and her answers to Wyn. When
she realized how her answers might be used, she had
broken down in tears, and Wyn had to dose her with her
best brandy.

She suspected they would use her as another example
of how professors shouldn't interfere in business, much
less politics. Probably the excuse would be the usual one
for a woman and an intellectual. *She was working too
hard, poor thing. And then she started poking into business and wasn't up to the stress.* What could you expect?

Actually, she figured her brother would try to prove
her incompetent. That meant a rest home—a country
club with guards for wealthy, neurasthenic, or otherwise
inconvenient people. She hoped the one they'd probably
park her in would have a decent library. Maybe the tranquilizers wouldn't be too strong, or she could spit them
out.

Well, the rest home could just wait. She had one last
lecture to give.

Wyn climbed the platform, arranged notes she knew
she would not use, and looked out at the students waiting
for her to speak. Faces pink and assured, with the familiar chin- or browlines of distant cousins, come to hear
lecture or scandal as they absorbed the academic airs and
graces suitable for the heirs of rulers.

There were ghosts in the room, too. Floating above
empty seats at the back (which were the places they
would probably have chosen) were other faces, the olive

skin and dark eyes of the students who had vanished because they were Citizens, to be engulfed by BuReloc. What would they have made of Sanders Theatre and this university Wyn had called home for most of her life? Could they see it for the tainted thing it had become?

Her voice rang out over the room with its pine- and sun-scented echoes. Aristocrat speaking with aristocrats, she could invoke references and languages that would have lost and shamed her LAU students. "We have been reared," she told them, "to admire *Realpolitik*. Consider, for example, the ways of Thomas Hobbes and his *Leviathan*. But must life, as he formulated it, be 'nasty, brutish, and short' to be considered 'real'? I find it interesting . . ."

There, she had used first person; that ought to bring her students' heads up. They *must* know: she would be detained today, taken away, whatever euphemisms they chose. No wonder Sanders had filled the way it did when elder professors were retiring.

". . . that Hobbes chose to translate Thucydides's *Peloponnesian War*, which contains Pericles' funeral oration. That speech is perhaps one of the most moving formulations of belief in an ideal code that we have from the ancient world, and the Melian Dialogue . . . Book Five, which is a debate between such an ideal code and a rather cynical *realpolitik*.

"I cannot quote Hobbes to you at this point. The book is out of print and I . . ." Wyn paused to let the irony sink in . . . "lost my copy in California last year. It is strange, however, how one recalls phrases in and out of context. For me, the most chilling phrase from Book Five comes not from Hobbes but from another translation. For all I can recollect, it may have been one of my own, done many years ago. 'For the strong do what they will, while the weak suffer what they must.'"

She could see the smiles, evoked by her mention of the California riot that had brought her back prematurely to the East Coast, altering to nods of approval. "We are used to agreeing wisely with such statements. To disagree, these days, marks us as naive, foolish, sentimental,

especially those of us who plan to enter the more active
fields of law and commerce. And yet, to have these words
spoken by a people who had earlier declared that they
honored the law and they honored the law that was above
the law is to hear a chilling moral progression. Or, as I
see it, a moral deterioration.

"As students, we are not just entitled to make such
judgments." She paused.

"We are required." Shock on those scrubbed, smug
faces. Had she ever looked so sure, so jolted out of her
composure? Memory shocked her: the day before the
riot.

Disappointed at hearing ethics when they had hoped
for scandal, her class was glazing out again. Perhaps only
a riot outside the windows would convince them of what
she had seen. But no such riot would taint the Yard if
she could help it. More than enough blood had been
shed on any campus.

*"Why, you goin' back there if you knows they gonna
take you?"* Her brother had been very, very right. Social
work, settlement house work hadn't been the answer.
But students in Harvard's "adopted" schools in the Dorchester and Mattapan Welfare Projects had received her.
First, because they had no choice. No Citizens turned
down help from a Baker from Harvard. Then once the
newsgrids had shut up and the Welfare rumor mills had
a chance to spread the word, they had bothered to listen.
Warily at first: like all the people who came into the
Projects when anyone in her right mind knew the only
thing to do was get out as fast as you could, this professor
had to be crazy. But maybe, just maybe, she was their
kind of crazy.

And maybe, just maybe, she was theirs.

It had been strange at first to teach basic reading
rather than Linear B or Homer. It had been stranger yet
to make home visits to grandmothers younger than herself but pregnant once again. And strangest of all to find
herself learning more from them than they could from
her.

Abandoning generations of "keep it in the family," she had asked their advice; and they had warned her. *"They'd never do that!"* she had protested to faces, black, white, and brown, old and young, all wizened from the same street wisdom and the street fights that erupted when that wisdom failed.

Was she expecting trouble? What kind? Given tough licensing laws and the penalties for illegal weapons, she'd better not pack a weapon. So her bookbag held books and papers, nothing more dangerous. A first-aid kit rode in one pocket. She had even sewn some simple jewelry and coins into the seams of her bag. With luck, the nurses in whatever rest home she was bound for could be bribed.

"You're pushing it, Wyn. I'm warning you." Sure enough, Wyn could hear the minatory singsong in her brother's voice. For years, it had been second nature in the family to yield to him when his face turned red, and he waved his finger at her as no teacher beyond the elementary grades had the ill-grace to do.

She had held the statement out to him, the statement of her holdings and the records she had found. Saying nothing. Letting the record speak for itself.

"So, you're blowing the whistle? Do you want to disgrace us all?"

"This illegality has done that already," she had retorted. Tactical blunder. She should at least have looked as if she were ready to deal.

She had tried to hire a lawyer the next day—not a Family member. The lawyer had sweated, hedged, gabbled of consequences that made him sweat through his shirt until even the silk of his tie hung limp. Ultimately, however, Baker money—even after it was besmirched by old Put & Call—convinced him to accept a retainer. And her instructions. She wondered if he'd stand tough if . . . when . . . she disappeared.

Subpoenas were delivered; the newswires went ghoulish with "need to know" and the implication of famous prey. But "you haven't heard the last!" her brother had promised. The elaborate contra-dance of bail, hearings, and indictments began.

So did the careful, cautious "it's for her own good" of her brother's people's investigation.

Carry money and small valuables. Wyn's Welfare Project friends warned her. *Don't stick to fixed habits. Watch yourself.*

But what about her life?

"Lucky if you keep it." She had herself seen the boy who had been set on fire when he refused to run borloi; the woman whose boyfriend had slashed her face; the ex-gangmember whose brothers stayed with him, as if on guard—and those were the lucky ones, who got to go on living.

"You stay here. We hide you."

She assured them she was protected, that she played a game circumscribed by law.

"You think? You step on his turf; he get you. You stay here."

She hadn't listened. And she hadn't run. She had no great faith in her ability to hide, in any case. And some bravura notion of being arrested at her work, taken from her classroom had pushed her back from the Welfare Projects to Cambridge and this final lecture.

After all, it was her students in California who had vanished quite literally off the face of the Earth, bound— as she knew now—for interstellar Devil's Islands like Tanith or Haven. They couldn't afford the luxury of grandstanding: she could.

He sayin' you crazy, her friends from Welfare, her students there, had told her. *Gonna put you away.* Even after two girls had dressed up like cleaning crew and raided the dumpster behind her brother's lawyers' office for shredded transcripts, Wyn had found it hard to believe that he would turn on her.

You turn on him!

She never had persuaded them of the difference between crime and revenge, had she? But, assuming he said she was crazy and tried to have her committed, she was hardly the first overprivileged woman to be punished that way for the crime of disagreeing with her family. How bad could a rest home be, after all? She had always meant to ask her aunt Dorothea, who had spent twenty years of her life in and out of them. Old now, and lucid on the days she bothered to stop drinking and dress to come downstairs, Dorothea had watched her as ironically as the women in Mattapan.

No point in thinking of that now. What's done is done. Where was she in this lecture? *That was right. Shake them up a bit with their own weakness. They only think they're safe, prosperous: what if someone stronger comes along and decides to take what they have?*

"... It is a sign of our own deterioration that we need to ask 'who are the weak?' Are they those who live in Welfare Islands, those who have turned their back upon our nation and our world for the dubious loyalties of the CoDominium? Or are they those who do not ask? The unexamined life, Socrates said, is not living. And we have failed to examine our own lives.

"It is thus we who are the weak ..." Wyn let the statement drop gently into the sunny, civilized theatre.

"... For we have forgotten. And we have forgotten to ask."

She had not forgotten, she protested as she moved into the final section of the class. A century or so ago, there had been a great classicist, a Jew, who had fled Germany. He came to a checkpoint and was stopped by a young soldier who searched his baggage. With the instincts of the hunted, the scholar *knew* that the soldier recognized him, knew him for a Jew and a fugitive. He waited for the man to lay his hand upon his arm and shout the words that would herald the start of his arrest and death. The soldier indeed spoke. *"You have a copy of Horace in your bags, Herr Professor."*

And so the professor had spoken of Horace, had lectured, risen on the wings of fear and eloquence till he taught as he had never taught before. And when his mouth dried, his voice broke, and his throat almost closed with weariness, the soldier spoke again. *"Danke schön, Herr Professor,"* he said. And stamped his papers and sent him on his way to freedom and to life.

Heads turned to stare out the blurred glass of the theatre's windows. Wyn's head went up. Again, the copper spoor of blood dimmed the air.

"Prowl car," muttered one student to his seatmate. His ruddy face paling. "It's white."

Psicops? No security but Harvard's own ever set foot in the yard. Were they going to make her out to be a dangerous lunatic?

Wyn's belly chilled, and her mouth dried. Her voice went hoarse, but she forced breath up from her diaphragm, and her voice rang out with a strength that surprised her. Could she turn back? she wondered. Even at the last, Antigone had been offered a choice: recant, retreat. She had not—and she had died. Too rigid, people called Antigone these days.

Like Antigone, Wyn had a brother who had betrayed his family. That had to be set right as best she could.

Perhaps Wyn should have been more discreet. She could not have been less foolish. Not when she knew. And she knew other things too: that there was always a payment for knowledge.

Now, she spoke to the kids who would never see this overcivilized room. The faces that she saw only in her imagination—the blackened eyes and bloodied mouths—seemed to relax as she spoke, then fade as if they were ghosts she had assuaged. Then, to faces leached by unaccustomed fear of their confidence, she spoke of the students they would never meet.

"They were dispossessed, you see, being weak; being only Citizens. You say that you are safe, being Taxpayers? Taxpayers you are; Taxpayers *we* are; and yet I tell you, when a government like that of Athens turns first upon its principles and then upon the people who still espouse them—as if ashamed before them—anyone can become the weak. And in that situation, one may only hope one has the strength to endure. If you take one thing from today's class, I suggest it be this: the *Gedankenexperiment* ... Einstein's term, which translates as thought experiment.... Assume that you have become 'the weak.' What will you do now?"

Pause to draw a long, much-needed breath and meet the eyes that challenged hers.

"You're quite right, of course. The question cuts both ways. What would I do?"

She looked down into those faces and nodded, a minute bow of conclusion.

"I should hope to be equal to the ordeal."

For a moment, she stood, catching her breath, assembling her papers and stowing them in her bookbag. To her astonishment, the students cheered her as if she were Lilith. Their red, opened mouths reminded her of students in the first riot she had seen and how their mouths bled as they fell.

She forced a smile and a rueful, modest headshake. Then, with a last look around the wooden vaults of the old theater, she slipped out a side door. Memories died as quickly as the echoes of old applause. She wondered who would forget first: her students or the kids from the Welfare Districts.

It took all the strength she had to leave Mem Hall and begin her usual leisurely stroll toward the Yard and her study in Widener Library.

"Professor Baker?" Outsiders, then, not to use a social title. They didn't call her "doctor" either: that would be reserved for medical types. So it was the rest home, was it? And so soon! She turned and eyed the two men and one woman as she might size up freshmen. Their tailoring was good enough to let them pass for Taxpayers, yet loose enough to let them move freely. She wondered if she could outrun them; she was certain it wasn't worth trying.

She inclined her head, then continued on her way.

"Could we talk with you?"

"I have office hours in the Library."

"We would prefer someplace more private."

She kept on walking. Quick steps sounded behind her and someone laid a hand on her arm. Wyn spun around, the arm holding her bookbag coming up in pathetic defense.

Two students strolled past. More emerged from the iron and brick gates that opened into the yard. Could she appeal to them?

The woman in the group had a hand in her breast pocket. Wyn wondered if she would produce sedatives or a weapon.

"Not here," she said. "And not in front of them." She gestured with her chin at her students.

They nodded, relaxing visibly that she was proving reasonable. That should be in her favor at a sanity hearing.

"This way," said the man in the lead. His voice held the deliberately soothing tones of a psychiatrist, though Wyn had never met a shrink who moved as if he did katas every morning. He took her arm—just a friendly meeting, wasn't this; and *smile* for the innocent kids, why don't you?

Past the Science Center. Past Mem Hall again. Past the dreadful ersatz Georgian of the Fire Station and onto the street. A white van, bare of logo, idled. Psicops indeed, Wyn thought. As well announce in the Freshman Union that she had run mad. The door was opened for her.

"I suppose," she said cautiously, "there is no point in talking you out of this?"

"Please get in."

No students were on the street. Wyn spun on her heel, preparing to run into the street, to shout; but the hand was on her arm again, urging her toward the car. And a lifetime of civility, of restraint blunted her willingness to make the scene that might have saved her. *We are the weak.*

The door whined shut. There was no release mechanism on her side of the vehicle. The car rose on its hoverpads and sped down Cambridge Street, out of the city, beyond Boston into the manicured exurbs where only the wealthiest Taxpayers lived. No one spoke to her.

"Damn!" the exclamation forced a grunt of surprise

from the man who sat beside her as lights and sirens erupted behind them.

"Why dint y'stay inna the speed limit?" he slurred as he hit his chin on the plexiglass dividing driver from passengers.

"I did!" protested the driver.

"Keep on going."

"*You* keep going, Taxpayer," the driver snapped. "It's not your license they'll lift; and then what do I have? A quick trip to a Welfare District?" He pulled over.

A prowl car pulled up. "You have custody of Professor Winthrop Baker? This warrant authorizes us to demand her release."

A flood of warmth, of gratitude, washed over her. Bless her lawyer and his timing!

"That's not a good idea," replied the psychiatrist. "She needs medical intervention . . ." His voice, so assured when dealing with Wyn, trailed off as he saw the sonic shockers that the newcomers held. Now *he* was "the weak." She wondered what punishment he would face.

He took the papers, leafed through them, and exclaimed before he could control himself. "But we . . ."

"Apparently, someone had second thoughts about security."

The psychiatrist eyed Wyn. "For *her?*"

Both men shrugged. "Whatever else you can say, he's thorough."

The man from the prowl car gestured at Wyn. "Out." The door opened. Wyn slid out. Her bookbag lay on the seat. When she bent to retrieve it, someone waved a shocker at her.

"Let her have it." Wyn seized its strap before anyone could countermand that.

"Whatever she's got in there, she'll need it where she's going."

The prowl car pulled round. Now Wyn could see the panel on its door. Bureau of Relocation.

She had been outplotted and outfoxed. Her fingers

rose to her throat, tightening convulsively on her poli
code that would call out to a force of her own choosing.

"Cancelled. Get in." The absence of even a pretense
of civility chilled her. Dispossessed and disenfranchised
like her students. And now she would learn what they
had endured. She heard an appalled whimper, flushed
with fear and shame, and began desperately to run. . . .

A wave of sound rolled after her and struck her down.

Antiseptic and old pain were in the air. Wyn turned
her head on what felt like a paper sheet on a too-worn
mattress. *I am not going to ask "where am I?"* she vowed.
She knew she was someplace medical: had to be, seeing
that her last memory was of taking a sonic shock.

You have *been to the wars, haven't you?* she asked
herself, astonished.

She determined to sit up and was astonished at how
weak she felt. What felt like the grandmother of all
migraines glittered and stabbed in her eyes.

"Coming around?" asked a man in a white coat so
worn that even the red staff and crossed serpents of his
profession were frayed. RYAN said the badge on the coat.
His eyes were blue, and his hair was graying. His face
bore the reddish patches of skin cancers, cost-effectively
(if not aesthetically) removed. To her surprise, Wyn
heard a South Boston accent. A contract physician? He
was a long way from home. The tones were efficiently
kind and blessedly familiar. She felt her eyes fill as he
propped her up and handed her a disposable cup.

"As soon as you can think straight, I have to talk to
you. There's not much time."

She gulped the bitter analgesic. The spikes sticking
into her brain seemed to withdraw, and the light diminished to a bearable level. Light from warped overhead
panels: no windows.

Damn all, had they taken her to a state institution?
She'd never be found, much less sprung from those rat-
holes!

"I don't have time to break this to you," the physician

told her. "You took a hit from a sonic stunner. You're at the BuReloc station in Florida. When I finish processing you, you'll be put on the first ship out."

If she started laughing, she knew she would never stop. Emigrants, forced or voluntary—wouldn't do for them to die in droves aboard a starship, now would it? And what was *she* doing here?

"May I make one call, please?" she asked. Her lawyer ... her family ... could she reach their Senator's staff? It would be a waste of breath, even if she could. They probably all knew and assented.

"What good do you think it would do?" Ryan asked her gently. "Records have you down as a political." His hand went up, blocking Wyn's sight of the scratched datascreen.

Wyn allowed herself to chuckle once, briefly. "So the son-of-a-bitch got to his Important Contacts, did he? Got named guardian of his crazy sister, the dangerous radical. No civil rights. And off she goes." She shook her head to clear it of the ghosts that threatened to storm her sanity: Hecuba wailing before the black ships; Andromache in a cart; Melos burning, the men dead and the weak led away into slavery.

"Nothing I can do?" She couldn't take that. She jumped to her feet, looking for the exit. She was taller than Ryan, stronger, probably, from years of all that good Taxpayer nutrition and exercise. She could push her way past. . . .

"For Christ's sake, don't try it, Ms. Baker!" The sincerity in that shout brought her around.

"This is kidnapping," she told him. "You know that." She paused to catch his eye, to underscore his awareness that they shared a hometown.

"In the name of God," she whispered, "could you make some calls for me?"

It was hopeless. Already, he was shaking his head. Wyn met his eyes. *I'm not throwing my life away the way you did.* Astonishment and fear that she had had chances he

could barely dream of, yet had blown them all showed
in his face. He was half afraid of her, half angry.

"Sure, you've been shafted." He spoke too fast, his
face now turned away. "Ms. Baker, five more years, and
I reach Taxpayer status, and my kids with me. We'll
never have what you threw away, but we'll get by. You
think I'm going to risk that? We're just little people.
Look: I can make sure you're fit to ship out. But I'm not
ruining my kids' lives for you."

He paused, and his face, already pocked with the scars
of skin cancers economically removed, flushed dark. "I'm
sorry, Professor. But it wouldn't do either of us a damn
bit of good.

"And you can hate my guts all you want. Damned if
I care. I don't have to do this, you know. There are
people out there who'd be grateful if I spent more time
with them."

Wyn bowed her head, fighting panic. *I'm not equipped
for this*, she thought. *Read, listen, stay at home; why join
the rat race?* she'd been told all her life. Her family was
too old for people like her to go haring around the universe. Space travel—she tried to recall what she knew of
it and was embarrassed she knew so little.

She wasn't going to live through this, she thought
abruptly. But other exiles had survived. If she were weak,
if she let her life slip away, she only let her brother and
his trained slaves win that much earlier.

Listen; remember; try to keep alive. "Now, you've got
one hour, one hour before you ship out. It's going to be
rough. And if you're as smart as your records say"—
incredulous headshake—"you'll help me prepare you to
survive."

I don't believe this. I just don't believe it. She shook
her head, waving away the offer of a trank. This was one
nightmare for which she had to be conscious.

"Go ahead, Doctor," she said in the crisp voice she
would use with her own specialists. "Maybe you could
start by telling me what I face."

"First, Lunabase, then Outsystem. Tanith, maybe, or

Haven." Coerced, perhaps, by her tone, he tapped in an inquiry on the computer, muttering under his breath as it beeped and sputtered. "There's a ship bound for Haven scheduled to reach Lunabase. Cold-weather world. I can make sure you're not dropsick, that your immunizations are up to strength, and that your circulation is in as good shape as it can be."

I'll live, Wyn vowed to herself. *Living well—living at all—is the best revenge. And I'll get back . . .*

He shook his head. Compassion replaced his earlier defensiveness. "Something else," he said. "I need your permission to inhibit your fertility."

Wyn burst out laughing.

"At my age?" she demanded. "Whom—or what do you think I'm going to meet on Lunabase. . . ."

"Lady, you listen to me. You're still at risk. And there's damn few contraceptives on board ship, and those'll go to the younger women, if they're lucky. If they're damned lucky. You *don't* want to be pregnant when a ship Jumps, believe me. Not with what they've got for medical care on board if you miscarry. . . ."

Wyn raised her eyebrows at him. "Doctor, I am not sexually active."

He shook his head at her. "Dr. Baker, you've got to understand. This trip's *long*. And it makes steerage look like a yacht. You won't be Dr. Winthrop Baker on board a BuReloc ship. You won't be much of anything except a female body. I can't tell you what to do with your own body. But if you've got any sense, you'll take the implant. It'll suppress menstruation, too. And believe me: you want that."

Ultimately, she did. Feeling vaguely queasy, she slid down off the examination table and dressed in the coverall he handed her, a coarse thing of greenish gray. *Ship issue?* she wondered and wondered even more to find herself curious.

"Better move it," said the medic. "But before you do . . ." he handed over her bookbag. "Your things are packed in it. I wouldn't let anyone handle that, if I were you. I added a few more medical supplies. You'll need them."

"Why?" she asked bluntly. "And how much?"

"I haven't sunk that low. Yet." He flushed, and the scars of his surgeries for skin cancer flushed darker than the rest of his face. "Guard this stuff; it's all you have. Your money's been impounded, you know," he told her. She hadn't. She was not surprised. "God bless. It's time."

She drew herself up and walked to the door, then whirled back to shake Dr. Ryan's hand. She forced him to meet her eyes, to see the respect—reluctant but genuine—in her own. She was glad his face brightened a little at it.

"Good-bye, Doctor," she said. "And thank you."

There was blood in the air. And the stinks of sweat, of packaged food gone rancid, sickness, and babies too long left unchanged assaulted Wyn, backing her against the stained white concrete walls of the processing center. She gagged, drew a careful breath, and then another.

Two Marines walked by, careful of their weapons and of the crowd of families awaiting processing as if they were criminals instead of willing immigrants. They walked right by her, their glances dismissing her: a middle-aged woman, tired, scared, and shabby—in other words, no threat and virtually invisible. Given the wailings and babblings all about her, she doubted if they'd even hear her.

Cold from the concrete spread into her back as she stared at the dusty light panels in the ceiling. Past her flowed the crowd: families with screaming children; brothers and sisters huddling together; here and there a solitary man swaggering toward the ship that would carry him into exile; the occasional woman, blowsy or terrified, shrinking against the walls: people angry, frightened, or numbed by what they faced.

Dr. Ryan's shabby office seemed like a paradise of reason and care by comparison. Hard to believe she had *ever* sat in a chair, been treated, and thanked someone like him in a cool, civil voice as if she had a right to care, without appreciating the privilege.

"Move it, sister." A trusty gestured to her.

Wyn moved it, her bookbag with her pathetic few supplies and her clothes, the jewels still sewn into the seams, bumping on one shoulder.

It was really happening. It was happening to her. Ahead of her, someone sank to his knees, moaning, and was shoved back to his feet and on ahead. No: no use in collapse, then. She walked toward the wire cages that held interviewers enthroned behind battered metal desks for processing. Her footsteps took on a rhythm that, gradually, she recognized. One of the Herald's speeches, she thought. *March to the ships of the Achaeans whenever the commanders of the army sound the shrill note of the echoing trumpet.* March into exile. March into slavery. Euripides had written that after Melos; and all the Athenians, blood upon their hands, had wept. She would have wept if she could find her tears and if they would do any good.

"Baker," said the trusty seated at the desk. His coverall, the same gray as the guards wore, was too tight and stained by food. He glanced down at the screen built into his desk. "Political." Wyn drew breath to make some sort of last appeal.

"Move it."

She stared at him. What about the records checks, the checks for medical clearance—?

"Move it, traitor bitch, or I call the guards."

He glared and gestured. A Marine ambled over, the bell-shaped muzzle of his sonic stunner gleaming. Wyn moved it.

The trusty pushed a button. A door opened in the wall, and Wyn went through, into a maze of narrow white corridors and then into the blinding yellow sunlight she would never see again. She drew a deep breath of air blessedly free of the taints of blood, filth, and old sweat. Moored at the end of it wasn't after all one of the black ships out of Greek tragedy, the blue eye warding off evil at its prow, but a huge-winged landing ship.

Ahead of her stretched a narrow gangway, crowded with guards and transportees. "Get a move on it," muttered a guard, gesturing at her with a prod and a whip. "Haul ass!"

Wyn moved it. Five more steps and she would be at the end of the gangplank where it fed into the ship. The Florida sun was warm, almost a benediction on her aching back. Before she entered the ship, she turned and took a hasty, hungry look at the violent crimsons and golds of the last sunset she would ever see on her world.

Moments later, the hatches clanged shut. She was shoved onto a padded shelf and secured like merchandise. The screams of the other transportees rose about her. Then the shrieks of the ship's engines drowned them out and seemed to hurl them all on top of her.

Wyn staggered in the unfamiliar, blessed weight of Luna Base's one-seventh gravity. Not much; but it would suffice to anchor the vomit, assuming her fellow prisoners had anything left in their stomachs. From acceleration to zero-G, the trip to Luna Base had been a horror. Not just the stinks and the slime, but the closeness. She had never thought of herself as overly fastidious, had daily worked up a good sweat running, but now she realized how much she needed space. Here, instead of elbow-room, she had cubic room. And precious little of it.

And this was the dream of space that she'd heard a few old-time physicists lament? Still, there had been that one glimpse of the Earth from space. *They've taken the dream and broken it. And it should have been ours*, she thought. She had never before cared to think much of it before.

Plato, she knew, had written of space, as had the Neo-Platonists. Dream-visions, all of them. All out of fashion. In the last gasp of this century, intellectuals had made it a fashion to spurn the idea. Her too, though she had never considered herself as subscribing to fashions in thought. If you surrender control of something, *someone* will seize it, she told herself. Of all her sins of omission and commission, she feared that abandoning the dream of space, the control over the ships that flew through it, was one of the things that had brought her to Luna Base, a convict, rather than an eager student.

Unsteadily, she walked down the corridor of this new prison, painted the gray green of Luna's rock. An intercom crackled over the straining air vents, ordering groups to this side and that. She saw a crowd of men young enough to be her students herded in one direction. Then the order subsided. Indecisive, the crowd from the shuttle milled. A few sat on the now-filthy bundles they still carried with them.

Their faces as expressionless as if they wore bronze helms with only slits for eyes and nose, the CD Marines in blue and scarlet stood guard.

Enlisted men. Wyn had met officers at this dinner or that. If these men had been officers—*what makes you think they wouldn't tell you you got precisely what you deserved?*

The crowd waited so long that even the CD Marines began to shift from foot to foot. Finally, the intercom crackled to hasty life.

"ALL HAVEN-BOUND . . ." Static drowned out the rest of the message, but not the shouts that followed.

"Rest of you, down there! Step lively, now."

Trusties in gray coveralls emerged from side doors. They had sonic tinglers; not as bad as the stunners, but nothing Wyn wanted to be hit with. Swearing, waving their weapons, with orders blaring so loudly overhead that it too felt like an assault, they herded Wyn and the other prisoners from the shuttle into a huge room, subdivided into pens. Doors—no, a port—began to slide shut as motors whirled and whined, building up to . . .

Was this the ship? No processing, no questions, no explanations: Had they just been herded on board?

She closed her hands to conceal the trembling in them. She had hoped that Dr. Ryan was wrong. Around her rose the cries and stinks of poorly tended children. It was like something out of the *Trojan Women*: herded onto the black ships, helpless and afraid.

"You come in with us, honey," came a voice. Wyn nearly wept for gratitude. Men, women, and children, thugs and citizens they might be, all lumped together. She had hoped, at least, that convicts would be separated from . . . from what? Law-abiding citizens? *Wyn*, she told herself, *up here we're* all *convicts*.

Then, the screaming started.

A girl, her mismatched skirt and jacket almost shredded, darted through the narrowing port, pursued by red-faced trusties. Unused to the gravity, she stumbled and fell, still screaming in two languages.

"They put him out! They threw him out the lock! Out *there!*" Her sobs doubled her over, and she gagged and retched.

Wyn started forward, but not before a shorter, much plumper woman grabbed the girl, raised her, and smacked her face sharply. "Quiet! You want to follow him? You want it all to be wasted?"

She gulped, drew breath for another scream, and the woman slapped her again. "Shut up! Or we'll all be in for it."

Wyn threaded through the crowd and knelt beside them. "What's wrong?"

"What's it to you?" The woman's eyes were ancient, suspicious, though her face bore the too-taut look of many plastic surgeries.

"We're not rats in a trap," she snapped back. "Was she . . ."

"Probably," said the older woman as she soothed the hysterical girl with the absent skill of too much practice. "Someone tried to protect her. They put him outside."

And when Wyn's face went blank, the other jerked her thumb. "Out the airlock."

Air bubbling, lungs bursting, blood freezing and boiling . . . Wyn fought to breathe and not to gag.

"Don't tell me you're gonna be sick on me, too. Kee-rist, I thought at least I'd stopped baby-sitting."

She bent her head, murmuring over the girl. . . . "You're called Nina? Pretty. Come on, little girl, you gotta show us you got guts, you gotta make sure the bastards don't get you, you can live through this, I've seen a hundred girls like you, and they all ended up rich and sassy . . . you'll see. . . ."

She glared at Wyn. "Do something!" she hissed.

Like what? She could see the men who had chased Nina into the hold, pushing this way and that. Only the crowds kept them from finding her this far.

Wyn rose and forced herself to draw a deep breath. "All right, you over there. Hide them!" Her coverall was stained. She needed a bath more than she had needed anything in her life, probably including air. And here she was, snapping orders.

Incongruously, people obeyed. "You—" she gestured with her chin at a compact man surrounded by his family . . . "See if you can't get the attention of the Marines."

His wife raised an immediate protest.

"Why . . ."

"Shut up!" snarled the woman who comforted Nina. "See what happened to her? It can happen to you family broads, too. Raped and your man breathing vacuum . . . All right, you men, turn your backs on the poor kid. She don't need to have men staring at her. Listen to the lady. She told you to get moving."

"Just do it," Wyn ordered. And when the man hesitated, "Please . . . if we don't hang together, they'll hang us separately. It could be your wife, your daughter . . ."

The man went. Wyn turned back to Nina. One filthy hand fumbled in a pocket and drew out a phial.

"Good stuff," approved her ally, recognizing the brand of trank. "Save it for emergencies."

"What do you call this?"

"A real pain in the ass." She took the drug anyhow and fed it to her patient. "Now swallow, or I'll rub it down your throat like I would a dog," she threatened, but her hands were gentle.

Nina obeyed. Wyn wasn't surprised at that or when the strong sedative hit her like a sandbag at the base of the skull.

Wyn looked up at the people who stood between Nina and the men searching for her. "You have to stand up to them," she told them. "This time it's her. Next time, who's it going to be? You? You? The little boy over there?"

"You think you can take care of your own family?" the other woman asked to mutters of "*puta*" and other words Wyn didn't catch. "When they have stunners, and you have what? Good hearts? Better you should have brains."

"We *have* to work together," Wyn repeated. "Make a start now. Even trusties have to sleep sometime, and they know it. And if there's a riot, they won't be trusties for long."

That drew feral grins from the men standing about. As if glad to turn their attention away from the girl now dozing on the deck, they formed a ring about her, their wives, their daughters, and the three women in the center.

A stir in the crowd announced the arrival of CD Marines, the bells of their weapons shining as they were pointed in Wyn's direction. In their center marched a midshipman, barely old enough for his freshman year, but a man and an officer already.

"What's going on here?"

The group opened up, looking at Wyn. *I won't speak from my knees like some wretched Hecuba!* But already, she had learned wisdom: she held her hands away from her body and rose, carefully.

"This young woman was raped by two of your . . . two of the trusties," Wyn said. "They followed her in here. She claims they spaced someone. . . ."

"My father!" wailed the girl, much to everyone's surprise.

A fierce scuffle broke out too close to where they

stood. "I'll get you all, you bastards!" someone shouted
thickly, as if he spoke through a mouthful of blood and
teeth. The midshipman gestured, and two Marines
fanned out. Shortly thereafter, the whine of a sonic stunner made her flinch.

A freshman would have blushed and looked down: not
this young officer. He took names, numbers, what details
he could extract from Nina, to whom he spoke with such
detachment that the girl could reply without sobbing.
Then he turned away.

"Sir!" Wyn called at his back. He pivoted and faced
her, impatient, but polite about it.

"What will be done now?"

"I'll have them in a pen before they're an hour older,"
he said. She could see the "why am I bothering to answer
her?" take shape on his face and pressed in with her next
question fast.

"And the girl? She needs medical attention."

He shook his head. "Ma'am"—the title slipped out—
"this isn't a passenger liner."

She held her eyes and raised a brow. He had the grace
to flush. Behind her came fearful murmurs, and she
looked away. *What if he checks my records? God only
knows what sort of thing my brother's put into my files.*

Deliberately, she let her shoulders sag, lowered her
head, just like most of the other women present. One of
the crowd. Just another convict. Don't notice me. Please.

His eyes went back, the interest, the respect extin-
guished. Then he was gone. The pen doors slammed
shut.

"We made ourselves some enemies," a man said. "We
better stick together and watch out."

There were nods all around. A few men patted each
other's shoulders, then turned, reassuringly to their families. The women murmured agreement.

"Hoo-boy, that does it!" announced ... Wyn looked
in vain for a name on the woman's coverall. *She looks
like a pro*, Wyn thought and knew that for the thinking
of her friends in the Projects.

"First time decent family types have done more than spit at me. Usually, they throw out the loners. This might not be so bad. Well, I always was up for new experiences."

Wyn raised an eyebrow and gestured. The woman laughed extravagantly.

"Well, not *this*, exactly, honey. You political?"

Wyn nodded, mildly shocked. She had supposed that prisoners would consider it . . . well, ill-mannered to discuss how they came to be on board one of the BuReloc vessels.

"Lady, aren't you? From back East."

"Boston." Her voice almost broke on the name. "I'm Winth—"

"Don't have to give me your name. 'Boston' will do fine. Call me Ellie. You get in wrong with some political stiff?"

"My brother."

"If it's not money, it's men. I've seen enough of both in my life."

The pause drew out, and Wyn knew she was supposed to ask about the person she was talking to. She thought she could guess. The silence grew demanding.

"What about you?" Wyn asked.

The woman sat back on her heels and laughed. "Boston, honey, you wouldn't believe it, but I'm a political too. Didn't pay taxes on my . . . if you want to be nice, we can call it an escort service." She wiped at her eyes. "Tax evasion! I've been pushing it, or watching my girls for twenty years, and they get me on lousy tax evasion."

To her surprise, Wyn laughed too. At Ellie and at herself, all New England righteousness companionably chatting with a madam. Ellie watched her narrowly.

"Yeah, sure," she said. "Even here, you're a lady and I'm . . . well what *am* I?"

"Brave, I'd say," Wyn retorted. "Besides, it's happened in the best of families." Hadn't one of the Philadelphia Biddles made a vulgar stir and dined out on it for years?

Again, Ellie laughed. "Boston, you kill me, you really do."

"God, I hope not, Ellie," Wyn found herself saying. "You're the first person I've met since the world caved in on me who hasn't bored or scared me to death."

"Shake on it?" asked the ex-madam. "It's not like I'm asking you to work for me, you know. I mean, you do know?"

Wyn laughed again and held out her hand for a brief handshake that Ellie broke off to warn Wyn about not showing off whatever it was she had in "that tacky green bag."

Wyn never learned the name of the ship. Once it had been a CD vessel—the *Gdansk*, she thought from seeing the name stencilled on a bulkhead. Now, decommissioned, turned over to BuReloc, it might as well be called the *Botany Bay*. Or, she thought, the ship of fools.

The days turned into a litany of grumbles. "Clean" became a myth; Wyn looked back even to visits to Welfare Islands as trips into a vanished Eden. Even the rickety bunks were scarce; the younger men traded shifts, so that the narrow beds, in stacks of four, were always in use. That provoked a rude snort from Ellie that Wyn ignored. A few people showed signs of gambling away bunktime: A meeting of the people in their bay stopped that and instituted a schedule of regular cleanings for their deck and for the inadequate refreshers that served them and, for all they knew, half the other convicts. After all, you couldn't expect Marines to clean up after prisoners.

It was like, Ellie announced one day, perpetually having cramps *and* PMS—and you didn't even dare scream or throw things. Not even Nina, who turned thin, silent, and jumpy. Every day Wyn expected her to burst out screaming so the Marines would come and remove her, but she never did.

She didn't bleed either. In these close quarters, they'd have known if she had. Ellie's question, too blunt to be embarrassing, brought the answer: the medics had worked on her before she left Earth. Wyn was profoundly relieved.

What the women did who had not inhibited their fertility, Wyn didn't want to think of. Wyn struggled against a claustrophobia that threatened to drive her frantic. Given no space and no activity and the bulky starches of convicts' rations, she felt herself sagging. Even the isometrics she began to work at with almost a religious fervor brought her little relief.

Day after day, the ship sped toward Jupiter. Day upon day was a nightmare of heavy gravity, bearing down upon the rickety welded bunks until, one ship's "night," some buckled, trapping a family beneath them.

The bunks were cut away, and Wyn tried not to retch at the stink of burning flesh when someone was less careful about the cutting than he might have been. Then the people beneath them were taken away, too.

She never saw them again. And when she tried to ask a Marine, Ellie—whom Wyn had privately considered nerveless—flashed her a glance of such fear that she shut up. When a few men slipped out on work assignments about the ship and returned with steel pipes to reinforce the bunks, Wyn helped them conceal it from the Marines.

From the one 'cast Wyn had watched years before while recovering from the flu, she knew that Alderson Jumps were instantaneous; transits from point to point were what occupied the days and weeks and months a ship actually spent going from one star to another. They had not yet left Earth's system, and Haven was more than a year away. Wyn wondered how she would stay sane that long.

At the orbit of Jupiter, the ship paused. After a nightmarish interval in which the low spin gravity failed as the ship took on fuel from the immense scoopship tankers waiting nearby—as "near" was reckoned in space. She knew that they had reached the point of the Alderson Jump when the alarms howled. People had time to scream once before everything blurred and stayed blurred for a long time.

After a featureless eternity of first lying on the bunks or the bulkheads, then of sitting staring at scratched, dirty hands, Wyn forced herself to move.

"At least with a hangover you can throw up," Ellie moaned.

There were people all about them who had not reached the sitting, staring, or moaning stage. Some never would. Later that "day," CD Marines herded trusties in to remove the bodies before people started to panic.

Thereafter, bunks were not at all scarce in Wyn's bay.

The 'cast Wyn had seen on BuReloc showed men and women earnestly about the business of rehabilitating themselves and making themselves fit colonists. She wondered who dreamed that one up.

She thought she could understand the convicts who suddenly began screaming and hurling themselves against the bulkheads. Certainly, she could understand the man whose wife died and who, next time the call came for work crews, went out and never came back. Either he'd run wild or—and Wyn hoped this—he'd seized the chance to enlist in the CD forces.

The filth, the uncertainty, the threats of violence, even the "days" and "nights" that passed, perceptible only by a diminution of the light from scarred panels roused her first into fury, then into frenzy she could not express. The woman in the bunk beside hers had foul breath; Wyn lay awake one night plotting how to suffocate her.

Ostensibly, a prison ship was just that—bare bones. In actuality, if you had money or valuables, you could buy almost anything . . . or anyone. Mindful of Dr. Ryan's advice and Ellie's street smarts, Wyn guarded what was in her bookbag, doling it out to the men on work crews to trade for medicinals, even an occasional treasure of food or drink, anything that would make her life and the lives around her a little less bleak.

She tried to rough out articles she'd never write, even a chapter of the book she had started before her arrest. But she would forget critical words in the Greek texts she had known by heart since she was a girl, and, overpowered by the confinement, the stink, and the hopelessness, her arguments raveled and faded into apathy. She began to think she had enough tranks left, probably, to kill herself: better so, perhaps.

"You think you're fooling me, Boston?" Ellie asked. "I've seen it when a girl gets like you. She's thinking of cashing in. And you know what I tell her?"

Let the old whore babble, Wyn thought. Maybe it would tire her out and she'd let everyone alone.

"I tell her to live long enough to spit on the bastards' graves, that's what I tell her. And what I'm telling you. You've done good here. We got a kind of law in this bay, and we all know it's you. If you check out, what's that mean to everyone else?"

Wyn raised a heavy eyelid. "What makes you think I care?" she asked.

"Boston, you're full of shit. 'Course you care. You got 'good citizen' all over you."

Wyn glanced down at herself. She had gotten very thin in the past months; that happened when you gave away your rations most of the time. "What I have written all over me is dirt," she snapped.

"Then clean up your act, will you? Thin as you are, how you going to survive the next Jump? And you got some graves to spit on, remember?"

"That's a long way back," Wyn objected.

"Then you're going to have to be in shape to make the trip."

There was no way back; Wyn had known that in her bones from the time she had boarded. But Ellie's mouth wobbled, and she ... my God, she was even crying. No one had ever cried over Wyn before. And now that she thought of it, she realized how quiet it was around where she lay, as parents kept their children quiet around her, hoping she would make the turn away from despair and back to them.

Wyn sighed and levered herself up. It seemed about a light year to the head, where she traded a gold pen for the chance to take a brief, blessedly hot shower. Thanks to a man released from cleaning detail, she had ship's chow from the CD galley and ate it with more appetite than she'd had for weeks. It gave her the strength to stomach ordinary rations the next day and all the days afterward. As soon as she could walk about the bay without staggering, she forced herself to do isometrics and to increase the time she spent exercising in the days that passed.

Another Jump, and she survived it. Now, she found herself restless, as she had in her first days on board. After prowling about the bay so often that people were heartily sick of it, she hacked her hair short and volunteered for cleanup duty.

It wasn't as if women were exempt from "volunteering." Usually, the Marines recruited female convicts for galley work or for cleanup in a place where they needed someone small, with a lower center of gravity. What else the women did in some cases was a matter of rumors—plus what Wyn personally considered the fairy tales of Marines and even officers falling for a particularly pretty girl.

With her hair cut short, scrawny as she was, her face pallid from long confinement, Wyn didn't think she was a sight to break the heart of some hapless CoDo officer, while midshipmen were a whole lot likelier to run the other way.

It was a relief to leave the bay, to thread through corridors and passageways she hadn't seen, but that she marked in the too-keen scholar's memory that even despair hadn't taken from her. The bite of antiseptics came as a positive pleasure, and so did the warmish water and watching the grimy bulkhead gleam beneath her scrubbing hands.

She grinned at the other woman and the men of her crew. As they scrubbed, they spread out, glad of the chance for at least the appearance of privacy. What a wonder it was not to have ten people crowded around you! Even the CD Marines seemed to have disappeared. No doubt they'd decided that a middle-aged woman was a damned unlikely candidate for running amok or storming the bridge.

She was kneeling on the deck, rubbing away at a particularly tough smudge when a kick from a boot sent her sprawling.

"Can't believe my luck!" came a voice Wyn had last heard thickened by blood after he'd been punched.

She levered herself up from the deck, murder in her eye, and the boot kicked her flat again.

Where had she seen that face before? Above a gray coverall . . . smeared with blood. That was right. He had been a trusty, one of the men who'd spaced Nina's father and raped her.

Pretend you don't recognize him. Lie your way out, she told herself.

"I said I'd get ya. Never thought I'd find you alone, though, and on your knees. Good place for you."

Wyn glanced down the hall. To think that a moment earlier, she'd been glad the Marines were nowhere in sight. She drew her breath for the loudest scream of her life, but the man pounced forward. A needle-thin knife flashed before her eyes as he grabbed her coverall with his other hand. The wet, flimsy fabric ripped, and Wyn gasped.

"Quiet, bitch! You're coming with me."

"What do you think you're doing?" she demanded.

"Getting some of my own back. You cost me a soft berth. Now you owe me, gotta make it up to me."

"That's stupid. You were breaking the law," she snapped. "What good does this do?"

"Good? Because I *can*. Like I could with the girl."

Adrenaline washed through Wyn. "Look at the man," she hissed. "Too bad they didn't space you too."

He backhanded her and she spat blood at him as he dragged her down the corridor.

Wyn struggled, trying to stamp on his instep, trying to bite the hand that held her, to pull free so that she could scream and run, but always, there was the knife in front of her face. It wasn't death she feared, nor being cut . . . it was her eyes! What if he blinded her! The fear made her tense her muscles so her bladder wouldn't give way.

A port was coming up, and he shoved it open onto what was little more than a closet. Long enough, Wyn found, for her to fall full length onto the deck, and for him to fall upon her. He barely kicked the door closed.

His breath was foul. If he—God, if he even tried to kiss her, she was sure she'd vomit in his face; and then he'd kill her. She hoped. In the end, that was about all he didn't try.

The strong do what they will. The weak suffer what they must. She told herself in an attempt to achieve distance from the spasms and grunts on top of her, the pain as he thrust into her unprepared and wholly unwilling body. She would not be weak. She would refuse weakness. Her hands balled into fists and she struck his back, brought up her knees (regretting that for the leverage it gave him), then trying to buck him off her body.

He was on his knees in front of her face all too soon thereafter, his knife in one hand in case she had any ideas about biting him where it would do the most harm. When he pulled out, she spat at him.

He slapped her, then rolled her onto her belly. *Beware of Greeks*, some fragment of Wyn's mind gibbered at her. This could do real damage, if he didn't kill her when he was finished. He'd have to kill her; she had seen him, and he had to know she wouldn't hesitate to report him. She heard something clang on the deck and felt her legs forced apart. Despite the horror, the metallic sound registered. He was using *both* of his hands. He had dropped the knife.

And there it was, about a meter away. It might as well have been a light year away unless she could grab it. A desperate plan, complete the instant she saw it, seized her mind and body. With what she hoped would sound like a hopeless moan, she collapsed onto one arm, and curled up into a ball, as if that pathetic maneuver could stop the painful invasion of her body.

But her left hand snaked out and seized the knife, bringing it beneath her toward her stronger hand, the right.

You want to die, you could fall on your sword right now, her mind warned her. Ellie's "spit on the bastard's grave" rang in her head. She jerked with her shoulders and thrust her hips up, as if fighting the man off. When he hurled himself back onto her, though, she was ready with the knife. And a lifetime's reading of the *Iliad* showed her exactly how to drive it into his chest below the sternum and twist it upward so the blood gouted out. Again and again, she stabbed him. His blood splashed her, hot, though she thought she never would stop shaking.

If his buddy was around, she was dead meat; she knew she couldn't force herself to retrieve the knife. She retched herself dry, spat on his body and staggered out of the tiny room.

Please God, this was no time for the Marines to come charging up! Instead of the Marines, she got a scared midshipman whose voice squeaked on the "ma'am" he shouldn't be calling a prisoner.

"In there," she rasped from a throat bruised from the grip of the dead man. Whom she had killed. She doubled over with dry heaves. "He fell on his knife," she willed the midshipman to believe.

The boy walked to the closet, opened it, then backed away. His eyes flicked over her half-naked and wholly bloodied body. No one could tell how much of the blood was hers.

"Terrible things, knives," he agreed with a maturity that stunned her. He moved in to support her. Boy though he was, she recoiled.

She didn't want to go to what passed for a Sick Bay on this sick, sick ship. No one ever returned from Sick

Bay. She would get back to her bunk, and she would ask Nina how you lived with this.

"Just let me get back to . . . I have friends there, they'll help me . . . No, no need to. I can walk on my own."

When the worst of the shuddering had left her weak, but quite calm, she retraced the corridors to the prison bay that had the feel now of a refuge. Her legs wobbled, and her groin burned, and she blessed Dr. Ryan.

She was no distant goddess now, no lady, no scholar to be spoken to with respect and touched not at all. Just a female body. She hit the buzzer and leaned on the port.

It slid aside.

Ellie was not the first to see her, but she was the first to guess.

"Jesus *wept!*" she said and started forward.

Nina reached her first and flung her arms around her. Ellie joined her, taking her face in her hands to examine the swollen, split lips, before steering her expertly toward her bunk.

"Come on, honey . . . Baby, you fetch me my little bag, will you?" she told Nina. "You take this cloth, wet it good . . ."

Feet padded off fast. Wyn wanted to sag against Ellie's reassuring, female bulk, wanted to hide her face. If she'd been more cautious . . .

"Not your fault!" hissed the other woman. "It's not."

She guided Wyn through the ranks of cots. Men sat on many of them, but they turned their faces away as the women passed, granting them the respect of privacy.

She didn't want to be tended and cleaned, but Ellie was quite inexorable. With antiseptic salve on her face, antibiotics and painkillers in her system, and her groin bound up in soft cloth—Ellie must have traded for a diaper from one of the mothers—Wyn was put to bed and covered with the least smelly of the blankets they were issued.

"I spit on his grave," Wyn whispered to her. "He had a knife and he dropped it . . ."

"*Good* girl, Boston. You're a champion." Ellie hugged her. A tear splashed down her face and onto Wyn's. "Dammit, you'd think I'd have seen it all by now. Here . . ." She reached behind her. "Drink this."

To Wyn's surprise, it was whiskey. She pushed it away. . . . "What about the painkiller?" She hadn't been raped and committed murder just to die because of an alcohol/drug problem, dammit.

"This stuff doesn't react with alcohol. Don't worry about it. Just you get stinking drunk, and we'll take care of you."

"Bring my bag," she muttered. She still had jewels sewn into its seams. She had to pay Ellie back.

Ellie pushed her back down. "Y'know, Boston, you can be a real asshole sometimes. Shut up and drink."

The whiskey burnt the cuts in her mouth, then seared as it went down. Field surgery used to use alcohol as a painkiller and cleaner, Wyn knew, and it was working now. After awhile, the lights dimmed. When she was certain no one was watching her, Wyn cried silently, her face buried in the shabby blanket. After awhile, she drifted.

A little after she woke, the ship Jumped. Her last thought before the Jump and the first one thereafter was that it was a shame that the ship couldn't perish in the antiseptic heart of a star.

The cuts and aches faded. After awhile, so did the nightmares and what Wyn came to regard as a deplorable tendency to flinch from men's voices. Boredom replaced weakness and fear. At one point, she even tried to teach Ellie Greek.

"You're outta your mind, Boston, you know that? Strike a deal with you. I don't tell you about my business; you don't teach me that stuff."

Ellie's business: clearly, she intended to resume it once they landed. "Hey, stands to reason this Haven they're sending us to is no garden spot. They've got miners there, and where there's miners, there's girls. Now, I'm way too old to start out turning tricks again, but I'm a damn good bookkeeper . . . work my way in and work up to a share in the place."

"Is that all you want?" Wyn must have been half stupefied by boredom or the question wouldn't have popped out.

"What I want? I *want* to have enough credit so I don't have to OD on pills and booze when I get too old to work and the food runs out. I *want* to be my own person. You need money for that, in your own name, under your own control."

Wyn could see the wisdom in that. She only wished she were as certain of her future as Ellie.

What would await any of them on Haven? What awaited her? She knew convicts worked and worked hard. They were charged for their passage. They were charged for their lifesupport. They were charged for the wretched coveralls they wore and the food, even when they didn't get full rations. Charged at rates, she suspected, she wouldn't pay for luxury travel.

It might be possible to repay all that by some form of indenture ranging from apprenticeship to slavery, depending on the employer/owner. And then you'd have to start all over to save the money for passage back to Earth.

No, that wasn't even a possibility. She had known that from the start. Her exile was final.

If she were going to survive, better not regard it as exile, but as a new life. How would she manage?

A glance about the bay showed her fellow exiles in a new light. The strong ones—casual labor. The other politicals—maybe they could be used as clerks. The wives and daughters arrested with their men? Women's work, the answer occurred to Wyn immediately. In a low-tech society, cooking and cleaning would doubtless be handed right back to them. Even the children: she recollected that even in the Plymouth Colony that had become her home state, indentures started young.

It looked as if she was about to suffer from her own

ancestors' management tactics. She wondered if she were up to it; she'd lived off Baker wealth, Baker fame, Baker connections her whole life and counted herself lucky. At the same time, she knew, she had inherited the Baker conscience—*a double portion, since my brother clearly didn't get any*. And that conscience had a bad way of surfacing at inconvenient times to reproach her or, as it had this time, get her kicked off-world.

So now you get the chance to prove yourself, Wyn. Just what is it you think you can do? An interesting question, wasn't it? What kind of trade could a displaced aristocrat with a talent for languages take up in middle age?

Anyone on Haven need a butler? A nanny? Sure, she could teach. But with "political" written large on her dossier, would they trust her within five parsecs of a school? What *had* her brother paid to have written into her files?

She feared she would soon learn.

A few more Jumps and gravity shifts, and the intervening weeks and months passed. Atrocious as their rations had been, they became shorter. They began to sleep more, waking to eat and invent new versions of old curses on the purser, who pocketed the cost of their food. They shed the unhealthy bloat that comes of eating too much starch, became thin, then gaunt as they stinted themselves still further to make sure that the children, at least, had enough.

Haven would be too rough a world for children stunted by malnutrition, she had told one woman, the mother of three, and the word had spread.

One last Jump. One last interval of sitting in a daze. The variable gravity wobbled sickeningly, then steadied at a level that made her ache in every joint. To Wyn's surprise, gossip helped her identify this as mercy.

Then, one ship's "night," while the prisoners were groggy and disoriented, crew and CD Marines burst into the bay and ordered them out. *Now.* On the double, if not faster.

"My God, just smell them! Like pigs, these convicts," muttered one Marine. The ensign overseeing the transfer didn't silence him.

Wyn scarcely had time to grab her precious bag before she and the rest were herded to shuttles. She staggered a little in the unaccustomed G, then sucked in her breath as if someone had kneed her in the belly as the shuttle broke away from the ship in which she had spent more than a year of her life and whatever illusions she had brought on board. Zero-G brought her empty stomach flip-flopping perilously close to her mouth, and then Haven's own gravitation and the shuttle's braking rockets took hold: she was heavy, heavier than she had ever been; and her vision reddened. It wasn't fair; she was going to burst, and she hadn't survived the trip just to explode in reentry because the pilot poured on the G's. There were no hatches; she wouldn't even see the sky in which she would die.

From the shuttle's cockpit came a steady drone of affirmatives and static. "Beginning final burn ... mark ... Splash Island coming up on the horizon ..."

My God, were they going to land in *water*? Wyn forced herself not to scream, to unstrap herself and claw at the nearest bulkhead: not to be trapped, not to sink in this steel trap, plunging further and further till it burst asunder, and her lungs ...

She wanted to scream a protest, but "uuuhhhhh!" was all that came out, more breath than pain.

And then they were down.

In the water.

On whatever Haven this world might be.

The stench of steam and overheated metal rose about the port. Clutching a bag that felt heavier than any suitcase she had ever packed in her life, Wyn tottered toward the port. A blackened metal ladder led down from it to boats that bobbed in the black water far too much below. Even as the ship floated, she could feel Haven's gravity, heavier than the ship's. It felt heavier than that of lost Earth, though she knew otherwise.

Her feet trembled on the rungs of the ladder; the boat's crew steadied her as if they hated touching anyone as filthy as she was. Could they smell it through the steam and the traces of this new world?

It took forever for the launch to fill. The thin crying of hungry children rose in the alien air.

"Where are we going?" she asked.

To her surprise, she was answered. "Splash Island," replied a man with a twisted arm. He grinned and pointed across the dark, dark water. Lights gleamed from translucent sheds on that Island.

"There's Splash Island. Pro-ces-sing . . ." he sounded the long word out. "Over there . . ." a sweep of his arm . . . "you got Docktown. And beyond it, The City. Castell City."

A combustion engine roared into fetid life, then back-fired so loudly that at least two people screamed and the launch jolted dangerously. The ferryman laughed, exposing broken teeth.

"You don' wanna fall in. *Believe* me. We can't fight what's in there, and I ain't goin' back for ya. Keep your arms inside the launch."

I haven't a coin for the ferryman, Wyn thought. In the next instant, she realized she was wrong. The coin shone in the night sky, dominating it, more crimson than copper, baleful as the eye of a cat. Another shone upward, reflected in the dark, dark water.

Ship's rumor called Haven's bloated primary the Cat's Eye. Funny: on Earth, it had always been the dog who had been sacred to Ares. Cat's Eye and its reflection glared at each other. It was a world of War, Wyn realized at that moment; and this Charon, this convict who'd served out his life here, ferried her across the water to start a new life.

Haven's gravity took her as she climbed out of the launch, and she stumbled to her knees. Her hands scrab-bled, then filled with mud. *Dear Earth, I do salute thee with my hands,* the mournful pentameter from *Richard II* rang in her thoughts. Wrong again. Haven's ground was dirt, soil: it never would be *earth*.

"Why are we so heavy?" wailed a child. Its cries were quickly hushed as if it knew Haven were no planet for weeping.

And yet, with the Eye above and the reflection below and the lights of Docktown and Castell City shimmering over the water, it was beautiful.

Moving like invalids their first day out of bed, the convicts shuffled toward the Processing Center.

"God, I am too damn old for this," Ellie moaned. "Feel like I got lead boots on. All over me. Or maybe that's just crud."

"Men on one side ... women on the other ... all right, move!" came the order. "Kids with the women."

Men and women clutched each other, dismayed. They had all been together for so long that separation came as a threat. Down long, shabby corridors they were herded. Wyn noticed that the women guards hustling her and her friends along were unarmed. The corridors opened into a room that smelled, blessedly, of clean steam and water, dripping from nozzles set into the ceiling.

"All right, everyone strip. And scrub good!"

The soap they found in squeeze bottles nearly took off their outer layer of skin, and Wyn had never felt anything as good. Steam billowed about them, mercifully hiding their bodies. But at that moment, she wouldn't have minded if they hadn't separated the men and the women.

Tugging a fresh coverall (for which she'd no doubt be billed, too) over damp skin, Wyn caught sight of herself in one of the cracked, water-beaded mirrors still clinging to the walls.

"Look like a New England schoolmarm," she muttered to herself. In fact, she reminded herself of the frayed sepia photos of her aunt (never mind how many greats) Phoebe, who helped found a girl's school in India, then went on to China to fight against footbinding.

She wasn't as much slim as lean now, starved down

into endurance. And at some point during the journey into exile, her eyes had traded a scholar's abstraction for a veteran's wariness.

"Not bad," Ellie shook her head. "Don't know why you act like you're ready for an old-age home."

"You're not recruiting me for your line of work, are you?"

Both women laughed, a little raggedly. After decontamination would come Processing, and then Assignment. But what contamination had her brother put in her file? They wouldn't let her anywhere near students, would they? She might be lucky to find herself hauling scrap in a mine until she collapsed.

Medical processing rid her of fears she'd contracted some disease from the man who raped her. Her arms were sore from immunizations when she was Processed—identification, classification interview, and a battery of tests. She identified them as out-of-date aptitude and personality evaluations, plus an ancient IQ test. Practically meaningless; and yet whatever future she might have could ride on them. Her palms began to sweat, and she pondered each answer as carefully as the girl next to her.

For deportees to survive on Haven, matters were simple. Someone had to buy their contracts for work in town, in the mines, on farms, or wherever: almost anything was better than going it alone. The only other options were farming—usually with inadequate supplies and equipment and in Haven's outback—or to become one of the walking dead who loitered around Docktown seeking casual work or a quick deal.

Further down the hall, Ellie squirmed in her chair. Wyn knew the woman was thinking, *I'm too old to go back to school.*

As the tests ended and they were returned to holding pens, Nina turned to her. "Boston, what are we going to do?"

"We have to wait to be assigned," Wyn said. She just wanted to sit down and rub her temples. How many years had it been since a test had psyched her out?

Nina came close to her, dark eyes wide with terror. "I heard . . . there's mines here. A place called Hell's-A'-Comin' and I'm afraid, Boston. Where there's mines, they need girls, and . . ." The big eyes overflowed.

Wyn put her hands on the girl's shoulders. She glanced about helplessly. Ellie was nowhere in sight. What would Ellie say to this girl? She could practically hear her, _"Boston, no way I could make a working girl out of this one."_

So many lives had been broken. Against that, what did the life of one girl matter? Plenty: Nina had been Wyn's shipmate, and she looked to Wyn for help. Wisdom from the Welfare Projects blurted from her mouth.

"We're probably being watched," she whispered. "Mess your hair. Slouch. Act anti-social."

"Anti-social?" Oh God, now she had to give examples.

"Drool or pick your nose or do something that's a real turnoff. Dammit, don't _laugh_! And, Nina, you want to do me a real big favor? When you start this little act, turn your back on me, okay? I don't want to watch."

Wyn sat alone in the detention pen, wondering who would emerge from an inner office to claim her. Everyone knew, when applying to graduate school, on about what day the letters of acceptance or rejection would be delivered. And everyone waited for mail that day, for the precious thick or damning thin packets delivered the old-fashioned way. She had sat on admissions committees since then and knew how candidates were discussed. How were her new . . . her new masters discussing her?

The door slid open slowly, and a guard entered. Wyn rose, quickly enough for deference, slowly enough to preserve her own illusions. "This way," the guard said.

No statement that Mr. so-and-so had bought her contract? She started to raise her eyebrows, then thought better of it.

She was brought to a tiny room. In it sat a man dressed in rugged, all-weather clothes conspicuous only by the shimmer of the gemstones he wore on one hand and on the slide about his neck. She had seen such a stone only once, when her niece Caroline had wed that improbable

Texan and Shreve's had had to set the veritable boulder
he gave her in platinum. It had been vulgarly large, but
the stones this man wore as baubles made it resemble a
seed pearl. The man rose as she entered. Her eyebrows
did flick upward at that.

"Ms. Baker?"

She inclined her head.

"I've been studying your file. Oh. I'm Dan Carmichael,
private contractor at the Kennicott Mines over Hell's-A'-
Comin' way."

She froze. She had always been able to identify euphemisms. And from her days working in the Projects, she
recognized this man. *I know a pimp when I see one.*

*"I said I'd get ya. Never thought I'd find you alone,
though, and on your knees. Good place for you."* Her
callused hand went out to brush the back of an empty
chair, and she shut her eyes against the pain, the viola-
tion, and thereafter, the feel of her hand driving steel
into flesh and hot blood spurting over her wrist.

He was aiding her to sit; in an instant, he would shout
for help, she knew it. She summoned strength from the
core of rage she had learned to nurture—"spit on the
bastards' graves"—and shook her head.

"I am too old to . . . I believe you call it, 'turn tricks.'
Not to mention my lack of other attractions."

He stared at her. *I'm not going to faint.* When he
seemed to be sure of that, his laughter rattled the flimsy
partitions of the room.

"Varley owes me a favor. He said I ought to meet you,
that you were likely to wind up near the top. It stands
to reason. The governor flags all the politicals; and hell,
lady, you're something special even in the way of politics.
Can't think of a job I could offer you, unless it would be
teaching. . . . My gals tend not to have kids. Down the
road, though, it's sure going to cost plenty to send the
ones they do have to Company schools."

"I would hardly think so," Wyn murmured.

"Some of 'em do, though. And sooner or later, they'll
need schools. Well, that's down the road. . . ."

Frontier schoolmarm. Wyn, you are going back all *the way—at least, if you're lucky.*

"You might tell me something, though. That little girl, the one who talked to you, then started . . . ugh! That's all an act, isn't it?"

Nina had cried in her arms. The urge to protect her like a student made Wyn shiver.

He can check to see if you're lying, her good sense told her.

"She was raped at Luna Base. When her father tried to help her, they spaced him. She won't earn back your investment," she said crisply. Then, inspiration struck.

"Sir . . ."

"Lord, you speak fine!" He shook his head at her.

"Sir, if you have access to the BuReloc files, you should know that there is one woman . . ." How could she phrase this appropriately? ". . . in your line of work. We called her Ellie . . ."

Wyn slid forward on her chair. Sure enough, built into the computer panel on the table was a screen for observing the prisoners awaiting assignment. There sat Ellie. Obviously, she had finished processing later than Wyn. "That one."

The man's fingers tapped on the keyboard. A guard emerged and shepherded Ellie out of the holding pen into the cubicle. One quick glance, and she had sized up Carmichael. A grin, a pass of her hand across her hair and coverall, and she looked younger, flushed, even pretty. Wyn blinked. So that was how a real pro did it.

"Dammitall, Boston," she blurted. "I thought you said you didn't want my line of work!"

"Ellie . . ." It was Wyn's turn to flush as she realized that she had never known her shipmate's last name, "I would like you to meet Mr. Daniel Carmichael, who manages . . ."

What *was* the proper way to introduce people in their line of work. Apart, of course, from the obvious. Aha! What had Ellie called her business when they'd met back on Luna?

". . . an escort service at Hell's-A'-Comin'."

She glared at Ellie, willing her to hold out her hand first. The lady always indicated whether she wished to shake hands.

Ellie shook her head, then Carmichael's hand. Only then did she start to grin.

"Thank you, Ms. Baker," Carmichael intoned, his voice hollow with laughter.

"Boston, you never told me your name was Baker," Ellie said. "One of *those* Bakers? And you let me . . . hoo-eee! I'm surprised you even spoke to me."

Wyn shrugged. Both Ellie and Carmichael watched her with growing amusement.

"Is that how you learned to keep a straight face? You ought to come to work with us . . . make you the standup comic."

Wyn smiled at her. So few words, and it was all arranged. *I ought not to approve,* she thought. *But there is Hell's-A'-Comin', and the brothels are real; and no question, the women in them will do better with Ellie to look out for them.*

"Or I could play the piano in the parlor," she said slyly.

"Got a keyboard instead," Carmichael said. His face reddened as he lost the struggle against a great shout of laughter. "Sure you won't reconsider?"

Wyn smiled. "I'll take my chances."

"Ya know, Boston, you can be a real asshole sometimes," Ellie said.

"I'll be fine," Wyn assured her with more confidence than she felt. "You'll make so much money up at the mines you probably won't even recognize me next time you see me. Or want to talk to me."

"You'll still be respectable. Still Boston," Ellie said and hugged her. The next instant, she was all business. "Where's those papers?" she demanded. "Isn't there someplace I got to sign? You want it in blood or what?"

More keystrokes, and the contract whirred out from a

slot in the console. Tongue between her teeth, Ellie signed and handed the papers over to Carmichael.

"Ms. Baker, I thank you," he said. Then he hesitated. "Here's for luck. The way you're thinking, you'll need all the luck you can get on Haven." He lifted the slide with its glowing gem, a tiny replica of Haven's giant moon, from about his neck and threw it over Wyn's. "Will you get a move on it, Ellie? We open for business at 20:00, and we need to find you a decent dress."

Ellie followed her new employer out the door. ". . . gave away a fortune, and you ought to see the stuff she's still got hidden in that green thing she carries. . . ."

Silence. The tiny room seemed suddenly cold, echoing. Wyn was relieved when the guard escorted her back to the holding pen. Quickly, she stuffed her new lucky charm into the green bag. At some point, she might be able to sell or trade it. And there was no sense in being a walking target.

There were no windows in the pen. It smelled like every other pen in which Wyn had been deposited with a grunted "wait here." It shouldn't, Wyn thought. This was an alien world; somehow, she had expected it would look and feel different. She wanted out, to fight for whatever future Haven might offer her; she wouldn't get that future sitting here.

"Ms. Baker?" Not a guard this time, but a man dressed almost drably, in what Wyn was suddenly sure was "solid citizen" clothing. Once again, she trotted down the hall to the interview cubicles.

"Ms. Baker, I am Thomas Bronson." He waited for her to acknowledge his family name and to take the hand that he—a vast concession—held out to her.

"How do you do?"

"I assume that your trip here was rather trying."

Wyn inclined her head and nodded again when Bronson waved her to a seat. A Bronson of Kennicott here on Haven? Must be from a minor branch of the family. Not old enough to be a failure, shipped out to the frontier; not young enough to be an heir, proving himself. Probably just old enough to be desperate to make one last push to better himself here, if not lift himself offworld.

"The governor alerted me when your file crossed his desk. Yours was marked for two reasons: politics and high intellect."

"The charges against me were false," Wyn said levelly. "All of them except terminal folly." *And you can't file an appeal back on Earth for that.*

"Most unwise to launch a frontal attack against entrenched authority." He steepled his fingers. Recognizing the tone of Official Pronouncement from many dinner parties, Wyn nodded: *you expert; me, unworldly professor. So tell me, Mr. Bronson, have you bought my contract? And what do you need me to do?*

"I would not do it again," she said.

"So you have learned from the experience?"

"A very great deal, sir," she said. She had learned to study those in power, to figure out their weaknesses and survive by playing upon them. She had been a trusting fool, and then she had been helpless. She would not willingly be helpless again.

"It is your knowledge of Earth that I could find useful. . . ."

"My knowledge of Earth?" Wyn allowed herself to smile. "Mr. Bronson, I left Earth more than a year ago on what I fully expected to be a one-way trip. And I think neither of our families would say I knew much about the real world when I lived on it."

"Still," he said. "Your family's contacts. Your education, the way you speak."

She glanced at his hands. He wore a wedding band. That told her: *outpost mentality.*

"Do you have children, Mr. Bronson? School-aged children perhaps? And the local schools—are they adequate to those children's needs?"

Years of faculty/parent conferences and student advising made him easy to read. Shipped out from Earth or maybe born here: an early marriage to a local woman unable to keep pace with his ambition or supply their children with whatever polish he thought they ought to have.

He'd bought her contract for politics. But teaching them could be her insurance policy once he'd mined out her few Earth names and networks.

His face lit. "I have taken up your contract." Wyn inclined her head. "Please think of it merely as an employment contract. My children, of course: and we could use an executive assistant, discreet, cultivated."

In short, a major domo, their resident status symbol from Earth.

You won't get a better offer, she heard Ellie's voice.

No doubt, he would pump her for details of Earth politics, out of date as they were. No doubt, he would mine what connections he thought she had about as thoroughly as Kennicott went into the hills by Hell's-A'-Comin'. And in return?

Maybe, just maybe, I can strike back.

The idea did not provide the angry pleasure it once had. She had learned something, after all. If Bronson was a power here and relied on her, she too would have power of a sort, even a chance to shape a place that was not already hopelessly corrupt.

Even her tie to Ellie and Carmichael at the mines might be worth something. Exiles made what choices they had to: anything to cease being "the weak." Anything they could stomach. Ellie's and Carmichael's work might be cleaner than the game she was offered.

She thought she could manage. Life on board a BuReloc ship toughened her to the point where she thought that maybe, just maybe her ancestors—who had *not* been pampered aristocrats—might not find her a weakling. She was well up to this game, she thought. In fact, even if Bronson could produce passage back to Earth, she thought she would spurn it in favor of the promise she saw for her on Haven. She would not always be "the weak," fated to suffer what she must.

It was not often a person got a second chance. Hers
sat across from her, folding up the contract of her indenture and tucking it into his jacket.

Bronson rose, and she rose with him. "We would be
obliged if you would begin at once. Tonight, we have
an important dinner. . . . You will, of course, join us."
He looked pained. "There is the matter of suitable
clothing . . ."

Hadn't Dan Carmichael said the same thing to Ellie?
No, Wyn didn't think she'd stop speaking to Ellie.

"When I earn it," Wyn said. She had a sudden crazed
vision of stripping open the seams of her faithful green
bag, extricating the pearls she had sewed within it, and
wearing them with the coverall that was the convict's
badge.

He flinched. "Consider it a condition of employment.
You must appear . . . presentable. One of the Hamiltons
will be there."

Well, thank you, sir! She was a Baker; of course, she
was presentable. Then she thought about what else his
statement might mean. She intended to teach. But there
was always that other way. Marry one's way up and out.

At her age?

Why not even that? After all, when Great-Aunt Phoebe
had gotten thrown out of China, she'd come back to
Boston, and she'd married (which branch of the family
was it?) . . . But Bronson was waiting for her reply. Wyn
copied Ellie's, even to the downcast look and the breath
held long enough to let her blush.

Decent clothes, fabrics that didn't chafe. And chances
to stop being "the weak." She could hope. It was dignified to hope.

*Count no man happy until you have seen the hour of
his death.* She recalled the old caution from Herodotus.

But don't write him off till then either. Or her.

Bronson escorted her through the Processing Center,
and onto the launch bound for Castell City. A light snow
was falling, and the fresh air filled her with new hope as
she gazed at the huge, feline primary reflected in the

water. When the launch docked, Bronson made half the dockyard stare by handing her, dressed as she was in convict's gray, down from the boat. She nodded thanks, then followed him out into her future.

"And the town being now strongly besieged, there being also within some that practiced to have it given up, they yielded themselves to the discretion of the Athenians, who slew all the men of military age, made slaves of the women and children, and inhabited the place with a colony sent thither afterwards of five hundred men on their own." (Thucydides, *The Peloponnesian War*, translated by Thomas Hobbes, University of Chicago Press, Book 6, p. 372.)

Yuri Ilyich Kronov scowled as he slapped the wet snow from his coat and hat and hung them, sodden, on the rack by the radiator. Moscow was a misery of slushy wet snow, and his office, like every building in Russia during the winter, was an oven. By the time his coat and hat were dry, he was perspiring freely, and had stripped down to shirtsleeves.

Kronov was a clerk in the Moscow branch of the Bureau of Relocation, whose offices looked across Red Square to Saint Basil's Cathedral. Today the cobblestones of the square were covered in a gray-black soup of half-melted snow and half-dissolved banners and leaflets. Another Russian Nationalist rally had been staged without permission two days ago, and the sweeper trucks were waiting for the snowplows, who were waiting for the sweepers, both thus ensuring that nothing interfered with their drivers' vodka intakes. Kronov sighed. He wondered when it had all started going to shit.

Kronov's musings ceased with the abrupt rattling that shot through the building's heating pipes like machine gun fire. He took his hammer from the desk drawer and was crossing the room to administer the only repairs he knew when the door opened.

"Good morning, Yuri Ilyich." Genadi Ivorovich Kirichenko bustled in with a new armload of papers for him. Kirichenko was Kronov's supervisor, a CoDo representative from the Ukraine, and Kronov detested him. Kirichenko was a party *apparatchik* without peer, unofficially a self-made millionaire, and only too willing to talk about both to anyone who'd listen. It was an open secret that he'd bought his seat on the CoDominium council.

"Good morning, Genadi Ivorovich." Kronov looked at the hammer in his hand, idly considered planting it in Kirichenko's forehead, then decided it wasn't worth the aggravation it would bring him. Almost, but not quite.

"Had quite a round-up over the weekend, old man," Kirichenko said, and Kronov winced. Educated at Oxford, Kirichenko affected English expressions in Russian. He wore French shoes, German suits, and American cologne, and complimented himself on his international good taste. In short, he was a thoroughgoing boor.

Oblivious to Kronov's stony silence, Kirichenko went on: "Two or three hundred of those Russian Nationalist chaps rounded up in St. Petersburg." Kirichenko pronounced it *"chee-yeps."* "Moved them down south last night to the holding facility at Riga."

Kronov's head shot up. "Riga? That's in Latvia. Why weren't they sent to the detention center here in Moscow?" He immediately regretted his tone. Privately, Kronov was a staunch supporter of the Russian Nationalists, but that support had to be very private, indeed. The *Pamyat* movement, fiercely pro-Russian, nationalist and openly racist, was an embarrassment to the Soviet hard-liners who so fanatically supported the CoDominium. It was thus as strictly censured in Russia as was the Ku Klux Klan in the United States. Only scientific research institutions were more closely monitored.

Kirichenko shrugged. "No room. The one here in Moscow is full up. Besides, what difference does it make? Their kind all wind up deported in the end, anyway."

Kronov's paranoia put deeper meanings into Kirichenko's tone, and he too shrugged in dismissal. "Of course. Just seems inefficient to me. How are we to cycle them through for deportation when they spread them out like that?"

Kirichenko beamed. "Afraid of a little hard work, Yuri Ilyich? That's no way to get to the top, mate." Kirichenko's mangled British idioms were becoming unbearable, and his use of Kronov's patronymic was entirely too familiar, but Kronov indicated no offense.

"Tell you what," Kirichenko said, putting the files on Kronov's desk. "Here's the paperwork; consolidate the names, and ship the deportees anywhere you like. Just be sure to maintain the dispersal ratios, and you can take the rest of the day off."

Kronov looked up over the rims of his spectacles at Kirichenko's departing smile, wave, and inevitable "Cheerio." The crack about taking the day off was an insult to Kronov's intelligence. The task as given would take Kronov the better part of twelve hours, and Kirichenko knew it. CoDo dispersal ratios were designed to ensure that not too many forced deportees of the same political stripe went to the same world. A mob with common cause was trouble anywhere.

But in practice, BuReloc's human cargo was moved with no regard whatsoever for the dispersal ratios. Only when there were special instructions, like this, which pertained to particular groups, like the Russian Nationalists, were the ratios taken seriously. Kirichenko had just saddled Kronov with the most onerous task available at BuReloc's Moscow desk.

Miserable Ukrainian pig. Kronov could scarcely keep from grinding his teeth. *If the* Pamyat *has its way, he'll be back where he and the others like him belong: grubbing potatoes and begging crumbs from Russia's table. Ukrainians, Latvians, Lithuanians, Estonians; all those worthless hangers-on who enjoyed the protection of Soviet Russia for decades, then tried turning their backs on her when the Dark '90s hit us and shook things up so badly for a while.*

Uncharacteristically, Kronov had a flash of insight. He turned to the ancient Soviet-made *Agat* desktop computer and waited while it accessed its files with agonizing slowness. Deportee lists were exceedingly detailed and very well-documented, a legacy from the vast amounts of CIA, NSA, GRU, and KGB staff workers BuReloc had inherited. With a grinding rattle and a loud crunch, the *Agat* produced a spreadsheet screen showing deportation figures sorted by nationality and destination.

Now, let's see, Kronov thought (generations of surveillance had bred out any Soviet citizen's capacity for talking to themselves aloud when alone). *A nice out-of-the-way place, with a lot of Ukrainians.* He thought about the treatment his nationalistic countrymen would be getting in Riga, and shrugged. *Even Latvians would do, I suppose.* In the end, he decided on Estonians, whom he didn't like any better than Lithuanians or Latvians.

The place was a large Estonian colony on a harsh little moon called Haven. Kronov snorted; they'd named their area "Tallinn," worked hard, and had begun coaxing decent farm land from the alien soil. *So much the better.*

Well, let's see how they like having a few thousand Russian patriots for neighbors, Kronov thought with grim satisfaction as he began the paperwork.

Kirichenko's instructions regarding the dispersal ratios could go, along with Kirichenko, straight to hell. If confronted, Kronov would claim that he'd taken those instructions no more seriously than Kirichenko's obvious jest of taking the rest of the day off. Or that, had Kirichenko been serious about the holiday, he'd obviously intended Kronov to process the work in the most expedient way possible and then go home.

With any luck, Kirichenko himself will be censured for sloppiness, Kronov considered, then indulged himself in the pleasant fantasy of processing Kirichenko's unplanned and permanent vacation. It helped to pass the time.

It was midnight before he'd finished, but he was tired only with the fatigue of a man finishing a job well done.

Kronov turned off the lights in his office, putting on his coat as he closed the door and headed for the elevator.

Kronov thought about the Russian Nationalists— his Nationalists—arriving in the Tallinn Valley, finding all that good farm land prepared and ready for them by the unwitting Estonians. Then, naturally, subjugating those Estonians, and establishing a more natural order to things on *that* world, at least. Unconsciously, he shrugged.

There can be no other outcome. We Russians are, by definition, rulers of other, lesser peoples.

The elevator had arrived, and he took it down to the street. The weather had cleared, and Kronov looked up at the brilliantly starlit sky.

Too bad it couldn't have been Ukrainians, he reflected.

But Estonians would have to do. It changed nothing. Russians were Russians, Balts were Balts, and that was that.

Hang Together

HARRY TURTLEDOVE

Anton Päts awoke in darkness. He had gone to bed in
darkness, with neither Byers' Star nor Cat's Eye in the
sky. He would go to bed in darkness again, for this
stretch of truenight lasted more than forty hours.

His heart thudded in his chest as he rose. The Tallinn
where he had grown up was by the sea. Tallinn Town,
in what the Estonian departees who'd founded the place
had named the Tallinn Valley in memory of their lost
home, was at the equivalent of about 2,500 meters. He
would never be used to thin thin air, or to the unrelenting cold that pierced a man's bones like an awl. Tallinn,
the real Tallinn, had had winter, yes, but it had known
summer, too. In the Tallinn Valley, it was always
November.

His wife and daughters and son-in-law still lay snoring
in the big communal bed, huddled together for warmth.
He let them sleep. He pulled on his boots and a wool
cap, then rubbed his hands, the gnarled hands of a man
who had fought the land for years with only hand tools
as weapons. The heat the rubbing yielded was faint and
fleeting. He cherished it anyhow.

A guttering tallow dip gave just enough blood-colored
light to let him make his way to the door without tripping
over the shoes that lay everywhere. He went outside.
The wind nipped at his cheeks above the border of his

305

bushy brown beard, now heavily streaked with gray. Even
the patterns the stars scrawled across the sky were meaningless to him. No one had ever bothered naming
Haven's constellations, and without names they had no
power. The stars were lost to him and his anyway, lost
forever.

In front of his wood cabin stood a pole, cut from as
tall and straight a tennis-fruit tree as he'd found after
long searching. At the top of the pole fluttered a large
flag, a horizontal tricolor of blue, black, and white. He
took his cap off to it, as he did every time he went
outside. Though he was light-years from Earth, he would
not let the idea of Estonia die in his heart.

Not that Tallinn Town is much like the true Tallinn,
he thought with more bitterness than he usually felt after
close to two decades on Haven. Here were no stone
towers, no medieval walls, no jutting spire to mark St.
Olaf's great church. Here were only cabins much like his
own, and unending labor to harvest enough oats and barley and rye and vegetables to keep people and animals
going from one day to the next.

His gaze traveled over the low rooftops toward another
pole, even taller than his. In the darkness he could not
really see it, could not see the banner that flew from it,
but he knew they were there.

His upwelling bitterness threatened to overflow. God
knew the CoDominium cared little for what happened
to politically unreliable deportees once it dumped them
on Haven. Still, it had taken either more than the usual
run of bureaucratic indifference or diabolical cunning to
saddle Tallinn Valley with a load of exiled Russian nationalists. Their red-white-blue banner with the bicephalous
imperial eagle was twice the size of his Estonian flag.

Breath smoking around him, Päts clumped back to the
barn to milk the cows and sheep. The animals grunted
in sleepy surprise and complaint as he threw open the
door. They had not evolved to spend forty-odd continu-
ous hours in darkness, and did not care for it one bit.
Two cows kicked him as he milked them, both just above

his knee. He was swearing and limping as he walked down to the river to check the vegetable plot.

Weeding by starlight was something he hadn't anticipated when BuReloc dumped him here (there were a lot of things he hadn't anticipated when BuReloc dumped him here). He had to do it, though. Turnips and onions, like cattle and sheep, hadn't evolved to spend so long a time in the dark. They went dormant. The local plants kept right on growing. If he wanted to keep his vegetables unsmothered till Byers' Star rose again, his trowel had to stay busy.

The knees of his trousers were thickly padded, to keep his own knees warm as he crawled along on the frigid ground. After a while, the cold seeped through the padding. Päts keep weeding all the same.

After a couple of hours, he heard footsteps coming along the path. He glanced up, expecting his son-in-law. But it was not Konstantin. The broad-shouldered silhouette limned by starlight and the wan illumination of Cat's Eye's lesser moons wore a bulging fur cap with earflaps. That meant it was a Russian; like Päts, Estonian men generally favored wool headgear.

Letting the gloom hide his scowl, Päts said, "Good day," in Russian. He spoke it fluently enough, as did most of his compatriots. Only a handful of Russians in Tallinn Town had bothered to learn more Estonian than *täi*—louse.

This Russian paused now, peered toward him in the gloom. "Who—? Oh, it's you, Päts," he grunted—in his own tongue, of course. "Maybe you think it's a good day, but then you're already at your plot. You cursed Estonians took all the land close by the town when you got here. Me, I have another hour's walk before I can even begin my work."

"We didn't know more people were going to be settled here, Iosef Trofimovich," Päts said, as patiently as he could. He addressed the Russian by first name and patronymic, more politeness than Iosef Mladenov had granted him.

Mladenov grunted again. "We are as many as you. These plots should be shared out more fairly. One day, they will be shared out more fairly, whether you like it or not—and the fields as well, where again your holdings keep ours at arm's length from our own homes."

Päts wanted to rise up and brain Mladenov with the trowel he held now in a clenched fist. Only two things held him back. First, though Mladenov was short, he was hard and strong, and likely carried a trowel of his own. And second, even if Päts did stretch him dead and bleeding on the ground, that would be just the start of internecine strife in Tallinn Town. Life on Haven was hard enough without neighbors at one's throat.

But the Russians—! Päts clenched his teeth, tore a weed out of the ground, ripped it to pieces, and threw the pieces aside. The Russians drank too much; the first thing they'd done after the BuReloc trucks chugged back toward Shangri-La Valley was build themselves a still. They worked too little; they weren't used to the idea that they had to keep busy even if no one was watching. On Haven, if you didn't keep busy, you starved.

Worst of all, they were *Russians*, members of one of the CoDominium's two leading states. Even if they were politically crazy Russians, they still found more sympathy in Shangri-La Valley than any Estonian could hope for. Päts and his fellows had had to beggar themselves with the bribes they needed to bring a handful of ancient bolt-action hunting rifles to Tallinn Valley. He knew for a fact that these Pamyat fanatics had Kalashnikovs, maybe worse.

That gave him a third reason for leaving Iosef Mladenov alone. If the Estonians and Russians did go at it, he was afraid his people would lose. But oh, Päts longed for the days when Tallinn Valley had belonged to the Estonians alone. Were the Russians not content with tyrannizing their homeland for centuries? Now did they want to steal this place of exile as well?

As if to underscore his worry, another Russian came padding down the path in soft felt *valenki*. The fellow

cheerfully whistled Prokofiev as he walked. He too
paused when he spied Päts stooped in his plot. "Is that
you, Anton Avgustovich?" he asked. His voice was light
and young. Päts recognized it at once.

"*Da*, Sergei Dmitrovich, it's me," he said resignedly.
Here was a friendly Russian. All things considered, he
preferred the surly Mladenov.

"How are you this fine day, sir?" Sergei Izvekov went
on.

"I am well," Päts said.

"And your charming daughter Ana, she is also well, I
hope?"

"She is well," Päts agreed. Ana was his young daughter—more to the point, his unmarried daughter. Izvekov
had been sniffing around her for the better part of a T-
year. Päts had not been able to discourage him this side
of a thrashing. One of these days, it might come to that.

Perhaps finally taking a hint from Päts' string of short
answers, Izvekov went on his way. The Estonian
returned to weeding. In the darkness, he did not see that
one of the plants he was pulling up was a fireweed
sprout. The acid in the leaves burned his fingers. He
swore, foully. Between Russians and fireweed, his mood
was black.

He hardly brightened when his son-in-law, Konstantin
Laidoner, at last came to help him. "Took you long
enough," he growled. Even having his own language in
his mouth again hardly gave him pleasure.

"I am sorry, father of my wife," Laidoner answered.
"I did not want to leave right after I woke. Sarah felt
unwell. I think she is pregnant, father of my wife."

Päts' mouth fell open. Sarah, pregnant? His Sarah, who
had been born on the hellish flight out from Earth
aboard the *Red October*, whom he had held in one hand
as if she were a potato, whose dirty linens he had
changed, whose skinned knees he had kissed miracu-
lously back to health? He knew she was a woman now.
With a communal bed in his house, how could he help

knowing it? But in his heart, she remained eternally his little girl. Pregnant?

In his heart now came fear. This was a valley, though by Earthly standards the equivalent of highland country. She could deliver safely, if everything went well. If things went not so well, the nearest real doctor with real instruments was thousands of kilometers away. Would the CoDominium fly such a doctor to Sarah's aid? Even imagining that set scornful laughter echoing in his mind.

As was his way, he covered fear with gruffness. "Get down here and weed with me, Konstantin. If she is pregnant, she'll need all the turnips we can coax from the ground."

They worked together until the little plot was free of native plants. Then they got up and trudged out to their field to do the same thing. The barley and rye looked to be doing well; for some reason, the oats were having trouble. No doubt an agronomist could have solved the problem in a few days, but if no obstetrician would come from Shangri-La Valley to care for a woman, what were the odds of anyone flying out to check on some plants? If people outside the main valley couldn't make it on their own, that was their lookout, as far as what passed for a central government was concerned.

"Now what?" Laidoner asked after they had finished weeding and doing what they could for the ailing oats (which mostly consisted of making sure they had enough water and manure).

"Gather the eggs, unless one of the women has seen to the hens by now. Slop the pigs. Churn the butter. Check the cheeses, to see how they're doing. Jaak says he'll make some new boots for us when one of those sheep's-milk wheels is ripe. Always something to do, youngling, always something to do. I remember back on Earth when I was your age, not long before they shipped me out. I'd sit around in a tavern for hours on end, drinking beer and telling lies to friends as idle as I was."

Konstantin had headed back to Tallinn Town before

Päts could finish the sentence. As he started after his son-in-law, he wondered how many times he'd told that tavern tale. Too many, evidently. Konstantin must have known it by heart.

A couple of Russians came down the road toward Laidoner. One of them carried a hoe on his shoulder, as if it were a rifle: the Russians were on their way out to cultivate too, then. Instead of making way for Konstantin, they blocked his path. "Let me by, please," he said.

"Let me by, please," the one with the hoe echoed, mockingly mimicking his accent. "If it weren't for troublemakers like you, Estonian scum, the *rodina* never would have had to suck up to the Americans to make the CoDominium. And they never would have shipped us to this Christless place for speaking the plain truth that Russia should be Russian. Grab him, Gleb; let's pound some respect into his stupid, ugly face."

Laidoner sprang to one side, but the Russian called Gleb grabbed him and wrestled him to the ground. The fellow with the hoe stood over them, waiting for a clear chance to swing it.

Päts plucked a knife from his boot and ran toward the fight. He blindsided the Russian with the hoe. The Russian hit the ground like a sack of flour. Päts sprang onto him, jerked up his chin by the beard, set the edge of the knife against his windpipe. "Get away from my son-in-law," he snarled at Gleb, "or I'll let all the air out of your friend here." To emphasize what he said, he let the knife dig in a couple of millimeters. The Russian he was sitting on wailed.

· Gleb rolled off Konstantin, who got shakily to his feet. "You cut my brother, Estonian louse," Gleb said, "and we have war in this valley."

"That didn't worry you when you thought you had the drop on one of us," Päts retorted. All the same, Gleb's words gave him pause. He did not want war with the Russians. He did not want to live with them, either, but no help for that now. Reluctantly, he got off the fellow he had tackled. He kicked him in the ribs, about half as hard as he wanted to. The Russian took it like a man, which only annoyed him more. "Go your way and we'll go ours," Päts said to Gleb.

"We'll go," Gleb said. "This time. Come on, Boris, let's get you on your feet."

After a couple of tries, Boris managed to stand. Even so, he walked with a list, as if he'd sprung a leak on one side. Gleb picked up the hoe. He looked back at Päts, who stayed in a knife-fighter's crouch. The two Russians turned and went on down the path. Snatches of Boris' words floated back: "—castrate that bastard—think he broke one of my ribs—"

"Come on, Konstantin," Päts said. "It's over."

"This time," his son-in-law said, echoing Gleb.

"Yes, this time," Päts agreed. "Russians." Back on Earth, they had outweighted Estonia a hundred to one, and used their weight to hold the land down whether the Estonians liked it or not. Here in the Tallinn Valley, the numbers of the two groups were more or less even, but the Russians still behaved as if everything was theirs by right. The arrogance of conquerors— With a distinct effort of will, Päts made himself shove the Russians into the back of his mind. "Are you all right, boy?"

"I'll live," Laidoner answered drily. "They didn't have a chance to do much to me. Thank you, father of my wife. And speaking of Sarah, I'd sooner not tell her of this. I don't want her to worry, especially not now."

"All right," Päts said. Konstantin was right; if Sarah was pregnant, she needed to take things easy. *If Sarah is pregnant, you're going to be a grandfather.* Somehow that thought had taken this long to catch up with him.

After dealing with the pigs and the cheeses (the women had gathered the eggs), Päts and his son-in-law went back to the house for food; working in the cold left a man with a land gator's appetite. Even before he opened the door, Päts smelled the creamy richness of soup on the kettle. Saliva flooded into his mouth.

He sighed with pleasure as he went inside and walked over to the fireplace to warm his hands. Konstantin stood beside him, soaking up heat like a tamerlane basking on a rock. The kettle hung over the fire. Päts peered down into it, smiled at what he saw: barely, carrots, and pork shanks all bubbling together. "It's almost ready," his wife Eva called from the kitchen.

"Good," he boomed. "I'm starved."

Eva came bustling in: a small, fine-boned woman gracefully going from gold hair toward silver. She tilted up her face so Päts could kiss her, but she was more concerned with the soup. She dipped in a hand-carved wooden spoon, tasted, frowned. She went back to the kitchen, returned with salt. When she tasted again, she nodded. "Sarah! Ana! Blow out the candles in there and put away your knitting. It's ready."

Päts' daughters hurried into the front room. They were younger versions of their mother, and reminded him of how lovely she'd been when he won her. Was Sarah a touch paler than usual? In the ruddy firelight, it was hard to tell.

Eva ladled soup into bowls. "Let's eat here by the fire," Päts said. "Too cold to go back to the kitchen." No one argued with him. When they had all sat down, they bent their heads as he said grace. Sometimes he wondered why he should thank God for marooning them on Haven. It was, he supposed, preferable to the bullet in the back of the neck he might have earned for what the CoDominium called attempted subversion of the state.

"This soup is wonderful, mother of my wife," Konstantin Laidoner mumbled around a pork bone. He tossed the bone into his bowl, went back to the kettle to fill the bowl once more. When he sat down again, he said, "You should eat more, Sarah, put strength on yourself." Eva nodded vigorously. She knew, then.

Sara said, "I try to eat, Konstantin, truly I do. But I have no appetite. I—" She broke off abruptly and ran for the front door. Päts heard her retching outside. Eva had been sick too, all the way through both pregnancies.

When Sarah came back in, she was shamefaced and white as a ghost. Päts got up and enfolded her in a bearhug. "Don't you worry, my little girl. Soon enough all this will be done and we will have a new child in the house. Everything will be fine." *If Tallinn Town is not in ruins by the time the birth comes due*, he thought but did not say.

Ana said, "Let me put on some water to make you herb tea, Sarah. It will help settle your stomach." She made a face at her sister. "You're going to have everyone waiting on you now. I'm jealous. Maybe I should—" Without finishing, she went into the kitchen for a pot, then outside to get the water.

Maybe I should—what? Päts wondered. *Get pregnant, too?* He was sure Sergei Izvekov would be happy to help her. If Ana could halfway talk about it, she might want him to help her. Päts scowled. Before he let that happen, he would break the Russian over his knee like a stick.

"Why so glum, Anton?" Eva said. "You should be happy—you don't learn of the coming of your first grandchild every day."

"It's nothing," Päts said. Eva looked at him shrewdly. It was not nothing, and she knew it. He knew she knew, too. After they'd lived with each other for more than twenty T-years, keeping secrets was next to impossible. But she did not press him. Sooner or later, it would come out, and he knew she also knew that.

Maybe, he thought, the trouble with the Russians would blow over. It had before, more than once. Then he would not have to tell Eva anything. But he did not believe it. The Russians hadn't tried beating up Estonians for the sport of it before. From there to fires and murders and civil war in the valley was only a short step.

He yawned. Whatever the Russians were going to do, he hoped they wouldn't do until he'd had another sleep. By the time he woke up, Byers' Star should be in the sky. Things never looked as bad in daylight as they did toward the end of the long dark.

"I'm going to bed," he announced, hoping Eva might join him there.

But she said, "I'm not sleepy yet. I was the last one up. There are always things to do, too, light or no light."

Living on a world with patterns of light and dark so different from those of Earth made people take wildly differing sleep patterns. As he rather grumpily tramped toward the bedroom, Päts hoped he and Eva could come back into synch before too long. Sarah and Konstantin never seemed to have any trouble with that, but then, they hadn't been married long. He chuckled to himself. Once the baby came, they'd spend less time in bed.

He pulled off his boots and cap, buried himself in covers. Aside from saving space and making a house easier to build for people who hadn't been carpenters till they were forced to be, the major advantage of a communal bed on Haven was that the people in it kept one another warm. Now he was by himself, and chilly as well as lonely.

Konstantin came in just as he was dropping off. The youngster wasn't the person with whom he'd hoped to share the bed, but warmth was never unwelcome, not here. The two men snuggled close together and slept.

Sunlight stealing through gaps in the shutters woke Päts. It was not the brilliant sunlight he remembered from his younger days on Earth, not with Byers' Star so far away. But it was incomparably brighter than lamps or candles. Päts found himself smiling as he got out of bed. Just leaving the house and being sure where one was going had a bracing effect on a man.

The soup was still in the kettle. Päts fed the fire to heat it up, had himself a bowl as big as the one he'd enjoyed before he slept. As he did every so often, as he doubtless would till the day the minister prayed over his grave, he wished for a cup of coffee to get him moving quicker. They imported such luxuries in the Shangri-La Valley, but the Shangri-La Valley was a quarter of a way around the moon. BuReloc transportees in the hinterlands made do with what they could turn out for themselves.

As he ate the last few spoonsful of soup, he thought about what he would have to do once he got outside. The pigs first, he decided. Pretty soon he would have to decide which of this latest litter to keep for breeding and which to turn into hams and bacon and pork roasts and pickled pigs' feet and ... Just thinking about it made him hungry again.

He pulled his cap down over his ears. Byers' Star was still low on the horizon, and would not yet have brought any warming to speak of. For that matter, speaking of warmth and Haven in the same breath was a waste of a good breath.

Päts headed outside to salute the Estonian flag. No sooner had he opened the door than something went *craack!* past his ear and buried itself in the far wall of the front room. He stood gaping for a split second, then threw himself flat.

No second shot came. He needed two tries to get to his hands and knees; he was shaking in every limb. Adrenaline brought a stronger waking rush than he'd ever dreamed of from caffeine. Not far from the doorway was a stick. Päts put one end inside his cap, held it high. Only after the silence continued did he climb to his feet.

He heard his son-in-law running inside the house. The young man did not step into the doorway, for which Päts gave him credit. He said, "Are you all right, father of my wife? I have the rifle."

"Good lad," Päts said. "I think the skulking son of a whore shot once and fled." He drew himself to attention before the Estonian colors. The salute he made was not the casual gesture of greeting he sometimes made, but one of soldierly precision. "By God, I will have a reckoning for this, Kostantin." He tramped toward the Russian half of Tallinn Town.

"Where are you going?" Laidoner called after him.

"To see Iosef Mladenov," Päts answered grimly. "Either we will have a stop to this game or we will have war. One way or the other, you will know when I come back—if I come back. If I am not back in three hours, avenge me."

"I will come with you," Konstantin said.

Päts shook his head. "You are younger than I am, and your wife is pregnant. We can't afford to lose you. And if the Pamyat maniacs mean fighting, we can't afford to lose two finding out."

When he entered the Russian section, in which he set foot but rarely, Päts felt he had stepped into another world. The very shape of the houses changed, as did their look: they were brightly painted, and roofed with wood shingles. The thick smell of cooked cabbage huge in the air. The streets were dirtier than in the Estonian part of Tallinn Town, with dogs here and there digging through piles of refuse for scraps. One raised its head and growled at Päts. He growled back.

The few Russians about stared at him as he tramped grimly along. He ignored them. He had never called on Iosef Mladenov before, but he had no trouble finding the man's home. That imperial banner might as well have been a beacon, just as his own Estonian flag was. He wanted to spit at the flagpole in front of Mladenov's house as he walked past it, but held in his temper by main force.

He released some of it by pounding on the door. It shook under the weight of his fist. No one answered. He pounded again, harder, leaned his face up to the peep-hole. Another eye was looking back at him. "Mladenov?" he growled.

"He's sleeping," the man on the other side of the door said.

"Get him."

"He's sleeping," the Russian repeated.

"Get him, *metyeryebyets*, or his house and this whole God-damned town will come down round his ears while he lies there snoring."

"Don't threaten me," the Russian said.

"I do not threaten. I promise. If I walk away without seeing him, we fight. If he tries to hold me, we fight, too. The war starts unless I am back safe with my people in three hours—no, nearer two and a half now. *Now get him.*"

He felt the Russian move back from the door. "Wait," the fellow said.

"I will wait. But remember, the more time you waste, the more likely you waste lives with it."

He stood outside Mladenov's front door, blowing out steam at every long, furious exhalation. In less than five minutes, the door opened. Iosef Mladenov glowered out at him. "What do you want, Päts?" he said, making his voice rough and deep to show he was not afraid of the taller Estonian.

"A reckoning, Mladenov, and past time." Päts gave back rudeness for rudeness, disdaining to use the Russian's first name and patronymic. "Someone took a shot at me from hiding. If you aim to fight, we will give you all the fight you want. If you want to play the assassin's game, you will find we can play that, too. But God help Tallinn Valley if it starts."

Mladenov did not back up, but some of the fierceness left his face. "You'd better come in," he said grudgingly.

Päts went in. Mladenov waved him to a chair. He sat. Mladenov sat too, on a couch against the opposite wall. He did not offer the Estonian food or drink. The fellow who had argued with Päts was not visible. Small shuffling noises from around the corner said he probably lurked in the hallway there. Päts was willing to bet he'd be armed. It didn't matter. He wasn't going to start fighting here—he hoped.

"It is only from the goodness of my heart that I speak to you," Mladenov said. "After you set on Gleb and Boris Suslov—"

"After I *what*?" Päts roared, his good intentions blown away in a blast of fury. "Those two lying bastards thought they'd have some sport with my son-in-law. I saw and heard the whole thing, and stopped them from doing worse than they did." He rapidly told the Russian leader what had happened. "Let them deny it to my face, if they dare."

"That is not the tale they tell," Mladenov said, but he sounded oddly hesitant. He might not like Päts, but he knew the Estonian was not a man to lie.

"I don't care what tale they tell," Päts said. "I think, Iosef Trofimovich, that if you Russians listen to tales without checking, and if you go shooting from ambush, we will have war to the knife, and maybe none of us will live through it. Do you want that? You will not find my people such easy meat here as back on Earth."

"We would win that war, Anton Avgustovich." Mladenov's words were still harsh and threatening, but now he addressed Päts in the polite fashion. "Still, as you say, it might cripple winners as well as losers. And I agree, shooting from ambush is a coward's sport. I will speak further with Gleb and Boris as well. But if you think you Estonians will keep forever all the best land in the valley and that closest to town, you had best think again."

"We were here first, and we were the ones who made those lands into what they are today. If you think we will throw away all the labor we have invested in them, you are the one making the mistake," Päts said.

"Then war will come," Mladenov said flatly. "One day I will burn that flagpole of yours, Anton Avgustovich, and the flag of what you wrongly reckon to be a nation. Nations are groups of people strong enough to survive. You do not qualify. It is up to you, Estonian. If you want to fight now, we shall fight now. If not, we will fight later. *Nichevo.*"

It can't be helped; there's nothing to be done about it. The Russian word could mean either. Both filled Päts with fury and despair, for he was pretty sure he held a losing hand. Behind what he hoped was an impassive mask, he calculated furiously. The odds of BuReloc's dumping more Estonians into Tallinn Valley were slim to the point of vanishing. The CoDominium's apparatus of control and repression was all too likely, though, to haul out more Russians. The longer till the conflict, the worse his own people's chances. As he took a deep breath, he wondered if Mladenov would let him leave once he chose war.

Before he could speak, someone pounded furiously on Mladenov's door. The Russian who had stayed discreetly in the hallway leaped into the front room. As Päts had guessed, he held a Kalashnikov. The change lever was set on full automatic. A burst from less than two meters would turn a man into blood pudding.

But the pounder was no Estonian intent on rescue or revenge. He spoke pure Russian, with a broad peasant accent like Mladenov's own: "Iosef Trofimovich, come quick! Some fucking horsemen just rode in, down from the plains. You'd better come to talk to them."

Mladenov bounced to his feet. "Tatars!" he snarled, as if it were a curse. To a Russian, it was; back on Earth, their wars with the steppe nomads had gone on for centuries. Mladenov turned to the fellow with the Kalashnikov. "You come with me, Yevgeny, and bring the assault rifle. I want them to see we have it." He suddenly seemed to remember Päts. "You'd better come too, Anton Avgustovich. The Tatars won't care whether your people are Estonians or Russians—they'll only know you're farmers, and farmers are prey."

He and Yevgeny hurried out of his house without waiting to see whether Päts would follow. Glumly, Päts did. His mind whirled as he struggled to adjust. For the past twenty T-years and more, BuReloc had been dumping disaffected Soviet Asiatics onto Haven along with everyone else. He'd thought the nomads would have taken longer to reach the steppe north of Tallinn Valley, but here they were. And Iosef Mladenov, curse him, was right about one thing—the nomads were a worse danger than the Russians.

Half a dozen of them—four on ponies, two on muskylopes—waited in the center of town. They wore round fur hats, sheepskin jackets, and shiny black boots. Every one of them had a rifle on his back and a big showy knife on his belt. Cartridge-filled bandoliers criss-crossed three chests.

One of the Tatars, a fellow with a great beak of a nose and a sweeping black mustache, stared down from horseback at the townsmen who hurried up to meet him. "You are leader?" he demanded of Mladenov. His Russian was fair.

"I am Iosef Trofimovich Mladenov. I and Anton Avgustovich lead, *da*," Mladenov answered, pointing at Päts. The Estonian wondered whether Mladenov wanted him to share the trouble or was really including him. The latter, he decided reluctantly. Whatever else he was, Mladenov was no fool. If Estonians and nomads made common cause, the Russians in the valley were doomed.

Did he want to lead his people in that direction? He looked at the Tatar. The fellow was studying Tallinn Town the way a fox—or on Haven, a tamerlane—studied a chicken coop. He said, "I am Isa Bektashi, son to Suleiman Bektashi, chieftain of the clan of Aydin. He intends to take you under his protection, to keep you safe from other, less kindly clans that are coming to roam the steppes."

"To protect us? To keep us safe?" Päts repeated. Estonia had heard those words so many times back on Earth, usually from Russians, sometimes from Germans. "Isa Suleimanovich, tell your father we have no quarrel with him, but we can protect ourselves."

"That is so, by God," Mladenov said. He looked back and forth between the nomad and Päts. Päts wondered if he resented being upstaged. The Estonian bared his teeth in a humorless grin. Mladenov had named him a town leader—this was what he got.

Isa Bektashi said, "Think again. You would not do well to anger my father."

"We do not want to anger him," Mladenov said. "We do not want to serve him, either. Let us live at peace with one another."

"Not so simple," the nomad said. "Our women, they need the valley to give birth."

That was always a problem on Haven. Only in the lowlands was there enough oxygen to let a woman bring a baby to term and to undergo labor with a decent chance of living through it. Päts said, "Your women will be welcome here, Isa Suleimanovich. We shall not molest them. We are civilized men, not savages."

Bektashi shook his head. "You say *welcome* now. What if, one fine day, you say *not welcome*? What happens to clan of Aydin then? How can we leave selves open to wounding by infidels? You come under our protection, let our riders into valley to make sure all goes well."

"*Nyet.*" Mladenov and Päts said it in the same breath. The Russian went on, "This is our valley, our land. We will protect it ourselves—from you, if need be."

One of the Tatars behind Isa Bektashi made as if to unsling his rifle. The Russian named Yevgeny brought his own weapon up to his shoulder. Mladenov glanced around to the houses by the square, as if to check warriors hidden in them. So far as Päts knew, there were no warriors. He admired Mladenov's quick thinking.

Bektashi barked something at his follower in his own language. The fellow took his hand off the rifle. Yevgeny relaxed, fractionally. Bektashi glared at Mladenov and Päts. "This is your final word?"

They looked at each other. They both nodded.

"You will regret it," said the nomad chief's son. He made his horse rear and spin round on its hind legs, then trotted north out of Tallinn Town. The other riders followed him.

Päts looked at Yevgeny and Mladenov and started to laugh. Mladenov scowled. "I do not see anything funny here, Anton Avgustovich," he growled. "Nothing."

"No?" Päts said. "Here is the war between us, all at once forgotten because we have a worse problem. From my enemy, the man who gladly would have killed me half an hour ago, you've turned into my ally and my friend. Do you see no joke there?"

"Put so, maybe I do," Mladenov said. "When the choice is between fair land and no land, it makes the choice between fair land and better land seem of small importance, doesn't it?"

"So it does, Iosef Trofimovich, so it does. Your leading men and mine need to sit down and talk things over, I think. Those nomads look damnably well armed. If we want to keep this valley for ourselves, we won't hold them off with words alone. We'll need all the guns we can get our hands on ... and we'll need to work together." The words left a bad taste in Päts' mouth, but he knew they were true.

So did Mladenov. "It shall be as you say, Anton Avgustovich." He looked no happier about the prospect than Päts was, but went on nonetheless: "We will need sentries at the mouth of the valley, to warn us if the nomads come. We have a few two-way radio sets, to get word quickly back to town—"

"Do you?" Päts said in surprise. "We tried to get some, but our applications went nowhere. Of course, we are not Russians, either." *One more reason to be glad my people are not going to fight these* Pamyat *bastards*, he thought. Walkie-talkies would have given them one more big edge. Fight the Russians ... he looked down at his watch. "I have to go, Iosef Trofimovich, right this minute, or my own people will start the war coming after me."

"Can't have that, not now," Mladenov said. "Shall I come with you, to start working out a rotation for sentries?"

"Come if you care to," Päts answered. The Russian leader was no coward, not if he was willing to beard a band of armed and angry Estonians in their den. He would have been easier to dislike as a more thoroughgoing villain.

The Estonians were almost out of their den when Päts and Mladenov reached them. They were forming up by the flag in front of Päts' house. Some carried spears improvised from knives and poles, a couple bore hunting bows, while all those who owned firearms had them.

"Wait!" Päts shouted.

"Father of my wife," Konstantin Laidoner said in glad

surprise. Then he saw who was with Päts. "Why have you brought the Russian here? We were all getting ready to come and rescue you." He sounded disappointed at missing the chance to fight. He was still a young man.

"I am here, as you see. And all of us, Estonians and Russians alike, have a worse enemy than any who lives in this valley." Päts used Russian so Mladenov could follow what he said. He went on, "I will let Iosef Trofimovich here speak of that."

Seeing the Russian leader as anything but a menace was new and different for the Estonians. Seeing him as someone who had important information, information that could actually help them, was not only different but difficult. But he spoke effectively and to the point—he did not lead his own community by accident. He finished, "You Estonians know I do not love you. I think you have acted unjustly by not sharing out the lands in this valley more fairly. Still, neither have you tried to enslave me or my people. That is what Isa Bektashi will do. If we don't beat back the nomads now, we lose all chance to quarrel among ourselves later."

The Estonians were not a people to show much of what they felt, not among themselves, still less to an outsider. They talked in low voices, using their own tongue. Finally Jaak Vilde switched to Russian: "Iosef Trofimovich, we are with you. As you say, we can always fight among ourselves. This other fight does not look likely to wait."

Mladenov crossed himself. By the gesture, he set himself apart once more from the Estonians, who were mostly Lutheran. Somehow, it did not matter now. Päts said, "Let's start planning now, to work out how best we can hold what is ours."

Tallinn Valley's opening onto the steppe was several kilometers wide. Till now, that had not mattered; till now, there had not been enough people on the steppe for it to matter. But the gap was too big to fortify in a hurry. If the clan of Aydin attacked, they would have to

be met inside the valley. The most sentries could hope
to do was give early warning.

Accordingly, none of the young men who went out to
stand watch carried guns—they were too vulnerable to
being picked off by Tatar raiders, and the folk of the
valley did not own enough firearms to risk them thus.
The youngsters went forth proudly all the same. The
Russians and Estonians who had rifles slung them on
their backs as they went about their chores, ready to fight
at a moment's notice.

But hour followed hour, and nothing happened. Cat's
Eye joined Byers' Star in the sky, making the valley as
light and bright as it ever became. Byers' Star slowly
sank, leaving Cat's Eye alone in the sky for more than
forty hours. Then Byers' Star returned and Cat's Eye
sank. Finally, a hundred thirty hours after Byers' Star
first rose, both it and Cat's Eye were gone from the
sky—full night was back for another twenty-two hours.

That stretch worried Anton Päts—who could guess
what deviltry the Tatars might try when no one could
see what they were up to? At his urging, Mladenov doubled the number of patroling sentries. The Russian
wanted to light watchfires through the darkness, but Päts
talked him out of it: "They'll let Bektashi's men see
where we are but they won't do us a bit of good, looking
out onto the steppe."

For all the farmers' precautions, Nikita Tukachevsky's
relief could not find him when he came out to take his
place. The word needed a while to filter back into Tallinn
Town, for Tukachevsky had one of the valley's precious
radios, which he was supposed to pass on to his relief.
The Estonian who was to replace him had to track down
the sentry to the west before he could send word to
anyone in the valley that something was wrong.

Armed searchers went out at once, but found no sign
of the luckless Tukachevsky until Cat's Eye returned to
the sky. Päts was part of that search party. He carried
his rifle at the ready, his hands tight on it in the nervous
grip of a man who knows war only from stories.

"Over here," someone called, and Päts, a couple of hundred meters away, trotted through mixed grass and native Haven shrubbery to *here*. He heard how much noise he made as he ran, and knew he needed to do better—he sounded like a herd of drunken muskylopes with the mating frenzy upon them.

Tukachevsky lay sprawled and dead. His trousers were around his ankles, and he had been mutilated. Päts sucked in a sick breath. A word was carved in sinuous Arabic script on the young Russian's forehead. Something bloody had been stuffed into his mouth. Päts reached down to pull it out. He found he was holding Tukachevsky's severed penis. With a groan, he dropped it by the corpse. His stomach heaved; he fought against being sick.

More searchers, Estonians and Russians both, came up and formed a circle around the sentry's maltreated body. Some looked frightened, some looked fierce. Most seemed both at the same time. Several Russians made the sign of the cross.

Päts said, "This is a warning to us. The Tatars think to make us afraid with it." He remembered the feel of what he had just touched. He was afraid, all right. But he did not let that show in his voice: "The truth is, it warns us what we can expect if we give in to them—and not just we men, but our wives and daughters, too. You and you and you, take this poor lad back to Tallinn Town for burial. The rest of us, well, we will watch and we will wait. The time for revenge will come."

The men nodded, one by one. The fear had gone from most of their faces, and some of the ferocity as well. They just looked grim, as men will do when they face a dangerous job from which they cannot escape. Päts had seen that look on old pictures of veteran soldiers from the days of the Great Patriotic War. He'd thought it obsolete. Now he suspected he wore it himself.

The nomads gave the folk of Tallinn Town another twenty hours or so to mull over the fate of Nikita Tukachevsky. Then horns blared an alarm from the central square of the town. A bonfire was kindled there, its col-

umn of smoke a warning the enemy was on the way.
Anton Päts was in his garden a few hundred meters out
of town when the alarm went up. He swore in Russian
and Estonian, got up from his hands and knees, and
looked north.

Bektashi's men did nothing to conceal their presence.
On the contrary—fires flared as they threw torches into
the fields. Päts swore again, horribly. Even if the nomads
were beaten, Tallinn Valley would suffer on account of
them.

The forward assembly point for the farmers was a couple of kilometers north of Tallinn Town. Alternating
between a jog and a fast walk, Päts hurried in that direction. By the time he got close, the rifle on his shoulder
seemed to have doubled its weight. Other men hurried
up with him—everyone who had a gun, and a good many
who did not.

"What happened?" Päts asked.

Sergei Izvekov said, "The radio let out a squawk. One
of the sentries—I think it was your Eugen"—he pronounced it *Evgen*, trying to make it into the Russian
Yevgeny—"said, 'Help! They're—' and then that channel
went dead." *And Eugen, a good man with three little
children, dead with it*, Päts thought.

"Form a firing line," Iosef Mladenov shouted. "Take
cover where you can, and make every shot count. Think
of your mother, think of your wife—"

"If that doesn't do it, think of your neighbor's wife,"
somebody broke in. Mladenov tried to glare every which
way at once to find out who had interrupted his martial
address. He had no luck. The tension-breaking laughter
that rose from the amateur warriors said the gibe had
done some good.

Päts found a place behind a boulder too big to have
been cleared out of the field. Methodical as always, he
checked to make sure his weapon had a round in the
chamber and that the safety was off. Then he peered
round the rock to see how close the Tatars were.

A kilometer of ground still separated horsemen from

defenders. Bektashi's men were not advancing all out; they paused every so often to light more fires or simply to ride this way and that through the fields, trampling down long swathes of grain.

From five meters or so off to Päts' left, Sergei Izvekov called, "You see, Anton Avgustovich, they are no more soldiers than we. Bandits, yes, acting the hooligan for the sport of it, but not really soldiers."

At the far right end of the farmers' line, someone started shooting at the nomads. At that range, he couldn't have hit a farmhouse, let alone a rapidly moving man on horseback. Mladenov's bull roar called down curses on the nervous rifleman's head.

Bektashi's men whooped and came on, spreading out into a skirmish line as they drew close enough for a gunshot to have some chance of striking home. Päts thought there might have been fifty of them, about as many as the men they attacked. The nomads began firing too, some of them blazing away with weapons on full automatic. That meant bad shooting, but it also meant a lot of lead in the air. Through the noise of the gunfire came wounded men's screams and the shouts of the Tatars: "Allah! Allah! Allah!"

Päts peeked out from behind his boulder, fired at the nearest leather-clad horseman. He missed. Two bullets *spannged* off the stone close by, throwing stinging chips into his face. He lurched backwards, worked the bolt, peeped out again. Now the nomad was terrifyingly close. Päts snapped off another shot, heard a scream. The steppe pony the nomad rode went down as if it had run headlong into a fence. Päts shouted in triumph.

But the nomad had been in the saddle since boyhood, and knew how to take a fall. He lost his rifle, but hit rolling and came to his feet only a couple of meters from the boulder. At that point-blank range, Päts fired—and missed. Before he could work the bolt again, the nomad pulled out a knife and jumped on him.

Päts went over backwards. His gun flew out of his hands. He screamed as the nomad's knife grated along a rib; had the fellow stabbed two centimeters higher or lower, he would have been silent forevermore. He grabbed the Tartar's knife wrist with his left hand, tried to get his right on his opponent's throat. The nomad bit him, down to the bone. He screamed again.

He jerked up his knee. The Tatar twisted aside before it could slam into his crotch. In the tiny part of his rational mind that was still functioning, Päts realized that, while Bektashi's men might be bandits rather than soldiers, even bandits were apt to know more of hand-to-hand combat than farmers. Rather more to the point, he realized he was probably going to get killed.

A rifle roared, so close to Päts' ear that for an instant he thought it was the sound of his own death. But it was the nomad who jerked and convulsed, who splashed Päts with blood and brains and bits of bone, whose bowels let go, adding the manure pile to the battlefield stenches of burnt cordite and burnt meat.

Päts threw the corpse aside, scrambled up to his hands and knees—he remembered enough of where he was not to stand up. Sergei Izvekov was less cautious, or more foolish. Seeing as he'd just blown out the Tartar's brains, Päts could hardly complain. He did shout, "Get down!" A startled expression crossed Izvekov's face, as if he suddenly realized what he'd just done. He threw himself flat. "*Spasebo*," Päts added more quietly: "Thank you."

"*Nichevo*," Izvekov answered.

Päts thumped him on the back, reclaimed his own rifle, and looked out to see what was happening in the bigger fight. A lot of horses were down, and a lot of men. A couple of nomads had managed to get around the farmers' right flank. That would have been a lot worse had anything much remained of the rest of the plainsmen's assault. But almost all the riders there were either dead or galloping north as fast as their horses and muskylopes could take them. Well-led soldiers will accept hideous losses for the sake of a decisive victory. Bandits, as a rule, will not.

As Päts watched, one of the Tatars off to the right slid

from his muskylope and crashed to the ground. His rifle bounced away. He made no move to go after it. He would never move again. That was all the other would-be enfilader needed to see. He wheeled his mount and dashed after his comrades. He reeled in the saddle before he got out of rifle range, but kept his seat and kept on riding.

Sergei Izvekov had been watching, too. "*Bozhemoi*," he said softly. "We won." He sounded astonished.

"So we did," Päts said. He didn't sound anything but amazed himself. His ribs and his fingers started hurting again. He reminded himself to use an antitetanus ampoule for the bite. The nomad had had jaws like a cliff lion's. Päts looked down at his late foe's ruined head. That Tatar wouldn't bite anybody else, nor would his clansmates. They'd broken teeth on something harder than they'd expected.

All along the farmers' firing line, men stood up and exchanged congratulations with their neighbors. No, not all along the line: four or five men were down. Some thrashed on the ground, some lay still. Päts ground his teeth. Only in stories did the heroes win their victories without loss.

Now that the shooting was done, the cries of wounded animals and men dominated the little battlefield. Easily recognizable even from a couple of hundred meters away because of his blocky shape, Iosef Mladenov went out to a nomad who was clutching a shattered leg and shrieking. The Russian's rifle barked once. The nomad was quiet after that.

Mladenov headed for the next injured Tatar. "Wait, Iosef Trofimovich," Päts called as he hurried out toward the Russian.

Mladenov's face clouded over. "Don't bleat to me of mercy, Anton Avgustovich," he growled. "I won't hear a word you say. These damned Tatars don't understand the meaning of the word, and they'd only take it for weakness. And after what they did to poor Nikita, I wouldn't give it to them if they did understand. A bullet's a better mercy than they ought to have."

Päts did not answer, not with words. He raised his own rifle to his shoulder, aimed at the nomad writhing on the ground, shot him through the head. The plainsman jerked and twitched for a few more seconds, then lay still. Mladenov gaped at Päts, his pale eyes wide and staring. "You shouldn't have to do it all yourself," Päts said.

Taking turns, they finished four more of the attackers. When the nasty job was done, Mladenov said, "As well we did not come to blows ourselves, Estonian. I thought you and your people softer than you prove to be."

"As well we did not come to blows," Päts said, and let it go at that. He knew the bulk of the firepower that had defeated Bektashi's clan had belonged to the Russians. As if he had every right to it, he picked up the automatic rifle that lay beside the last dead Tatar. The fellow carried several spare magazines, and cartridges for two or three more on his bandoliers. Päts appropriated the ammunition, too. He felt Mladenov's eyes on him all the while, but the Russian kept his mouth shut.

Sergie Izvekov came up. The young man gulped a couple of times as he looked at the pool of blood under the dead nomad's shattered skull, but he'd caused the same kind of carnage not an hour before, to save Päts' life. In any case, battlefield courage was not the kind he was looking for now. He gulped again, then said, "Anton Avgustovich, may I speak to you about your daughter Ana?"

Päts peered down at the shorter Russian. When that long, measuring stare failed to send Izvekov fleeing, the Estonian let out a long sigh and said, "Speak, Sergei Dmitrovich. I should be poor-spirited indeed to deny you now. If Ana cares to have you, you will be part of my family, and a welcome part."

Mladenov boomed laughter and waggled a sausage-like finger under Päts' nose. "You see, Anton Avgustovich, one way or another, we Russians shall end up with some of your land."

Päts started to scowl. Then he looked round the battlefield. Estonians and Russians were embracing like brothers, strolling here and there together, gaping at the bodies of Tatars they had slain, trying to run down riderless horses and muskylopes. Had Bektashi's men not come, the only way the two sides in Tallinn Valley would have looked at each other was over open sights. And the plainsmen, though beaten now, were still out there on the steppe. Päts' eyes swung north. Bektashi's men or some new clan might swoop down at any time.

"If we cannot live as neighbors, Iosef Trofimovich, we will live as slaves," Päts said. "What's the American proverb? 'We must all hang together, or assuredly, we shall all hang separately'? Something like that. So better Sergei gets his land like this than manured with Estonian blood."

"Truth," Mladenov said soberly.

Päts threw one arm around his shoulder, the other around Sergei Izvekov's. Together, the three of them started slowly back toward Tallinn Town to let their women know they had won—this time.

The slamming of the huge, heavy front door downstairs woke ten-year-old Kyle Eng from a sound sleep. The Eng family mansion was otherwise quiet, and a gentle breeze carried the salty Pacific air into his room from the lanai. The surf broke softly, rhythmically, against the shore of Kauai, one of the Hawaiian Islands.

Kyle tensed every muscle in his arms and legs, freezing himself into position. When his father slammed the front door in the middle of the night, it meant he had come home drunk and angry again. Sometimes he just staggered into his den or off to bed; other times, he raged around the house, yelling at people or demons whom no one else could see. Other times, however, he stomped up the stairs after Kyle to yell and scream insults about his mother.

Now, those footsteps were pounding clumsily up the carpeted steps toward his room.

Kyle could only hope that his father was going

somewhere else up here. That wasn't likely, though.
His older half-brother, Tim, slept down the hall,
but their father never gave him this kind of trouble.

Tim was fifteen. His mother had died of an ill-
ness when he had been a baby, and as far as
their father was concerned, Tim could do nothing
wrong. He was also a very sound sleeper.

Kyle knew that his own mother had made his
father very angry, probably forever. Much younger
than his father, she had left them all several years
ago, taking a substantial amount of the family cash
and negotiable assets with her. By the time his
father's private detectives had tracked her down, she
had spent all the money and had taken up with
another wealthy man in Florida. The elder Eng had
successfully prosecuted her for theft, but he had
never recovered from the feeling of betrayal.

With Kyle's mother first missing and then in
prison, Kyle had continued to live in his father's
house.

Lying rigidly, pretending to be sound asleep,
Kyle heard the the crash as his door was kicked
in. It banged against the wall, making him jump.
He jerked the covers over his head as a shaft of
bright light from the hallway slanted into the
room.

"I ssee you, sson of a slut," his father slobbered
drunkenly. "You're awake!"

Kyle, with his eyes closed tightly, felt the covers
yanked away. Instead of just yelling at him as
usual, though, his father reared back and kicked
him with the hard heel of one of his expensive
imported boots. Kyle cried out, surprised at the
pain in his shoulder.

"Ha! Talked to your mother lately, boy?"

"No—" Kyle started, then shut his mouth as a
heavy fist swung down and punched him in the
back.

"It's our anniversary, y'know, your mother's and mine. Shoulda been our eleventh, today, boy!"

Kyle scrambled up on the head of the bed and tried to roll off, but this time his father's fist smashed directly into his forehead. White lights twinkled in his vision, and he momentarily lost his wits as he rolled back on his bed. When the next blow pounded against the side of his head, he barely felt it.

The youngster collapsed on the bed, blinded by tears, unable to move as the beating continued. Suddenly, vaguely through his confusion, he heard his brother's voice.

"Dad! Stop it!" Tim shouted in the doorway. He ran forward and grabbed the older man's arms from behind, pinning him. At a slender, rangy fifteen years of age, he wasn't strong enough or heavy enough to wrestle their father away by brute force. Even in his drunkenness, however, their father would not hurt Tim. The two of them struggled in an awkward dance.

"It's our anniversary," the older man repeated.

"C'mon, Dad!" Tim screamed, his voice cracking.

"Son of a sslut," their father sneered again. He stumbled, but let Tim swing him around toward the door. "Tell her I ssaid sso!"

Tim shoved their father out the door and then slammed it shut after him. Then he had to switch the light on. He stood facing it for a moment, breathing hard. Their father's footsteps shuffled uncertainly at first, then thumped back down the stairs.

Kyle was in shock, staring teary-eyed but without really crying. His head was throbbing. He watched as Tim knelt by the bed and looked at him closely.

"You're gonna have a lump or two," said Tim. He hesitated. "Kyle, can you hear me? Are you okay?"

"He'd never hit you, would he?" Kyle asked, in a voice on the verge of crying.

Tim's face hardened. "He's, uh, sick, Kyle. It's not you. And it's not me, either."

"He thinks you're perfect because your mother was good. And he hates me 'cause my mom is no good."

"Aw, Kyle." Tim looked flustered. He seemed like a grownup sometimes nowadays, but Kyle knew he really wasn't one. "Look. You want to go horseback riding with me tomorrow?"

Kyle nodded.

"You like horses, don't you? Like I do? When I grow up, I'm going to be a horse vet, a doctor, so I can be around them all the time."

"I want to be with you," said Kyle.

"Okay," Tim said gently. "But, look. I've got this poker game planned for tomorrow, too. So if you come, you have to keep this a secret. Okay?"

"Okay." In that moment, Kyle would have done anything for his older brother, even something far more difficult than just keeping a little secret.

"Are you going to be okay? Maybe I should wake up one of the servants to call a doctor for you."

"I'm okay," Kyle said meekly. "But what if he comes back?"

Tim paused. "You're coming to my room for the night. Tomorrow I'll move you in for good."

Kyle looked up, suddenly hopeful. "He wouldn't do that to you, would he?" he asked again.

"I'll never let him do that again, Kyle," Tim growled through his teeth. "Not if I can help it."

Suddenly Kyle threw his arms around his brother's neck. Finally feeling safe, he began to cry at last.

SONS OF HAWAII

WILLIAM F. WU

At age twenty-four, Kyle Eng sat stiffly in his chair in the courtroom, watching the judge. He could hardly believe that Tim was in this mess, not to mention his own mild-mannered self. Kyle, after a sterling performance at the University of Hawaii to earn a B.A. in political science and then an M.A. in public policy and urban planning, had embarked on a fast-moving career as a liaison between developers and local government. Now he and Tim were on trial here in Hilo for fomenting armed rebellion. It made no sense.

"Case 972-675," droned the uniformed bailiff. Like Kyle and Tim, she was a young Asian Hawaiian, older than Kyle but not much.

"Cute, huh?" Tim whispered, elbowing Kyle. He was slightly taller and had a bony, angular frame. "Hey, loosen up, little brother. You don't accomplish anything by sitting there stiff as a board. You gotta be like a cat, loose and flexible. That way you land on your feet." He jabbed Kyle harder and grinned.

Kyle reluctantly smiled back, rubbing the spot on his ribs. He was shorter than Tim and had a medium build. Tim even resembled a cat, but Kyle didn't.

Tim was charming, charismatic, and good-looking, quick to size people up and win them over. As he had planned, his education was in veterinary medicine, with a specialty in horse breeding. Their father had been dead for seven years, leaving them both a substantial inheritance in Hawaiian real estate and diversified investments.

The money had paid for their educations and had allowed Tim the luxury of investing in his own string of horses. He ran his own stable, breeding as well as riding. One of his hobbies had become reading equine history, including military developments, for relaxation.

Kyle's loyalty and admiration for him had remained absolutely firm. Their friends and colleagues supposed it was because Tim was so independent and quick-witted. The real reason was that after that night Tim had kept his promise to stay between Kyle and their father.

On a number of later occasions before Kyle had his growth, their father had started to beat Kyle again, but Tim had always been nearby. Twice, their father, farther gone into his drinking than ever, had finally turned on Tim and beaten him savagely. Tim had taken the punishment instead of Kyle, who had trusted him implicitly ever since. Kyle's home life had made him passive out of caution, and devoted to his older brother.

"The defendants will rise," said the bailiff, in a shrill but bored voice.

They stood. So did their lawyer, Jake Ishihara.

"How do you plead?" Judge Southforth, a black woman with a streak of gray in her hair right in the front, stifled a yawn.

"Not guilty," said Jake firmly.

The judge was clearly surprised. She looked at Jake for a moment. "You do understand the defendants are charged under the Unlawful Assembly and Treason Act as Amended? Their followers failed to disperse a violent protest when so ordered by the authorities. By this law, that constitutes a declaration of rebellion." She frowned and read from her notes. "As the law reads, 'Failure to disperse shall be considered a declaration of rebellion.'" She looked up pointedly.

"Your Honor," said Jake, "neither of my clients was

present at the riots, nor have they ever fomented armed rebellion in any form, at any time."

As they continued to talk, Kyle sat with nearly every muscle in his body tense. The problem was a wacky scheme of Tim's. Two years ago, he had started a political movement to turn Hawaii into a free-trade zone, to compete with the big Asian centers like Singapore, Macau, and Hong Kong. That part was ambitious, but understandable.

Kyle had signed up with him because the project had possibilities; besides, he had never been able to refuse Tim anything important. However, in order to attract attention and to create negotiating space, Tim had taken another step. He had suggested that Hawaii become an independent republic again, as it had been briefly long ago.

That move had not only drawn the unwanted attention of the authorities, but also a mixed following of anarchists, libertarians, entrepreneurs, fugitives, and opportunists of all kinds. Many of these followers had little use for each other, but they all understood that in a free-trade, independent Hawaii, they could have a fresh start. They had staged a number of protests on their own, several of which had turned into riots.

These incidents had clearly turned the local population against Tim's movement, despite his personal charm. As a result, Jake had convinced the brothers to waive their right to a jury trial. Jake had said he would have a better chance before a lone judge in arguing the distinction between his educated, establishment clients and the rabble who had rallied to them.

"Kyle, the younger brother," Jake was saying, "has been known as a reserved, responsible professional in many circles. Neither of my clients ever intended for Hawaii to become independent. That was a political trial balloon in the movement to make Hawaii a free-trade zone, no more."

"Considering the volume of tape of these riots," said Judge Southforth, "I had assumed you would just plead guilty."

"No, Your Honor."

"How do the people regard this?"

"Well." The prosecutor stood up, fumbling glasses onto his face. He was a paunchy, silver-haired man with a perpetual frown. "Every single one of these violent protests has been held in the name of Tim Eng for President of the Republic of Hawaii. We will introduce into evidence many media tapes of the rebellion and sworn testimony from rebels who have been granted immunity in exchange for testifying."

"That presidential campaign was a draft," said Jake smoothly. "My client had no part in that."

"You're out of order." Judge Southforth sighed. "All right. Let's get started."

Tim and Kyle were both found guilty.

They appealed, of course, and remained free on a very large bail during the process. Their family mansion and Tim's stables were all bonded. Kyle, who had never been in any kind of trouble before, was in shock.

On the other hand, Kyle was being carried along on the crest of Tim's wave. That was nothing new at all.

Maybe Kyle's biggest shock came when the appeal was denied. He had always seen his brother as being virtually unstoppable. Tim had never had any serious problems before, either. After their final court appearance, they remained free on bond, and Jake summoned them both to his office.

"I can't believe this," Kyle muttered, as they stood in front of Jake's desk. "This whole business is just insane."

"Aw, it's not that bad." Tim gave him a hearty slap on the back.

"It may be more serious than you think," said Jake gravely. He tapped a rolled document into his palm for a moment, then dropped it onto his desk. "Kyle, this is getting even more complicated. Would you excuse us for just a moment?"

"What? Uh, sure." Kyle was hurt. This was his business as much as Tim's. Still, Tim was in charge, as always.

While Tim and Jake turned away and began to talk, he slipped the document unnoticed from Jake's desk, out of pique as much as any other reason.

In the waiting room, Kyle turned his back to Jake's secretary and looked at the document. He expected to see some legal jargon about why their appeal had been denied. What he found was even more of a shock than the original verdict had been.

It was a copy of a letter from the Judicial Board of Appeals to the CoDominium, Bureau of Relocation, Secretary of the North American Region. Kyle's face flushed with panic as he skimmed the letter. It referred to activities by Tim he had never heard of: bribes so large that they must have come from their trust fund; financing and purchase of actual weapons for subersive groups; recorded meetings with known subversives.

Kyle frowned and read it again, more carefully. A quote from the prosecutor told him why these matters had not arisen at the trial. The prosecution had not felt their case was strong enough to get a conviction on them, and had feared that the defense might have discredited the entire treason case by picking apart the weak spots.

However, now that the prosecution had won, these points were once again part of the larger picture. The Judicial Board of Appeals concluded with a recommendation: that the Eng brothers be sent to the planet Haven, due to Tim's threat to U.S. national security and Kyle's well-known loyalty to his brother.

With an embarrassed glance at the secretary, Kyle drew in a long, slow breath and rolled the document tightly in his hands. So his brother wasn't as innocent as Kyle had always thought. Well, that didn't matter now. What did matter was where they were going.

They would never see Earth—and particularly Hawaii—ever again.

Tim and Kyle Eng had three more weeks in the local lockup before the next transport ship left for Haven. During that time, Kyle saw that through Jake, Tim made a number of deals that he did not discuss with Kyle. That was okay. Kyle was deeply depressed and could not escape the suspicion that his life was already over. What kind of deals could Tim make that would help them now?

They shipped out on an ore freighter called the *Olathe* with a number of other convicts, including many of their so-called followers. At least these had had the decency, or the stupidity, not to testify against them in exchange for immunity. Not missing any chance, Tim quickly made friends with as many of them as he could find, regaling them with stories of politics or parties with celebrities, or anything else that would entertain them. In the process, he managed to turn the immediate vicinity of the Eng brothers' bunks into a running poker game. Several of the largest deportees signed on with the Eng brothers as bodyguards.

A security guard named Rollo Henley was in charge of their section. Kyle learned soon that through Jake, Tim had bribed certain members of the crew to allow him to host the poker game. Tim was allowed to receive a modest house cut. Henley became a traffic cop, carefully limiting the number of deportees who could enjoy Tim's hospitality at any one time. It was a security measure, of course, and Tim smiled indulgently at the bribes Henley collected from eager poker players himself.

Kyle had to admit that Tim was good. He lost money, though never a large amount at one time, in exchange for goodwill and information about Haven. It was his company that both crew members and deportees really liked.

"What are those?" Kyle asked one night, just before lights out.

Tim was reading some kind of little booklet, and two more were visible in his open duffel bag. "This one's a report on Haven. Jake found it for me before we left. The others are phrase books."

"Yeah? What languages do we use in the mines?"

"We aren't going to the mines." Tim looked up and

grinned. "Relax, will you? We can't change what's already happened."

"Well, I certainly know that," Kyle said sourly.

"Aw, come on. What's wrong, little brother?"

"I don't get it," Kyle said. "How can you be so light-hearted about this? We're going to one of the most horrible inhabitable planets of all."

"It's a fourteen-month trip," said Tim casually. "We might as well make the best of it. I know you don't like poker, but I think we'll land with some goodwill and some solid information, too."

"I just don't see how you can be so cheerful about this disaster. I don't think Haven is very civilized. We probably have nothing better ahead than a lifetime of hard labor."

Tim was silent a moment. "Okay, look. I had Jake do some checking around before we left, and I have a deal with Henley you don't know about. But you have to keep this a secret."

Kyle hesitated, his heart pounding with sudden hope that his brother could land them both on their feet. "You don't have to tell me," he said. "I've learned to trust your judgment."

"Let's just say it's a self-contained freezer case," said Tim. "It's heavy, but once we've landed, solar power will keep the freezer going. On Haven, it'll be worth a fortune. That means it's worth our lives if anyone finds out about it."

"Don't tell me any more details," said Kyle. "But why won't Henley steal it, if it's worth so much?"

"On Earth, it's worth a lot of money, but it's not invaluable. In space, it's totally worthless. But mainly, he won't know what the stuff is, even if he breaks his promise and opens up the case to take a look. I doubt anyone on this ship can tell at a glance. On the whole, he'll make a big profit if he keeps his word and he'll be at loose ends if he steals the case."

"What kind of a deal did you make with him?"

"Right before the trial, I had Jake sell all of my real

estate holdings at fire-sale prices. The deal is, some of those buyers will give him a kickback when they resell. In turn, Jake has agreed to pay Henley a quarter million dollars if he returns with a password."

"What password?"

"The one I'll give him when we've landed safely on Haven with that case in hand."

"Don't tell me any more."

Kyle felt a little better. During the long trip, he observed that Tim was patiently asking crew members as much about Haven as he could. The information was spotty and colored with personal bias and faulty memories, but it was better than nothing.

Kyle took notes on what Tim learned, since that was not Tim's style of behavior. Kyle still felt that he was no more than his brother's shadow, a passive observer with nothing of substance to contribute. Still, he was very glad that Tim was there.

By the time the *Olathe* landed on Haven, Tim Eng was the most popular deportee on board. The circle of bodyguards in his employ had enlarged to a following that was informal but as loyal as a gang of deportees was ever going to be. Kyle didn't have the personality to inspire them the same way, but they understood that the brothers were a package deal.

The ship landed at Castell City on Splash Island. Kyle dreaded the moment. All he could picture was toiling in some freezing mine until he dropped.

As most of the deportees were herded into long lines headed into Castell City, Rollo Henley personally took Tim and Kyle aside. Their henchmen, numbering over thirty, were also drawn out of the line. Kyle shivered in the cool air of midday, watching.

"I've made the arrangements we agreed on," said Henley. He was carrying the heavy black freezer case. "Here's an address for you in Castell City, in the warehouse district. One of the guards at the processing center will take you there; he's already been paid, so don't let him gouge you. The time is midnight." He handed Tim a slip of paper.

"Midnight." Tim grinned. "How mysterious."

"I've also arranged your contingency plans. Call the number on that paper. If you need those arrangements, they will be made. If not, you can take the cost back out in favors here locally."

"Fair enough."

Kyle hated this. They were talking in code as far as he was concerned. He would just have to wait until Tim took him into his confidence, maybe in private.

Satisfied, Tim knelt, opened the freezer case, and glanced inside. Then he closed it again and held out his hand. "You're a man of your word, Henley. Thank you. And the word for you is, 'Temujin.'"

"Say again?"

"Temujin."

"Temujin?" Henley shook hands with him. "There aren't many men whose word I'd trust over this kind of distance."

"I have to trust Jake the same way, but I do," said Tim. "And I don't expect to get back there to check up on him. In your case, if anything does go wrong with Jake, you know where to look for me." He grinned. "In one of two places."

"Good luck." Henley slapped him on the back. "I'm going to escort your group in separately to expedite your processing. After that, you're on your own."

The processing was routine but boring. Kyle shivered in his standard deportee issue uniform as he stood in line, even after they were all inside the building. By now, he had already heard that Haven was very cold, its relatively small inhabitable area the best of a bad lot. This was no place for guys from Hawaii.

Soon enough, Kyle learned what Henley's bribes had been able to accomplish and what they could not. For instance, Tim's group was sent to temporary housing together pending placement, but they were simply stuck in a corner of a large room with a couple of hundred other people. They were told that they would be sent to various jobs tomorrow. In the confusion, however, Kyle finally got Tim aside for a moment.

"Would you mind telling me what's going on?" Kyle demanded. He rarely spoke to Tim so hotly, but he was frightened.

"Lower your voice," said Tim calmly. He turned Kyle's shoulder away and spoke low in his ear. "Henley has put me into contact with a guy in Docktown. That's where the big warehouses are."

"A guy?"

"Some kind of labor boss, supposedly."

"You mean a mobster." Kyle felt his stomach muscles tighten.

"I'm hoping to cut a deal. We'll all be better off working the docks and warehouses than down in the mines."

"What about this wonderful mysterious freezer case?" Kyle nodded down at it, on the floor between Tim's feet. "I thought this was going to save us from disaster."

"Once we find our place in this society, I'll know how to use it. Till then, just help me keep it safe."

"And what's going to happen at this midnight meeting of yours?"

"Of ours," Tim corrected. "We're all going."

The guard whom Henley had bribed, a stout, grim-faced man named Grabowski, kept his word. Shortly before midnight, he walked with Tim and Kyle through the cold, dark streets of Castell City. All of Tim's henchmen followed after them, probably as scared as Kyle was and just as determined not to let it show.

Kyle clenched his teeth to keep them from chattering. In the uneven streetlight, the warehouses loomed large and dark on each side of them. He carried the freezer case because they couldn't risk leaving it behind and Tim wanted to concentrate on other matters.

The walk took nearly an hour. Grabowski finally

stopped at the big bay twin doors of a warehouse. He pressed an exterior button that rang a buzzer inside. Then the big doors rumbled upward on their tracks.

Grabowski stepped away. Kyle decided he didn't want to risk getting involved. It was just as well.

Inside the doors, right in front of Tim and Kyle, stood a crowd of big, rough, brawny men in work clothes. Kyle estimated there were at least a hundred of them, though in the shadows he couldn't be sure he saw them all. The man standing in front was about fifty, with a barrel chest and thick bull neck straining at the spotless white dress shirt and expensive suit he wore. He was flanked on each side by a man dressed similarly.

"Which one of you is Tim Eng?" he demanded.

"I am," said Tim. "You're Demopoulis?"

He nodded once, slightly. His face was hard, nearly motionless as he spoke. "This meeting with me has already cost you a lot of money," said Demopoulis. "You don't get any of it back, no matter what happens. Now what's so important that you dragged me out here at this time of night?"

"We want to work for you," said Tim.

"No."

"We'll earn our way," said Tim. "No handouts. Just let us join you."

"No. Off to the mines with all of you."

"Any terms you want," said Tim, smiling his most disarming smile. "I'll make the deal with you and keep my guys in line. Maybe we can help you expand your operation."

"No. If that's all you want, our business is concluded."

Tim took a deep breath and put his hands on his hips. "It won't hurt you any to tell me why."

Demopoulis stared at him in silence. Finally, he gave just the faintest hint of a smile. "All right, it won't hurt me any. It sure won't." He pointed at Tim with a stubby finger. "This doesn't happen to me. Nobody reaches me from a transport ship that hasn't even landed yet and nobody comes to me with a bunch of soldiers lined up.

I don't know much else about you, hotshot, but you're not the kind of man who works for anyone else by choice. Not for long, anyway. You're too much like me. And I'm not giving you any foothold here in my turf. Got it?"

Tim stared back at him for a moment, and then laughed. "Got it."

"I don't think your men have got it yet," said Demopoulis. Suddenly, without moving, he yelled, "Get 'em, boys!"

The mob surged forward. Kyle yanked the heavy freezer case up to his chest and wrapped his arms around it, trying to back away. The thirty or so men behind him, however, were caught off guard. He collided with the guys just in back of him, who were preparing to defend themselves.

In the roiling mob, Kyle ducked low and managed to shove himself backwards and to the side. Most of Tim's followers were running, but the ones in the very front were outflanked and then surrounded before they could get away. Then sirens and the roar of large personnel carriers reached Kyle as he was shoved and buffeted in the crowd.

Shouts went up on all sides from the men around him, and the immediate violence was halted. Searchlights shot through the darkness, blinding Kyle. He could just see the silhouettes of armed, uniformed men leaping to the ground and spreading out in formation.

A strong hand grabbed his upper arm. "Easy, Kyle," Tim said softly in his ear. "We'll be okay. Stay calm. They're CoDo Marines."

"They're what?"

"CoDominium Marines. They'll just take us back where we belong."

"They sure got here fast."

"Fast, nothing. That Grabowski must have alerted them. He's playing all three sides, setting up this meeting for money and also making sure no real trouble happens."

"Everyone freeze," a loud voice ordered over a bullhorn. "Do not move. You are covered. Deportees remain where you are."

"No problem," said Tim easily, to Kyle. "The freezer case okay?"

"Yeah."

"Good. Looks like it's time for our contingency plan."

The CoDo Marines simply sorted out the deportees and herded them back to their facility, as Tim had predicted. When they returned, Kyle noticed that Grabowski was off shift. The next morning, Tim gave a friendly but apologetic farewell to his erstwhile followers. They took it well; what would happen to them now was no worse than what they had expected when they had first been convicted.

Kyle was surprised, though, after breakfast in the cafeteria. Tim, now carrying the freezer case himself, steered him out of the corridor to where Grabowski was standing. He still didn't smile much.

"Pretty slick move last night," Tim said to him with a grin.

"You could have been killed in the confusion," said Grabowski. "This way, Mr. D is happy; I keep my job; and you're still healthy."

"Like I said, pretty slick. Now, then. Where do we go now?"

"We'll get your duffels and go to the heliport."

"Is there going to be any trouble about not processing us for the mines?" Kyle asked.

"Not if you stay right next to me."

They did. By now, Kyle had decided that asking Tim questions in front of other people was a waste of time at best, and maybe a serious mistake at worst. As usual, he followed Tim's lead in silence.

Out at the heliport, they mounted a large cargo helicopter. Grabowski nodded briefly to the pilot and everyone was outfitted with oxygen. Then they took off with a suddenness that left Kyle's stomach lurching as the ground fell away under them. No one spoke as they flew over the Shangri-La Valley to the north, but Tim held a map in his hands and constantly compared it to the slowly moving map screen on the console of the chopper.

The chopper droned on. Eventually, Kyle saw first foothills and then a rugged mountain range beneath them. The chopper fairly skimmed over the peaks, at minimum altitude.

The huge mountains below them continued kilometer after kilometer. Kyle finally turned to Tim. "Where are we going now?"

Tim turned his map and marked a spot with his thumbnail. "To the foothills on the far side of this range. They're safer than the steppes beyond it."

"Foothills?"

Tim grinned, slapped him on the back, and leaned away.

Finally the chopper began to descend. Kyle watched in near-disbelief as he saw the rugged wilderness that grew larger in his vision. No sign of human habitation existed anywhere he could see.

The pilot tossed them both heavy parkas before they got out. All four of them debarked and the pilot opened the cargo bay. Kyle had thought he was beyond further shock, but he was wrong.

Two of the large, furry Haven creatures called muskylopes were inside the cargo bay. They were already in harness, to a wagon laden with goods covered by a tarp. Grabowski climbed up the ramp to lead them out.

"Oh, no." Kyle groaned aloud.

Tim jumped forward to help Grabowski. In a moment, the wagon was out of the cargo bay. The pilot immediately closed it up.

"All right," said Grabowski. "The wagon has dry supplies for two men for thirty days if you're careful and hunt on the way. The water will only last you a week if you ration, but refilling won't be a problem. You have heavy clothes, blankets, and sleep cocoons. The weapons aren't much by Terran standards—some old Armalite rifles with ammunition, several bows and plenty of arrows. Some revolvers, too. That's where most of your money went."

Tim took a moment to throw back the plastic tarp on the wagon and check the contents.

Kyle stared at the wagon sullenly. He could think of nothing to say. The only alternative was returning to Castell City and its mines.

Tim turned and offered his hand to Grabowski. "We're square."

Grabowski shook with him, but didn't smile. "You're too trusting. If Henley wasn't an old pal, I could have sent you to the mines and kept the money."

"Henley chose well. Thanks." Tim nodded to the pilot as well, and stood back. He and Kyle waited for the chopper to leave.

Kyle inhaled the cold, dry air and watched the helicopter rise into the sky. At last, more than leaving Terra and more than leaving Castell City, this was the end of everything he had known.

Except Tim.

"Climb aboard!" Tim called heartily.

As Kyle did so, Tim found a place for the black freezer case in the back of the wagon just behind the seat. He pulled back the plastic tarp to make sure the sunlight could reach the solar cells on the case and then hoisted his big duffel of cash and liquor alongside it. Then he mounted the seat next to Kyle.

"Where are we going?" Kyle asked. "Do you actually know what you're doing?"

Tim shook the reins and started the team moving north. "I never know exactly what I'm doing, *didi*. But I'll tell you where we're headed. You just keep an eye out for anyone following us. This is a pretty wild planet, I hear, and you're riding shotgun. Remember the target shooting we did as teenagers?"

"Shooting! I haven't shot in years." Alarmed, Kyle looked around in all directions. The land around them was a narrow valley surrounded by steeply rising, forested hills. It was totally deserted. Right now, it was hard to believe that anyone else could be within hundreds of miles of here.

"Aw, no need to panic," said Tim easily. "But you might want to break out one of those old rifles so we can look it over."

"Later," said Kyle. "I still want to know where we're going."

"To the northern steppes," said Tim. "You have the background material in your notes."

"I remember some of this," said Kyle. "But I have over a year's worth of notes and it's all packed up at the moment."

"I memorized the important parts," said Tim. "Listen. Several rumors tell of steppe nomads living up there. Mongol tribes, central Asian tribes . . . the crew members weren't sure. I don't think they could tell the difference. But there aren't many of them yet, and they're a long way from the CoDo authorities. I'm gambling that there's a good future to be carved out up there, over the mountains. We landed here so we could get started in private. The tribes on the steepes can be dangerous, especially if you just land abruptly."

Kyle was silent a moment. "How far is it to the steppes?"

"Nobody could tell me for sure. It'll be risky, but I have a line on a series of passes and valleys we can take. We'll have to be careful. Some of those valleys are already inhabited. I'm hoping to barter some of our Terran liquor for passage."

"And that mysterious black case of yours?"

"We'll camp early tonight. I'll have to brace the case up under the wagon somehow, out of sight. It only needs a few hours of sunlight every day to stay powered. It's a sure bet that if we meet people who want to search us, we'll have to let them."

"I think I'll take a look at those guns," said Kyle.

The trip northward was largely uneventful. The road led to occasional sources of water. At first, they relied on their stores for food during this part of the trip. Perhaps the hardest adjustment was getting used to the 87-hour day and constant cold, for two born-and-bred sons of Hawaii.

On the rare occasions when they encountered strangers, they both donned cartridge belts, stuck revolvers in them visibly, and held rifles at the ready. Still, they were careful to keep the rifles aimed skyward and to nod politely as they passed. Most of the strangers nodded back, just as warily, and went on. One lone wanderer on a tired horse tracked them at a distance for most of a day, but a warning shot from Tim finally drove him off.

Kyle took over the driving chores the next day. He felt that job suited him. Tim was a better choice for riding shotgun.

Eventually, they had to hunt out of necessity. In this endeavor, Kyle was actually a better shot, being more patient and deliberate. Before long, they had reached the first settlement, where two bottles of their best liquor and an extra rifle earned them a night's hospitality, including a dinner of hot, hearty, tasty, but unrecognizable stew.

Tim warned Kyle not to ask the origins of their hosts. Haven was a planet where most arrivals were starting over with their last chance in life and sometimes they were sensitive of strangers who pried. Still, Kyle eyed their hosts carefully. They were herders, certainly, but not of an East Asian descent. By their appearance, he surmised that they were perhaps of a Central Asian stock, of mainly Turkish ancestry. In any case, their hospitality was genuine and they sent an escort to take the brothers to their own northern border.

In like manner, Kyle and Tim journeyed on through the mountains from valley to valley. Several of their polite but heavily armed hosts indulged themselves in searches of the wagon's contents, but none stole them blind and none found the mysterious black case under the wagon. Each valley sent them on their way lighter in barter, but without harm.

Kyle had never been so cold for so long in his entire life, but Tim never said a word of complaint. Then, just as the horizon ahead began to show empty sky, they reached one final valley. Only flatland lay beyond the last, distant ridge.

As the wagon creaked patiently through the entrance to the valley, Kyle looked up ahead in surprise. Both the right and left slopes were settled, though only a few structures were actually visible on each side. The flat but fairly narrow, open valley floor spread in front of them also had one settlement he could see; a distant spot might represent another one. Kyle estimated the valley was no more than five or six kilometers across at the widest. He couldn't tell how long it was from here.

"These aren't nomads," said Kyle. "Look at this place. All those dwellings are permanent."

Tim took in the tableau at a glance. "That's right . . . but look at the differences. The western slope is built up with some wooden huts around that stone tower—hell, it looks like a little castle!"

"And the other slope is a cluster of little wooden houses nestled in the trees," said Kyle. "I see what you mean. But there's just as much stone and forest on both sides. What do you make of it?"

"You're the public policy expert," said Tim. "You tell me."

Kyle looked straight across the valley. An hour's travel ahead, he could see a small walled compound. The wall appeared to be made of stone with a smooth mortar facing. Inside, tiled roofs were visible on the buildings. A windmill stood over it.

"Well?" Tim prodded.

"Three notably different styles of architecture based on only one set of natural resources," Kyle said slowly. "I'd say they represent three distinct cultural backgrounds. From the distance between them, and the defensible nature of their architecture, they don't share a political system. On the other hand, they must have a workable coexistence, because the valley dwellings were made in part with stone from the slopes." He could also see livestock in all three areas, but they appeared to be of the same types. Both the valley and the slopes were cultivated in spots.

"What did the hillside people get from the valley?" Tim asked.

"I can't tell. Maybe free passage and the right to share-crop some fields in the valley, something like that."

"Which one should we approach?"

"Let's go straight through the valley," Kyle decided. "This road goes to that place on the valley floor."

"Does that mean they're the most important?"

"Maybe." Kyle grinned. "Maybe they just built the road."

In only a few more minutes, a flashing light caught Kyle's eye. It was reflecting the sunlight and came from the stone tower on the western slope. "We should have company soon," said Kyle.

He was surprised, though, to see that the five riders who came into view departed from the valley compound. They started at a leisurely pace on two horses and three muskylopes. As the wagon plodded toward them, however, and the gap shrank to a kilometer or so, the riders spurred to a canter.

Tim prepared their own weapons. Kyle saw that the riders had only two rifles among them. The others carried lances and wore machete-like swords in their belts.

As the riders finally came close, Kyle drew the wagon to a halt and braced the stock of his rifle casually on the seat, the barrel aimed up. So did Tim. They had this down to a routine now.

To Kyle's surprise, all the riders who reined to a halt in front of them were of the same racial stock as much of Hawaii, including themselves—Cantonese, judging by their fairly short, stocky frames, round faces, and somewhat broad noses. The northern Chinese tended to be taller than this and their skintone was too light to have originated in southeast Asia. They lacked the facial hair of Japanese men.

The first rider, a young man near their age, tried two languages before saying, "Hail, strangers," in accented English.

"Good day," Tim said carefully.

"You have business in this valley?"

"We seek passage to the northern steppe," said Tim. "No more."

All the riders bristled at this.

"What is your business on the steppe?" the chief rider demanded. "You bring them weapons?"

"No," Kyle said quickly. "We seek new land to live in, that's all. Peaceful passage."

The other four riders were now walking their mounts down each side of the wagon, surrounding it.

"I am Dafu Lei," said the chief rider. "You shall be guests in our house. Follow me." He backed his horse out of the way, not taking his eyes off them.

Kyle and Tim could only choose between complying or shooting, and the latter meant starting a fight with four enemies at their backs. On the other hand, no request had been made for their weapons. That was a good sign.

Kyle shook the reins and started the wagon forward.

Dafu Lei brought his mount into step.

"What is the name of this valley?" Kyle asked.

"This is the Guanggo Valley," said Dafu. "We are from the House of Lei, deportees from the planet Xanadu. The House of Hom is also from Xanadu. We are the only two houses in the valley."

"Who lives in the stone tower on the mountainside?"

"That is Castle MacLeod, home of Clan MacLeod. The Clans MacLeod, Munro, and Robertson live on that slope. They are from Covenant, and call their ridge the Highlands."

"What about the other side?" Kyle asked, nodding toward the wooden houses barely visible in the forest opposite.

"The Mozark Hills, they call them. The Coons, Gann, and McKay Clans live there. Deportees from Earth itself." Dafu's manner seemed to warm slightly. "We are called the Triad Clans, for the three backgrounds we have."

Tim was eyeing Dafu's mount. It was a small, sturdy brown horse. Kyle couldn't tell much else about it.

"Part Arabian, is it?" Tim asked.

"Half," said Dafu, proudly. "Half quarterhorse. She is very strong and healthy."

"Looks it," Tim said quietly.

The House of Lei was, as Kyle had seen from a distance, a small compound of several buildings with a courtyard surrounded by a high wall, all of stone. As they neared it, he was able to see that the family herded muskylopes and horses and raised some hardy, high-altitude crops.

The patriarch of the Lei Clan came out to meet them. His name was Lungho Lei. He was about fifty years old and introduced himself, in a reserved but courteous manner, as the original deportee who had begun this spread. Now he had four grown sons, of whom Dafu was the eldest, living here with their families, and several daughters. Also, some other Xanadu families of different surnames lived there under his protection, all working the land and tending the small herds.

Kyle and Tim were shown to a small unheated room in the main house and brought water for washing. The room had one window, barred with a decorative ceramic dragon sculpture fitted into the opening. There was no glass, only an inside wooden shutter. An electric lightbulb lit the room, powered by the windmill and an old generator elsewhere on the grounds.

They had been told to leave their weapons in the wagon, but had not exactly been forced to surrender them. Both brothers were more uncomfortable here than they had been in the yurts and tents of their other hosts. Their wagon was farther away from them and when the front gate was closed for the night, it was locked in and so were they. They were being watched closely.

That night, Lungho Lei hosted them at dinner in the company of his sons and the heads of the other families. From their manner and their dress, Kyle saw that this was a rather formal occasion, taking place in a modest hall that was the largest room in the compound. Guests were almost certainly rare here; those of Cantonese descent probably unheard of.

Lungho Lei's white hair was short, but he had indulged in a three-pointed white beard. He stroked it casually as he asked the brothers stories of their passage. They answered with small anecdotes, revealing as little of themselves as they could. Other members of the House of Lei spoke quietly among themselves at times but did not address Kyle and Tim directly. When dinner arrived, it was simple, but good.

Dinner was served by the grown and teenaged daughters of the community, but none of them were introduced. The young woman who served Kyle and Tim smiled at them shyly as she came and went. She was slender and pretty and Kyle found her looking at him several times when he happened to look up.

"What's your name?" he asked quietly.

"Linwah," she whispered. "Are you really from Earth itself?"

"Yes. From Hawaii."

Her eyes widened, but she hurried away, looking around her guiltily.

"So," said Lungho Lei, studying Kyle. "You have come north a very long way to reach us. You travel to the land of our enemies. Why?"

Kyle tensed. His mind went blank for an answer. The wrong response might get them killed, or at least turned back on foot without their wagon and belongings.

"We did not know they were enemies of yours," Tim said easily, landing on his feet once again. "To be honest, we seek only a safe place to settle."

"Which tribe do you seek?"

Tim shrugged, picking up a mushroom with his chopsticks. "We don't even know who the tribes are." He continued eating.

"Mongols of the Merkit, Naiman, and Mangkhol tribes predominate," Lungho Lei said quietly. "We of the Triad Clans hold the northern pass of this valley against them, as my—and your—distant ancestors once did against theirs on old Earth." He smiled. "The irony amuses me. The danger, however, is real."

"I hear," said Tim casually, "that a high, dry wind off the northern steppe has developed a high altitude desert nearby."

"It is a poor land," said Lungho Lei, nodding affirmation. "They raid us and, when they are not in evidence, we of the Triad Clans sometimes raid each other. Our feuds come and go, but they are matters within Guanggo Valley. Weapons for the Mongols are another matter, one of the outside. So are the nomads who graze to the south of us—and those who pass through their land unharmed."

"We have very few weapons," said Kyle.

Lungho Lei nodded and caught the eye of someone in the back of the modest hall. Two young men who were not in the dinner party strode forward briskly, carrying Tim's mysterious black case together in a large two-handed basket. They set it down with great care on the table near Lungho Lei.

As Kyle watched, they opened the case and turned it. The case was full of sealed vials of fluid and some other equipment he didn't recognize. Two small booklets were also in it, and some type of instruments in padded holders.

"Forgive my inhospitality," said Lungho Lei. "I had your wagon searched because you told us you seek our enemies. These vials would be of great value to them."

Kyle looked at Tim in alarm.

"We have recognized their contents," said Lungho Lei. "What breeds do you have here?"

Tim grinned and sat forward eagerly. "I have gametes

and zygotes from the finest Mongol horses on the face of good ol' Earth. Also the instruments necessary to use them and instruction manuals. All I need are healthy mares as either surrogate mothers or else good breeding stock to be artificially inseminated. There are plenty of them here and only a tiny fraction has to work out to start a string of tough, durable horses that has been bred to northern steppes and deserts for centuries."

"Such horses would make a man very wealthy in any valley," said Lungho Lei. He showed no outward sign of surprise. "In the land to the north of us, they could make a man into a king. This is why you seek the northern steppes."

Horses, Kyle thought. Of course. That had been Tim's hobby back in their former life. On a wild planet like this, they were far more valuable than any currency.

"Yes," said Tim, with a disarming grin. "That is true."

"But you have grazing land in this valley, as well," said Kyle. "Is there a place for two more here?"

Lungho Lei thought a moment and then returned to his dinner. While he ate in silence, no one else in the hall spoke. The two young men by the freezer case did not move.

Finally the white-haired man looked up. "You will remain here as my guests while I think on this. In exchange for your horses, I believe a place can be found for you." Then he finished his dinner, turning the conversation to casual topics.

Kyle kept an eye on Linwah for the rest of the dinner. She glanced over at him several times, but did not have another chance to speak. Kyle was flattered; for once, a woman had noticed him more than Tim.

Kyle and Tim did not speak until they had returned to their room. As Kyle sat down on a bunk, quiet footsteps stopped outside their closed door. A bar slid gently into place, locking them in. He looked at Tim.

"So close," Tim whispered. "The northern steppe is so close."

"I like it here," said Kyle. "This is a settled community. And we fit in—that is, we look like we do. It would be a safe place to start life over."

"We'd be followers," said Tim in a quiet but firm voice. "The best land in this valley is already claimed. Why wait twenty years for the old men to die off and then fight with their heirs for their inheritance? Out on the steppes with nomads, life is much more fluid. We can earn our way with barter and service at first, then strike out on our own. Any open grazing land belongs to those tough enough to take it."

"I'm no rider, at least not like you are. You really like this idea of living on the steppes?"

Tim grinned crookedly. "Don't you remember the old family history our grandfather told us about? How one of our ancestors in China did something for a Mongol emperor and was rewarded with marriage to one of his daughters?"

"Yeah, so?" Kyle shook his head. "Oral history isn't worth much over what, seven or eight centuries? What about it?"

"So that Mongol princess came from the line of Kublai Khan, and so back to Genghis Khan."

Kyle smiled with more amusement than he felt. "After that many generations, the blood is pretty thin."

"That doesn't matter. Look, you told me once that non-literate societies value oral traditions—they have to respect them and keep them and be honest with their spoken word because they have no other records. So I believe the story."

"Yeah, that's right. So you believe it. But what of it?"

"*So will the Mongols on the steppe.*" Tim eyed him earnestly. "Follow me yet? The distant sons of the Kha-khan arrive from Earth with the finest seed of Mongol horses ever seen since the thirteenth century. We'll be welcomed like heirs to the throne."

"I'm not so sure. Their current tribal leaders won't want to step aside. Even if you're right, they can just kill us and keep the freezer case."

"Aahh." Tim brushed that aside with a wave. "I know better than to go busting in making demands. I'll handle the tribal politics when the time comes, armed with that freezer case. I even have those phrase books to help with their language. But right now we have to get out of here."

"We can't," said Kyle. "At least, not until we've passed muster with them. They've locked us in."

"Funny you should mention that," said Tim, grinning as he cocked his head. Soft footsteps were coming down the hall.

The bar slid away and then Linwah slipped inside the room, carrying a bulging pack on a shoulder strap. In both hands, she lugged the heavy freezer case inside and gently set it down. She smiled self-consciously, looking at both of them.

"Didn't you notice she liked you?" Tim said. "I saw you two talking, and I got her aside for a moment on our way out."

"Hello, Kyle," she said quietly, in accented English.

"Hi," said Kyle, suddenly realizing what Tim had in mind. "You mean we're *escaping* from here?"

"She can't afford to get caught," said Tim. "She can take us to a small rear gate, but we'll be on foot—no wagon or mounts."

"Why are you doing this?" Kyle asked her suspiciously.

"I've never met anyone from Earth like you," she said earnestly. "That is, Cantonese from Earth. From Hawaii. You must be very brave to come all this way alone. I want to help."

"This is insane," said Kyle. "What is it, some adolescent infatuation? We can't let her get into trouble over us."

"She's the old man's daughter," said Tim. "He'll yell at her and then forget it. And after we start our herd, we'll send them both a couple of horses to make amends."

"Tim—"

"Listen, Kyle," Tim said earnestly. "This isn't a BurReloc

detention center or a Hawaii state correctional center, either. No sentries, no guard towers, no sensors or lasers. It's just a house with a wall around it. Her family thinks we're locked in and they're going to sleep."

"Everyone is asleep," Linwah confirmed. "Unless we are in a feud, we only have the animals to sound an alarm."

Kyle didn't know what to say. He looked at Tim, then at Linwah. She looked away shyly. Deep down, he didn't want to go. She fascinated him, not the least by her daring. After a lifetime of following Tim's every whim, though, he simply could not summon an argument now.

"Come on," said Tim. He stood up and bundled into his heavy outdoor clothing. Then he took the pack from Linwah, slinging it over his shoulder, and hefted the freezer case. "Linwah."

Kyle was also slipping on his outer clothing. Then he hustled after them, last as usual.

Linwah moved with quick, quiet steps, stopping frequently to listen. The floor of the narrow hallway was made of small stone and some type of fine mortar; the effect was similar to concrete, but rougher. Their gentle steps made no sound.

A small door in the back of the building creaked slightly when she opened it, but no one stirred. They walked out across the grounds in the dim light of Cat's Eye. The livestock were quiet as she led them in a faster walk to a rear gate in the wall.

Kyle couldn't help steal a glance at their wagon, and the two muskylopes hobbled near it.

"I'm sorry," she said as she unhooked the gate. "The front gate squeaks badly. And the dogs would bark at the sound of hooves if you rode out. My family would be roused."

Kyle looked at her, into her eyes. She was only a word away from going with them. In that moment, he felt he had never seen a woman more exciting.

"This will be fine," said Tim. "Come on, Kyle. Even on foot, we'll reach the northern pass by morning."

"No," Kyle said suddenly.

"What?" Tim was half out the open doorway when he turned.

"I'm staying."

"Kyle!" Tim stared at him. "Are you crazy? This is no time to argue—"

"I'm not arguing. I'm staying. You go. Now."

"Didi—"

A dog barked, then another. A horse whinnied. They had raised their voices too loud.

Linwah gasped and ran for the house as fast as she could.

"Too late to worry about noise," Kyle said. "Come on!" He ran for one of the muskylopes. It shied, startled, when he threw a bridle over it. "Get on!"

Tim didn't need any urging. As Kyle buckled the bridle, Tim clambered on, the heavy freezer case threatening to swing free of his hand, and stretched forward for the reins. "Jump, Kyle!"

"I'll stall 'em!" Kyle shouted back. He yanked a rifle from the wagon and tossed it to him. "Go!"

Tim caught the rifle in his free hand and held it by the crook of his elbow. Then he yanked open the freezer case and grabbed a handful of frozen vials, whichever ones he happened to snatch. He tossed them on the ground. "You'll need 'em!"

Kyle swung a cartridge belt over Tim's head as Tim threw down one of the instruction manuals and a set of instruments rolled in their padded holder.

"Go!" Kyle slapped the muskylope and sent Tim riding out through the rear gate. Then he ran to hook it shut. Tim needed every second.

Lights had already come on in the compound. Kyle scooped up the frozen vials from the ground, leaving the other items for later, and ran to the rear door, hearing the hoofbeats of Tim's muskylope. For the first time in his life, he was acting without thinking, and he launched himself at the first dark shadowy figures that came running down the hall toward him, still clutching the vials clumsily.

Kyle thrashed around as much as he could. His two assailants shouted to each other in Cantonese and were soon joined by others. They got in each other's way, however, in the narrow hall. Since Kyle's purpose was not to escape, but to create a diversion, he just kept struggling.

More shouts sounded in other rooms, down other halls. By the time Kyle's assailants had a firm grasp on all his limbs, he could hear mounts being tacked up outside. Someone else had heard Tim's hoofbeats, too.

In moments, Kyle had been dragged into a well-lit room to face the grim visage of Lungho Lei, dressed in a coarse brown robe.

"So," said Lungho Lei. "You return our hospitality by fleeing? You have more interest in the northern steppes than you admit."

"He chose to stay!" Linwah shouted in English, then changed to Cantonese.

After a moment of quick talk with her in Cantonese, Lungho Lei switched to English again. "Where is your brother?"

"You know where he is gone. But I wish to stay and I have my fee." Kyle held out his vials. "The manual and instruments are outside. Can you keep these frozen?"

Lungho Lei nodded at someone, who quickly took the precious vials. Those holding Kyle released him.

"So. My daughter tells me that when your brother chose to escape, you refused. She also confesses that she chose to unbar your door. How do I know you will not unbar our gate some night when your brother chooses to return with his Mongol friends?"

Kyle looked into the old man's face, knowing it was at last time for him to land on his own feet, without his older brother to help. The white-haired man looked back sternly, but not angrily; he spoke with reasonable concern, not paranoid suspicion. What Kyle said next would determine his life and maybe his death. For one more time, he would have to trust his older brother to protect him and care for him even from a distance, as he always had since their childhood.

"I ask for your daughter in marriage." He bowed, imitating the old Chinese style he remembered from some immigrants. "We shall give you grandsons and work your fields. We shall raise fine horses for you. This will be my land, too, and my brother will not raise his hand against it."

The old white-haired man stared back, his face impassive. He glanced at Linwah, who looked down, reddening, but smiling, too. Then Lungho Lei nodded to Kyle, less deeply, in return.

"It is enough. Welcome home."

FROM: Consul-General Edgar Blair
       Government House, Castell City
       Haven, Tanith Sector

TO: Director Stephen Scannell
     CoDominium Colonial Service
     CoDominium Headquarters, Luna Base
     Luna, Earth Sector

DATE: October 18, 2089

Dear Stephen,

I regret the necessity of having to ask an old friend for yet another favor, but the situation here on Haven grows graver with each passing day.

According to Admiral Hartman, Commander of the CD Naval Force for the Tanith Sector, there are no troops or ships to be spared in our attempt to police Haven. Local records indicate that Haven was—well, not peaceful—but under CoDominium *authority* until the discovery of those cursed shimmerstones. Now that the Haven Gem Consortium is no longer the sole official exporter of shimmerstones, theft, piracy and everything but outright war has broken out among the miners, "exporters," and thieves who control the discovery and exportation of Haven's most valuable export.

While the 201st Provisional Marines and the Haven Volunteers have returned law and order to Castell City and the populated areas of the Shangri-La Valley, the same cannot be said for those areas in the fringes of the valley and elsewhere. Highly trained bands of brigands and bandits menace both miners and small communities alike.

Population figures have at least tripled since the discovery of those damnable stones. The Haven Constabulary, with a total force of 179 men, can only patrol and maintain order over a fraction of even Haven's limited habitable area.

After the "strike"—here we call it the Revolt—succeeded in breaking the Consortium's shimmerstone monopoly, many of the mercenaries deserted from their units before they went off-world and formed gangs and free corps to harass outlying miners and small towns. It now appears that several of those "outfits" (one calls itself the Iron Regiment and held out against the 201st for a month and a half before it was defeated) have obtained proscribed weapons, including T-680 tanks and Yak VTOLs, to give you an idea of how serious our situation here has become in the last few years. We have evidence that some of these "bandits" have been supplied *unofficially* by Xanadu and possibly even Sauron again. It is debatable whether or not even the under-strength 201st has the weapons and/or manpower to restore order and pacify some of these outfits.

We need help badly. Maybe you can convince Grand Admiral Lermontov to send a regiment of Marines. If something is not done quickly, I fear for the safety and welfare of the peoples of this beleaguered planet, to say nothing of its official representatives.

I will appreciate any help or support you can provide. Give my love to Blanche and the girls.

Your friend,
Edgar Blair

FIRE AND ICE

Eric Vinicoff

"Devil's Brewery ETA five minutes, Sarge," Darrow said conversationally. He wrestled the stick two-handed, while his gaze jumped back and forth between the instruments and the blurred terrain beyond the windshield.

The ice-sharpened faces and scraggy vegetation of the narrow rift valley shot by at 240 KPH, ten meters down and closer off each wing. Gale-force gusts slammed into the transport. It boogied, groaned, and scraped belly and wingtips. My fingers were putting dents in the duraplast of the copilot's seat armrests. "You sure you've done this before?" I demanded.

"More or less. The idea was, I believe, to avoid detection."

"And the ground."

"Bugger off."

"If I knew what that meant, I don't think I'd like it." But Darrow had chauffeured CoDominium Marines in some heavy action before deserting, so he might know what he was doing. I staggered back to the cabin to check on the rest of the squad.

The red-lit cabin looked like the ready room for Hell. Ski, Preacher, Toglog, White Cloud and Schmidt sat on the facing benches, field-stripping their weapons. One good thing about a black-budget pickup force was that you went first class. White Cloud, our sharpshooter, wore/carried a Gauss gun, while Toglog amped our fire-power with a Remington Enforcer over-and-under grenade launcher. The rest of us had CoDominium-issue Kalashnikov 7-mm assault rifles with ten-shot clips. Bandoliers, grenades, commando knives and white cold-weather combat suits with Nemourlon body armor rounded out the tools of our trade.

Toglog and Preacher were passing a flask of castor oil. Boozing on a mission was contra regs, but then so were we.

"Listen up, you grunts!" I yelled over the roar of the engines. "We're almost to our drop point! In case you've forgotten why we're taking this little joyride, I'll refresh your memory! A gang of shimmerstone hijackers is operating out of the Devil's Brewery! It's too well equipped to be local—probably a merc outfit! Our job is to find their base and wipe it! Any questions?"

"Yeah!" White Cloud grunted. "What's for lunch?"

"Your ass, if you screw up! Ski, get these yahoos ready to rock!"

"On it, Sarge!" The ex-circus strongman from Nowy Krakow was smarter than he looked, which was why he had been slotted for corporal.

I lurched back to the cockpit. Darrow was still hugging ground, but the valley had opened up into a dreary snow-bound steppe. The Cat's Eye hung in the morning sky like some god's lost marble. Haven was only marginally habitable for terrestrial life around the equator; this far north it didn't even try. The temperature was sub-zero, the air was unbreathably thin, and the native flora and fauna were equally deadly.

"Bloody right!" Darrow yelled eagerly. "That, I dare say, is our target."

I followed his gaze.

If Haven was the asshole of the galaxy, the Devil's Brewery was what came out. Tidal pull from the Cat's Eye had fractured and crumpled the planet's crust, letting out some of its boiling guts. Active volcanos mounted guard over several hundred square kilometers of lava rivers and lakes, fumaroles, geysers, and hot springs. Crevasse-shot ice and snow covered the tortured terrain, shaken by frequent quakes. Volcanic ash, rising steam and a permanent blizzard muted the crimson hell-fires.

I licked my lips in anticipation.

The transport knifed into the white-out of the blizzard. It bucked like a bronco on loco weed, and the screaming of the wind came loud and clear through the double hull. Something with the kick of a SAM slammed the transport upward. "Ice or magma from an explosive eruption," Darrow explained as he veered to miss—barely—a smoking gray cone.

Fire and ice. Mix them together, and you get hell. Like a soldier's soul. I went back to the cabin. "Get them strapped in, Ski! Could get a bit—"

CRAAAAAANG!

"—hairy!"

The cockpit was gone. Wind, snow and blood-red light exploded into the cabin. I jammed my arms into safety straps and braced. The cabin started tumbling. Preacher's "Now I lay me down to sleep—" and White Cloud's war cry were lost in a bedlam of crashing gear and tearing duralloy. The god who had lost his marble took his anger out on what was left of the transport: a roundhouse right, stiff uppercuts, then a flurry of jabs. The punches dribbled my head against the cabin plasteel, while the straps cut into and almost through my arms.

Then I noticed we weren't tumbling anymore. We were down.

The cabin lights were out. I gasped for breath, and the frigid air thrilled my lungs. Fumbling around, I found my helmet and put it on. The combat suit started compressing and warming the air before it got to me.

Shadowy shapes were moving and moaning happily in the red-tinted gloom. Switching on my helmet com, I growled, "Anybody have enough sense to suit up?" Silence answered me.

I found and checked out my Kalashnikov by touch, while Ski, Preacher, Toglog, White Cloud and Schmidt

reported. Preacher had lost a few teeth from his winning
smile, and we were all beaten up, but we were still armed
and dangerous.

"Ski," I ordered, "go forward and check on Darrow."

"On it, Sarge." A dark bulk crawled through the crumpled hatchway.

A moment later Ski was back on the com. "The Brit
is squashed against the rear cockpit wall. Messy."

Climbing to my feet, I announced, "Rest break is over,
grunts. Up and at 'em." Minus our aerial cover, our com
link to HQ, our retrieval, and one squad member.

Leaving the cabin wasn't hard; we had our choice of
cracks. I led the squad out into the teeth of the blizzard.
The slippery snow made standing hard and walking
almost impossible. Despite my suit, the cold and the banshee howling cut to the bone, amping my pleasant glow
from the crash. Everything was luridly red-lit, including
us. Visibility was a handful of meters.

"Have you had a revelation as to the location of the
hijackers' base, Sarge?" Preacher asked. He had gotten
the nickname because he was a Harmony from Castell
City, but he was an unlikely candidate for salvation. His
evangelistic yack was retaliation for the squad's ribbing.

"Well, it ain't here, so let's go find it. I'll take the
point—Ski, cover the rear."

"On it, Sarge."

I picked a direction, and started fighting through the
blizzard. The squad was strung out behind me.

An ice-covered lava flow was the closest thing to a path
available. It zigzagged between a tumbled ridge and a
deep fissure. Steam and heat roared up from the fissure;
I peered into it, and saw bubbling red magma. Wind-
driven snow and ash hammered at me.

We passed a hole in the side of a dormant cone which
was spewing pale gas. A fumarole. Spotting Schmidt
swaying a bit, I dropped back and slapped the filter button on his helmet. "Stay sharp, kraut. I'm not always
going to be around to wipe your ass for you."

The taciturn little New Rhinelander gave me a one-fingered gesture of thanks.

Forward progress came slowly and awkwardly. Walk. Slip and fall. Walk. Ground tremor knocks you down. Walk. A flying chunk of lava hits you. Walk. Step in a crevasse and trip . . .

"Does that lava pool over there look familiar, Sarge?" White Cloud grunted.

"No. Why?"

"I thought it might remind you of home."

"Droll. Very droll."

"Feed the squaw man some sugar," Toglog suggested.

"You cheap imitation Genghis Khan—!"

I let the squad yack. The com transmissions might attract attention, which was what I wanted.

We were in the lee of a steep slope when a sharp tremor started its white face sliding. I yelled, "Avalanche!" and scrambled to get clear. Preacher, Toglog, White Cloud and Ski made it too, but Schmidt disappeared under the pile of ash-darkened snow.

"Can't take him anywhere," I muttered. "Ski!"

"On it, Sarge." Ski went over to the snow pile. Lifting his right arm, he announced, "A magic trick that I learned in the Cracovia Traveling Show. Presto." His arm plunged into the pile, and came out holding a sputtering Schmidt by the neck.

"Too small. I better throw it back." Ski brushed snow off Schmidt, and put him down.

"Move out, you yahoos!" I growled. "Before the hijackers die of old age!"

The lava flow started up a volcanic cone too steep to climb. We angled across the boulder-littered slope, then slipped and slid into a gorge with weirdly eroded rock formations. Scrawny native grass and shrubs surrounded steaming hot springs. Slogging through knee-high snow drifts, exertion put an edge on my glow. Sweat was keeping my helmet's defogger busy.

Toglog was telling one of his innumerable and interminable war stories. He came from a tribe which roamed the steepe near Novy Tartary, and he was a model of traditional Mongol virtue. "—so I tied one end of the chief's guts to a tree, then I chased him around it until he—"

Suddenly something leaped down from a high ledge, so fast that it was a blur. Our reflex shots missed. It landed on Preacher, knocking him down.

It was a northern cousin of the cliff lion, white instead of grayish-brown, one hundred-plus kilograms of felinoid predator. Roaring like a shuttle engine, it sought Preacher's throat with its slavering jaws. Somehow he managed to get his forearm in the way. They thrashed about in a deepening hole in the snow, while the cliff lion tried to chew through Nemourlon. Preacher's Kalashnikov lay nearby.

The rest of us surrounded the pair, but nobody could get a clear shot. Preacher moaned as the powerful paws batted and raked him.

"Having fun?" I asked.

"Heavenly bliss," he gasped. I caught a brief glimpse of his crazy grin.

"Quit playing with that damned cat," I ordered. "We've got a job to do."

"Spoilsport." But Preacher managed to pull out his knife. He knew he would only get one chance, so he made it count. He plunged the blade behind the massive head, severing the spine. The cliff lion spasmed violently, then went limp.

Preacher rolled the carcass off of him. "The lamb shall lie down with the lion, and the meek shall inherit the Earth."

His forearm armor hadn't been designed to cope with large carnivores. It was intact, but the arm under it was crushed and mangled. I got out my medkit and tied a tourniquet. "Best I can do. Can you handle a rifle?"

Preacher looked blissed-out. "Amen to that, Sarge. I'm ambidexterous."

"Sarge didn't ask you about your sex life," White Cloud contributed.

"Soldier," I told White Cloud, "shut up and soldier."

Preacher retrieved his Kalashnikov, and we moved out.

A few minutes later we emerged from the gorge into a relatively open area. Deep snow smoothed over the uneven ground which climbed gradually into the whiteout. To our left a rocky rampart curved toward and then away from us; an irregular scarlet glow reflected from the thick clouds over it. Either an active volcanic crater or a lava lake. The blizzard was less severe here, just snow flurries and moderate gusts.

The back of my neck started itching.

"Stay sharp, grunts!" I growled. "This looks like a good spot for—"

The world split wide open in a blinding brilliance and a deafening bang. I found myself flying. I got a quick whirling view of rifle slugs kicking up sprays of snow, and the squad scrambling for cover. Then I crashed through a patch of ice.

"—trouble!" I finished.

Slugs chopped the ice around me, ricochetting off my body armor. One punched through and sent a thrill up my left thigh. Another mortar round went off a dozen meters away, showering me with snow.

The fire was coming from the rampart and the higher ground ahead. Spotting a car-sized boulder nearby, I dove behind it. "Sound off!" I ordered.

Ski, White Cloud, Preacher and Schmidt reported that they were okay. Toglog had taken a piece of shrapnel, but he was still ambulatory.

The hail of depleted uranium slugs kept up unabated. Chips flew as my boulder was whittled away. The mortars were zeroing in on our positions. We snapped off a few rounds to keep our hosts interested.

"I figure twenty, twenty-five hostiles and a pair of mortars," I told the squad. "Anybody got the boppers targeted?"

"On it, Sarge," White Cloud answered.

"Show us."

White Cloud snaked out of his crevasse. He was a

Dinneh Apache from the Badlands who had developed a taste for firewater and civilized warfare. Aiming the bulky Gauss gun, he fired two quick shots. The whining cracks echoed from the cliffs to our right. Two puffs of snow were kicked up on the top of the rampart. Then White Cloud was chased back into his hole by a flock of slugs.

"All right, it's hero time!" I growled. "You know the drill! On my mark . . . cover fire!"

Toglog's Enforcer coughed twice. The grenades chewed a piece out of the rampart where one of the snow puffs had been. Reloading, he took out the second mortar. Part of a combat-suited body tumbled down the slope, staining the snow red in its wake. Meanwhile White Cloud was working on the sniper positions.

"Charge!" I ordered. Instead of going around the boulder, which might have been expected, I went over the top. Then I zigzagged up the slope, using what cover there was.

A slug glancing off my thick torso Nemourlon knocked me down. I jumped back up and kept going. Spotting the hijacker, I drove him back behind his rock with a burst from my Kalashnikov.

Ski, Preacher and Schmidt were tight behind me, adding their fire. I figured to punch through the ambush straight ahead, then hit it from the flank and roll it up.

Two hijackers reared up to throw grenades. White Cloud picked one off, and Schmidt cut the other in half with a clip-emptying burst. The exploding grenades removed any doubt.

Then the ground shook.

Not another tremor, but a full-blown quake that rumbled for at least ten seconds. Everybody was knocked down. Snow slid and boulders rolled.

A fifty-meter chunk of the rampart crumbled. Three hijackers on top tried to get clear, but they didn't make it. The pool of lava behind the rampart poured through the gap like water through a broken dam. The snow in its path exploded into steam.

The lava flow was heading for Toglog and White Cloud. Toglog scrambled up the slope toward us, and barely avoided a very hot bath. But White Cloud was closer to the rampart. Facing the onrushing fiery red river, he waved the Gauss gun over his head and yelled in Apache. Probably swearing.

The lava rolled over him, and he was gone. I wondered what it felt like.

A rifle slug at my feet reminded me that I wasn't here on a tour. I spun, spotted the sniper kneeling behind a rock, and blew out his helmet with a luck shot.

Gesturing with my Kalashnikov for the squad to follow, I started up the slope again. Ski and Preacher flanked me to the right, Toglog and Schmidt to the left. Grenades hurtled down. We picked them off in mid-air. The explosions kicked up a snow-screen which hid us for a few seconds.

Bursting through it, I saw that the nine surviving hijackers on this side of the lava river had assembled about a hundred meters upslope. That suited me just fine.

"Grenades!" I ordered.

Yanking a grenade from my belt, I threw it high and hard. Ski, Preacher and Schmidt did the same, and the Enforcer coughed. The hijackers bagged a few of the grenades, but the rest went off around and among them. Bits of equipment and bodies shot out of the pink-tinted cloud. Four hijackers dove for cover and laid down withering fire. One writhed on the snow, screaming.

We hugged ground to avoid the storm of depleted uranium slugs. I popped up long enough to finish off the wounded hijacker, and caught a bell-ringing ricochet off the side of my helmet for my trouble.

Time to finish this. "Fix bayonets!" I ordered. I hoped the hijackers were still monitoring our transmissions.

I clipped my knife to the end of my Kalashnikov's barrel, and added a three count for molasses-slow Toglog. Then I growled, "Over the top!"

I jumped up and ran flat out right at the hijackers,

bayonet first. The deep snow was like quicksand under my driving legs. I heard the squad tight behind, yelling in four languages.

The hijackers' rifles spat desperately at us. A few ricochets felt like punches from the Fleet champ, but there were none of the clean hits needed to penetrate body armor. Not surprising. The sight of five red-flickering bayonets charging was enough to put a twitch in the most case-hardened marksman.

The hijackers were wearing combat suits like ours, only khaki instead of white. I targeted the big bruiser who seemed to be in command. He sidestepped my lunge, then clubbed me in the back with his rifle butt. I slipped and fell.

He was bringing the rifle to bear on my helmet as I rolled over. Too slow. I shoved my bayonet into his belly button, and eviscerated him with a Saigon Slice. He dropped on top of his steaming guts.

Getting up, I looked around to see who needed help. But it was all over. The other hijackers were down. So was Preacher; a full-auto burst had turned his chest into spaghetti with meat sauce. Ski, Toglog and Schmidt were cleaning their knives.

"What about the ones on the other side of the lava, Sarge?" Ski asked.

There were probably two or three of them, hidden by the clouds of steam. "Not a factor," I told him. "We'll be long gone before they can hike around it. Everybody ambulatory?"

We all had bullet and shrapnel wounds in non-vital areas, where our Nemourlon was thinner. Blood was still leaking from some of them. Schmidt was limping, and we were all dragging ass. But I got three affirmatives.

"Fall out for first aid," I ordered. Getting out my medkit, I patched my holes and gulped a keep-going pill. The others did the same. I kept a wary eye out for more trouble, but didn't spot any.

Ski and Schmidt, out of ammo, rearmed themselves with Skoda assault rifles, bandoliers and grenades that the hijackers wouldn't be needing anymore. "Who do you figure these guys were, Sarge?" Ski asked.

Unit patches had been cut off the khaki combat suits. "Mercs. Not a front-line outfit like Falkenberg's—not the way they pulled off this ambush."

"Too bad we didn't keep one alive," Toglog grunted. "We could have gotten him to guide us to his base."

"Mercs have a well-earned rep for stubbornness."

"My people have ways to make still tongues wag."

"There's a wagging one I'd like to still." I shouldered my Kalashnikov. "Saddle up, grunts! Time to get back in the war! I'm on point—Ski, take the rear!"

"On it, Sarge."

The blizzard started to pick up again. The air was thick with ash, and it stank of sulphur even after filtering. I plodded to the crest of the slope, with the squad strung out behind me. Then we slipped and slid down the steeper far side into another raw, broken gorge.

As we followed a boiling stream, I dropped back beside Ski and jacked my com line into his helmet.

"Why the private conversation, Sarge?" he asked.

"The hijackers couldn't have known for sure what they were going up against. They have heavy weapons, yet the ambush was strictly infantry."

"So?"

"So the ambushers must have been a ready-reaction force. Since they couldn't handle us, the real hammer should be in place by now, waiting for us."

Ski licked his lips in anticipation. "Up ahead, where the gorge widens into what looks like an old crater floor? Coming out we would be sitting ducks."

I nodded. "If I were the hijacker commander, that's where I'd hit us. So I'm going to take Schmidt and throw a surprise party of my own. You and Toglog keep going like you don't know any better, with lots of com yack. But go slow. When you reach the end of the gorge, take cover until we spring our surprise. Then join the party."

"On it, Sarge."

I had a private yack with Schmidt, while Ski did the

same with Toglog. Then Schmidt and I headed for the left wall of the gorge.

It was about eighty meters high and damned steep, but shot with enough cracks and ledges to make climbing possible. We pressed flat against the glossy black igneous rock to keep from being blown off, and an aftershock from the quake almost knocked us off anyway. Even with the pill's boost it was hard going; my glow had spawned a golden haze. Schmidt and I communicated by Marine hand-talk.

We reached the top, a wind-polished plateau that looked like the loneliest spot on Haven. The blizzard and the slick surface made running hard, but we did the best we could, paralleling Ski's and Toglog's trail until we caught up with and passed them.

We finally came to the end of the plateau. Dropping flat, we crawled to the edge and peered down through the snow and ash. A half-kilometer circle of chopped-up tundra was surrounded by low mounds; beyond it a row of young volcanoes belched lava, smoke and hellish light. But the scenery didn't interest me nearly as much as the hijacker force deployed around the gorge's mouth.

Forty or so soldiers were dug in, with two mortars and three .50 caliber machine guns among the riflemen. Backing them up were the two APCs they had come in, and a T-680 tank.

I jacked my com into Schmidt's. "I brought you along, because you've had heavy weapons training. Think you can handle the T-680's gun?"

Schmidt smiled thinly. "I have panzer diesel in my blood. But how do you plan to arrange the opportunity? Are we going to surround them?"

"Something like that. Did you have your usual sauerkraut for breakfast?" I shuddered at the thought.

"Of course," he answered, puzzled.

"Good. Give me your suit's fecal bag."

He handed it over, looking even more puzzled. I clipped it to my belt. Unjacking, I ordered, "Move out," in hand-talk.

We crept down the steep slope behind the hijacker force. We were in their line of sight, but our suits blended well with the snow, and they weren't expecting company from our direction. Nobody seemed to notice us.

Down on the tundra I signed Schmidt his orders. He took cover behind a rock outcrop, and I started crawling toward the T-680. I had learned infiltration in a school where the diploma was continued respiration. I became part of the snow-covered ground: cold, hard and silent. Soon the tank loomed over me like a fortress of duralloy and reactive armor. It had an anti-personnel sensor, but I hoped the local conditions were confusing it.

They must have been, because I reached the shadow between the tracks without eating a shell. The idling engine sounded like a huge carnivore's growling. I hunted along the low duralloy roof, until I found what I was looking for: the environmental air intake. Quickly I squeezed the contents of Schmidt's fecal bag and my own through the grating.

The filter system wasn't designed to cope with shit, and the T-680 wouldn't be on inboard air because it wasn't engaged. The two man crew would be wondering what they had parked over. If they weren't too worried about the opposition, they might—

Yeah. I heard the turret hatch pop, hobnail boots stomping down the treadshield, thudding into the snow. I slid my knife from its sheath, as a pair of khaki-suited legs walked around to the back.

When the hijacker leaned over to take a look, I uncoiled like a striking rattler. The finely honed carbon steel blade cleaved the thin Nemourlon below the hijacker's neck ring, and the throat behind it. Blood from his mouth sprayed over the inside of his helmet. With a bubbling sigh he folded into the snow.

Knife in hand, I retraced his steps and started up the T-680's flank. I had to get to the hatch before the remaining tanker caught on and buttoned up. I reached the top of the turret, when a slug *spranged* off the camo-finished duralloy between my legs.

Three hijackers were running toward me, firing bursts from their Skodas as they came. More depleted uranium hammered the duralloy around me. They must have alerted the tanker because the hatch started closing.

A slug punched through the Nemourlon, skin and muscle over my right hip. The sharp thrill energized me. I scrambled to the hatch. Three shots rang out from Schmidt's rock, and the hijackers went down. But others weren't far behind. I dove through the last sliver of hatchway.

The interior of the T-680 was dim, cramped, and mostly hard edges that I hit on my way down. A sidearm barked. Slugs bounced off my chest armor, ricocheting around the interior. I landed on something soft: the tanker. I brought my knife up to cut his throat, but wiped it clean and sheathed it instead. One of his own tumbling slugs had taken the back of his head off.

I heard somebody climbing up the outside, and unlimbered my Kalashnikov to welcome him. But it was Schmidt who jumped down from the hatchway. "Button up, Sarge!" he snapped. "Company on my heels!"

Slugs *clanged* futilely against the T-680's armor, punctuating his warning.

I slid into the driver's seat, while Schmidt climbed back up to the turret. I hadn't played tanker for a long time, but it was like riding a bike. I buttoned the T-680 up. Ignoring the angry banging of rifle butts on the hatch, I took off my helmet. The thick reek of shit and dead meat was like perfume.

"Ready for action?" I yelled over the engine rumbling.

"*Ja!*" Schmidt had taken his helmet off too.

Grenade explosions slammed us, but it would take a lot more than that to damage a T-680. "Engaging!" I yelled. "Take out the APCs!"

I put on the driver's VR helmet; the view was like I was outside, except for the superimposed displays. Two hijackers were trying to plant their grenades under the left tread. My hands and feet worked controls by touch. The T-680 lurched back, twisted, and lunged forward. The hijackers became red stains on the tread they had been trying to blow.

Through the swirling snow I spotted both APCs closing in, hoping to recapture or at least disable their prime piece of armament. The remaining riflemen cautiously flanked them, while the mortars and machine guns were frantically being repositioned. The T-680 shuddered as the APCs' .50 calibers tried to cut a tread; the only damage they could hope to inflict.

I spun the T-680 and charged them. If Schmidt couldn't hit them, I was going to try to run them over. The turret traversed. The tank shook from the cannon's recoil. A fireball erupted a handful of meters behind the lead APC, spewing smoke and steam, leaving a pool-sized crater. Two hijacker riflemen didn't exist anymore; the rest were running for the gorge mouth.

"Pretty sloppy shooting, grunt!" I yelled up at Schmidt. "Maybe they will laugh themselves to death!"

The APCs were curving away from us in opposite directions. The cannon roared again, and a near-miss knocked the lead APC on its side. A third round blew it sky-high in a beautiful mushroom of orange flame and black smoke.

"I might make a soldier out of you yet!" I yelled.

The fleeing hijackers ran into more trouble. Grenades and sharpshooting cut down the first six, driving the rest to cover near the gorge's mouth. Ski and Toglog had joined the party.

The remaining APC was hightailing it at max speed. Schmidt was firing as quickly as he could reload. The first four shells missed the zigzagging target, but the fifth nailed it.

I swung the T-680 around. A quake opened a crack in the tundra in front of us, but we jumped it before it got too wide. Ash from the line of volcanos was turning the snow black. The surviving dozen or so hijackers, caught between Ski and Toglog and us, were digging in for a last stand around the mortars and machine guns. Nobody was trying to surrender, which was smart, because we weren't taking any prisoners.

Switching to the twin anti-personnel machine guns, Schmidt scythed the hijacker position. Slugs from their .50 calibers and Skodas rattled off the T-680's armor, while mortar shells hammered it. All they accomplished was to throw off Schmidt's aim and to get me a refresher course in kraut obscenity.

The turret kept traversing, and the anti-personnel guns kept buzzing. Snow and frozen ground erupted. Hardware crumpled. Bodies shredded. The position was pretty well reduced by the time we reached it, but I rolled over it a few times to make sure.

I spotted a white-suited figure limping from the gorge's mouth, and drove over. It was Toglog. Stopping in front of him, I popped the turret hatch. "Schmidt, get rid of the tanker corpse and help Toglog in!"

"*Ja*, Sarge!"

Toglog had acquired a few more minor wounds, and he was packing a Skoda instead of his Enforcer. "Grenades all used up!" he explained as we patched ourselves and gulped more keep-going pills. It was a good thing that we had transport again; we were all running down despite the pills.

"What happened to Ski?" I growled at Toglog.

"One of the .50 calibers carved him from head to toe! Fine weapons—too bad you crunched them!"

"You would want to stagger into combat carrying a field piece! Forget it! The fun and games are over, you yahoos—time to do the job we came to do!"

"We still don't have anybody to ask where the base is!"

"Don't need to!" I tapped buttons on the command console, and a map appeared on the tac screen. "The auto-con will show us!"

Following the map course, we set out for the hijackers' base. I drove, and Schmidt stood by in the turret just in case. Toglog didn't like the cramped quarters; he rode on top of the turret, enjoying the scenery.

Rounding the volcanos, the T-680 wove through a region of geysers and hot springs. Blasts of steam turned the tank's interior into an oven. The highjacker force's outbound tracks had been covered by fresh snow, and visibility was down to a handful of meters, so I had to rely mostly on the auto-con. Picking a way through the rough, dangerous terrain kept me pretty busy.

"Expecting another attack, Sarge?" Schmidt asked.

"It's the one you don't expect that fries your ass! Keep your eyes open, and that wound under your mustache zipped!"

But the trip was uneventful, except for a few quakes, avalanches, crevasses, and a hail of lava chunks that almost knocked Toglog off the turret. I could see how the hijackers had managed to operate here so long without being discovered. What I couldn't see was how they managed to operate here at all.

The T-680 climbed through a pass in a nuked-looking ridge. In the middle of the snowbound lava field beyond, I could make out a lone dome-shaped hill. There were streams and some vegetation on its lower slopes, but the wind kept the glossy black summit swept clear.

"According to the auto-con," I yelled, "that's our target!"

"I don't see any base!" Toglog replied over the com. "Just rock!"

"Stay sharp anyway! Just in case that rock falls on us!"

The auto-con guided the T-680 down onto and across the lava field, toward a cavelike hole in the hill's flank. The mouth was about thirty meters across. A thin column of steam rose from it.

The back of my neck started itching again.

"Schmidt, lob a few shells into that hole!"

"You think the base is in there?"

"I think it's—"

KRUUUMP! An explosion under the front of the T-680 lifted it. It landed hard. More cannon shells erupted into flame and dark smoke around us, and .50 caliber slugs jackhammered off the armor. Toglog was thrown into a snowdrift. He popped up, chased the tank, climbed the left treadshield, and took cover behind the turret.

"—damned likely!" I finished.

"Where's the fire coming from?" Schmidt yelled.

I checked the tac screen. "A cannon and three machine guns in bunkers upslope from the cave!"

"Got 'em!"

"Then get 'em!" I switched on my com. "Last chance to come aboard, Toglog!"

"I was born on the steepe!" he answered. "I won't go to my ancestors in an iron yurt!"

"Have it your way! See what you can do about those machine guns!"

I sent the T-680 racing toward the cave mouth at max speed, through flame and smoke, slugs and shrapnel. Schmidt had the cannon in action, blowing huge chunks of snow/dirt/rock out of the hill.

A blast rang the T-680 like a bell. A treadplate was blown loose; I cut speed to a crawl before it could jam. Smoke came down from the turret, followed by a coughing yell from Schmidt. "Scratch the cannon!"

I was watching a combat-suited figure zigzagging up the slope. Machine gun bursts kicked up snow at its feet. "Cover Toglog!"

"Ja!" The twin anti-personnel guns dueled with the three hijacker .50 calibers. One silenced. Two. Then Toglog went down, his left arm a red-spurting stump.

Too late, Schmidt nailed the last machine gun.

Another near-miss from the hijacker cannon slammed into the T-680. It was still moving toward the cave mouth, but at turtle speed it would be scrap before it could reach cover.

Suddenly I noticed that Toglog's corpse had moved. Following the red trail upslope, I spotted it near the slit through which the hijacker cannon fired. Rearing up, it tossed four grenades liberated from a hijacker through the slit. A moment later the whole part of the hill blew out. Snow and rubble slid over Toglog, all the way down to the lava field.

The T-680's sensors picked up a strong energy reading from the cave mouth. "Hose the cave!" I yelled. "Now!"

The anti-personnel guns buzzed. Two lines of tracers disappeared into the cave's darkness, sweeping back and forth, up and down.

Something big and airborne shot out of the cave mouth. It screamed low over the T-680.

KRAAAAANG! The T-680 was blown over on its back. I tumbled down into the turret behind Schmidt, banging my head thrillingly. Fire and smoke filled the interior. Finding my helmet, I put it on, then helped Schmidt find his. The tank's electrical system shorted out spectacularly. In the darkness and sudden silence I fumbled for the hatch's manual release. "Are you ambulatory, grunt?" I growled.

"*Ja.* Barely."

"Follow me." I felt wonderful, but my body wasn't obeying orders the way it used to. I had to get tough with it. Grudgingly my hands worked the crank. The hatch opened partway, revealing red-lit snow. I squeezed through, with Schmidt tight behind.

We scrambled to get clear. The screaming overhead got louder. Looking back, I spotted a stubby fighter—a Yak VTOL—coming around for another pass. Flying and fighting in a blizzard wasn't easy, but the hijacker pilot had had quite a bit of experience. The fighter was one of those which had been raiding the shimmerstone camps. It had used up its load of eggs on the T-680. Now it was chewing up tundra with its wing-mounted aerial cannons, closing on us fast.

One other thing I noticed: it was trailing dark smoke. Schmidt hadn't missed completely.

"The cave!" I yelled. We staggered, zigzagging, toward the dark opening. Schmidt looked as blissed-out and played-out as I felt. But we still had a job to do. We kept going.

The strafing line missed us by a meter or two, pelting

us with snow and frozen dirt but nothing worse. The Yak banked right to avoid the hill and swing around for another pass.

Tried to, rather. The dark smoke thickened, and the Yak plowed straight into an upper slope. The orange fireball briefly outshone the nearby lava flows.

We reached the cave mouth and kept going.

The glossy black shaft was as smoothly bored as my Kalashnikov, probably a gas vent. The floor had been paved, painted and lit like an airport runway. It plunged several hundred meters into the hill at a thirty-degree angle. We did too, as fast as we could.

Near the bottom, three hijacker riflemen appeared, heading our way. We all spotted each other at the same time, and opened fire. Our shots echoed hollowly in the blizzardless silence.

I emptied my clip into the lead hijacker, blowing his left leg off at the hip. He dropped. Schmidt nailed his hijacker too.

But the third one kneeled, aimed, and fired a short burst. Schmidt was knocked backwards. Blood gushed from his chest, subsided, then stopped.

Ejecting and slamming in a new clip, I fitted the last hijacker with a new eye between the other two. He slumped as I ran by him.

I stumbled to a stop at the bottom of the shaft. My legs were just about all out. Hugging the stone wall, I edged around into the cavern beyond.

The "hill" must have been formed by a giant volcanic gas bubble. The gas had vented, leaving a cavern about two hundred meters across. The hijackers had simply moved in and set up shop. Floodlights in the bowl ceiling lit a circle of tarmac. Prefab buildings, fuel tanks and equipment ringed the perimeter. In the middle three more Yak VTOLs were being prepped by ground crews, to deal with the attack. They didn't seem to know that I was it.

Slugs chipped the rock wall over my head. Two hijackers in ground crew outfits were running across the tarmac toward me, firing their rifles as they came.

I dove, rolled, and scuttled under a truck. More slugs chopped up the tarmac in front of me. I cut loose with my Kalashnikov, driving the two hijackers to cover behind a pile of crates. More armed hijackers were converging on us from the buildings.

I looked around for the ammo dump, but it wasn't wearing a sign. The golden haze was now almost blinding. I felt so good that I just wanted to lie here enjoying it. But I still had a job to do.

Only one option left. I headed for the nearest Yak.

I zigzagged across the open tarmac, firing wildly, hoping to interfere with the hijackers' aim. The closer pair stayed behind their pile of crates, but the charging group sent bursts of slugs my way. A ricochet off my back knocked me down. I managed to get up and keep going.

Thirty meters to the Yak. My last clip scattered the crew prepping it. I dropped the dead weight of the Kalashnikov, and kept going.

Twenty meters. A slug punched through my right shoulder, shattering the joint. It was the best thrill yet. I found myself rolling on the tarmac, moaning ecstatically. I lurched back to my feet, and kept going.

Ten meters. I heard yelling behind me, getting louder. Something exploded to my left, probably a grenade. I staggered, but kept going.

I hit hard, curved duralloy. The Yak. The shooting stopped. Afraid of damaging their expensive fighter. I slid along the fuselage to the hatch. Opened it with my good hand. Jumped halfway inside.

Somebody grabbed my leg. It wasn't working very well, but well enough to kick free. I squirmed the rest of the way in. Wrestled other hands to get the hatch sealed. Fists banged. Voices yelled.

I crawled forward to the cockpit. Into the pilot's seat.

The hijackers had surrounded the Yak. Skoda fire hammered the fuselage, spiderwebbing the windshield glassite. My good hand fumbled with the controls. I had never flown a fighter; a few hours of sim-training had been considered adequate to cover such a low-probability scenario.

That was okay. I wouldn't be going very far.

Skipping the checklist, I swung the wing and tail jets into VTOL mode and fired them up. Thrust pushed the hijackers back. The Yak rose a couple of meters and hovered sloppily.

The hijackers were running toward the shaft mouth, to keep me from leaving. Two of them were prepping shoulder-launched SAMs. The Yak bristled with firepower, all operated from the weaponry officer's board out of reach behind me.

The flow of blood from my shattered shoulder was filling the inside of my suit. I could hardly move, but I managed to bring the Yak's nose around.

I felt better than I had ever felt before. Better than I had thought I *could* feel. And the best was yet to come. The golden haze was darkening. I could barely make out the cluster of towering aviation fuel tanks.

Somebody finally figured it out. An explosion rocked the Yak. Red displays flashed. Smoke filled the cockpit.

What had it been like for you, grunts? Fire and ice merged. The ultimate orgasm, resisted yet lusted for. Just like I lusted for it.

I shoved the throttles in all the way. The jets swung to flight mode. Screaming, the Yak leaped forward.

The dim tank-shapes grew. Filled the windshield.

Flam/shock/crush/blind/tear/burn/flay—
YEEESSSSS!!

Somewhere in Haven's equatorial region there was a well-hidden facility which didn't officially exist. Certainly the CoDominium didn't know it existed, or else the sky would have filled with warships paying an unsocial call. For it was a military research center sponsored by the government of Sauron. To circumvent the CoDominium's strict technology restrictions without giving away its ambitions prematurely, Sauron established such facilities in out-of-the-way sites. Haven was about as out-of-the-way as you could get.

In a well-equipped but otherwise spartan private office, a man known to most of the staff only as the General sat behind his big desk. Switching off his computer terminal, he leaned back to consider the report he had just read.

The goal of Project Fury was to augment the performance of a soldier by surgically reversing his pain and pleasure centers and suppressing his shock reactions, on the theory that if he enjoyed rather than feared suffering he would be more agressive. From a strategic point of view the field test's telemetry and follow-up data seemed to validate the theory. A lightly armed commando squad had defeated an overwhelmingly superior force and destroyed its base of operations.

Unfortunately it had been a triumph of utter recklessness over good soldiering. The men's behavior had been erratic, to say the least. They had sought engagement at every opportunity, even when avoidance would have served the mission better. They had wastefully expended their minimal manpower. Casualties had been one hundred percent.

A death wish was the psychologist's term. The assumption that survival instinct would offset the self-destructive tendency of the pain/pleasure reversal had proved incorrect. The men had become addicts, subconsciously seeking more and more intense experience of all.

The problem was inherent and insoluble. Expensive super-soldiers who kamikazied in combat would be unreliable as well as unaffordable. So, insofar as augmenting the performance of the Homeworld's military forces was concerned, Project Fury was a failure.

The General stared into the half-lit gloom. His mouth twisted into a grim smile.

But not a total failure. In any war there were certain high-risk objectives which required elite, strongly motivated commando units. So-called suicide missions. Whenever the need arose, he would have the tools for the job.

FAREWELL TO HAVEN

His Excellency Arthur John George Waltham, the last CoDominium Consul-General ever assigned to the Byers' System, gazed out the quad-glazed windows of Government House at the last Haven sunset he would ever see. Behind him, workmen bustled busily, finishing the herculean labor of packing ten years of diplomatic life into crates for shipment back to Terra. He sighed. His baggage was packed and the diplomatic niceties were almost completed. Soon, fifty-four years of CoDominium governance would end. At noon tomorrow, on the seventieth anniversary of the discovery of Byers' Star, he, Allison, and the children would take the dubious honors of the Haven Volunteers, turn the government over to the locals, and embark upon the first leg of their long journey home.

Home to Terra. Now he smiled. He had missed the civilized days and nights of Earth, the civilized climate of Victoria, the civilized people of Melbourne.

It was the people he missed most of all, he

decided. Haven harbored nothing but barbarians and criminals: boorish religious fanatics, crude hafnium miners, angry, volatile transportees. God, how glad he would be to leave behind the problem of what to do with a million new political and criminal deportees each year. Or the tougher one of how to enforce the writ of the CoDominium Senate now that the Marines had left to deal with worse problems elsewhere, and he had only the Haven militia, the "Volunteers" to back him up. His smile grew broader. Let the locals solve their own problems now, and see how they liked it.

"I know that smile, you've been smiling it entirely too much recently."

He turned, smiling even more broadly at a beauty that even ten years of marriage on Haven (and four children) had not been able to mar.

"You always could read my mind, Allison. Yes, I was thinking how wonderful it will be to get you and the children back to civilization and civilized people once again. Haven is not the place to raise a family, not a sane one anyway."

"Now, Arthur, you know not all Haveners and transportees are evil psychotics. What would the children be like by now if we didn't have Nanny Kinaston to look after them? She hasn't just seen to them while we have been off being Diplomatic, she has given them a better education than they got in the government schools. I'm just wondering how we will be able to get along without her."

"Yes, dear, I know she has turned them into a fine set of young gentlemen and ladies, but you must admit that she is one in a million. With three generations of conservative-Havener-religious and radical-transportee-political fanaticism behind her, it's a wonder she managed to get an education, learn civilized manners, *and* keep her sanity. *I'm* wondering what we can do to thank her."

Allison stood pondering that problem for a moment, her head tilted to one side, her long black hair drifting down over one shoulder. "I don't suppose we could arrange to take her back to Terra with us this late in the game? She could take care of the children on the trip home." She smiled her own private smile, the one with the left corners of her mouth and left eye trying to come together. "It would be just like the trip out . . . a second honeymoon."

He was delighted with the idea. "Of course! I've never met a Havener who didn't want to get off this rock." He frowned briefly. "The waiting list for emigration is about two million names long, and they only let a thousand or so get off in any given year." He slapped the windowsill with a happy violence that had heads turning and his aide strolling hurriedly to his side. "What good is it being the Consul-General of an entire planetary system if you can't let someone leave it? I still have sixty hours in office, and by Jove, I'll see it gets done if it is my last official act!"

His Excellency Arthur John George Waltham, last and former CoDominium Consul-General for the Byers' System, his wife, and their four children, departed Haven sixty-eight hours later. They left laden with public honors, burdened with private chagrin, and unaccompanied by Nanny Kinaston. She had turned them down.

It was not that their invitation had been refused, though it had. It was not that they had never before encountered a Haven patriot, though they had not. It was the manner of the refusal that took the edge off the bright happiness of their departure and provoked random attacks of irritability during the year-long trip home; the words themselves.

When asked if she wanted to return with them to Terra, Nanny Kinaston stared at them with what could only be described as horror.

"You want to take me to Terra," she cried, clutching her throat, "where all the criminals come from?"